Blood on the Warpath

a novel about trust

by

Robert Luis Rabello

Dedicated to the glory of God, and to my
stepmother, Carolyn

As you loved my father, may your life always
overflow
with love. Thank you for your compassion, your
hospitality and acceptance of me as your son.
With love,

Robert Luis Rabello

Summerland, British Columbia

November 2020

I'd like to acknowledge my beta readers, Don
McGill, Lorna Hartman and Nirmiti Mittal for
their feedback. Additional thanks extend to my
colleague, Fiona Smith, for her editorial
expertise.

Prologue: Time to Kill

Brenna Velez felt her husband's hand touch her shoulder and gently glide down her back as he sat down. The scowl on her lovely face faded under the warmth of his attention, morphing into wistful sadness. She abandoned the sheet music on a nearby chair and shut her eyes as his lips neared hers, met, and lingered far longer than they typically permitted in public, at least at home in Tamaria.

"What's wrong?" he asked.

The young woman huffed a short, sharp breath as she reached for the music collection again. "The judges gave me three hours to review these pieces," she told him. "They're expecting me to perform them in some kind of elimination round this afternoon."

Lieutenant Garrick Ravenwood, her husband, knitted his brow. "Isn't that the point of the competition?"

"It would be, if I'd never seen these pieces before."

"So you know them?" he asked.

Brenna nodded. "I played every one of these when I was little. This one," she said, referencing a particular composition, "gave me no trouble when I was five."

Garrick pulled her left shoulder into his chest, kissed the top of her head and squeezed her strong, solid upper arm. In addition to being an accomplished pianist, his wife could wield a bow and sword with deadly expertise, and her muscular shoulders testified to years of faithful practice. Many people underestimated, or even dismissed her at first glance. Her petite size and Lithian heritage endowed Brenna with a youthful appearance – a woman's body on a girl's frame – distracting men and women from discerning the more important virtues of her intelligence and character.

Yet within four weeks, Brenna would celebrate her 30th birthday. Although still considered a young woman among her own people – as Lithians often lived hundreds of years – Garrick knew the depth and breadth of her capabilities from near-constant experience in her company since they'd met. "Well, they'll be in for a surprise," he said.

While she should have felt affirmed by his expressed confidence, Brenna searched his gaze for the disapproval she expected and noticed a subtle expression of triumph in his eyes. "You don't have to rub it in," she replied.

"Why are you looking for my displeasure?" he inquired, mildly annoyed that she'd challenged his assertion. He'd not uttered a word of critique about the music festival since the day before their departure. "I'm here to support you; not judge you."

She suspected he wasn't being truthful, but rather than forcing a confrontation, she let his words stand without challenge. In her culture, that meant at least tacit approval. But Garrick was not Lithian, and ever sensitive to her manner, disposition and perspective, he discerned her disbelief. When she didn't respond, he put his index finger under her chin and coaxed her gaze into his.

"This is not about me," he assured, quietly. "I voiced my concerns before we left home, but we both agreed to come here, and I want you to do well. I want you to shine."

"I just want you to be happy," she countered. "Can you set aside your worry – at least for a little while – so we can enjoy our time before you deploy again?"

"I'm doing the best I can," he assured, confident in the truth of his statement. Although suppressing his instincts wasn't easy, he was trying. "Will you trust me?"

Brenna examined her own motives in prayerful contemplation. She couldn't suppress the nagging thought that he'd been right to oppose her participation in this oddly coincidental competition, even though they'd experienced none of the dangers he'd articulated about a stirring insurgency and government repression since their arrival. Yet in addition to the low-difficulty pieces she'd been assigned for the first round, Brenna recognized none of the other festival participants, a fact that amplified the memory of her husband's opposition to attending.

They'd traveled by train from Marvic, Tamaria's capital city, and arrived in the Nordan Coastal Colony without incident. Almond-eyed and dark-haired soldiers, armed with carbines, paced through the central station in Helsing – the regional capital – clad in blue uniforms and combat armor, wordlessly eyeing the Heran, Kamerese and Vatheran tourists who queued behind stern-faced customs agents. Their incomprehensible language complicated all official interactions, and their contempt for native Kurians easily extended to Garrick, whose taller stature, blonde hair, fair skin and pale, rounded eyes spoke of a distant, shared heritage between local people and the Tamarians.

Neither Garrick nor Brenna knew much about the Nordans. While the lovers could understand most of the spoken Kurian tongue – though not its written form, which featured a different script – Tamarian was not mutually intelligible. Since neither of them spoke Kamerese – the de-facto regional bridge language – they had to rely on Azgar vulgate to communicate until their arrival at the Seashell Resort. Here, many staff spoke Tamarian well enough to understand the young foreigners.

The mysterious invitation and accompanying brochure, which Brenna had received in the mail a few weeks earlier, boasted of a bilingual staff. Garrick hadn't believed it, given the distance between his country and the coastal colony, but he'd been wrong about that. Brenna didn't hold that mistake against him, partly because he'd admitted his error and apologized to her for assuming that he'd been right.

She loved that about him. She also loved his considerate, caring attitude toward her. Garrick's listening ear, and recognition of her value, bolstered Brenna's confidence. His rugged face, grey eyes, and beautiful body honed to perfection by swimming and weightlifting, stirred her desire, her admiration. A natural soldier and born leader, he possessed uncanny instincts when under threat, and had a very quick mind that usually inspired her to take his concerns seriously.

The reason Brenna had been so strident in rejecting his worries centered on Garrick's struggle with combat trauma. His last deployment left lingering, invisible scars whose pain too often bled into their relationship. He'd behaved irritably, even toward her. His hyper-vigilance during every social outing exhausted everyone who loved him. Brenna dismissed his paranoia about potential threats as irrational; yet for a moment, in her introspection, she realized that her own desire to get away from Marvic – from Garrick's troubled siblings and the racial pressure imposed by a xenophobic society – along with her personal, competitive instincts, diminished the importance of his concerns in her view.

And she didn't want to treat him that way.

Concluding that she'd been harsh in her judgment, Brenna closed her eyes and whispered a prayer of gratitude for the man who loved her. In a rare act of public affection, she snuggled close and murmured contentedly, raising her gaze to meet his.

"I trust you," she promised.

"Do you want to practice?" he asked, thinking that she might want to go over the pieces before her first performance that afternoon.

"Maybe later," she replied with a winsome inflection.

Garrick smiled. "So, we have some time to kill?"

"Oh?" she replied, flirtatiously. "You have ideas?"

He slid his hands alongside her bosom, desire rising in his eyes. "I'd like some time with *The Twins . . . .*"

***

Months of meticulous planning, of a thousand carefully considered details dovetailing together, came to life like a tree flower bearing ripening fruit. As Esteban Orozco sat in the Seashell Resort's auditorium, listening to yet another half-talent-would-be-pianist slaughter an obscure composition in the elimination round, he felt satisfied that this operation had gone well thus far.

Most of the performances he'd heard had been cringe-worthy. Esteban loved music and would have enjoyed hearing skilled players compete, but only one talent in this show mattered. As long as the Velez woman showed up, the countdown to battle could proceed. He'd seen her name on the docket, but because he didn't know what she looked like, he'd had to wait to identify her.

Confident that the dim-witted Nordans knew nothing, suspected nothing, and could do nothing – since their Colonial Army would suffer a quick defeat – Esteban sensed success. As long as his insurgent allies controlled the ports and prevented reinforcement, the mercenary believed that the training and weaponry his organization provided to the rebel Kurians would squelch resistance from the Nordans long before their formidable navy could supply additional men and material from their distant home islands.

He'd already been working on a contingency to help with that issue, as the Nordans depended on seaweed processing to create the oil that powered every ship, great and small, in their navy. Commando teams had been intercepting and burning seaweed shipments for weeks. Once the operation moved into its final stages, the lack of available fuel would limit naval operations. A full embargo might even bring the mighty Nordans to their knees. Their arrogance would end, and their resource-rich colony would finally open to anyone with the ambition to take it.

For his plan to fully succeed, Kameron's Tamarian allies would have to join the fray and cut off rail supplies from the Vatherans in the north. But Esteban had been told by sources close to the Kamerese king that the Tamarians, weary of war, did not want another conflict on their border. The Tamarians had to be compelled, and that's why he'd organized this music competition.

The young woman was Lithian, but had served with the Tamarian Expeditionary Force during the Kamerese Civil War, where she'd earned the highest military honor for action in combat. That meant she was valuable to them, and her demise would create a political crisis.

When she finally stepped onto the stage, Esteban raised his brow. She was a tiny thing, much smaller than most of her competitors. Her long, black gown featured two dark green triangles that flared toward the hem from the sides of her broad hips. The Lithian woman modestly put her right hand over her bodice when she bowed, then sat at the piano and lifted her head for a moment, as if meditating before she began to play.

From the moment her hands touched the keys, Esteban found his breathing stilled by the sheer beauty her slender fingers coaxed from the instrument. He'd heard other contestants struggle with that piece earlier in the day, yet this woman played the composition as if she'd written it herself.

Graceful, passionate sound filled the hall. Perfect arpeggios and flawless scales blended rhythm and melody. The Velez woman, confident and poised, paused before beginning the more challenging second movement, where her fingers danced over the keyboard like fairies in a forest glade. The third movement, full of throaty chords and big scales, presented no challenge for her. The degree of skill she displayed demonstrated lifelong devotion to the instrument, but how could such a young-looking waif play so well?

It didn't matter. Esteban now knew what she looked like and could identify her to his combat team. He arose toward the end of her performance to verify her room number and make final preparations.

The time to kill had finally arrived.

Shame

"*Tora Ni,* targets acquired," Lieutenant Sato whispered into his radio. He glanced at four other men on his team, noting that everyone else had their eyes fixed on the beach. It would have been hard to look away. Wordlessly, he refocused attention to the objective.

Long ago, some clever Nordan engineer created an artificial lagoon to take advantage of the extreme tides along the colonial coast, producing electrical power by virtue of the rising and falling sea level. Its breakwater also sheltered a calm, brackish lake from strong ocean currents.

Additionally, its shallow waters warmed during the daylight, making it an ideal location for swimming during long, hot summer days like this one, where even the wind off the sea carried warmth. With sweat staining his uniform, Sato secretly wished that he could cool off too. Without doubt, the young couple emerging from the water had come to this desolate spot for that reason.

Sato believed he had correctly identified the woman. Petite, with strong arms, thick thighs and a muscular back, her tapered ears, black hair and the slight slant to her eyes plainly announced her Lithian heritage. He'd not expected that she might also be beautiful, as the womanly shape on her slender frame stirred his heart in a way that he'd not experienced before. The fit, broad-shouldered young man in her company could have been Kurian – his blonde hair, round eyes and pale skin matched the profile – but if this woman was the piano player mentioned in Sato's orders, the man was most likely her husband, whose file identified him as a junior officer in the Tamarian Expeditionary Force. He looked fit and formidable.

Blood on the Warpath: *Shame*

After splashing each other and laughing at their own antics, the couple kissed in a sensual, lingering manner. Their hands began wandering so much that Sato wondered how far this conduct would lead. When they finally stopped, he felt silently – if mildly – disappointed.

Still, he gazed at the scene in fascination. Sato had always been intrigued by the slim, dark-haired, and almond-eyed women of his Nordan Islands home, but had never known affection from anyone other than his own mother. This woman seemed exotic and too muscular for his taste, but her sensual behavior quickened his heart.

Sato disciplined himself to think like a soldier. He'd been trained to embrace death, not love, and it shouldn't matter to him that these two would soon face slaughter.

But he couldn't help feeling that it would be a shame to see such a pretty thing die . . . .

***

Brenna took the towel that her husband offered, wiped her face dry, then bent forward to wring water from her hair as Garrick rubbed his head with his own towel. She put on a pair of dark glasses and kissed him after he'd finished. "Are you feeling better now?" she asked.

Three days with little to do had passed since their arrival at the Seashell Resort, punctuated by Brenna's performances and the personal time they'd spent together between her practice sessions. Garrick had already finished reading two philosophy books and made it halfway through a third. He nodded, knowing he needed vigorous activity to keep negative thoughts under control. Exercise often restored his natural geniality.

Blood on the Warpath: *Shame*

Neither of them had ever seen the ocean before. Awed by the brute power of thundering waves crashing into the rocky shore during a storm on their second day, Brenna felt reluctant to swim in the sea. After the raging waters turned placid the next morning, she'd watched other resort guests enjoy the beach near their hotel, and reconsidered.

While the attitude of wealthy tourists concerning beach attire – or the lack thereof – should have reassured the Lithian woman, Brenna's post-marital modesty compelled her to avoid wearing her swimming suit in public. Understanding this, Garrick searched a local map and discovered the hidden lagoon. After hearing her dominate the semifinal round of competition, he'd convinced his reticent wife to join him in the long walk from the resort to this isolated pool of delightfully warm water.

Thinking they were alone, he stripped and twisted the moisture from his swimming trunks before drying off, dressing in shorts and a casual shirt for the return trek. The fabric of Brenna's Lithian swimming suit mysteriously shed its wetness at her will, losing its alluring semi-transparency. She toweled off her shoulders, arms and legs before slipping into a silky, button-down blouse.

Brenna, who'd always competed against top quality musicians, usually had to work hard to win. She honed her skills for hours nearly every day and had an unbroken track record of music competition victories that extended into her early childhood. This event seemed strangely beneath her, and as her admiring eyes watched Garrick dress, Brenna couldn't shake the persistent suspicion that she should have trusted his instinct. Perhaps her easy dominance at this competition revealed something hidden, something sinister, something deadly . . . .

However, staying at the Seashell Resort had been a restful experience for the lovers, especially because the Nordan Colony was far more cosmopolitan than anywhere in Tamaria. On the surface, people seemed more tolerant of ethnic differences, which meant Brenna was not subject to the relentless and often overt racism heaped on her in the High Land. To their shared relief, no one cared if she held her husband's hand, playfully bumped her hip into his, gazed at him longingly, embraced in public, exchanged a brief kiss now and then, or spoke in a foreign language. The experience felt liberating for both of them.

After wriggling into her skirt and putting on her sandals, Brenna took her husband's hand in her own. Rather than following the road back to the resort, they decided to walk along the shore.

***

Sato lifted his eyes from the binoculars. How could he confirm that these two were the actual people he'd been tasked to track if he couldn't personally verify their identities? Keeping his frustration in check, the lieutenant reached for the radio microphone again. "Targets on the move, heading south on the beach."

"Copy *Tora Ni. Shīgōrudo* is now aloft. Target acquisition confirmed. Relocate to primary."

High overhead – far beyond hearing range and barely visible in the bright summer sky – a Nordan airship flew in a slow, racetrack pattern. *Shīgōrudo*, the seagull, would observe the targets from its lofty perspective and report to headquarters until *Tora Ichi*, the special forces team inside the Seashell Resort, picked up tracking responsibilities.

Sato and his team abandoned their position and hustled back to the service road connecting the lagoon's long-derelict powerhouse with the coastal highway. They'd hidden their transport vehicle in the trees, with Chief Engineer Sergeant Sharuko and Weapons Sergeant Funimaro on guard. Both men were alert and reported no contact at their remote site when Sato and the rest of the team arrived.

Transportation Sergeant Goro climbed into the driver's seat, gave one pump of the seaweed oil injector and turned the key until the compression-ignition engine coughed to life. Sato sat in front, while Warrant Officer Kanazane took the second-in-command position in the bed of the truck.

While this large, cumbersome and noisy machine could outrun a horse, Goro kept his speed in check to avoid stirring dust. With few vehicles on the road – mostly sluggish transports ferrying supplies between densely populated coastal towns and the occasional army convoy – haste might draw attention to Sato's team. They'd all been briefed on the importance of stealth, of blending in with the background of normal activity to avoid alerting the enemy of their task. Sato suspected that his team was part of some larger operation, but he didn't know the details.

He'd been told that the Nordan Colonial Army depended on the success of this operation to maintain control in a region seething with insurgency, intrigue and overflowing with foreign spies. Sato, selected for this mission because of his success on previous assignments, felt duty-bound to carry out his orders in an honorable manner. He'd signed up for adventure, and the army fulfilled its promise of travel to exotic locations like this one.

Blood on the Warpath: *Shame*

With his mind drifting toward thoughts of his distant homeland, Sato remembered his family and their humble repair shop in Hokunagai. Seaweed oil exhaust mingling with the unpleasant smell of a nearby cannery reminded him of the fishing boats his father and four older brothers would service in the harbor. That laborious lifestyle, full of repetitive tasks, permeated by grease and the lingering reek of fish, lay at the root of Sato's strong desire to escape.

Knowing that expressing such sentiments would have brought shame to his family, the young man quietly worked for his father throughout his school years, never daring to express how he felt, until a military parade and recruitment drive came to Hokunagai on Empire Day. Flag-waving children led the procession, while attractive women handed enlistment leaflets to young men in the crowd. Sato's life changed the moment his eager fingers accepted one.

Joining the army provided salvation from his damnation to endless drudgery. Caught up in the pervasive patriotic frenzy sweeping through the Nordan people, most of Sato's family – sensing his unspoken discontent and worried that he might run off to a big city and disgrace his parents – showered him with praise when they learned of his enlistment. Signing up also saved face for his father.

Of course, *Oji* Okisama didn't approve. But he had no say in his nephew's upbringing. Most people considered him a pacifist, secretly allied with anarchists and other undesirables, but no one ever accused the man of stupidity.

"Your head is full of foolish fantasies!" he'd warned. "War is a terrible business, not some grand adventure. In the end, you will bring sorrow to your family and shame upon yourself!"

Those sentiments festered in Sato's soul. He prayed to the gods that his uncle's prophecy would never come true, that his honorable service and devotion to the Nordan Empire would gloriously shine in the annals of history. He dreamed of a long and illustrious career, full of valor and unbroken success . . . .

But he secretly worried that *Oji* Okisama was right.

***

A reflection, a golden glint in the black sand, caught Garrick's eye. Initially he dismissed the sight, but after seeing another flash, and then a third, the young officer stopped. "What's that?" he asked, pointing up the beach.

Brenna squinted behind her dark glasses. Her visual acuity in daylight fell somewhat beneath what purebred humans, like her husband, could see. On bright summer days near water – and after a fresh snowfall – she wore shades to avoid glare-induced blindness. "I don't know," she replied. "Maybe a seashell, some broken glass, or metal."

Curious and wary, Garrick led his wife well above the aromatic, oceanic debris marking the highest tide, where brass casings lay partly buried – yet easily visible – in the dark, volcanic sand. As they approached, he saw many more, and on closer examination concluded that this isolated place beneath a black basalt bluff had recently been used for target practice.

He stooped to pick up an abandoned casing, scowling as he turned it over to examine the marks on its rim. "That's odd," he remarked, pointing to numbers stamped around the firing pin hole. "Do you recognize these?"

Brenna shook her head. "No, but I take it you do?"

Blood on the Warpath: *Shame*

Thirty-caliber shells were very common, but a feature of these looked familiar. "I saw this stamping pattern in rebel casings during the civil war in Kameron."

With her heart quickening, Brenna's brow raised. "So these are generic Azgar munitions?" she concluded.

Garrick nodded worriedly, knowing that arms factories did this to obscure the origin of their bullets. Governments often bought these to discreetly supply insurgents, and since Brenna knew this as well, he said nothing more.

Her curiosity piqued, noting what looked like a firing line in the dark sand, Brenna knitted her brow. "The Kamerese civil war ended eighteen months ago. Why would the Azgar send ammunition into Nordan territory?"

Slipping the shell into his left pocket out of habit, Garrick shrugged. "Maybe someone smuggled these over the border. Judging from the amount of brass on the ground, I'd say an armed group of at least platoon size recently used this beach for training."

The self-righteous expression arising in Garrick's eye annoyed his wife. "The music festival invitation stated that this area remains firmly under Nordan control, and that violence is limited to the northern and northeastern regions of the colony," she replied.

Knowing how desperately she wanted to start a family, Garrick believed that Brenna would never deliberately put their lives at risk by traveling to dangerous territory. "We're fairly close to the Kamerese border," he soothed. "Maybe one of those fringe groups who've been trying to overthrow King Alejo is training here."

That sounded reasonable, but no less perilous. "Then it's wise to head back," she replied. "I'd hate to get caught in a crossfire."

Blood on the Warpath: *Shame*

Although unarmed at the moment, Garrick usually carried a .45 caliber handgun with him. Due to the romantic nature of their excursion, he'd thought better of leaving his weapon on the beach while swimming and had locked it in the strongbox of their hotel room, where Brenna had also stored her boot knife. Her composite bow and a quiver of arrows remained hidden behind a dress in their closet. Now, he suddenly felt vulnerable.

Leaving the shooting range behind, Garrick led his wife around a rugged rock formation that, at high tide, spilled into the sea. Little pools of clear water left behind by the retreating sea created homes for anemones, starfish, sea stars, crabs and mussels. As a young girl, Brenna had eaten freshwater cousins of these creatures and knew they were delicious. "You want one?" she asked.

Garrick, however, lacked her sense of culinary adventure. "No, thank you," he stated. "I don't want to eat slime-sucking critters from the ocean floor."

"You have to cook them first," she quipped. "Vibriosis infection can be fatal if you eat them raw."

"All the more reason to abstain," he replied.

Just then, a shift in the wind's direction brought a whiff of smoke, originating from a fire a few hundred yards further south. The conflagration appeared unusually large, given the wet nature of their treeless, seaside surroundings. Out of curiosity the lovers approached to investigate.

Flames consumed a pair of wide, shallow-draft boats with curved prows carved into dragon heads. The smoky kelp oil smell mingled with the unpleasant aroma of burning human flesh. Realizing the murderous nature of the scene, Brenna recoiled. She scanned the beach, but noticed no footprints. The killers must have escaped by sea.

Three bodies, all of them male, lay on burning piles of dried kelp loaded on the boats. Each had been shot in the back of the head at close range. Standing downwind, Garrick reached for a shell casing and picked it up.

Brenna could see the bullet caliber differed from those they'd seen further north. "Handgun?" she asked.

Garrick nodded. Examining the rim stirred greater confusion. "Not from the same arms factory, either. I saw markings like this last summer on the Saradon . . . ."

"The Saradon?" Brenna asked, reluctant to stir memories of the nightmare experience he'd endured on the eastern plains. "Where were they from?"

"Captain Hougen told us these were made in Vathera and sold to the Perans. Tanarak tribes raided Peran armories to steal the weapons they used against us."

That made no sense. Brenna bowed her head to intercede for the victims while her husband respectfully remained silent, as he did not pray. At length, she spoke again, her brow knitted with worry. "This looks like a premeditated killing," Brenna stated. "But how could the Vatherans be involved when we're so far south?"

Her conclusion resonated with Garrick. The Nordans boasted a very strong and capable navy. They'd ended organized raids from the north many decades earlier. "Maybe drugs, maybe revenge, maybe a warning," he mused. "In any case, it's a shame."

***

"*Tora Ni* in position," Sato announced into the microphone. "Targets not visible."

A moment later, the familiar voice on the other end of the radio replied, "Be advised, *Tora Ni*. Change in tasking order. Your team will interdict four Kurian terrorists. New targets are an armed kill team in a rowboat half a mile north of your position, heading south to suspected insurgent dock. Coordinates follow."

Sato suppressed a curse as he hurriedly wrote down and verified the given location. This was not the mission he'd been briefed to carry out, but he understood that destroying seaweed shipments disrupted vital supplies for Nordan fuel factories. The locals had to be taught a lesson about who was in control . . . .

Although his commanders did not think of Sato as tactically clever, the nature of his new orders didn't require finesse. Glancing at the coordinates on his map, he noted that the Kurian terror team's destination lay south of the Seashell Resort in a tiny cove that lacked road access.

After consulting with Warrant Officer Kanezane, Sato selected a spot on the map where his team would unload, hike over a low ridge, then prepare to engage their objective. Dune formations noted on the map might become useful in providing cover.

Taking down their radio for the fourth time since their arrival delayed their departure. Sergeant Shinji worked quickly while Sato described his hastily-formulated attack plan with the rest of the team.

"Funimaro will take up a position on the ridge, about thirty yards from shore," he explained.

Turning to the weapons specialist, Sato outlined his intentions. "Wait for my signal," he concluded.

"The team will clear the dock and this shed building before the targets arrive. Funimaro will wire both and carry out the demolition upon our egress. Any questions?"

Shinji nodded. "Sir. Do you want the radio on the ridge with Funimaro?"

Sato shook his head. "No. If we encounter rebel forces and get pinned down, I will call for reinforcements."

"The garrison is many miles away," Medical Sergeant Yosai noted. "If we run into a large unit, it will take some time for help to arrive."

"Then we fight with honor," Sato replied.

***

Long daylight hours stretched the afternoon well into evening. Garrick and Brenna donned formal attire for their final meal of the day and watched the Daystar dipping near the northwestern horizon from their second-floor hotel room before heading to the Seashell Resort's restaurant.

Though he'd wanted to admire his lovely wife during the meal, Garrick's attention frequently drifted toward another table, where several Kamerese men had gathered.

"Why do you keep looking over there?" Brenna asked.

Worried that his bride might think him paranoid for sharing his thoughts, Garrick replied, "Casually glance at that table and pay attention to how often they look at us."

"Okay," she responded, trying not to show concern. Accustomed to attracting both pleasant and boorish masculine attention, she initially suspected they were just leering at her. Brenna's lips tightened in irritation. "What they're doing may be rude, but it's common."

Garrick reached across the table, took her fingers in his and lowered his voice. "Look at the way they're dressed and how they carry themselves. They're all fit, clean-cut and they behave with a swagger I don't see in the other resort guests. They gesture with a full hand, rather than pointing. They defer to the guy on their left, who looks a little older, and whenever they talk to the waiter, they're very polite."

Brenna stroked her husband's hand, unconcerned about the men at the table, but growing worried about Garrick. "They're soldiers, or ex-soldiers. Maybe they recognize a common spirit in you. They're not threatening us in any way. Why are you troubled?"

Maintaining a calm demeanor while his heart began to race required great self control. Garrick took in a deep breath to regain composure. "They're looking at us like we're the enemy," he replied.

"They're Kamerese," she soothed. "They're your allies."

Withdrawing his hand, Garrick took a sip of water and wiped his mouth with a cloth napkin. "The people who funded the terror attack on the palace before my brother's wedding were Kamerese," he reminded her. "The people who captured and tortured you were Kamerese . . . ."

Growing angry, Brenna's eyes burned. "That's not fair!" she retorted sternly. "I'm still struggling to forgive. You don't have to remind me of what I went through!"

Garrick let his gaze wander down the right side of his wife's neck, where an ugly scar from a rebel machete marred her otherwise flawless form. She'd earned Tamaria's highest honor for wreaking vengeance on her captors in the aftermath of that experience, but had suffered spiritual torment for months thereafter.

"I'm sorry," he conceded, watching her expression soften. The men arose from their table and left. "I don't want to ruin everything. Let's enjoy our evening."

They ate what she considered a mediocre meal of seafood, vegetables and rice. Bronwyn, their newlywed sister-in-law, could have taught the resort chefs a thing or two about putting food together. However, in the pleasant company of her husband, Brenna didn't complain.

Despite the fawning demeanor of her waiter, whose spoken Kurian sounded close enough to the Tamarian tongue for her to grasp, Brenna struggled to communicate. Their waiter, who misunderstood everything Garrick said, had a much worse time with the Lithian woman's heavily accented speech. He mistakenly brought wine for her meal that she refused to touch, fearing that drinking might jeopardize her likelihood of getting pregnant and carrying a healthy baby to term.

Anticipating the warm delights he knew she'd lavish on him later that evening, Garrick tried to let go of his concern and focus on nurturing his wife's happiness. Yet a persistent sense of imminent danger lurked in the fringes of his mind, an internal warning that wouldn't go away.

***

From the moment *Tora Ni* approached the new tasking site, everything went wrong. Sergeant Goro lifted his foot from the throttle at a roadblock obstructing a straight section of the highway. A low ridge covered in dense vegetation rose to the west, while to the east, recently logged forest stretched for nearly 100 yards. Beyond this, thick temperate forest rose.

Two unshaven Kurian men, brandishing bolt-action hunting rifles whose worn stocks told quiet tales of long use, stood nervously in front of a log they'd cut and dragged across both lanes of the road. One held his hand up to halt the truck.

"What do we do, sir?" Goro asked.

Sato, believing that this affront to Nordan sovereignty was best dealt with by threatening irresistible, overwhelming force, didn't immediately respond. Instead, he reached for the intercom mike on the dashboard. "Insurgent Kurians ahead," he announced to his men in the back. "Deploy when we stop."

The younger of the local men, wearing worn, ill-fitting fatigues supplied by some foreign army, nervously pointed his rifle at the vehicle while the other picked up a radio receiver and rapidly spoke into it. As the truck stopped, Sato felt the tailgate open and heard his soldiers scurry out. Confident in his authority, the Special Forces officer opened his door and hopped to the ground.

"What is the meaning of this?" he shouted in Nordan, expecting the local men to understand.

"This road is closed," the blonde-haired Kurian replied. "You have to go back."

Sato, thinking that the radio might yield valuable intelligence, directed Sergeant Shinji to confiscate it. He returned his attention to the younger man who – seeing he was outnumbered – had wisely lowered his rifle. "Drop your weapon!" he ordered.

When the man didn't immediately comply, Sato pulled his sidearm and aimed it at the young Kurian's head. "Drop it now, or die!"

Three seconds passed without a reply. With tension building, Sato believed that his honor, his authority, and the safety of his crew depended on compliance with a clear order. He pulled the trigger twice, his aim accurate and lethal. In a panic, the Kurian radio operator reached for his weapon, but the Nordan lieutenant calmly turned and shot him, too.

None of Sato's men questioned his judgment, as they also expected absolute obedience from the colony's subjects. They'd all witnessed similar brutality and believed their rank as overlords entitled them to weed out undesired elements in the colonial population.

"Dump the terrorists in the ditch," Sato ordered with a dismissive gesture. "And get this log out of here!"

Moments later, as Chief Engineer Sharuko evaluated the best way to clear the road, gunfire erupted from the tree line to the west. Sharuko took a bullet to the back, which lodged in his armor, but another struck his left shoulder, tumbled into his cheek and spiraled into his brain.

Sergeant Goro fell next, clutching an entry wound in his thigh that quickly darkened his combat pants. He screamed in pain, calling for Ozu, the medic.

Sato and his surviving men scrambled for cover before orienting to the threat and returning fire. The unexpected resistance quickened Sato's heart, as Nordan military supremacy typically guaranteed quick submission. Yet for the first time in his brief career, the insurgents were fighting back. This was also his first combat loss, and for a moment, the reality stunned him into inaction.

Weapons Sergeant Funimaro took the initiative. He carried a .30 caliber light machine gun, and with it, began laying down covering fire to suppress the enemy.

"Get Sharuko and Goro into the trees!" Sato shouted, gesturing for his men to move. "Let's go!"

Ozu Yosai and Moto Kanazane bravely retrieved the bodies of their fallen comrades, while Sato, Funimaro and Shinji fired across the timber cut. Once repositioned under cover, Kanazane blew a whistle, signaling the others to retreat while he fired to the east to cover their movement.

The team reached the trees without further casualties. Sato climbed the low ridge to observe any threats on the other side. He didn't need binoculars to discern that a company-sized force had been alerted by the gunfire. "Funimaro!" he called. "Get that machine gun up here! And Shinji – alert *Tora Chichi*. We need support, now!"

Communication Sergeant Shinji shouldered his rifle and carried his heavy radio gear uphill. By the time he arrived, out of breath and temporarily unable to speak, Sato had found their coordinates on the map.

Tora Chichi – Father Tiger – coordinated all units available for operations. The garrison at Svalgen, some fifteen miles distant, could not respond in time to save Sato's team. If the Kurian insurgents attacked in earnest, *Tora Ni* would run out of ammunition before vanquishing the enemy. Insurgents never fought with honor, never displayed courage. They'd always run from aggressive attack, but something had changed, and Sato became the first Nordan officer to face determined colonial resistance.

Egress to the north, where the town of Briminger and the Seashell Resort lay, would save his men. However, failure to meet his mission objectives would also bring shame to his unit and his reputation, two outcomes that Sato couldn't bear.

But after he explained the situation and gave his coordinates to *Tora Chichi* over the radio, Colonel Utemaro sternly advised Sato to hold his position. "You will direct naval artillery fires from the *Yoizuki*. Stand by . . . ."

Kanazane carried Sharuko's lifeless body uphill, then retreated to help Yosai move Goro to the summit. Sergeant Funimaro set up his machine gun on the reverse slope, with a roughly 120-degree field of fire covering the beach. Dozens of men – lacking cover of any kind – moved about in confusion, below.

While Yosai worked to stabilize Goro, the rest of *Tora Ni* positioned themselves on the ridge and prepared to fight. Tense moments passed. With the heat of the day waning, anxiety inspired sweat on Sato's brow. He didn't want to die, but he didn't want to be shamed, either.

While the lull in firing inspired inaction by the insurgents, who'd come out from several low buildings on the dark beach, the Kurians who'd taken out Sharuko and wounded Goro soon began advancing from their cover in the trees to the east. They moved cautiously, in a ragged, undisciplined line, through the stumps and debris littering the ground. Kanezane noticed them first. He silently motioned for Sato, requesting permission to engage.

Knowing that it would take time to calculate a firing solution for the naval guns, Sato shook his head.

Lack of discipline among the Kurians quickened the inevitable conflict. As the group from the tree line neared the Nordan truck, a few took pot shots at its windows. As they approached, one threw a grenade inside. The ensuing explosion alerted the men on the beach, who assumed that battle had renewed. With a collective shout, they swarmed in a disorderly mob toward the ridge.

Sato didn't have time to consider his options. Faced with overwhelming odds, he gave the order for his *Tora* Team to commence firing. It went well, at first.

The Nordans slaughtered more than ten of their enemies within moments, their rifles and machine gun blunting the Kurian charge. As confusion dispersed the men on the beach, Nordan fire pinned them down behind the dunes and grass. The insurgents began shooting back, forcing Funimaro to move into a different position, as the machine gun attracted a lot of attention and return fire. Individual rifles were far harder for the enemy to spot.

Meanwhile, the terrorists from the east began advancing uphill. Faced with an attack on two fronts, Lieutenant Sato honored the threat by splitting his firepower. He assigned Kanazane and Shinji to the smaller group advancing from the road, while he, Yosai and Funimaro on the machine gun defended their position facing west, toward the sea. All he needed to do at this moment was buy time for naval assets to position themselves for his defense.

Sato picked his targets carefully. As the enemy closed in and fear smothered his soul, the Nordan officer felt his heart rate rise. He uttered prayers to the gods – not for mercy or deliverance – but for courage to die honorably. His Special Forces team had not been equipped for a prolonged firefight. They'd trained for stealthy ingress, carrying just enough ammunition to accomplish a specific task. As their magazines emptied and they loaded their limited reserves, *Tora Ni* grimly faced the possibility that these moments might be their last. While every man wanted to survive, their social conditioning compelled them to linger in a circumstance where wiser soldiers would have fled.

Blood on the Warpath: *Shame*

Three miles to the west, the destroyer *Yoizuki* set a course that ran parallel to shore. She raised her four-inch guns and launched a targeting volley that crashed into the waves on the shore. Sato set his rifle down and reached for the radio microphone, directing fire further east.

With each of her four main guns able to sustain a ten round per minute rate of fire, *Yoizuki* pounded the insurgent Kurians with a fury they could not endure. Caught in the open, their bodies succumbed to high explosive shells that shredded their torsos into smoking hunks of burning flesh.

Hearing the naval artillery hammering on the far side of the ridge, the insurgents attacking from the east fled down the road. Kanazane and Shinji shot a few in the back, but the need to conserve ammunition constrained them. The Nordans, sticking to their orders and combat doctrine, did not pursue.

After Sato called off the barrage, his disciplined team held their fire. Quiet settled on the scene. They waited, none daring to express relief, while Sato examined the beach with his binoculars. Satisfied that the insurgent threat had been quashed, he spotted the small boat he'd been ordered to interdict and ordered Funimaro to sink it.

Two bursts from the machine gun sent the wooden vessel and its crew beneath the reddened waves. That was one less terror team to contend with, but as its cargo of stolen seaweed floated out to sea. Sato shook his head at the waste of a valuable commodity. What a shame!

***

Later that evening, as Garrick danced with his wife in the resort's ballroom, he caught a fleeting glimpse of other men whose appearance and demeanor marked them as soldiers. But their flatter faces, skin tone and almond eyes identified them as Nordan, rather than Kamerese.

He turned with his bride in his arms and briefly locked his gaze on a Nordan soldier, who quickly disappeared into a crowded arcade. Not wishing to alarm his wife, Garrick held his tongue.

Yet Brenna, who'd witnessed his hypervigilance and lived through the worst of his combat trauma, felt her husband's tension rise. She knew this response and whispered a prayer for grace on his behalf, but misinterpreted the problem. "Are you okay?" she asked.

"I'm fine," he replied.

"Please don't lie to me," she warned. "I love you and I deserve your honesty."

Garrick willed his emotions under control. He'd come here to support her in the competition and had no desire to argue. "We're being watched," he told her.

Brenna sighed. "We're close to the border," she reiterated. "A lot of Kamerese vacation here."

He shook his head. "This guy was a Nordan, probably an empire soldier. He was trying to be discreet, but when I made eye contact with him, he took off."

Desperate to soothe her husband's concern, Brenna gazed into his eyes with the center of her brow raised and a little frown turning down the corners of her lovely lips. "Maybe he's part of the security detail," she soothed, a twinge of desperation creeping into her voice. "I've seen more than one of them around."

"Maybe so," Garrick replied. "But why was he watching us? Why did he leave the moment I noticed?"

She dropped his hands and shrugged in disappointment. "I don't know." Brenna turned away from the dance floor with her husband following close behind.

He caught up with her at their table. "Brenna," he pleaded. "I know you want this time to be special for us. I know you want to relax and enjoy yourself. I'm not trying to wreck this for you, but something isn't right."

Fighting off an acerbic remark, Brenna bowed her head and closed her eyes to pray for patience, feeling Garrick's hand rest gently and respectfully on her shoulder. Despite his unbelief, he never interrupted her prayers and waited silently for her to finish. Afterward, she asked, "Would you feel safer upstairs?"

Garrick nodded, knowing that she would have preferred to stay on the dance floor. He hated letting her down, however, upstairs they could defend themselves with his handgun and her bow. The beach, with its soft sand beneath their balcony, offered an exit if they had to flee. Here, unarmed in the crowd, their options were limited.

Knowing his wife well, he set aside his anxiety for a little while longer. Garrick slid his hands down the back of her arms. "How about one more dance?" he offered. "We can head to the room afterward."

Brenna smiled and followed him back into the crowd. She pressed her body into his as the band played a romantic melody, grateful that after months of volatility, he could finally moderate his apprehension. Held in his close embrace, Brenna swayed in rhythm to the music, wishing she could enjoy moments like this more often.

Her veteran husband understood that his combat trauma complicated their marriage, compelling her to tolerate irritable behavior. Brenna deserved better, and in attending this music festival with her, he'd been determined to treat her with the kindness and affection she deserved.

Still, he remained alert, occasionally glancing around while he held his beloved bride close. Growing gradually more confident, he relaxed until the sensation of his woman's soft body pressing against his own wrought the comfort only she could provide. As the music ended, her smile warmed him.

"Let's go," she recommended.

Their sensuous mood heightened as they scurried upstairs, and the sound of her giggling resonated down the hall when they arrived on their floor. But the playful mood between them evaporated as they discovered a note on their door, written in the Kurian script that neither of them could read. Worse, the security deadbolt, which their key did not open, had locked them out.

"What's going on?" Garrick complained, partly concerned that the note might represent a threat, and also frustrated that he couldn't act on his longing right away.

"Maybe we should check with the front desk," Brenna suggested, caressing her husband's arm soothingly.

Garrick nodded, asserting control over anger that simmered as they walked back downstairs. At the desk, he pushed the note across the marble counter to an attractive young woman wearing a business suit.

The desk clerk leaned forward spoke quietly in fluent Tamarian. "Another guest has requested that you move to a different room," she said.

Brenna, thinking this might be racially motivated, sighed and cast her glance downward. No matter where she went in Tamaria, bigotry haunted her steps. She'd long ago grown weary of resisting the problem and resigned herself to whatever outcome awaited.

Seeing this response, the hotel clerk lowered her voice and related the lie she'd been ordered to tell them. "Apparently, the frequency and volume of your intimacy is disturbing to the people next door," she added with a flirtatious smile. She found the soldier handsome, well-formed, and secretly envied his little Lithian woman. "In light of the complaint, we thought that moving you next to an empty suite would better accommodate your needs."

Hearing this, Garrick nearly burst out laughing, as he'd worried that someone had been watching, rather than listening to them. "Moving us would be kind of you."

The clerk motioned for a porter before continuing. "We will assist your relocation at our expense, and offer a complimentary dinner with drinks in the hotel restaurant for your inconvenience."

Brenna blushed and cowered behind her husband. How embarrassing!

The new, larger room – located at the very end of the hall – featured lavish appointments that included a bigger bed with satin sheets, and a spacious bathroom with a jetted tub, rather than just a shower. Double doors opened to a balcony that directly overlooked the sea. A chilled bottle of wine, warm towels and lights set to amplify a romantic mood completed its ambiance. After the porter brought the balance of their belongings from the other room, Garrick stood on the balcony with Brenna, watching the Daystar set.

Blood on the Warpath: *Shame*

The smell of the sea air and the lovely view over the ocean set the tone for talk that wandered into his appreciation of her beauty. Brenna leaned her head into his shoulder, nuzzling his chest as he slid one arm around her back while his other hand rose to her soft, heavy breast.

Brenna loosened her gown, seductively pulling its straps down her shoulders while she gestured toward the room with a tilt of her head. "Come and love me," she beckoned in a sultry tone . . . .

***

Footsore and sullen, Sato led his team back to their observation post. Twilight, lingering in the northwestern sky, compelled them to settle down for the night. Although a launch from the destroyer *Yoizuki* had picked up their casualties and the intelligence they'd recovered from the insurgent camp – including the Kurian radio – the survivors of *Tora Ni* returned on foot, taking a route through the hills to avoid contact.

Sergeant Shinji set up the radio. Sato notified *Chichi Tora* that they'd arrived in position. With the wind off the sea picking up and *Shīgōrudo* heading for its hangar, *Tora Ni* would be the eyes of the operation through the night. Sato assigned his team a sleep, observation and patrol schedule, ensuring at least two men would be on watch.

Unable to sleep, Sato stood on the ridge overlooking the surf as the stars appeared. With the twin moons facing the Daystar in the west, the night grew very dark as twilight slipped over the horizon. In the east, the Great Eye Nebula cast its eerie, blue glow into the deepening shadows.

Uncertain he'd properly handled the conflict at the roadblock, Sato grew introspective. Should he have turned the truck around and infiltrated the ridge overlooking the beach on foot? A profound sense of responsibility for Sharuko's demise settled on his soul, partly because the engineer's death seemed so pointless, and partly because it happened so suddenly, so unexpectedly. Perhaps, had he chosen differently, Sharuko would still be alive, and Goro would not have been wounded.

The radio squawked. Shinji responded to the call, then notified Lieutenant Sato of a revision in their orders. "Targets have successfully moved to the second floor suite on the north end of the guest quarters," he reported.

"Copy," Sato replied. He tried to observe the building through his binoculars, but the lights were off and he couldn't see anything. After notifying the watch team of the change, he stretched out on his bedroll, worried about how to explain the engineer's death to Sharuko's family.

***

Late that night, after loving Brenna until he could offer nothing more, Garrick gently held his wife close, stroking her hair while she prayed. He never scoffed or ridiculed the vulnerabilities his woman revealed in her orison, allowing her to openly express faith with an authenticity that provided a window into her soul.

Brenna felt esteemed because he honored her convictions, even though he didn't share them. They'd arrived at this mutual respect after several conflicts over their contrasting belief systems nearly ruined their relationship. The compromise worked well for them.

He'd learned to hold her quietly in these moments, enjoying the sensation of her warm body and smooth skin while she emptied her soul and expressed gratitude for her abundant blessings. This built trust between them, while maintaining personal integrity and relational respect.

Suddenly, Brenna stopped. She looked up at her husband with widened eyes that appeared bright in the darkness. "Something's wrong," she cautioned.

Alarmed, Garrick glanced at the safe where his big handgun lay and asked, "What is it?"

"Allfather put a verse in my head," she told him. "It's a warning. It came out of nowhere . . . ."

A moment later, the sound of booted feet on the hardwood hallway floor froze the young couple in fear. In the ensuring silence, Garrick felt his heart pounding. Brenna's breath fell on his bare shoulder. He could hear her whispered prayer, her beautiful, prosodic phrasing that mysteriously stirred courage in his soul. A masculine grunt, followed by a loud bang and the sound of a door slamming against a wall, stirred the frightened lovers into action.

The sound of suppressed gunfire echoed down the hall. Garrick turned on the table lamp, squatted in front of the safe with his heart pounding, and quickly dialed in its combination. He reached for his handgun and a loaded magazine, which he slapped into place.

He'd not come here to die, but Garrick would defend his bride, even at the cost of his own life . . . .

Realizing that the attackers had broken into their previous room – and that they'd continue searching until they'd found their quarry – Brenna had little time to respond. The Lithian woman gracefully rolled off the bed and reached behind her long dresses.

As Garrick activated the light, she strung her bow in a swift motion, grabbed a handful of arrows from her quiver and hastened to the double doors leading to the patio.

"The light will lead them here," she warned in a whisper, encouraging Garrick to shut it off.

Stepping into a strong wind that rippled her filmy gown, Brenna glanced at the beach below as her eyesight adjusted. With the twin moons new and the Great Eye blazing, the night looked bright to her, but would appear completely dark to Garrick and their attackers.

Another crash followed as the door to the adjacent, empty room slammed into the wall. This time no gunfire ensued. The kill team was conserving ammunition – a sign of professional killers – not poorly trained radicals.

Grunting, Garrick lifted the bed onto its side and positioned himself at a steep angle to the short hallway serving as the room's entrance. Constrained by his love for Brenna and unwilling to risk her life if he could buy time for her to run, Garrick chambered a round, flipped his weapon's safety off and took aim at the portal. "Please go!" he urged. "I'll cover you."

Yet Brenna couldn't bear to let her husband face death alone. She slid behind the outer wall with arrows readied in her right hand, raising her bow just inside the doorjamb as a ram smashed the lock on their room's door.

Men wearing Nordan uniforms and balaclavas, looking for targets with sight-mounted flashlights, burst into the suite. Brenna loosed three arrows in rapid succession, their deadly shafts slamming into the soft flesh just above the body armor of her would-be killers. She heard the third one curse, recognizing a foul phrase she'd heard many times as a prisoner in Kameron . . . .

Surprised by this unexpected resistance, the surviving attackers blasted the room with gunfire before retreating. "Garrick, run!" she begged, slinging her bow over her shoulder. Brenna crawled over the rail, hung onto its lower crossbar, steadied herself, then dropped to the sand.

The unmistakable thunder of Garrick's .45 caliber semi-auto handgun erupted overhead. He fired four times as the enemy pressed into the room again. During a momentary pause in the action, gloved hands dragged fallen kill team bodies backwards. Deafened by the roar of his weapon, he didn't hear Brenna pleading for him to flee.

Just then, a grenade rolled into the room.

Garrick flipped the bed onto the explosive and dashed for safety. Brenna screamed for him to jump as he burst onto the patio. The grenade went off, its over-pressure showering the room and the beach beyond in splintered glass and debris. Too pumped with adrenaline to realize he'd been hit with shattered glass, Garrick climbed over the rail, steadied himself, then dropped onto the sand.

Brenna heard sustained gunfire and saw another masked soldier appear, using the mounted light to search for his targets. She was too far away for him to see, but she had no trouble seeing him. An arrow whispered demise into his ear just before it struck him in the throat, and a second followed one heartbeat later, killing his companion.

With only one arrow left, the Lithian woman cried out in desperation. "They can't see you! They're firing blindly and won't hit you if you keep running!"

Barely able to hear her screaming as the momentary deafening of his handgun's roar began to fade, Garrick stumbled onward. "I can't see, either!" he shouted.

"Just follow my voice," she pleaded, dreading that he might get hit in the back by a surviving shooter. "I'm over here! If you run to the sea I'll find you! Please don't stop!"

Automatic gunfire sprayed from the patio into the darkness. Garrick began hearing rounds whistle into the nearby sand until another arrow whisked over his head, forever silencing the would-be killer's carbine. The Tamarian officer ran as fast as he could until his feet hit the wet shore. He paused, then felt his wife's soft hand on his arm.

"You're bleeding!" she stated in a ragged, terrified voice. "Have you been hit?"

"I don't feel a thing," Garrick panted.

Brenna turned her attention to his injuries, confident they were too far away from the hotel to be seen, even with a flashlight. She wiped the black sand from her husband's bare back, shoulders and neck with a furrowed brow. "It's glass," she announced. Deftly, Brenna picked shards out of his flesh and tossed them into the waves. Whispering a prayer, she put her lips on his bleeding skin and felt a power surge through her flesh.

He felt a familiar, supernatural warmth flowing through his body – a sensation that always accompanied Brenna's healing. The lovers locked themselves into a tight embrace as foamy waves caressed the dark shore at their feet. A ferocious firefight began inside the resort. Sustained gunfire and shouting voices echoed over the beach. In the terror of that moment, neither Garrick nor Brenna wondered who was shooting at whom.

The Lithian woman sobbed until her fear faded, convinced that Allfather had again honored her faith and spared her husband's life. He'd made it out wearing only his underwear and holding his gun, but he was still alive.

Garrick thanked her repeatedly. "Bless your *Malleah Shevonne*," he stated, referring to Brenna's paternal great-aunt. "Bless the day she put that bow in your hands!"

With his arms wrapped around her, Brenna could feel his heart pounding. She prayed in gratitude for his deliverance until he let her go.

"We can't stay here," he stated at length. "Let's go back to the lagoon. I saw a barn on the far shore where we can shelter until morning."

***

Excited chatter over the radio motivated Weapons Sergeant Funimaro to awaken Lieutenant Sato. "Sir, I think you need to hear this," he said.

With an alertness that belied his exhaustion, Sato approached the radio. He heard gunfire over the voice of *Tora Ichi's* Communications Sergeant. Sato heard the man explain that they were pinned down in a firefight.

Sato turned to Funimaro. "Get everyone up," he ordered. "Prepare to move out."

Because he didn't have the authority to take initiative on his own, Sato used a different frequency to hail *Tora Chichi* and request instructions. Colonel Utemaro came straight to the point. "Secure the beach," he ordered. "Make sure your targets don't get away."

"Yes sir!" Sato replied.

But how could the foreigners survive a firefight? With *Tora Ichi* stalled by the enemy's resistance, how could the targets escape? And if they had, how could his men track them on such a dark night?

"I saw lights flashing near the back of the hotel and thought I heard gunfire too," Funimaro admitted. "I wasn't sure because it's hard to hear in all this wind."

"We're stationed here to observe, not engage," Sato replied. "If the colonel had wanted us doing anything else, he wouldn't have put us out of range."

Minutes later, *Tora Ni* left their position and marched toward the Seashell Resort. Gusty onshore wind blew spray and covered the sound of their labored breathing as they strode through deep sand and dune grass. Soon, the gunfire ceased and an eerie calm settled on the scene.

On a balcony overlooking the beach, three gunsight-mounted lights shone into the darkness, each of them pointing at odd angles. Noting singular arrows protruding from the necks of dead, carbine-wielding men, Sato ordered his squad to move a nearby picnic table beneath the balcony. He sent Funimaro up first, with the surviving squad members covering him, waiting for the sergeant to signal safety. Moments later, Funimaro gestured for Sato to join him. The Nordan officer reached for the safety rail, pulled himself up and climbed over.

Broken glass clinked beneath his booted feet. Stepping over what looked like fallen colonial soldiers, Sato drew his sidearm and carefully entered the darkened room. It smelled of burnt fabric, loosened bowels and an intriguing scent he did not recognize. Unable to see clearly, he reached for a dead man's weapon and shone its light into every corner, noting bullet holes in the walls, an overturned bed, burn marks and evidence of over-pressure in reading lamps knocked off tables, wall pictures ripped from their hooks and a shattered mirror.

Blood on the Warpath: *Shame*

Knowing that *Tora Ichi* was supposed to have prevented violence, Sato tried to make sense of the chaotic scene. Aside from coagulated blood in the short hall at the entrance, he saw no sign that the room's occupants had been injured. A petite woman's clothing and a man's shirts and pants hung neatly in the closet. Undergarments lay in broken drawers.

The occupants had either left in a hurry, or had been taken hostage. Toiletries in the bathroom hadn't been touched. Shattered mirror glass lay sprinkled over the shaving kit and hair brush. Two pairs of shoes lay in the hallway. Examining the closet, Sato found a quiver containing 14 arrows stashed behind a collection of formal gowns. Why hadn't the archer taken all of them?

Sato returned to the balcony to analyze the fallen soldiers he'd seen there. All three wore copies of Colonial Guard uniforms, but after lifting their balaclavas Sato concluded these were round-eyes posing as Nordans – each one slain by a single arrow that struck a finger's width above their chest armor.

Archery had long been an important practice among the Nordan warrior class. Even after the adoption of firearms, regular archery and horsemanship competitions attracted large crowds from all across the home islands, with cash prizes and honor heaped on the winners. Sato's familiarity with archery enabled him to recognize how skillfully these arrows had been loosed. He couldn't determine the range from which they been let go, but the precision and consistency of each hit astonished him. On a dark and windy night, it wouldn't have been easy to wield a bow with such skill.

Hearing voices speaking accented Nordan somewhere down the hall, Sato put his gun away, climbed back over the rail, and dropped to the table. "Scan the immediate area for evidence," he ordered. "Our targets are not here."

As the men spread out from beneath the balcony, Warrant Officer Kanezane approached Sato and spoke in a lowered voice. "It will be hard to track anything, even at first light. There are too many footprints in the sand and we may trample on clues."

"The foreigners are hotel guests," Sato replied. "They don't know the area, they left in haste, didn't take any of their belongings and it's too dark to have gone far. If I were them, I'd head to a place I'd been before."

"The lagoon, perhaps?" Kanezane replied.

Sato nodded. "That's likely."

Kanezane remained skeptical. "That's a long way to go in the dark."

"Perhaps, but the woman is Lithian, and I hear that they see well in conditions like this. We'll do our diligence and settle in for the night. We all need rest."

Sato had Shinji set up the radio and made contact with *Tora Chichi*. Colonel Utemaro's voice boomed on the other end. "Report, lieutenant."

"Sir!" Sato began. "We've secured the beach, searched the area and set up a perimeter watch. I believe our targets are armed and dangerous. We found three insurgents, wearing Nordan uniforms, slain by arrows I suspect were loosed by one of our targets."

"Have you apprehended the foreigners?"

"No, sir. They were long gone before we arrived."

Colonel Utemaro paused before responding. "Search and find them," he ordered. "Don't stop until you do."

"Sir, it's dark. We can't see anything and we risk destroying evidence . . . ."

"Find them," the colonel replied impatiently. "We need them alive. Search the area and report your success to me."

"Yes sir!" Sato replied.

Aware that his weary men could not follow those orders, Sato handed the microphone back to Shinji. "Shut the radio off," he said quietly. "We'll rest here for the night and search for the foreigners at dawn."

***

Garrick's feet ached from stepping on sharp, volcanic rocks. He'd stubbed his toe twice, unable to see in the impenetrable dark, but Brenna's confidence kept him going. Determined to keep up with her relentless pace, he pushed his body onward with brute will and discipline, never once complaining about discomfort.

Nearly 40 minutes after leaving the Seashell Resort, the lovers arrived at the mouth of the lagoon. Surf pounded against the breakwater, sending fountains of spray high into the air that glimmered prettily in the ultraviolet spectrum. Brenna paused to watch the awe-inspiring sight, knowing that Garrick could see nothing of the beauty she observed.

As the young couple waded across the shallow water to the far shore, the thunder of waves on unyielding stone faded, and the squishy sensation of wet mud oozing through toes soothed Garrick's sore feet. On the far shore stood an old, abandoned barn that occasionally sheltered amorous, teenaged couples. A burned-out fire pit and a blanket draped over a pile of straw hinted at recent use, but the rickety building lay empty now.

Blood on the Warpath: *Shame*

Weary Garrick waited in the darkness while Brenna checked their surroundings for threats. When she returned, he pulled his bride onto the blanket and quickly fell into a dreamy slumber of confident moral clarity, soothed by the abundant comfort of his faithful wife.

Brenna held his hand against her breast and sniffed as a tear spilled from her eyes. Remembering how easily she'd reverted to killing, her imagination sought a different outcome, one that would have preserved life rather than taking it. Drawing back her bow had been so natural, so much a part of an identity rooted in childhood. Brenna, who'd been raised in a violent era, among violent people, knew that despite her piety and desire to transcend profane methods of imposing power, she faced the same struggle as an adult that had haunted her childhood. She'd learned nothing from the aftermath of vengeance she'd meted out against rebel soldiers in Kameron, and it made her feel sad.

Her breath came in little gasps as she prayed, desperate for absolution, longing for fundamental reform of this well-concealed flaw in her devout character. But Allfather seemed far away, she felt spiritually adrift, and Brenna evaluated her recent choices in a different light than had been the case before she'd loosed her first arrow.

Garrick had been right all along. He'd not gloated in triumph, yet she knew she should have been quicker to listen and slower to dismiss the concerns he'd raised. Brenna's virtuosic confidence, coupled with her desire to get away from Marvic and have Garrick all to herself, had blinded her to a truth he'd been trying to reveal. Killing people on foreign soil would not easily be explained to investigating authorities, especially with the language barrier they faced.

Blood on the Warpath: *Shame*

Brenna, who'd relied on charm, sex and persuasive skills to convince her husband that they'd be safe at the festival, now concluded that she and Garrick had been lured here. Someone had carefully plotted to kill them and very nearly succeeded. Yet the resort staff must have known about this and taken steps to protect them. Why else had they been moved? Those extra moments had given them time to arm and defend themselves.

Brenna *believed* that Allfather sent her a warning during her prayers, before the shooting began. So why hadn't they fled instead of standing to fight? Why had she trusted in martial training and not faith?

After much heartache and remonstrance, Brenna finally cried herself to sleep. She fell into a restless slumber filled with violent dreams and tainted in deep shame.

***

"Get up!" Sato shouted.

The nearly naked man lying on the straw instinctively reached for his handgun, but five raised carbines deterred him. He obeyed, the shame of being caught wearing only his underwear reddening his pale face.

Single, and having never seen a well-endowed woman wearing a filmy negligee, Sato struggled to keep his eyes on her partner, whom he wrongly presumed represented a greater threat. "I said get up!" he reiterated, shoving the young man's thigh with his booted foot.

They didn't understand. The man merged in front of his partner, holding out his left hand and desperately speaking barbaric gibberish that even multilingual Sergeant Shinji couldn't comprehend.

As she began uttering nonsense in a vowel-dominated language – her cadence and posture likely indicating prayer of some sort – Shinji reiterated Sato's order in the Kurian tongue. Her praying stopped. The young couple wordlessly glanced at each other and arose – he with both hands held aloft, while she modestly crossed her arms over her bosom and glided slightly behind him.

At least they understood Kurian.

"Identify yourselves!" Sato demanded in Nordan.

Shinji translated into Kurian, but the responses from the man and woman made no sense. They understood the colony's language, but neither could speak it.

The young man tried speaking in the Azgar vulgate, a tongue Shinji had studied, but one that required great effort to translate because he was not fluent. Sato listened while Shinji struggled with conversation, letting his eyes wander back to the raven-haired girl. She looked stunning and strong up close, save for a disfiguring scar that ran from her right ear, down her neck, to her collarbone.

"He told me his name is Black Trees and that the woman is his wife," Shinji said at length. "Her name is Velez, which sounds Kamerese. If I recall, those are the targets, right?"

Sato, who'd just received a wrathful reprimand from Colonel Utemaro over the radio, grunted. *Black Trees? What kind of a stupid name was that?*

Shinji continued, "He thinks we're allied with the kill team who attacked them last night. He demands we stop threatening them."

Feeling disrespected, Sato would have shot the arrogant foreigner right then and there, had he not been under orders to capture him alive. "Take their weapons."

After Funimaro confiscated the bow and handgun, Sato lowered his carbine and his team followed suit. "Tell him we're here to investigate the terrorist attack on the resort last night. He should not be asking questions. He answers to us, or he will die like a dog."

Shinji translated into Kurian – which was easier for him to speak than the common tongue – but the haughty foreigner expressed no gratitude.

"The men who came after us were wearing uniforms like yours," he replied. "This is your colony. Your people are in authority here. After last night, what makes you think I trust you any further than I can spit?"

But as the translator related that message, Brenna stood on her toes and whispered in Lithian, "Those men weren't Nordan. They were Kamerese."

"Are you sure?" Garrick asked quietly. In the darkness he'd not seen the attacker's faces and couldn't identify their nationality.

Brenna nodded, her eyes wide with fearful memory. "One of them called me *vaca diabla* after I hit his comrade with an arrow. It means *demon cow*. That's what the rebel guards called me at the *Casa del Matados*."

Garrick uttered a quiet curse. "Then they were likely the soldiers we saw at dinner. I could tell they were checking us out . . . ."

The multilingual Nordan interrupted their conversation. "Shut up!" he demanded. "You will speak to us, or you will not speak at all. My lieutenant wants to see your passports. He also needs to know about your involvement in the insurgent assault against the resort and its guests."

Unfazed, Garrick gestured down his nearly naked body. "Does it look like I'm carrying identification? Uniformed soldiers burst into our room, tried to kill us, and you think we're involved? Are you insane? We're the victims here. We barely made it out alive, and you're treating us like we're criminals. Neither of us had time to dress, much less fumble around to find our passports."

"We found you two in possession of deadly weapons," Shinji told him, shaking his head. "And you look like a native Kurian to us. You have no right to make demands. Answer our questions, or we'll kill you."

Careful to control his exasperation, Garrick responded in a calm tone. "We don't want trouble, but we can't prove our identity without going back to the resort. If our passports survived the grenade blast, I'll show them to you. But I'd rather you let us get dressed and take us to the Tamarian embassy in Helsing."

"That's not possible," Shinji told him. "The Colonial Authority will debrief you. They will decide your disposition. We have no say in the matter."

Frustrated, and noting how the Nordans were openly staring at Brenna and making her feel very uncomfortable, Garrick said, "Then at least have the decency to stop leering at my wife. Have you no shame?"

Trembling with indignation, Garrick climbed aboard a bus that the Nordan Special Forces team had taken from the Seashell Resort. One of the soldiers, who'd shown an inkling of humanity and offered Brenna his rain poncho, looked at Garrick, then spat in disgust. He gave the Tamarian officer a shove to encourage haste, shouting something in Nordan that Garrick didn't understand.

While the bus featured comfortable, padded seats, the Nordans didn't let the lovers sit together. One soldier forced Garrick to the back at gunpoint and kept a wary eye on him. Another pushed Brenna into a seat near the front and sat across the aisle with his rifle pointed at her.

Garrick heard the officer talk over a static-plagued military radio until the ethanol-fueled bus engine sputtered to life, its noise and vibration drowning the unintelligible conversation. The officer appeared unhappy as he put the hand piece down. *What was going on?*

Brenna looked over her shoulder with sadness reflected in her expression. She'd come here to perform, not to create trouble, and the difficulty of communicating with these mean-spirited foreign soldiers and their odd language multiplied her frustrations.

The resort's bus seemed quaint and inefficient when compared to the sleek, hybrid trains and quiet street cars of Tamaria. Even the much-maligned Electric Personnel Transporters of the Tamarian Expeditionary Force, with their limited cargo capacity and horrible handling over rough terrain, seemed highly advanced in comparison.

As the vehicle picked up speed along the gravel road, the roar of its engine increased to the point where the Nordans had to shout at one another in order to be heard. The driver slowed, then turned right onto a highway. That meant they were heading south.

Garrick maintained a stoic demeanor, despite his worry. Since the barn where he and Brenna had spent the night lay more than a mile from the nearest town, if the Nordans had wanted to kill them, he and Brenna would have perished in that isolated place. No one would have heard the gunfire. That meant someone wanted them alive.

Their direction of travel suggested they were either being taken back to the hotel, or to a military base near Briminger, the town located to the southeast of the resort. Unable to act on his outrage for what he considered humiliating treatment, and anxious to protect Brenna from harm, Garrick waited for the Nordans to make a mistake.

Dense coastal forest rose alongside the two-lane highway, occasionally revealing a lake or rocky outcrop that broke the monotony of dark green conifers laden with grey road dust. The region's wild beauty evoked primeval wonder in Garrick, until the huge, old trees dominating the roadway verge yielded to wide swaths of sloppy logging debris, where fir and cedar trees that had stood for hundreds of years recently succumbed to axe and saw. While the local forest had been managed for as long as people lived in the region, this harvesting method seemed glaringly indiscriminate. The Tamarian soldier concluded that the Nordans likely considered this region's timber and mineral wealth worthless if left in place. Therefore, the colonizers had no interest in conservation.

A few minutes later, the driver slowed and turned right at a junction. Garrick felt relieved, as the change of direction meant they were heading back to the resort. Perhaps, once he and Brenna presented their passports to the Nordans, the foreigners would let them go.

***

When the bus arrived at the resort, Sato ordered Kanezane to keep the prisoners under guard while he spoke to the Coastal Colony Officer. After being chewed out for shutting off the radio – despite claiming he'd been preserving its battery – and being ordered to consult with a civilian who'd not been involved in the operation, Sato felt frustrated. He had no patience for stupid bureaucrats.

However, the man waiting for Sato was not some low-level civilian hack. Oshita Koji – the Colonial Chief for the Southern Coastal District – had come up from Helsing, the regional capital, to assess the aftermath of the terror attack. That had to mean trouble.

Shortly after he entered the lobby, Sato received a quiet warning from Abjörn Olsen, the resort's administrator. The silver-haired Kurian had spent the night desperately trying to restore order in a chaotic situation. He looked exhausted. Addressing Sato with respect, he urged the Nordan officer to watch his tongue.

"The Chief is already upset," Abjörn cautioned. "We moved the clients like we were told. We increased our security, and did everything your people asked of us. This bloodbath has been a disaster for the resort. A good word about our cooperation would go a long way right now."

Sato hadn't known the targets were deliberately moved by the resort staff – as his task had been focused on observation and backup – but he understood the logic. Moving the targets gave *Tora Ichi* more time to take out the insurgents after they'd initiated the attack. In Sato's mind, Colonel Utemaro had done everything reasonable to avoid bloodshed.

Strictly following his orders, Sato needed proof that the detainees under his care were the actual targets. Until then, he couldn't be certain that he'd fulfilled his mission. Since he'd already screwed up by not searching for the escaped foreigners during the night, Sato didn't want to turn over his captives – as he'd been ordered to do – until he could prove they were the right people. Serving as a tool for some civilian functionary did nothing to increase Sato's confidence, as the Colonial Authority had a reputation for interfering with military operations.

"Tell Mr. Koji that I must verify the identities of my prisoners, first," Sato replied. "Once I have done so, I will report to my superior before releasing my captives."

"He won't like that," the administrator warned.

"Well, then he can take that up with Colonel Utemaro. I have orders, and I intend to follow them."

Sato returned to the bus. The lovely foreign girl, whispering gibberish with her head bowed and her eyes closed, ignored his commanding voice. "Tell her to take us to their room," he ordered Shinji.

When she continued with her prayers, rather than following Sato's translated orders, he grabbed a fistful of the woman's hair, pulled her from her seat and shoved her out of the bus. "Do as you're told!" he shouted.

The round-eyed soldier stood and protested loudly. But rather than listen to Shinji's translation, Sato pointed his side arm in the man's direction, quickly quieting the Tamarian's threatening tone and posture.

"Keep an eye on him!" Sato ordered. Turning to Shinji he continued, "Bring the radio. Come with me and translate for the foreign girl."

***

Brenna had endured humiliation before, but as a warlord's daughter, she'd never let an adversary think he'd gained the upper hand with her. Glaring on the warming pavement as a pair of Nordans came out of the bus, the Lithian woman locked her eyes on the leader while the radio operator told her to take them to her room.

Silently, controlling her contempt, Brenna complied. Grateful that the borrowed rain poncho offered modesty that diminished soldierly ogling, she led the Nordans upstairs, past damaged doors and bullet-riddled rooms until she arrived at the end of the hall.

The resort staff must have removed the bodies already. Dried blood stains on the carpet, spatter on the walls and spent shell casings testified to a lot of death during an intense firefight. Garrick hadn't done all this damage with four shots. What else had happened here?

An ocean aroma drifted through open curtains torn by gunfire. The shredded mattress, shattered furniture and bullet impacts sprayed across the far wall shouted a story of extreme violence. Brenna shuddered, knowing that Garrick had stayed behind to defend her.

"Show us your identification papers," the radio man ordered sharply.

Barefooted Brenna gingerly stepped over the bed fragments, reached for a drawer and rummaged through it to find their passports. After retrieving the documents, she made eye contact with the Nordan officer.

"I would like to get dressed," she said.

After looking at the passports and hearing the translation, the man grunted and made a motion with his hand, suggesting she go ahead. In response, Brenna made a circular motion with her fingers, indicating that she wanted the men to turn around. Her stern expression belied the vulnerability she felt. They complied, but the officer locked his eyes on her reflection in a broken mirror.

Brenna selected a camisole, skirt and blouse from a drawer, turning her back on the Nordans while she dressed herself. She took boots from the closet, and after clearing her throat to request privacy again, recovered her boot knife from the open safe and discreetly slipped it into its holster. She located the *Auðr*, a mystical money bag stripped from a giant she'd slain, and stuffed it into her *bug-out* bag.

The radio operator approached and spoke in a suspicious tone. "What are you doing?" he demanded.

Brenna pushed Garrick's *bug-out* bag to the back of the closet with her foot, reached for her quiver and pulled it out. "You took my bow," she replied. "I want it back."

A discussion with the lieutenant ensued. Moments later, the Nordan soldier said, "We arrested you in possession of dangerous weapons. You will be questioned by the colonial authorities about your role in the attack.

"If they determine you were not involved, they will return your arms. What they do is not up to us."

Brenna tightened her lips. "Then let me get some clothes for my husband," she replied. "He should be presentable for the interview."

***

"I don't know what kind of half-wit plan the army was running here," Oshita Koji complained. "But this is an epic disaster. You had a team in place who could have prevented the insurgents from attacking before a single shot was fired, yet you bungled the mission."

Sato stood firm, his gaze fixed on the wall behind the older man. He had to respect Koji's authority, but he didn't like doing so. "Mr. Koji, I have carried out my orders honorably. If you have a problem with the planning and execution of this operation, you will have to take that up with Colonel Utemaro."

Koji stood, leaning his broad frame against the resort administrator's desk. "The Tamarian embassy phoned me three hours after I'd gone to bed last night. Their lady ambassador knew about this Lieutenant Ravenwood fellow and the Brenna Velez woman before I did. This attack happened in my territory, on my watch, yet I had to find out about it from a foreign government.

"Somebody told them, lieutenant. I promise you the informant didn't come from the ranks of my people. That means there's an agent here at the resort, or among the crew participating in this operation. I have interrogated the entire hotel staff and guests. No one knows anything.

"Since most of *Tora Ichi* perished in the incident and the rest are in hospital that leaves your men as my prime suspects. Find the traitor and hand him over to me."

Sato shook his head. "No one on my team had any contact with a foreign government, sir. We've been under strict orders to maintain secrecy since the beginning of this operation. We were trying to prevent an international incident, not cause one. My men have conducted themselves with great courage and honor. There is no possibility of treason among any of them."

Although he remained calm, inwardly, Sato felt terrified. He'd ordered Shinji to shut off the radio, in contravention of orders – something for which Colonel Utemaro had already reprimanded him – and now this civilian bureaucrat accused his men of contacting the Tamarians to shame the colonial government. While the allegation sounded absurd and was unlikely to cause permanent career damage, Koji had the power to make life miserable for a mere lieutenant in the short term.

"You'd better come up with an explanation for how the lady ambassador knew about this debacle of yours," Koji warned. "After I question your foreign captives, my next call will be to Colonel Utemaro . . . . ."

***

Grateful that Brenna had brought him clothes to change into, Garrick sat in one of the resort's empty second-floor rooms. "I've told you," he reiterated. "I'm not going to tell you more until I hear from my embassy and rejoin my wife."

"Let me be clear," Oshita Koji, who spoke fluent vulgate, advised. "You're a foreign national in Nordan territory. You have no rights here. Answer my questions."

"Or what?" Garrick asked, emboldened by his belief that the Nordan military officer hadn't been happy to hand him and Brenna over to civilian authority. "If any harm comes to me or my wife under your care, you'll be dealing with my government. Is that what you want?"

Koji grew impatient. Despite being large and strong for a Nordan, he'd failed to intimidate the foreign soldier. Further, the Tamarian officer's arrogance could not be deflated without harming him physically and thereby escalating an already precarious situation – a fact he seemed to understand. While Koji had the authority to kill the Tamarian soldier and his Lithian wife, the Chief knew that reporting the death of foreigners would complicate a delicate political situation. The Colonial Authority didn't want a diplomatic spat with the Tamarians, who were allied with the Kamerese, the Nordan Empire's rival.

Choosing another tactic, Koji strode to the room's phone. When the resort's administrator, who'd been manning the front desk during the crisis, answered, the Colonial Chief spoke tersely in Nordan, then hung up.

Garrick heard his wife's meek voice speaking short phrases from the room next door. He couldn't tell what she was saying, but it didn't sound like she was cooperating with her interrogators, either. Although he didn't pray, Garrick secretly hoped that the Nordans would handle Brenna gently. He felt inwardly terrified that they might abuse her, and silently vowed to do anything in his power to make that stop if it started.

The ringing phone interrupted his reverie. Mr. Koji answered and spoke briefly to the person on the other end before putting his hand over the receiver. "This is the Tamarian embassy in Helsing," he said.

Uncertain of the Colonial Chief's intentions, Garrick took the phone. "Lieutenant Ravenwood," he announced.

After introducing herself as Greta, an embassy staffer, the woman rattled off Garrick's military ID number to verify her authenticity. "Please confirm," she requested.

"That is correct," Garrick responded with relief.

Greta spoke in fluent and rapid Tamarian. "Are you safe, lieutenant?"

"Yes ma'am," he replied. "They've detained us, taken our identification and confiscated our weapons."

"Don't worry," Greta assured. "We know you were targeted in a terror attack, and they know we know. I don't think they'll be foolish enough to mistreat you."

"What would you like me to do?" Garrick asked.

"Cooperate with the colonial authorities," Greta suggested. "We're working to secure your release. The current situation in the colony is tense, but if you can, find a way out of there and get to the embassy. . . ."

Greta's voice ended abruptly. Garrick heard no static on the line, only silence. "Hello?" he inquired thrice. Shaking his head, the Tamarian officer handed the phone back to Mr. Koji.

The Colonial Chief put his ear to the receiver, then barked an order at one of his aides. "Now," he said, returning his attention to Garrick, "I've offered a gesture in good faith. You've spoken to your embassy. Reciprocity is in order."

"Again, I'll tell you what I know when you bring my wife in here," Garrick promised. "You have my word."

Koji nodded, then barked another order at his aide. Moments later, a soldier pushed Brenna into the room. Relief washed over her lovely face as her husband suppressed a smile. They did not embrace, but mutually reached for each other's hands and stood close.

"Now, tell me what happened," Koji demanded.

"Men wearing Nordan uniforms came to our room intending to kill us," Garrick replied, standing. "Come with me and I'll show you." Though he'd not yet seen the damage done to the building, as he led the way, Garrick also noted more than one firing position and a lot of blood on the carpet. There had been a nasty fight here.

"This is where we'd been staying before the staff moved us," Garrick stated, gesturing toward the room with a broken door. "The attack team went here first, expecting to find us inside."

"So you believe the terrorists were targeting you?"

Garrick nodded. "Last night during dinner I noticed several men watching us. We'd have been staying here, but the resort staff moved us into a suite down the hall."

Curious, Koji asked, "Why would they do that?"

"A woman at the front desk said our intimacy was disturbing sleep for the guests next door," Garrick replied.

Remembering his look at the resort's register, Oshita Koji knew that no one else had been booked into this corridor. When he questioned the resort's administrator, about this, Abjörn Olsen said, "The army told us to keep these two away from the other guests. We moved them last night, as ordered by the commando team leader."

"When did they move you?" Koji asked Garrick.

"After dinner, maybe two hours before the attack," Garrick replied. "The new room they gave us is at the end of the hall, with a balcony overlooking the beach."

Koji nodded. If the hotel staff was cooperating with the army, then Lieutenant Sato was unlikely to know anything more about the threat against these young foreigners. The army had a policy of keeping its operational details hidden from junior officers, in the event that front-line troops were captured. Had the army used this Tamarian couple as bait? And if so, to what end?

"We were in bed, getting ready to sleep, when we heard boots in the hall and the door being breached," Garrick continued. "We had little time to react."

"You were arrested in the possession of deadly arms," Koji stated. "We found insurgents slain by arrows and gunshot wounds that match your weapons. Why did you fight back, instead of running away?"

Brenna looked to the side, her face flushed with guilt. She merged behind Garrick as he explained. "We didn't have time to dress and get out. I covered the exit with my .45 so my wife could escape."

Koji pointed at Garrick. "So you had the handgun. You're telling me she's the archer?"

Garrick nodded, pointing at the balcony. "She fired from the edge of the rail, using the wall as cover."

Eyes widened, Koji shook his head. *How could this little waif kill five men – armed with automatic weapons no less – using only a bow? Aside from her womanly form, she looked like she'd left her mother's care not more than a few months ago . . . . Who were these foreigners?*

"The kill team rolled a grenade into the room," Garrick continued. "I dumped the bed on it and climbed over the patio rail as it went off. The blast knocked me down. We escaped along the beach and sheltered in a barn for the night. That's where your soldiers found us."

While the story sounded plausible and fit the details of the scene, important questions remained. "Who'd want to attack you?" Koji asked.

"We have no idea," Garrick replied.

"If that's true, why did you bring deadly weapons on a trip to a music festival?"

"We take them everywhere we go," Garrick stated. "The fact that we needed to use them here demonstrates the wisdom of that practice. If we'd not been armed, we'd likely be dead right now."

Brenna winced, hearing her husband say this.

Koji, preoccupied with Garrick's testimony, didn't notice. "Hmm," he mused, concluding that he needed to go over Lieutenant Sato's head. Changing the subject to get the foreigners out of the way for the moment, Koji asked, "Have you eaten?"

When the couple shook their heads, Koji ordered them taken to a secure room down the hall with an armed sentry at the door, and told his aid to arrange breakfast.

Garrick stooped, pretending to tie his shoe as the others filed out. He picked up a bullet casing from one of the attack team rifles and slid it into his pocket.

Moments later, behind a closed door, Garrick took Brenna into his arms and held her close. His strength reassured his wife, while her softness comforted him. "We need to find a way out of here," he whispered.

"I haven't finished the competition," she replied softly. "If I leave now, I'll forfeit."

Surprised, Garrick replied, "You think they're going to continue after what's happened? While I was waiting for you on the bus, I saw people leaving in droves."

"I haven't heard that they've cancelled my round this afternoon," she stated. "If it's all the same to you, I'd like to keep my undefeated streak alive."

Garrick understood that music occupied a central and important role in Brenna's life, but he'd never witnessed his wife acting so competitive before. "I spoke to someone at the embassy by telephone," he explained. "She said we need to find our way back there."

Brenna took hold of her husband's hand, gazing into his eyes, imploringly. "This is important to me."

"I know," he replied quietly. "But someone used this event to isolate and attempt murder against us. Even the Nordans realize we were the targets for that kill team. We've been followed and watched ever since we arrived. I think there's a political struggle going on that involves the Kamerese, and that's why we were targeted. If the Nordans figure that out, they'll blame us."

"How can you be sure?" she asked.

Garrick pulled the cartridge out of his pocket and showed his wife the rim stamp. "Recognize this?"

Brenna's heart raced. "Is that from the beach?"

"No," he replied. "This one came from our room. The Nordans think the attackers were insurgents, but you heard one of them speak, and I'm sure we saw them at dinner. The evidence points to a Kamerese operation, like the attack on the palace gate before we left home."

Falling quiet for a moment, Brenna recalled the epithet one of the dying men hurled at her. "Okay. If you're right, I agree that we need to leave. But how? They have our passports and weapons. We're stuck in here with an armed guard at the door."

Garrick rose to check the window. Cobblestone pavement stretched across a loading area, two stories below. He discovered, when he cranked the window mechanism, that it had been designed for ventilation, not escape. It would not open sufficiently for either of them to get out, no matter how he tried to force the hinge further. Frustrated, he sat back on the bed. "This Koji fellow seems pretty sharp. Once he figures out the Kamerese are involved, he may conclude that we were complicit and have us executed."

Brenna stood on her toes to peer at the view outside, noting the long drop to hard pavement, below. She turned to face her husband and pointed at the door. "So we have to make our way to the embassy in Helsing, and the only escape is past an armed guard . . . ."

"We'll find a way," he soothed. "We just have to be patient and wait for them to do something stupid."

Brenna felt hemmed in and suppressed rising panic, knowing she could do little else but wait. "I don't want to die," she said, "But I don't want any more killing, either."

She'd become sensitive about taking life ever since an operation at *Casa del Matados* during the Kamerese Civil War, where she'd fought with great skill and courage. For her bravery in the fight, she'd been awarded a Medal of Valor, an honor she didn't think she deserved.

In her view, the desire she'd felt for vengeance conflicted with her faith. Brenna believed she'd been tormented by evil spirits in the aftermath of the action and didn't want to repeat that experience. As the horror of that time whispered from her memory, Brenna felt the need for solitude and prayer. Unable to leave the room, she gripped her husband's hand and prayed in silence.

Several minutes later, a young steward with a cart arrived outside the room. After talking to the guard, he opened the door and brought in breakfast. Leaning into Garrick's right ear the Kurian whispered cryptically, "Freedom is coming soon," before turning to leave.

What did that mean?

The meal consisted of toasted and buttered rye bread with jam and cheese, canned salmon with Kamerese rice wrapped in seaweed, and herring. Hungry, and uncertain of when they might eat again, the young couple devoured every morsel on the platter.

***

"We were tasked to monitor the targets and provide back-up for *Tora Ichi*," Sato insisted. "I have handed the foreigners over to you as directed. My orders have been completed and I must report to the colonel."

Koji shook his head. "I am not satisfied with your story. Why were these two selected for surveillance? The hotel manager told me he moved them as directed by the army. Why is that? And further, after they escaped, how did you find them so easily?"

"Operational details are above my pay grade," Sato replied, speaking truthfully. "I don't know anything about the targets except that the man is a soldier, and his Lithian wife plays piano. We were ordered to hold them for questioning after *Tora Ichi* eliminated the insurgent threat.

"We deduced they'd fled on foot after last night's firefight, and the most logical place to look for them was at a nearby lagoon where we'd previously observed them swimming. If you need more information than that, you will have to speak to Colonel Utemaro."

Koji appraised the young officer with a critical eye. Everything he'd learned thus far suggested the army had bungled an operation, but Koji hadn't climbed the Colonial Office leadership ladder by luck or nepotism. Hard work, diligence and intelligence propelled his successful career in the Foreign Service, and Koji wanted to be certain that he had a good grasp of the scenario before taking on the Special Forces. The army's tentacles of power reached directly into the Emperor's inner sanctum. It could be dangerous to take them on without strong evidence of their incompetence.

At that moment, Koji's aide knocked on the office door. "Come in," the Colonial Chief ordered.

"Forgive me, sir," the aide said with a bow. He placed a folded paper on the desk in front of Koji and quickly left the room.

Sato noted that when the Chief read the note, his brow lifted and he caught his breath, ever so slightly. That couldn't be good . . . .

"Does the army think that these two foreigners are involved in the insurgency?" Koji asked.

Sato shook his head. "I doubt it. The girl is a musician, not a killer. She's too small to hurt anyone. I suspected the soldier might be a local until I examined his identification. Neither of them can speak either Kurian or Kamerese. That makes them unlikely accomplices."

"What were you supposed to do after you'd apprehended and questioned them?" Koji asked.

"My team was tasked with escorting the foreigners to the Tamarian embassy in Helsing."

"Yet you knew nothing about the lady ambassador's concern for these two when I spoke to you earlier. Don't lie to me, lieutenant!"

Sato remained ramrod straight. "I did not contact the embassy. I have never spoken to anyone there, nor has any member of my team."

Koji shook his head. The army had to know that the Tamarians and the Kamerese were allies. But now, having read a confirmation that the dead attackers were Kamerese, not Kurian, he suspected the Tamarian soldier and his pianist wife had been part of the operation.

"Get out of here," he ordered dismissively. Koji called his aide into the room after Sato's departure. "Tell the guard to bring those foreigners to me."

***

An explosion thundered through the far wing of the resort. With the window rattling in its pane Garrick shielded Brenna beneath his body as they both took cover behind the bed. Clattering gunfire rose in a deadly chorus, punctuated by shouting and the sounds of human terror.

While Brenna prayed, a long burst from an automatic weapon echoed down the hallway. Multiple bullet impacts splintered the door, followed by a cry of pain and a thud as a body slumped against it. Garrick huddled behind the bed with his wife in his arms, waiting as her whispered petition continued lofting heavenward.

The door knob turned, then opened violently, as if kicked. It slammed against its stop and then into the right shoulder of a boy no more than 12 years old. As two others hurried down the hall, he recovered his balance and clumsily held an automatic rifle to his shoulder with his index finger dancing dangerously near its trigger.

Garrick held his hands aloft and open to show he had no weapon.

The boy – pale-skinned and blonde – stopped, his face reflecting uncertainty as he made eye contact with a man who could have easily passed for a native. Potential kinship motivated the lad to point his gun barrel to the side. Indecision washed over his face.

He crossed his fingers, tapped his chest twice, then ordered, "Get up!" in his native tongue.

Garrick and Brenna both stood to their feet.

Behind the strong, grey-eyed man the boy beheld the loveliest woman he'd ever seen. Her diminutive form stirred his desire, yet she seemed pitiful and afraid. His breath stopped. His pulse quickened. No native girl looked like this, but she didn't look Nordan, either. While he'd sworn to kill all foreigners, her face and form softened his heart and dulled his resolve to duty. The boy stepped back into the hall, then jerked his head toward the door. "Go!" he ordered, expecting that he'd be understood.

The lovers wasted no time. Brenna took her husband's hand in hers, peeked down the hallway as shouting insurgents and the sound of booted feet on stairs filled the pause in gunfire from outside, then scurried to the room they'd occupied the night before.

"I put the *Auðr* in my *bug-out* bag," she said. "Should we take anything else?"

Garrick, who'd endured the mild disdain of Brenna's rolled eyes for his paranoid insistence that they should pack *bug-out* bags in the event of an emergency, didn't pounce on her former dismissal in triumph. "Let's get our toiletries and your boot knife."

She nodded, as gunfire rattled down the hall.

He bent to kiss her, as the danger of their situation fanned the fire of his longing for her. Garrick suppressed his passion, increasingly aware of a familiar, heightened sense of being alive that always accompanied combat. The addicting rush triggered acute awareness of sound and peril that had served well in the past to help him survive.

Hearing only small arms fire from the west end of the resort, Garrick checked the balcony for threats. Once satisfied, he beckoned for his wife, climbed over the rail and stood on a table conveniently positioned below.

It hadn't been there last night . . . .

While Garrick had packed an emergency rucksack with critical supplies, Brenna's *bug-out* bag looked like a zippered cloth cylinder with a broad shoulder strap. She passed it to her husband, then gracefully stepped over the rail and dropped to the table with a little bend in her knees and a bounce in her breast. Brenna shouldered her bag and inquired, "Which way?"

He pointed toward the southeast, where a broad, black beach faced the ocean, and followed his fleet-footed wife as she fled across the strand, away from the sounds of fierce combat. Even encumbered by her bag, her tireless stride proved impossible to match. Breathing hard as battle sounds faded into the gentle crashing of waves on the shore, Garrick followed Brenna's rapid retreat.

Several minutes later she paused beside an outcropping of rock, where a bluff overlooking the water encroached upon the narrowing beach. When he finally caught up, Garrick – though strong and fit – noted that his wife was neither breathing hard, nor sweating. This gift of her Lithian physiology meant she always, easily outran him. "We're losing the shoreline," she announced, pointing to a palisade rising in the southeast.

Garrick had a very good memory for maps and an understanding of terrain derived from a combination of experience and military training. "If we climb the bluff, we can find cover in the trees and head due south to Briminger. There's a chain of hills running east to west from the shore beyond the town. We should be able to see Helsing from the ridge crest."

"How far is it?" she asked.

"At least twenty miles," he replied.

Brenna stood on her toes to kiss her husband's lips. He tasted a little salty. "Not far for a soldier," she said.

"At your pace, I'll be dead long before we get there."

With her brow raised the Lithian woman replied, "Then you'd better lead the way."

***

A truck bomb, similar to the explosive detonated against the palace gate in Tamaria weeks earlier, had taken out a large section of the Seashell Resort's eastern promenade and VIP entrance. Billowing smoke rose from the wreckage while the human carnage caused by the blast remained untreated. Many lives slipped away under the swarm of indiscriminate firing that shattered glass and splintered the fine cedar of the resort's facade.

Hotel security, with the advantage of protected positions and clear fields of fire, defended the eastern and central entrances, beating back an unorganized charge of insurgent fighters who'd threatened to overwhelm them. Yet it was only a matter of time before the attackers prevailed, and everyone in the hotel knew it.

Low on munitions and grievously outnumbered, Sato fought to save the Colonial Chief from certain death. He turned to Kanezane, awaiting orders near the front desk. "Strip the dead of their weapons and ammunition. Collect as much as you can carry. Take Yosai and get Chief Officer Koji and his staff to the west service entrance." To Funimaro, who served as the back-up driver, he said, "You and Shinji will help me drive the bus over there."

"Sir, the rebels are blocking the access road," Funimaro said. "We saw them deploy from the east."

"Then we'll drive around the building on the beach," Sato replied, hoping that might work. "Let's go!"

Using a side door, the Nordan Special Forces team fired a smoke grenade to cover their advance across open ground to the bus. With thick, sooty vapor lingering in the still air between opposing sides the enemy could also move forward, but this was a risk Sato felt he had to take.

Funimaro coaxed the ethanol engine to life, as breathless Shinji put his heavy radio down on a seat. Sato broke open a rear window and pointed his carbine toward the insurgent positions to cover their escape. Because he could see nothing, he didn't fire to conserve ammunition.

Inside the building, Kanezane and Yosai fought their way across the lower west wing floor, where young patriot fighters – having attacked the resort from the beach to the south – controlled both levels. Although the Kurians fiercely defended the hallway, the noise of gunfire, punctuated by the screaming of wounded child soldiers, marked progress for the Nordan Special Forces. Their superior training, firing accuracy and fearlessness gave them a significant advantage over their young adversaries.

Fleeing in terror from ruthless, professional soldiers, the surviving Kurian patriots retreated upstairs in disarray. Kanezane crouched in the hallway as Yosai pounded on the office door and shouted for Chief Koji.

Kanezane heard running on the upper floor. "Hurry!" he urged. "We don't have much time!"

Outside, Funimaro drove the bus around the building. He nearly got stuck in the dark sand, but had enough momentum to overcome friction until the big machine heaved onto pavement at the south side of the resort's west wing. There, a large roll-up door provided access to the hotel's store room and kitchen.

As Funimaro hit the brakes, movement caught his eye. He noticed a small, dark-haired woman rapidly fleeing southward on the beach, followed by a husky, blonde-haired man. Weren't they the foreigners that *Tora Ni* had been tracking?

Sato and Shinji dashed out of the bus and hurriedly opened the big door. "Kanezane!" Sato shouted.

Around the corner, the Warrant Officer heard his name. "On the way!" he replied, just as two Kurian fighters reappeared at the end of the hall, and another group arrived at the base of the grand staircase, taking up positions behind them.

Intense gunfire overwhelmed all sound. Kanezane and Yosai nearly expended their munitions reserves trying to push down the hall with Chief Koji, his aide, driver and bodyguard – who wielded only a sidearm – in tow.

Turning left, the Special Forces duo emptied their magazines before dashing down the wide hall to the kitchen and loading dock. Sato and Shinji moved forward to cover the retreat, urging everyone to hurry.

Two rounds struck Koji in the back. He stumbled as his bodyguard returned fire while his Kurian attackers sought cover. The Colonial Chief struggled to move under his own power and quickly became deathly pale.

Shinji gave Kanezane his rifle, then put his shoulder beneath Koji's and carried the bigger man down the corridor to the bus. *Tora Ni's* tactical retreat succeeded and as the engine roared to life, Shinji worked hard to staunch the Colonial Chief's bleeding. He used compression dressings and pressure to no effect. Oshita Koji, shivering and whispering his wife's name, died shortly after the Nordan Special Forces got underway.

***

High clouds diffused the Daystar's light, limiting shadows while holding warmth close to the ground. As Garrick and Brenna fled from the sound of surf, the still air remained heavily laden with the scent of seaweed and salt. Coastal rainforest clung to the high ground overlooking the ocean. Old trees on the palisade summit, flagged from their lifelong battle with wind rushing inland, stood still in the uneasy calm.

Despite his outwardly confident demeanor, Garrick struggled with internal terror. Unarmed, outnumbered, and unaware of what potential threats lay ahead, an unwelcome vulnerability plagued his soul. Accustomed to facing peril with courage, relying on extensive training, readied rifles and artillery that could ruin any adversary's day, Garrick suppressed rising, persistent anxiety. His natural, masculine desire to protect his beloved belied a harsh reality that he could do very little to prevent harm to her without a weapon in hand.

Yet for as long as he'd known her, Brenna had needed no one's protection. Despite her small size, even with a boot knife she was formidable in close combat. That reality didn't erode the disquieting dread of their exposure to uncertain peril. Because Garrick didn't want to burden his beloved – whose whispered prayers in Lithian comforted her while doing little for him – he kept his apprehensions unspoken. Ideally, he wanted to reach the Tamarian embassy in Helsing by nightfall, but Garrick had never been to the city and no idea where to begin looking. The language barrier would further complicate matters, as he could not read street signs, nor could he expect any of the locals to understand anything he said.

Neither he nor Brenna knew who could and should not be trusted, especially in light of the fact that their erstwhile Kamerese allies had been responsible for the failed assassination effort. Was some rogue faction trying to drag Tamaria into another war, or was this part of a clandestine effort by the government in Kameron City to gain the upper hand over their Nordan rivals?

Subsequent Special Forces hostility, along with their smug sense of superiority, inspired Garrick's contempt. The abrupt end to his telephone conversation with the embassy, followed by a shockingly large explosion and a horde of surprisingly well - coordinated Kurians attacking the resort added to his rapidly multiplying concerns.

Why had the young insurgent encouraged their escape? What did his odd salute mean? Garrick felt puzzled, but at present, the only thing he and Brenna could do to preserve their own lives involved running, and he'd never keep up with her if they had to flee in earnest.

Brenna concluded her prayers with a kiss toward the heavens and damped eyes that she wiped dry on her forearm. Brenna's heart overflowed with regret for arguing with her husband about attending the music festival, as now it seemed obvious that he'd been right while she'd been wrong. The Lithian woman felt a spiritual urging to confess her error and ask forgiveness, confident that he would embrace her and gently extend grace, yet her sensitivity to his demeanor, tone and body language warned the young woman to wait until they were safe before expressing contrition. She sniffed, keeping a leaky lid on her emotions.

Perceiving Garrick's apprehension, and knowing his desire to protect, Brenna trusted his judgment and let him lead. His uncanny knack for doing the right thing when under threat inspired confidence as she watched him pick a cautious path uphill, frequently glancing over his shoulder to see whether or not they were being followed.

Brenna prayed to let go of her disappointment, as she'd never before defaulted from a music competition. The roots of her earliest memories, stirred by the feel of piano keys on her fingertips, reached into a comforting time before the birth of her beloved sister, Cassie. Brenna recalled the size of her *Amair's* hands, his encouraging words while they sat together at the keyboard. *Umma's* smile at the sound of a familiar hymn formed the foundation for Brenna's enduring love of music.

Learning the piano also instilled discipline. Hours of scales, sight-reading, music theory and an endless regimen of learning new music, of practice and preparation honed her natural talent. When she started performing, all of that effort wrought success. Brenna dominated competitions because she pursued excellence relentlessly, working harder than any of her competitors.

Now, for the first time in her life, she'd not be accepting the accolades of an applauding audience. Their praise actually meant less to her than did the sense of accomplishment she'd always felt by maintaining her undefeated streak. That personal drive to compete found expression only in music and the martial arts, where her diligence, commitment to excellence, stamina and strength either distinguished her from all competition, or saved her life when she found herself in desperate straights.

Yet the ease she'd previously felt among the colonists and other guests at the Seashell Resort had transformed into foreboding. While Garrick could blend in among the Kurians, Brenna's dark hair resembled that of the Nordans, whom the insurgents clearly wanted to kill.

Breathless as he reached the top of the bluff, Garrick glanced over his shoulder. His widened eyes and raised brow strengthened Brenna's concern.

"We have company," he warned, pointing down the beach. "They must have seen us running from the resort."

Brenna turned, her heart pounding as she noticed Nordan soldiers following their footprints the beach.

***

After a harrowing escape from the Seashell Resort and the untimely death of Colonial Chief Koji, Sato felt stressed and pressured. With his squad understaffed and munitions low, *Tora Ni* needed resupply to survive.

Funimaro, who'd driven along the beach rather than trying to ram through an insurgent roadblock, sank the bus to its axles in soft sand too near the resort for comfort. Because it would be dishonorable to abandon Koji's body, *Tora Ni* had to find and defend a position.

An outcropping of rocks lay ahead, and beyond it, a bluff rose from the sea. Worried that the bus tracks would lead the insurgents straight to their location, Sato ordered Kanezane – who had the .30 caliber machine gun with two 20 round magazines left – Yosai and the Colonial Chief's men to take up a defensible position in the rocks. He split 25 rounds of ammunition evenly among them.

"The tide is coming in," he noted. "Hopefully that will cover our tracks. I will radio for help."

Yet when Sato contacted *Tora Chichi* to report and request evacuation. Colonel Utemaro, sounding unusually stern, expressed dismay upon hearing of Colonial Chief Koji's demise.

"This reflects badly on your leadership," the colonel complained. "I expect a full report of the incident when you return to base. Bring the foreigners with you."

Eyes widened in terror, Sato paused.

"I saw the foreign girl and her man running down the beach," Funimaro admitted.

"Are you sure it was her?" Sato clarified.

Funimaro nodded rapidly. "I'd recognize her *oppai to o shiri* anywhere."

Sato winced at the vulgar reference to the woman's body parts. Though he'd gazed at her reflection while she dressed and agreed with Funimaro – the girl had a form not easily forgotten – he found such talk impolite. He would never speak of a woman in such an overtly degrading manner.

"I'm afraid the foreign targets escaped to the south during the attack," Sato reported.

Colonel Utemaro cursed. "I'll arrange amphibious transport within the hour. Report to me immediately."

As the colonel ended the call, Sato heard gunfire aspire over the pounding of his heart. A horde of Kurian insurgents swarmed down the beach toward his position. Knowing he could not defeat them, the Nordan officer felt less fear over the colonel's castigation than he did the terror of dying on this forsaken beach without honor.

He sent Yosai and one of the Chief's men to check the shore for evidence of their targets as the prophetic words of *Oji* Okisama echoed eerily from memory – *War is a terrible business, not some grand adventure.* Lieutenant Sato took up his position in the rocks, loaded his last magazine and waited for the inevitable end to arrive.

***

Progress slowed within a few steps into the forest. With no path to follow, Garrick and Brenna worked their way through lush undergrowth choked with mossy deadfall that made their steps uncertain. What appeared to be solid ground covered in moist, green ground-hugging plants often yielded suddenly beneath their feet. Wild thornberry shrubs and devil's club grew in the shade of large ferns, tugging at and tearing fabric. Brenna fell once and Garrick twice. Their labored breathing and the crack of breaking branches beneath their feet displaced the fading, distant sound of waves on the shore.

With the prospect of getting lost looming in his mind, Garrick paused to pull a map and a compass out of his *bug-out* bag. Brenna watched him orient their position in silence before he shouldered his backpack and held the map out for her to see.

"The beach is less than a mile south of where we're standing. Anyone without a dog will have a tough time tracking us through here. But I'm concerned about twisting an ankle or breaking a leg. We can't run if we can't walk, and we'll make better time on the sand than through all this undergrowth."

Brenna swatted an insect and pointed at the map. "They'll expect us to go that direction. If we head east, we can follow the highway down to Briminger and maybe take a bus to Helsing instead of walking all that way. Soldiers on foot will have a harder time following us through the forest than they will on the beach."

Garrick acknowledged her wisdom, folded the map and slid it into his left pants pocket. He turned eastward, ascending a gradual slope where hemlock and cedar trees remained untouched by Nordan axes. While the redwoods growing around their home in Tamaria's palace complex stood over 200 feet tall, high elevation limited their growing season. In this mild, coastal climate, massive cedars dwarfed the largest trees Garrick had ever seen.

Pausing occasionally to listen for sounds of pursuit, Garrick and Brenna – harried by biting bugs – slowly worked their way southeastward for the better part of two hours before arriving at an abrupt scarp. Here, an ancient glacier had ground against the remains of a small, long extinct cinder cone, shearing off its southern edge and pushing crushed basalt to the sea.

From its summit, the young couple noted several smoke columns rising high above a settlement at the edge of a bay, due south of their current position. Garrick examined the scene with a pair of binoculars from his bag before handing them to Brenna.

"That's Briminger?" she inquired.

Garrick nodded. "There's nothing else on the map."

Brenna handed the binoculars back to her husband. "It doesn't look promising. If there's violence and looting going on, the Nordans are likely to be out in force."

He scanned the dark strand, holding his breath while focusing on young men walking south along the shore. "Perhaps. But it looks like we have a new threat. I see insurgents wandering around the beach right now."

"Really?" she asked, requesting the binoculars again with a rapid gesture. "The Nordans must have lost us."

"We could go further east and bypass the town," he suggested. "It looks like forested lowland on the map."

Knowing that they weren't dressed for traveling over this type of terrain, Brenna hedged. She'd already torn her skirt a couple of times, Garrick's trousers suffered similarly, his shoes were filthy with foul-smelling muck he'd stepped into, and her boots – though flat-soled – were better suited for fashion than hiking.

"We'll have no moons again this evening," Brenna stated. "We can climb down before nightfall and wait for darkness at the bottom. The tide will be out by then and I can lead you down the beach without anyone seeing us."

That would put them close to the town and delay their arrival at the embassy, Garrick mused. If the Nordans were busy restoring order, their attention would be focused inland, not out to the sea. Perhaps he and Brenna might slip through any active patrols undetected.

Garrick paused, his eyes glancing down his bride's beautiful form. "That's a good idea," he replied. "But what do you want to do between now and this evening?"

Brenna furrowed her brow and frowned. She could see a longing in her husband's eyes that quickened her pulse and stirred in her soul. Danger heightened their mutual desire and she didn't want to disappoint him. "Can we talk first?" she asked. "I need your forgiveness."

***

The Seashell Resort, now engulfed in flames, sent a thick plume of smoke aloft that rose in a lazy drift to the east. Sato watched the horde of rebel fighters advance toward the listing, stranded bus.

"Fix bayonets and hold your fire!" he warned. With the tide washing the wheels of the bus, he'd hoped the Kurians would lose interest and give up their pursuit of his team. He prayed to the warrior gods to that end.

But it didn't happen. The enemy kept coming.

"Be brave!" he whispered. "Die with honor!"

Time slowed. Sato's heart beat fast. His breathing shortened. The sounds of the sea, of gulls crying overhead, and of the futile prayers of surviving *Tora* members vanished from his consciousness as the horde approached. He knew there were too many insurgents coming and too few bullets to kill them.

A man barked orders in Kurian as the mob approached the bus. Hundreds of young soldiers raised their rifles and continued to advance.

"Farewell, mother . . . ." Sato murmured. He turned to Kanezane and shouted, "Fire!"

The .30 caliber machine gun slaughtered the enemy's front row. Panic swept through their ranks as members of *Tora Ni* selected targets on the flanks of the insurgent formation.

They'd achieved surprise, but the advantage that entailed faded quickly as the machine gun ran out of ordnance, its rapid firing replaced by the overwhelming thunder of rifles responding in superior numbers.

With a great cry, the Kurians surged. Their weapons blazed. Yosai, to Sato's left, jerked backward in a spray of arterial blood. Next to him, Shinji went down. Kanezane dumped his rifle and picked up a weapon from his fallen comrade, firing three times before its magazine emptied.

The enemy swarmed up the rocks. Sato locked eyes with a blonde-haired, teenaged boy just as Funimaro met his end. The Nordan lieutenant pulled his trigger and spent the last of his ammunition. As the boy fell, Sato charged forward and forcefully thrust his bayonet into the heart of one last enemy before an insurgent struck him down and blackness forever enveloped his consciousness.

***

Brenna encouraged her husband to recline. She leaned against him, swallowing her pride and searching for the right words to speak. Her prayers for safety and pleas for mercy quietly lofted heavenward, but that familiar lightness of spirit she craved eluded her.

"I'm sorry for doubting you," she admitted. "I should have listened and trusted your judgment, but I let my own feelings, my longing to compete again carry more weight than your concerns. Instead of listening to you, I insisted that I have my way. That was wrong of me."

While Garrick could have exploited her vulnerable soul with withering criticism, doing so solved nothing. Instead, he responded gently. "I *know* how much this meant to you," he replied. "I know you wanted to shine at the festival, and that you wanted to spend time with me. I also know that you'd never deliberately endanger us.

"I'm not keeping score with you. I'm not worried about who's wrong and who isn't. I don't need to prove my worth or my wisdom because you inspire confidence that you're committed to me, and that's far more important in my view than being right. Let's not dwell on how and why we got here. We need to focus on getting home safely."

Of the many reasons Brenna loved Garrick, the sensitive and intelligent way he handled conflict with her ranked very high on her list. His conduct and the way he spoke proved that he consistently valued her views, even when they disagreed with his own. She leaned her head against his chest, her silence speaking more to him than she wanted to admit.

"You're worried about something else," he continued. "Please, tell me what's wrong."

Brenna closed her eyes and pushed a short breath from between her open lips. "It's the killing," she admitted. "Why didn't we just run, Garrick? Why did we fight?"

He stroked her cheek with his right forefinger and kissed the top her of head. Knowing his wife well, he chose his words carefully. "I stayed behind so you had a better chance of getting away, and you stayed because you wanted to save my life. What we did was motivated by love, not thirst for revenge."

"The outcome is the same," she replied quietly. "Somewhere in Kameron, those men will be mourned by the people who loved them."

Garrick shook his head. "Someone sent and paid those men to kill us. They went willingly. If you hadn't covered me, they'd have filled my back with bullets and you'd be the one shedding tears right now.

"I don't think you should fret about your courage. I'd argue that the morality of your actions far exceeded those of the people who tried to murder us."

"Okay," she conceded. "I understand your point. But after my experience in Kameron, I swore I wouldn't go on a killing spree like that ever again. I felt spiritually tormented by what I'd done, yet last evening it seemed so easy to fall back on violence. I don't want to be a woman whose faith is stained by shedding blood."

Garrick took her hand in his. "That's not who you are," he assured. "You were rightly angry after escaping from the *Casa del Matados*. The rebels deprived you of food, cut your hair and would've done worse if your maiden clothes hadn't protected your virtue. So they beat you without mercy, made you watch unspeakable horrors committed against others, and in the end, even tried to cut off your head with a machete. Your feelings after enduring all that are understandable. Responding to mistreatment with anger doesn't change who you are."

"Perhaps not, but it does reflect an ugly reality about me that I'd rather not confront. I don't want to live that way." Brenna herself pressed into her husband's embrace. "Now I've put us into peril, and I'm worried that we're going to see a lot more death before it's over."

She's probably right, Garrick mused, though he left the sentiment unspoken. The abrupt end to his phone call with the embassy, the attack on the Seashell Resort, and the smoke rising from Briminger all suggested that much more danger lay ahead. Now they had no identification, no weapons, couldn't speak the local language and carried only basic necessities in their *bug-out* bags.

Remaining low-key during the afternoon reduced their need for nutrition, but hunger eventually drove Garrick to open one of his boxed military meals. Each of these contained adequate calories for an active soldier, consisting primarily of dried fruit, tins of meat paste or stew, brittle rye bread and sweet granola bars. They did not cook the food out of concern that smoke from a fire would reveal their hidden location.

With their interpersonal conflict resolved, quiet, affectionate kissing reignited their passion. Confident of their safety for the moment, Garrick slipped his hand beneath Brenna's blouse, tugging at its hem to pull the garment over her head. With a little smile, she willed her Lithian undergarments loose and basked in his affection.

***

Disappointed by the previous evening's failure, Esteban Orozco took satisfaction in the successful attack against the Seashell Resort. Notifying the Tamarian embassy had, just as he'd believed it would, forced the Colonial Chief to investigate. Now, with Koji's lifeless body at his feet, the Kamerese mercenary felt hopeful again.

The operation had cost many dozens of young lives, but Esteban had convinced their leaders that the time had come to throw off the shackles of Nordan dominance, and patriot casualties were the price they paid for that freedom. The dead foreigners littering the rocks proved that Empire soldiers were not invincible. They died like ordinary men.

A Kurian functionary who spoke passable Kamerese approached Esteban from the side and cleared his throat to get the mercenary's attention. "We found these, sir."

Esteban reached for the documents. Opening them, he discovered they belonged to the Velez woman and her soldier husband. He raised his brow. How fortunate!

"Any sign of these two?" he asked.

"No sir. Just the passports."

"Organize a team and search for them," Esteban replied. "Spread the word and offer a reward for their capture. They couldn't have gone far."

***

As the Daystar settled beyond the sea, the lovers dressed for the evening, packed up their belongings and cleaned their stopover site before threading their way downhill. A waxing, onshore breeze blew the smoke from Briminger further inland, but as darkness descended and the Great Eye rose in the heavens, its light paled against an orange corona illuminating the town.

Brenna led the way, holding her husband's hand, announcing any obstacle she encountered loudly enough for him to hear over the rising sound of surf. She could see glowing minerals peppering the shoreline rocks and pools of oil floating on the surface that had leaked from Nordan vessels in deeper water. Under these conditions, the windswept, sandy strand lay open to her vision for at least as far as Garrick could see at high noon.

About thirty minutes after they'd begun walking, Brenna stopped. Garrick blindly bumped into her back.

"What's wrong?" he asked.

"I can see people patrolling the beach," she stated.

"How many?" he asked. "Are they armed?"

"A lot," the Lithian woman replied, fear edging into her voice. "And yes, they have guns. But worse, I see hunting hounds."

Brenna, who could run down a horse on foot, stood no chance against a large dog bred for pursuing prey over open ground. She'd learned that lesson being chased by Azgar Deathwolves three years hence and didn't want to repeat the experience. It would be even worse for Garrick.

"How far away?" he asked.

Brenna shook her head. "Close enough that if we move too much, the animals will notice."

"I didn't know dogs could see in the dark."

"It's not dark," she replied. "There's a lot of light in the sky. It's just not light you can see . . . ."

Garrick thought for a moment. "Our *bug-out* bags can float," he reminded her. "And I can swim far better than any dog."

Brenna eyed the surf warily as a fragmented childhood memory flashed into her mind. She recalled dark clouds over the *Mari Halinnea* – the beautiful, inland sea of her homeland – on a day when wind-driven waves crashed hard onto the beach. When her sister, Cassie, momentarily vanished beneath one of them Brenna screamed in terror and went after her, but a powerful wave knocked the young girl down, sending her tumbling through turbulent, sandy water until – feeling completely disoriented – her *Amair's* strong hands saved both her and Cassie from drowning.

The disquieting memory lingered, informing her discomfort. "I'm not sure," she replied, skeptically. "Maybe we should slink back into the forest and wait."

Knowing that not only had Garrick inherited his father's championship skill in the water, but that he'd also grown up swimming in a glacial-fed lake, Brenna wanted to believe he could swim around the threat. However, she'd always considered swimming a recreational activity and lacked both speed and stamina in the water. "What happens if we get separated, or get caught in a rip current that drags us out to sea?" she continued, expressing what she considered legitimate and rational concerns. "We didn't come here to drown."

Garrick set his *bug-out* pack down and removed a tether with snap hooks on either end. After clamping one hook around Brenna's bag handles he did the same to his own pack. "Hold the bag to your breast," he advised. "It'll keep your head above water. The tether will keep us from drifting apart. Our clothes will get heavy and drag us down when wet, so we're better off in our underthings."

Brenna blew an irritated breath between her lips as she slid out of her skirt and rolled her blouse into the bag. He stripped to his underwear and stashed his clothes as well. The moment they stood and headed toward the sea, their movement alerted the hunting hounds, who began barking and lunging against their leashes.

Suddenly, a flare arced into the sky and burst high over the landscape. Loosened dogs dashed forward, men began shouting, and gunfire peppered the shore. Hurriedly, the young couple sloshed into water so frigid it nearly took Brenna's breath away.

Determined to escape, Garrick led his wife through the surf and began swimming as the ground gave way beneath their feet. Bullet impacts splashed nearby. Using a powerful side-stroke, Garrick pulled Brenna into the dark and heartless sea, frustrating a band of Old Order Kurian insurgents – patriotic men who'd taken a solemn oath to purge their land with sacred violence – restoring its rightful order by killing all foreigners.

Waves that looked placid and gentle from a distance evoked terror in Brenna's soul as the cold water rose above her head, blotting out her view of the horizon. Clinging to her tethered *bug-out* bag, feeling the steady pull of her husband's powerful motion in the water, Brenna slid into the trough between wave crests and held her breath as her face plunged beneath the surface.

Swimming with skill developed by long experience in the water and refined by military training, Garrick dragged his frightened wife through the swells. The sound of the surf dampened the baying of hounds, but the sharp report of rifles firing quickened his already pounding heart. Struggling with panic and feeling vulnerable as he pulled himself through the waves, Garrick urged his strong body into extraordinary effort to save himself and his beloved.

Another flare arced overhead, blinding Brenna and illuminating the sea. Bullets whistled into the water nearby. Garrick heard Brenna gasp and cough as she struggled to breathe. "Have you been hit?" he shouted.

"No," she told him. "Don't let go. Don't leave me!"

Terror trembled through her voice. Brenna didn't make demands and resented anyone giving orders to her, a cultural convention of good Lithian manners overruled by fear. Garrick encouraged her to pray. He didn't *believe*, but he knew she'd draw comfort from her petition.

Amid the towering waves, the sound of fading surf, the whisper of drowning bullets, and her feet swishing the water, Brenna's prayer aspired above the heaving, swirling sea. She felt powerless as desperate words left her lips and mysteriously lofted heavenward.

A salty taste lingered on the Lithian woman's tongue. Cold water slapped her cheeks and stung her eyes. Prayer felt feeble among the surging swells. While the snarling sea appeared bright – reflecting UV light her tetracromat eyes could see – Brenna's flesh trembled and weakness whispered surrender into her fearful spirit. Resisting its siren call, she prayed that Allfather would strengthen Garrick and preserve their lives.

A long time later, a more distant flare arced into the starry sky. As the sound of gunfire and the baying hunting hounds fell into memory, Garrick realized that the glow of burning Briminger had drifted much further away than should have been the case, given the strain that pulling Brenna through the water inflicted on his youthful vigor and stamina. He remembered his combat water safety training and realized they'd become caught in a current that had rapidly dragged them down the coast.

Angling back toward the shore, Garrick fought against being rolled onto his face. Many years earlier, swimming in the much colder, wind-driven waters of Broken Wing Lake, he'd learned to twist his torso against the rolling motion. This required more effort, tapping into endurance he'd reserved in the event of an emergency. Growing wearier with each stroke, he needed to rest.

"Brenna!" he called, breathlessly. "I need . . . a break . . . for a minute."

Pausing in the midst of her prayers, the Lithian woman complied. "Are you getting tired?" she asked.

"I . . . just need to . . . catch my breath," he replied, uttering a response intended to encourage her, rather than state a disconcerting truth. "I'm okay . . . ."

This happened again, a third time, and then a fourth. She heard his labored breathing, worried that he could not long continue and they'd drift away to their deaths. *"Allfather God,"* she prayed. *"You who made the stars, the sea and the land. You who spoke life into being, who crafted me in my mother's womb, who has protected and sustained my every breath; I cry out for your help.*

"We are weak and weary, while the ocean waters are strong and cold. We are frail against the deep, but you command the waves and they obey. You hold our lives in your mighty hand. Save us!"

Moments later, Garrick felt something brush against his back. He froze in terror. "Brenna! Hold still!"

She opened her eyes and stopped her kicking. The billows lifted her head high enough to see the distant shore. "What's wrong?"

Panting to recover his breath while clinging to his *bug-out* bag and the tether that bound him to Brenna, Garrick noted a tall dorsal fin – outlined against the light of burning Briminger – moving swiftly through the sea between them and the shore. "We're not alone," he replied, instinctively thinking it wise to remain still. "Don't move."

Brenna, who could see quite well, gasped when she noticed the shape and the size of the dark shadow swimming just beneath the surface. Whistles and clicks resounded in the water. "I think it's a whale," she said.

A strange sound, like a blast of air, arose from behind them. Startled, Garrick heard the sound, but could see nothing. Brenna turned, with widened eyes, as five slender, gleaming, curvilinear shapes cut swiftly through the waves. "There are more of them," she warned.

Garrick felt the water surge around his body as something very powerful swam beneath him. He tried to hold still, but the sound of breaching and a sudden blast of air alarmed him. Against the blackness he saw a patch of white and the gleam of an eye, close enough to touch.

A moment later, the whale slapped its tail flukes on the water and vanished beneath the billows. Blending with the whistling sounds, Garrick heard Brenna's fervent prayers and didn't interrupt her. He scanned the horizon for the feeble glow of burning Briminger, heard a sudden rush, then felt an irresistible thrust pull him forward. As his back slammed against smooth, wet skin, he nearly lost his grip on the tether that bound him to his bride.

She shrieked in surprise and terror as the fragile fabric tied around her *bug-out* bag hooked onto the whale's dorsal fin and dragged her helpless body along. Brenna would have let go, but a familiar voice in her head spoke with calm assurance, *"Don't be afraid, little one. I am with you. My creatures know my voice and obey."*

"Hold on, Garrick!" she admonished. "Stay strong!"

Struggling to keep his head above water, Garrick reached for the whale's towering dorsal fin and pulled his head and chest out of the water. Clinging to the tether with his left hand, he craned his neck in a futile effort to see where they were headed, but it proved impossible for him to tell.

While these cetacean hunters often swam close to the surface, they usually breached only for breathing. Yet this animal remained no more than a handbreath beneath the sea, as if aware that his charges didn't tolerate being submerged for very long.

Flanked by her family, the whale's great strength propelled her streamlined body far faster than any man could swim. A chorus of whistles, clicks and high-pitched squealing accompanied the rhythmic release and inhalation of air as the pod raced toward the shore.

Brenna pressed her hand on top of her husband's as the undulating mammal cut through the waves. Praying in gratitude, she wistfully longed to share the assurance and renewed peace that her faith provided; yet knowing that her secular-minded lover did not *believe*, Brenna kept her counsel to herself.

Just when exhausted Garrick didn't think he could hold on for another second, the whale drifted to a stop, drew in a deep breath, then sank into the water. As suddenly as the creature had first appeared, she vanished, leaving the young couple on their own.

Hearing the sound of surf, Garrick renewed his grip on the tether and began swimming again. Within a few strokes, his feet touched the sandy bottom. The weary soldier stood and pulled his wife into shallower water, where she stood and they walked into a cove on the shore. There, Brenna uttered fervid, teary prayers of gratitude as she held her husband in a tight, trembling embrace.

***

With her emotions calming Brenna tilted her head, pressing her soft bosom into Garrick's belly. Something terrible had happened here. Shell craters, dismembered bodies and abandoned weapons lay strewn about the cove where they'd come ashore. Everything lay silent and still.

The stench of rotting flesh mingled with the smell of the sea. Brenna shuddered as horror haunted her soul. Terrifying memories of combat – of cowering in a Tamarian trench, helplessly enduring heavy Azgar shelling for days on end – roared from her past.

"What's wrong?" Garrick asked, kissing her forehead as he caressed her shoulders.

Knowing that he couldn't see very well under these conditions, Brenna unzipped his waterproof *bug-out* bag and fumbled through it for a flashlight. Wordlessly, she beamed its light over the shore while looking away.

Garrick's eyes widened. "Naval artillery, no doubt," he concluded. While the sight gave him pause, his tactical mind recognized an opportunity. "Let's dry off and pick up some weapons."

Brenna shut off the flashlight to avoid attracting attention. She offered Garrick his towel and a fresh set of clothing before taking off her camisole and underwear. Unlike his outfit, she could will hers to dry and easily shake the salt out of its high-tech fabric. After toweling off her shivering body, she wore the same camisole again, with fresh underwear, a clean blouse and skirt.

After putting on shoes, Brenna led Garrick further ashore, carefully stepping around debris and any object that looked like it might be an unexploded shell. She turned away when he activated flashlight in order to preserve her night vision.

Garrick picked up an automatic rifle, checked and emptied its chamber. "These are like the Vatheran guns the Tanarak used against us," he told his wife gravely. "They give one man the firepower of a whole squad."

Remembering his earlier commentary on the subject, Brenna replied, "So the Vatherans are involved in this. What's in it for them?"

Nudging a dead man's jaw with his boot, Garrick noted Kurian features. A quick check of other bodies nearby revealed that they were all local men, likely insurgents, who'd been spotted and dispatched by the Nordans. "Selling weapons to an insurgency generates tidy profits for gun makers," he stated. "Do you want one?"

"Can you find something small?" she asked.

Garrick picked up a sidearm, which he checked and cleared before handing it to Brenna. "I'll find some ammunition," he said. "There's enough laying around here to start a small war." Garrick clicked his tongue and shook his head. "This is worse than I thought."

He slung the rifle over his shoulder, grabbed a combat fighting knife that had never seen action, then stuffed four magazines, four grenades and one box of rifle rounds into his *bug-out* bag. Munitions for the .30 caliber handgun were far more sparse. He only found two extra magazines with eight rounds each.

"Let's get out of here and find a safe place to sleep," he recommended. "I can hardly keep my eyes open."

In silent agreement, Brenna took her husband's hand and led him down the beach. They crossed over a formation of large rocks and onto a wide expanse of open land where dunes lapped up against the boulders in the north, and the long bluff of a more ancient shoreline to the east. Finding a sheltered place twenty yards from the water, the lovers coiled into a tight embrace and collapsed into restless slumber.

***

Brenna awakened at the sound of a scream. A familiar tingle stirred in her flesh as dawn splashed the horizon in pink light. She longed to linger in close contact with Garrick, but the sound of a child's crying compelled action. Reluctantly moving Garrick's hand from her breast, the Lithian woman arose and peeked at the shore.

"What's going on?" Garrick asked, groggily. A headache and thirst warned that he needed water.

"I see four Nordan women on the beach," Brenna replied quietly, her heart torn between desire and action. "They're huddling around a child who's been hurt."

Knowing her well, Garrick reached for his wife's clothes. "Here you go," he offered, finding her particularly attractive at that moment. The Tamarian soldier turned from her intoxicating aroma, put on shorts and a shirt, popped an analgesic tablet into his mouth and took a long drink from his canteen before loading the rifle, slinging it over his shoulder and following Brenna as she scurried across the sand. He questioned the wisdom of coming to anyone's aid in their current circumstances, but also realized he couldn't stop his wife from acting on the compassion that defined her character.

Brenna's rapid approach alerted one of the women, who pointed and chatted excitedly in the Nordan tongue. Brenna held her hands out to show that she was unarmed, yet her exotic appearance inspired suspicion. Three women stood behind the injured child and her mother. One of them pointed a handgun at Brenna.

Garrick pulled his rifle around and fired a burst into the sand, well left of the Nordan women. "Drop it!" he ordered in vulgate. "Drop it now!"

The tallest of the women understood. She gestured for her handgun-wielding companion to set the weapon down, which – after understanding that she was seriously outgunned – she did.

Brenna pressed forward. She made eye contact with the woman she presumed to be the child's mother and pleaded, "Let me help," in vulgate.

A quick translation resulted in a testy exchange between the Nordans, which ended abruptly as Garrick drew near, shooed the women away and retrieved the handgun from among their cockle-collection buckets. He expertly checked the weapon, noting with a smirk that its safety was still on and no round had been chambered, then removed its magazine and slipped the ammunition into his pocket. He slung the rifle over his shoulder before handing the emptied handgun back to its owner.

The mother clung to her child, scolding Brenna and pushing her away as the girl cried in agony. Her resistance wasn't helping.

"Tell that woman my wife can help," Garrick ordered impatiently. "She's not going to harm the girl."

"A gentle tone builds trust," Brenna responded mildly. "That's what we need right now."

She was right. "Okay," he clarified, calming his demeanor. "My beloved can heal the child. Let her work."

After another flurry of foreign talk, the willowy, vulgate-speaking woman replied, "My sister says you rebels will kill us all and take everything we have."

Garrick responded gently. "Look at us. Listen to us. We're not native people. I'm Tamarian, and my wife is Lithian. We're trying to get home, not cause trouble."

His confidence, charisma and transition to a non-threatening demeanor soon convinced the Nordans to set aside their mistrust for the moment. Most of them did so.

More translating followed. Brenna watched hope displace fear in the mother's eyes. The Nordan woman nodded tentatively, relaxing her grip on her daughter.

Brenna prayed, feeling familiar power rise in her body and tremble through her fingertips. She examined the injury with a critical eye. "This looks like some kind of sting, or poison," she remarked. Turning to Garrick, she asked, "Can you carry her to the sea?"

The multilingual woman translated as Garrick knelt, gently cradled the preteen girl in his arms and carried her to the water. He squatted in the shallows, allowing his wife to wash the child's legs and feet.

"I see thin spines in her flesh," Brenna stated, pulling out her Lithian boot knife to scrape them away.

The mother screamed at the sight of Brenna's blade and tried to pull the girl out of Garrick's arms. Irritated with this behavior, Brenna touched the mother's hand. "Sleep!" she commanded, and the Nordan woman mysteriously slumped into her surprised sister's embrace.

Fear spread through the other women. Who were these foreign people? With the girl still in Garrick's arms, no one dared do anything rash. Wide-eyed, they watched Brenna dip her Lithian blade into the water and delicately scrape the child's lower leg, ankles and feet. Then, she gracefully bent down and kissed the girl's wounded flesh.

To the astonishment of the watching women, all swelling and redness vanished from the child's skin. The little girl stopped her sobbing, gazing at Brenna in wonder.

A moment later, the child climbed out of Garrick's arms, reached for Brenna and held her in a tight embrace, muttering Nordan gibberish. Garrick stood, making eye contact with the tall woman. He held his palms to the side and shrugged. "See?" he said. "We're not here to hurt anyone, least of all a little one."

Brenna touched the mother's hand again. "Wake up. Everything's okay now."

The woman roused as if from a deep sleep. Momentarily disoriented, she accepted her daughter into her own arms and listened to her sister explain what had happened. The mother stared at Brenna as a tear traced down her cheek. She released her daughter and bowed low, speaking Nordan in a hushed and reverent tone.

Seeing this, Brenna recoiled. "Don't honor me!" she warned. "I am not worthy of your worship!" The Lithian woman backed away, sheathed her boot knife and trotted briskly into the dunes without looking back.

Wisely, Garrick watched her go but did not follow. Allowing Brenna to retreat and gather her composure, he turned to the girl's aunt. "My wife is a very devout woman. She finds it irreverent when people bow to her."

"Honorable sir, it's our custom," the tall woman countered. "We bow to show respect."

"It's not her intent to sully your customs," Garrick replied. "She believes that by bowing to her, you're disrespecting the god who gives her authority to heal on his behalf. She's rather sensitive about that sort of thing."

"You see that power at work, yet do not honor this god of hers?" the woman asked incredulously.

"No," Garrick stated flatly. "I can't explain how she does the healing, and neither can she. It's a mystery."

Puzzled, the Nordan woman scrunched her brow. Her eyes lingered over Garrick's well-formed, muscular body, noting the salt crusted onto his arm and chest hair. "You've been in the sea," she noted. "Let us offer you a hot bath and a meal as a way of expressing our thanks."

Uncomfortable, untrusting, and sensing that Brenna needed to be alone, Garrick glanced at their partially filled buckets and hedged. "We should be on our way," he replied. "It looks like you still have work to do."

"Please, honored sir. If we don't repay the debt, our ancestors will disapprove. The Sea Scorpion sting is deadly. My niece was already suffering paralysis and could have died. We're obligated to repay the favor."

Garrick pondered for a moment, reluctant to stomp on local customs. These women likely had a far better understanding of how to get around than either he or Brenna could boast. Perhaps they might be able to help. "We're heading for Helsing," he admitted. "Our papers have gone missing and we're a long way from home. Can you help us find a way to the Tamarian embassy?"

The woman, recognizing the passive construction of his statement and concluding that he and the foreign woman had their documents taken by someone in authority, spoke rapidly to her sister. Concern appeared on the other women's faces. Hands moved to frowning lips. Brows furrowed and much whispering followed.

"That's not possible," the woman said at length. "The city is besieged with armed insurgents. They have guns like yours and will kill us if we go there."

Garrick swore in Tamarian. "Do you have a telephone?" he asked. "We don't want to put you in danger. I just need to talk to someone at the embassy who can arrange our passage home through Kameron."

More talking ensued, generating nods and sounds of affirmation. "A bath, a meal and a telephone call," the multilingual woman stated. "If that is agreeable to you, we will consider our debt repaid."

He nodded. "Okay, but no contact with the civil authorities, the military, or the police," Garrick insisted. "And you do not speak to anyone about us."

The expression on the woman's face proved tough to read. Did she question his integrity? "No need for that," she replied. "We will send for you when we're ready to go."

***

Garrick found Brenna in the midst of her morning prayers. She looked beautiful as poetic words spilled over her alluring lips. Her aroma aroused him as she gestured to a presence Garrick could not see. Despite his disbelief, in the divine, he felt confident that her rituals were rooted in spiritual rites, not insanity, and let her pray in peace.

Distracted by his headache and a longing for intimacy he struggled to resist, Garrick reached for his canteen, crept away and drank deeply enough to empty the vessel entirely. He watched the Nordan women digging diligently in the distance until Brenna called for him.

She'd begun brushing her hair, a sight he'd found calming since the earliest days of their relationship. Yet her face showed a weariness he'd not seen in a long time. "I can't believe that woman bowed to me," Brenna complained. "What was she thinking?"

"Her sister told me it's a cultural thing," Garrick explained. "It's about respect, not reverence."

Brenna, who'd struggled with physical distraction during her prayers, didn't want to argue. After being miraculously delivered from the sea, she experienced a longing to express her gratitude. Healing the little girl offered that opportunity, but the mother's groveling with her face in the sand rattled the Lithian woman. She continued brushing. "I'd like a bath with you," she admitted sensuously, setting her brush down and crawling over to him. Brenna swayed her body in a seductive manner as an expression of longing filled her dilated eyes. She licked her salty lips as the telltale stirring of *Y Newen* pressed through her blouse. As she drew close, the influence of her swelling pheromones aroused him again.

Garrick reached for her, their lips meeting with a tenderness founded on lifelong commitment and deep concern for one another. However, they both knew this was not a good time to express their mutual passion. The amorous couple needed a safe, private place until her fertile season passed, which usually took several days. Being unable to act on Brenna's receptivity complicated their escape and created frustration for both of them. So he placed a gentle kiss on his wife's forehead and deflected her attention. "We should eat," he recommended. "The women will come for us when their buckets are full."

Disappointed and struggling against dissatisfaction that her romantic vision for the music festival had been spoiled, a little frown turned down the corners of the Lithian woman's lips. She sat on her bedroll, stifling her emotions. "What do we have?" she asked.

"Honey muesli squares, pemmican biscuits with blueberry jam, and dried apricots," he replied. "We have tea and chocolate, but I drank the last of my water, and if we start the gasifier to desalinate more, we'll have to wait for it and the water to cool before we can leave."

Brenna didn't feel like eating. She nibbled through a muesli square and two of the biscuits with jam. Preferring apricots to chocolate, she slipped the candy into her bag, thinking that it might be a nice treat for the child. Before she'd finished packing up, the Nordan girl showed up and excitedly urged them to follow her.

***

High overhead, Ensign Okura Kenichi – operating the optical sensors on *Shīgōrudo* – scanned the beach far below. He'd just about passed over the scene before movement and an unusual sight caught his eye.

Adjusting the lenses for maximum magnification, he zoomed in on the beach. He saw Nordan colony women walking in the company of a tall, broad-shouldered, blonde-haired man with a rifle slung over his back. At first, he presumed the man to be a Kurian insurgent. But since the weapon was not ready for action, he did not appear threatening to his companions, who walked alongside or followed behind in a casual manner.

Changing the angle of his camera, Kenichi noted that one of the women didn't look Nordan after all. She had dark hair, but her form and manner of dress differed from the others. "Lieutenant Ido!" he called. "I have just reacquired the missing targets for *Operation Tora*."

Ido came over to verify. Peering into the device, he grunted in affirmation. "I will contact Colonel Utemaro."

That action reset the Nordan military's efforts to find and recapture the foreigners. Colonel Utemaro called the garrison commander at Mageshima, outside of Helsing. A squad of Nordan military police went on alert, awaiting location details. Tasking orders for *Shīgōrudo* shifted from surveillance of insurrectionist movements near Briminger to maintaining visual contact with the two foreigners.

Kenichi kept them in his sights, wondering why these people merited such interest.

***

Sakura and her mother, Yua, carried buckets full of cockles on poles across their shoulders as they followed the foreign couple. Ichika, Yua's eldest daughter, walked alongside Izuma, their family servant, who'd brought a gun for protection. Her incompetence when facing a threat proved that she was only good for one thing . . . .

Yua wouldn't have drawn the weapon at all. In her mind, outsmarting the little foreign witch was wiser than shooting her. The strapping, round-eyed man in her company hadn't threatened anyone until stupid Izuma pointed the gun. Better to know the enemy's weaknesses than react with thoughtless provocation.

Emiko, Sakura's daughter, danced to the head of the procession, chatting in vulgate with the armed stranger – who claimed to be a Tamarian soldier – and his mysterious wench.

"How can you call her a sorceress?" Sakura asked quietly. "Emiko's legs were already suffering paralysis before the foreign woman came. The Sea Scorpion sting is a death sentence, but look at her now."

Yua scowled. "Her man admitted the healing power is not hers. She must be channeling demons."

Sakura didn't often cross her mother. In this situation, however, she believed that Yua's superstition was unfounded. "Then why did you suggest letting her and the soldier into our home?"

"We can take his weapon when they enter the house," Yua stated. "While they're in the bath, I'll contact the colonial authorities. They can't hurt us while they're naked and unarmed. It's better to keep your enemy in plain sight than to turn away. And if we didn't offer them the bath – where we can watch them closely – they might have followed us home to rob and kill us in our sleep."

"The ancestors will not be pleased with your attitude," Sakura warned. "The foreign lady healed Emiko and the soldier could have easily shot and killed us with his rifle. She came running in answer to my prayers and put an end to Emiko's suffering. How do you know the ancestors didn't send her?"

"You're blaspheming!" Yua spat. "Those people do not sacrifice to the gods, nor do they honor the ancestors. I saw her reaction when you bowed in respect. What kind of sensible person responds that way?

"And you've already forgotten that the woman knocked you out with the touch of her hand and awakened you in the same way. It's obvious to me that she's in league with evil spirits."

After thinking about this for a minute, Sakura replied, "Then let's send them on their way before we get home. We can give them the old boat to repay our debt and appease the ancestors."

Yua shook her head. "That is out of the question. You heard Ichika. These people have no documents. He claimed that they'd lost them, but who loses their passport on a holiday? Only thugs and terrorists hide their identities. Round-eyes can't be trusted.

"We must report them. It's honorable to ensure they're arrested. If need be, I will offer Izuma to the soldier to keep him distracted."

Sakura felt shocked to hear this from her mother. "Why would you think such a thing? Can't you see that he adores his wife?"

"Men are all the same," Yua countered. "Izuma is very skilled in these matters. He'll be unable to resist."

Choosing silence over the discomfort of maternal conflict, Sakura watched the foreign couple closely. She noted their constant close proximity and the kindly, gentle tone each one used when speaking to the other. Passion simmered beneath their shared courtesy, evident in sensual, longing glances, sustained smiles and a playful demeanor as they bumped hips while laughing at Emiko's antics. His listening reflected respect for her views – while her eyes hovered on him with deep admiration.

Izuma would have a tough time taking the rugged, Tamarian soldier's attention away from his beautiful, blue-eyed bride. His devotion, expressed in word, tone and behavior, inspired aching envy in Sakura's heart. She longed for the same degree of honor the Tamarian lavished on his wife, but Sakura's fisherman husband considered her a liability, a mouth to feed, a disappointment who'd not given him a son. She did not feel loved.

Yua's duplicity grated against the desire to be adored like the foreign woman. Sakura, distracted by her mother's perspective, pondered the source of the little Lithian woman's power. Even if she didn't acknowledge the gods, how could saving life be the work of demons? That made no sense.

***

Unaware of the conversation going on behind them, and trusting that the Nordan women represented no threat to their safety, Garrick and Brenna laughed at Emiko's efforts to pronounce their names.

"Blenna and Gelick," the girl said, pointing at each of them in turn.

She spoke vulgate, though not as fluently as her aunt, and with a heavy accent that sometimes obscured the meaning of her words. Despite this, Emiko – whom they learned from her relentless prattle had recently turned nine years of age – expressed herself with wit and a remarkable sense of humor in her second language that testified to underlying intelligence.

For Garrick, the experience of being in Emiko's company tapped into his concealed longing for a daughter of his own, someone who could carry on his family's name. He felt a little sad that Brenna had, thus far, been unable to carry a child to term. Knowing she'd feel terrible if he mentioned this, the soldier drew a bit nearer to his wife, displayed more public affection than he'd ever dared in Tamaria, and silently wished that she could be his partner in raising a family.

Emiko's call for a race toward an isolated jetty extending into the sea switched that train of thought onto a different track. The Nordan girl paused, taunting them to join her, and while fleet-footed Brenna could have easily prevailed in such a contest, the Lithian woman just shook her head and shouted, "You go ahead. We had a late night and I'm too tired for running."

An old boat with a sturdy oil-injection engine lay at the end of the rickety pier. It had a different, more practical shape when compared to local vessels of similar size, and could accommodate nine passengers – provided that everyone sat very close to one another. Emiko climbed in with the confidence of long familiarity, urging her new friends to follow.

Garrick helped the women load their heavy cockle buckets, then watched Ichika go through the procedure of priming the injector and heating the glow plug before pulling on the cord that spun the sputtering, noisy and polluting engine to life. It coughed like a thing alive, spewing blue smoke in its wake as the engine twisted the boat's propeller into action.

While the boat was not fast – Brenna remembered riding on hydrofoil sailboats across the *Mari Halinnea* that skimmed the waves at breathtaking speed – and it seemed decidedly low-tech to her and utterly wasteful to Garrick, it beat swimming. Because Brenna felt safer in a boat than she had in the sea, she paused to pray in gratitude.

With her weary head resting against his shoulder and the sensation of her silky hair brushing his skin, Garrick scanned the shoreline, watching local fishermen sort their previous evening's catch. None of them gave the passing boat a second glance, and since none were armed, he feigned disinterest. Because he didn't share the faith that inspired his woman's confidence, the veteran soldier maintained observational vigilance, ready to act if needed. He noted that Ichika piloted the boat around a point where a little fishing village stood, then into a cove on its southern side. She pulled into a near empty marina, cut the engine and secured the boat to a pier.

Their journey had taken less than ten minutes, and it would likely have been faster to walk. "Why did we take the boat when we could have saved time by walking across the point?" he asked.

"We always do," Emiko answered, bounding onto the dock, where an old rowboat maintained a lonely vigil.

Garrick made eye contact with Ichika, who scowled as he handed her a cockle bucket. "Natives," she spat. "They hate us, and we hate them."

As Brenna glanced in Yua's direction, the old woman glared in disapproval and something close to a sneer raised her upper lip. Uncomfortable with conflict, Brenna slid behind her husband and looked away.

***

Unlike the run-down Kurian village they'd passed on the point, the neat and tidy huddle of wood and paper houses of Chīsana Mura lay on the summit of a low hill overlooking the sea. A stone path, inlaid with gravel and kept meticulously free of weeds, led through manicured coastal firs, past vegetable garden plots where old men and women diligently worked and watered – pausing momentarily to stare at the foreigners before returning to their tasks – then beneath a red and black wooden arch guarding a terraced area where massive stone blocks supported several houses.

The entire village, enclosed by a stout wall, appeared simultaneously alien to the lovers, yet fitting and appropriate in this environment. The air smelled of the sea, fish, kelp oil and acrid engine exhaust from a generator providing electrical power. Small children gawked at Garrick and Brenna as they passed other houses on the way to their destination.

The Nordan women's home had its own wall with a gatehouse. Its curved roof, post and beam construction and sliding panels portrayed an esthetic of simplicity and beauty. A veranda, featuring storm shutters on the outside edge, ran along the building's perimeter.

Inside, the aroma of its rice and rush straw mats mingled with the scent of cedar. Ichika instructed the guests to remove their shoes in a sunken area between the front door and the rest of the house, much like the Tamarian custom of leaving shoes in the outer vestibule.

A terse exchange between Yua and Ichika drew the attention of an elderly couple, who slid a screen aside and peeked at the foreigners with stoic faces.

"Honored sir, we would like you to hand over your weapon," Ichika insisted. "This is a place of peace."

Concerned that the rifle might be used against them, Garrick cleared its chamber and removed its ammunition magazine before giving up the gun. "What about her?" he asked, referring to Izuma.

Ichika took the weapon from Garrick. "We store all firearms in a gun safe. Now, Izuma will show you to your room and let you know when your bath is ready."

She seemed a little quick to isolate her guests. In Tamaria, custom dictated that the host offer water to everyone entering a house. Garrick, still suffering from a headache, expected Ichika to do this. When she turned to walk away, he interrupted her with the request. Ichika spat a quick order to Izuma, who bowed in response.

The slender servant woman led the young couple to a sparsely-furnished room on the back side of the house that overlooked a lovely garden. Watercolor art graced the walls. Its furniture included a richly lacquered table, a lamp, and a thin mattress laying directly on the floor mat.

Moments later, Izuma returned with a pitcher of water and two cups. She left these on a cloth she placed on the table, bowed and closed the sliding door.

"Are we supposed to stay in here?" Brenna asked.

Garrick shrugged and shook his head in honest ignorance. "I don't know." He dug through his bag to find another analgesic tablet, reached for the pitcher, poured water into the cups and drank until his belly felt full.

Brenna sipped her water, listening to the sounds of Nordan conversation through the paper-thin walls. While she'd not given up the handgun in her *bug-out* bag and knew that Garrick had ammunition and grenades in his, a sense of vulnerability nagged at her. "Do you think we're safe here?" she asked.

"No," Garrick replied. "We're surrounded by a wall and the only way out is by sea."

"Then maybe we should leave," she suggested. "I don't want to be rude to these people, but the way the grandmother stares and sneers makes me uncomfortable. I think we should thank them and be on our way."

Feeling sore from the previous evening's exertion, Garrick longed for the soothing comfort of a hot bath. He didn't admit this, as he hated the way soldiers under his command groused about their misery and had long ago decided that he should avoid complaining. "A bath would do us both good," he reminded her, "and they've promised we could use their phone to contact the embassy."

Brenna tightened her lips. She could see the fatigue in Garrick's eyes and knew he needed rest. Gazing at him stirred her desire to the extent that she had to look away to exert control. *Y Newen,* the Lithian fertile period, typically began when a married woman felt safe. Yet oddly, the danger they faced had triggered her cycle this time, and Brenna felt frustrated that she couldn't act on her craving at the moment. This house, with its thin walls and sliding doors, oozed mistrust – undermining her desire for intimate contact. "Maybe we can slip away at night, while everyone's asleep," she offered.

"I'd be happier to do that with the rifle on my back," he replied. "I don't see that happening unless Ichika returns it."

"She doesn't concern me," Brenna stated. "The whispering grandmother is plotting something, and I don't think we can trust her."

***

In a cleaning shack to the side of the house, Yua and her daughters stood around a water basin with her father-in-law, Haruto, and mother-in-law, Kaori. Working together, the family could clean and sort the gathered cockles quickly enough to keep them alive.

After scrubbing the shells, family members tossed them into a long stone tray filled with fresh seawater. While a small, wind-powered bubble aerator added oxygen, Izuma would change the water periodically until the living creatures expelled all the sand in their shells.

Kaori questioned her daughter-in-law about the negative attitude she displayed to their foreign guests. "You say the woman is a sorceress, yet the Sea Scorpion is the messenger of misfortune and death. This woman cannot be in league with demons if she saved Emiko."

"So you would forbid me from reporting them to the authorities?" Yua asked. "How will the Colonial Office respond when they learn we've harbored our enemies?"

"Enemies?" Haruto responded. "Ichika told us that the soldier could have killed everyone, but did not. You saw that the woman healed Emiko. These are deeds of restraint and kindness, not the actions of our enemies."

Yua shook her head. "Don't be fooled, honored father. She is the Fox, full of cunning and deceit. She bears an evil scar on her neck and fled when Sakura bowed in respect. She put Sakura to sleep with a touch and brought her back the same way . . . ."

"I didn't know what she could do," Sakura interrupted. "I feared for Emiko, but I was wrong."

"You are still wrong," Yua corrected. "She has cast magic and you are under her spell."

"I forbid it," Haruto announced, ending the discussion. "You will not contact the Colonial Office. We have strangers in our house, and we will extend hospitality as our people have always done. We will feed them and let them rest before they go on their way."

Yua bowed her head, but her spirit did not comply.

***

"New orders from Admiral Kobashigawa," Lieutenant Ido announced. "We will aid the defense of the Mageshima Garrison by reporting on insurgent movements near the base. We will observe and direct naval artillery, if needed."

Ensign Kenichi thought the constantly changing orders illustrated confusion in the command structure, but he kept his objections quiet. "Yes sir! I will note that our targets have just entered Chīsana Mura for reference."

Ido nodded. "Very well."

The airship turned inland. With the border close by, its pilot made sure the aircraft didn't wander over Kamerese territory, on the far bank of the *Rio Attavela*. The Nordans didn't want to provoke a rival foreign power.

Kenichi noted a lot of smoke rising from Helsing. He'd already seen the senseless destruction of Briminger, where wild rebel mobs had run loose in the town wielding guns and firebrands. Now, the insurgents threatened a similar attack on the regional capital. This time, however, the army garrison at Mageshima could defend the city.

At least, he hoped so.

To Colonel Kuribayashi, commander of the Mageshima Garrison, the chaotic situation he faced called for courage and decisive action. During the violent attack on Briminger – several miles north – he'd ordered an evacuation of all nonessential personnel, coordinating his efforts with Lieutenant Governor Maseo Kurou in Helsing.

As reports of terror attacks arrived, he trusted that his defensive deployment would beat them back. Anticipating that the rebels might arise all over the city at once, he'd dispatched his troops and artillery to defend power plants, water and sewage stations, government buildings, telephone exchanges, and radio towers.

His reserve troops fortified the garrison perimeter, with the biggest gun tubes in his inventory set in strategic positions. There would be no evacuation for the soldiers defending Helsing. They would fight to the last man.

An aide approached with a phone message. "Sir!" the warrant officer said. "A woman in Chīsana Mura phoned. She claims that the foreigners wanted by the Special Forces are staying at her house."

The colonel grunted in affirmation. He picked up his telephone and relayed the message to the military police commander, who'd reserved a squad for this task. "Take them to the pick-up point on the river," he ordered.

Within a few minutes, eight military policemen loaded their weapons and climbed into a truck headed for the Nordan village of Chīsana Mura.

***

Brenna slid into the warm, soothing water. She tilted her head back to wash the salt out of her hair and smiled as her handsome husband dropped his towel and descended into a large, circular hot spring pool.

Izuma left them with soap and a skin scrubber before slipping behind the changing screen. Brenna lathered up her hands, then washed and rinsed her face before offering to scrub her husband's back. She made a game of it, tickling and exploring his body with her fingers, a favor he returned until the two of them began giggling like playful children.

Moments later, Garrick's expression turned serious and he quickly spun around. Noting the change, Brenna watched Izuma lead Kaori to the pool. The servant woman removed the old woman's towel and helped her down the submerged stairs. Haruto followed, easing himself into the water as Izuma slipped out of her gown and began washing her elderly mistress.

If the Nordans sensed unease from their guests they didn't say anything, and their faces reflected no indication that they discerned discomfort that their unusual behavior inspired in their visitors. Brenna glided behind her husband while he moved to the far side of the hot pool. Garrick turned his head when Haruto addressed him.

"So, you are a soldier," the old man stated, speaking the Azgar language with the ease of long mastery.

Garrick nodded uneasily. "I am."

The old man grunted in affirmation. "I thought so. You carry yourself that way. Where did you serve?"

Garrick outlined his experience, beginning with the Azgar invasion of Tamaria. He mentioned officer's training briefly before explaining his action in the Kamerese Civil War. "In my last deployment, the TEF defended our border against incursions by a plains tribe called the Tanarak."

"You've seen a lot of action for a young man," Haruto observed. "And we share a mutual enemy."

Puzzled, thinking that his host was mistakenly referring to the Kamerese, Garrick inquired, "What enemy would that be?"

"The Azgar," Haruto replied. "You speak their tongue quite well."

"As do you," Garrick observed. While the old man's accent sounded a little odd, he articulated his words clearly enough that Garrick had no trouble understanding. "I learned vulgate in school. What about you, sir?"

"Hmm," Haruto mused, remembering. "As a youth I served in the Fourth Marines of the Imperial Navy. The Azgar invaded and overran our southern colony islands, and I spent two years in a prison camp before they released me. I learned their tongue out of necessity."

"I'm sorry to hear that," Garrick stated. "But you are fortunate to have survived. I've heard that Azgar prisoners are not well-treated."

Haruto shrugged. "They're not, but that was long ago. We are here now, and I wish to express gratitude to your woman for saving my great granddaughter."

"It was not I," Brenna replied. "Allfather uses me as the conduit for his power. It is he you should thank."

"Then I will light incense in his honor," Haruto responded as Izuma began washing his body.

Sensing something mildly erotic in the young woman's touch, Garrick felt increasingly uneasy. He hurriedly scrubbed and rinsed his hair. Reaching for his towel, he climbed out of the hot pool's far side, offering a hand to Brenna – who refused it and pulled herself out of the water without help. Garrick gave her a towel and vanished behind the men's changing screen.

Izuma helped Kaori dry off and wrapped her in a towel before returning to the tub. Noting that the old woman sat on a bench behind the changing screen as if waiting, Brenna asked in vulgate, "Would you like me to help you get dressed?"

The elderly matron, understanding fully, shook her head. "Izuma will come when she's finished servicing my husband. It won't take long."

Hearing Izuma's slurping sounds with widened eyes, Brenna peered around the screen before quickly looking away. "What she's doing doesn't bother you?"

Kaori watched with interest as Brenna stepped into her panties – wondering how the tiny woman dealt with such a big, heavy bosom. The old matron stared shamelessly, also intrigued that Brenna had no body hair. "I have no interest. Men are men. What she does for him is a trifling thing. It's just release. There is no love in it."

Brenna raised her brow in disapproval. She'd been raised by devout parents who taught the value of sexually satisfying a single, lifelong partner, but also stressed the sacred nature of intimacy for procreation. The activity Brenna witnessed in the pool inspired mild contempt, as ranked as morally unacceptable in her view. Though she tried to avoid judging, condescension crept into her voice as she replied, "I don't see it that way."

"You don't want Izuma to service your husband?" Kaori said, sounding mildly surprised. "It would relieve you of the burden."

"No!" Brenna responded, a little too quickly. "Loving Garrick is a privilege, not a burden. I want him, and he is mine. I don't need help from your servant girl."

"Suit yourself," Kaori stated.

In the uncomfortable silence that followed, a whistling sound arose from the sea, growing louder as it arced overhead. Kaori reached for Brenna's arm in fear. The Lithian woman controlled her racing heart as dark memories of Azgar and rebel Kamerese artillery raining death from above rose from their long-suppressed vault. A rumbling crack resounded in the distance.

Taking in a deep breath and uttering a quick prayer, Brenna reassured her hostess. "Don't worry," she said. "It's naval artillery. They won't be targeting us here."

Another round screamed overhead. "How can you tell?" the old woman asked.

"If you can hear it, you're safe," Brenna stated. "It's the ones you can't hear that kill you."

Kaori trembled. "How do you know this?"

Brenna put on her Lithian camisole and willed it into place, noting and ignoring Kaori's curiosity about how the garment worked. "The Azgar invaded my homeland," she stated. "I lost people I love in the fight against them, and learned more about artillery than I care to remember."

Standing and touching the scar on Brenna's neck, the old woman inquired. "The Azgar did this to you?"

Struggling to retain composure and trembling from the terrible memory, Brenna shook her head. "No, honored grandmother. That came from a Kamerese rebel who tried to kill me with a machete."

Although she was an old woman with little concern for social etiquette, Kaori felt sympathetic and withdrew in respect. "Duplicitous insurgents!" she complained quietly. "They talk about freedom with a forked tongue. All they want is death and destruction."

***

From high in the sky, Ensign Kenichi watched swarms of Kurian fighters surging through the streets of Helsing, indiscriminately killing, looting shops and setting fire to property. With the army garrison hard pressed and outnumbered, *Shīgōrudo* moved into position to direct naval artillery.

Radio contact with spotters on the ground gave the general coordinates where vicinity commanders believed the firepower was needed. Ensign Kenichi refined these for Lieutenant Ido, who subsequently passed the references on to the navy commander.

Four ships of the Nordan Imperial Navy had recently steamed into position offshore in response to earlier intelligence reports concerning imminent rebellion. These vessels, sent to deter aggression, now aimed their guns in anger. The heavy destroyers Hanazuki and Shimakaze – each with two dual turret six inch guns on their decks; the cruiser Haruna – with four dual turret 14 inch guns; and the Musano – the largest and fastest of the Nordan Navy's capital ships, which featured three triple turret 15 inch guns – trained their formidable firepower against the rebel Kurians attacking the defenders of Helsing.

Ranging fires scattered surviving insurgents, who had no idea of the horror the Nordan navy was about to inflict up them. Once Kenichi verified that the rounds were hitting their intended targets, Lieutenant Ido gave the "fire for effect" order.

Bright flashes and a series of spreading shock waves rippled through the city below. Flames and showers of debris from shattered buildings formed plumes of smoke and dust that smothered visibility. Kenichi did not know the extent of the murderous fury meted out on the rebel forces below, and in his fascination with the hypnotic beauty of the moment, he systematically called out adjustments that spread this rain of death further and deeper without a second thought or trace of remorse.

His response focused on duty, on performing his assigned task with precision. He did not concern himself with larger questions rooted in the reasons for rebellion. In his mind, the Kurian backlash against Nordan rule deserved a crushing, humiliating defeat, and he felt honored to take part in that process.

More than a mile to the west of where the shells were pounding, the military police from the garrison at Mageshima encountered a roadblock and were pinned down by sniper fire. The crew abandoned their vehicle and took shelter in a storefront before regrouping, climbing inside stairs to the roof and fighting their way forward.

***

Heavy shelling continued through the afternoon. Rising heat and humidity induced sweat and discomfort, magnifying the danger of explosions in the distance. Garrick, concerned that he and Brenna might get caught in a deadly crossfire, evaluated their surroundings for an exit with a quiet intensity that his wife knew well.

Brenna worried about him, but said nothing.

After the awkward and somewhat humorous experience of eating sticky white rice – which neither Garrick nor Brenna had ever seen, as rice grown in Kameron was brown – vegetables and fish with finger sticks instead of cutlery, Ichika led Garrick to the telephone. She spoke to the operator in an effort to reach the Tamarian embassy, but couldn't get through.

"I'm sorry, honored sir," she told him. "We will have to wait and try again later."

Yua listened as the handsome, husky foreign man spoke to his woman in a strange, vowel-dominated tongue. Judging from the way they lingered on the veranda as he pointed to various landscape features in the area, the Nordan woman surmised that the couple were in league with the natives and had to be planning some evil deed.

Why hadn't the military police arrived?

Sakura, suspecting from the way that her mother kept spying on the foreigners, believed the older woman had not obeyed grandfather. As Emiko showed their guests the wishing garden, Sakura noted a wistfulness in their eyes as they talked, the longing glances they directed to one another, and again dreamed that she could be honored in her husband's mind in the same way the foreign man lavished attention on his woman.

By late afternoon smoke from the burning city began drifting toward the sea. Tadeo, Sakura's husband, returned from fishing with a familiar weariness in his demeanor. He smelled of salt and sweat, having worked very hard for a meager catch with his crew. He bowed curtly to the foreigners before heading to the hot pool for a well-deserved bath.

Hiromi, son of Haruto and Kaori – also the husband of Yua – listened impatiently to his wife as she explained her theory of the foreign woman as the personification of the Fox. "She has powers," Yua whispered gravely. "She's in league with demons. I am waiting for the military police to arrive and arrest them."

"Does my father know of this?" Hiromi asked, understanding that Haruto always honored the ancestors by extending hospitality to strangers.

"He does not," Yua replied. "I told him about the woman, but he refused to report them."

"What kind of duplicity is this? It's not your place to defy my father's authority. You bring dishonor to this house when you disobey my father's wishes."

Yua shook her head vigorously. "I have saved us from shame. If the colonial authorities learn that we have sheltered the enemy, we will be sent home in disgrace and everything we've worked to establish here will be lost."

"Then why did you bring them to my father's house in the first place? You should have left them on the beach where you found them."

"Don't you see how this works in our favor?" she asked with a gleam in her eye. "We'll earn praise from the authorities, who will likely increase our fishing quota. That will help you get a bigger, more modern boat and you won't have to struggle with a marginal catch."

Hiromi sighed. Did she have a point?

***

Late that night, Haruto awakened to the sound of urgent pounding on the front door. He roused his wife. "They're here. Go now!" he ordered. "Save our guests!"

While Haruto put on his robe and went to the front door, acting senile and stalling for time to the best of his ability, Kaori retrieved her guest's shoes, and awakened Ichika. "Get the foreign man's gun. Be quick!"

As she padded down the hall Kaori met Sakura, who'd had her sleep disturbed by the noise. "What's happening?" the younger woman asked.

"Your mother lied!" Kaori responded. "She called the military police and reported our guests. Go and wake up the foreigners. Show them the trap door and tell them to take the old rowboat out to sea."

Sakura, who spoke only a smattering of vulgate, bowed to her grandmother. When she entered the room where the foreign couple were staying, they were both already awake. An unfamiliar scent of alluring femininity lingered in the air.

"You come!" she urged. "You take things. You go. I show where. Take rowboat. Flee! Danger!"

As they dressed, Ichika showed up with the rifle Garrick had taken at the cove. "The police are here for you!" she warned, wrinkling her nose. What an unusual and sensuous aroma! Had Sakura interrupted this couple's intimacy? Scurrying to open a window, she permitted a stiff breeze from the sea to clear the air.

Garrick pulled up his pants, slid into the sweaty shirt he'd worn the previous day and took the weapon from Ichika's hand. "Pull out your gun," he suggested to Brenna in Lithian. "If I load this thing it'll make noise."

To save time, Brenna wore only her Lithian camisole and a skirt. She pulled the handgun from her *bug-out* bag and followed Sakura toward the side of the house. They scurried as angry voices rose at the front door.

Sakura brought them to a pantry where glass jars filled with preserved fruit gleamed on shelves. She moved a rug aside and opened a trap door. "Go!" she urged.

"Can you see down there?" Garrick asked in Lithian.

Brenna shook her head. "We'll need your flashlight. UV doesn't penetrate the ground."

As Sakura closed the trap door overhead, Garrick, concerned about being cornered, loaded the rifle. Pure darkness enveloped the lovers as he fumbled through his *bug-out* bag for the flashlight.

Shouting and booted footfalls trembled through the house, inspiring urgency. Garrick found the light. Its beam illuminated a long, steep corridor with no apparent end. He slung his bag over his shoulder and led the way downhill, with the scent of the sea rising with every step.

Above them, the military police followed Yua into one of the rooms. An open window overlooked the garden. "They were in here," the woman asserted.

While the rest of the family stood in silence, two military policemen shone their flashlights around the room. Not far from the futon, they found a small pair of women's panties.

"See!" Yua stated in triumph. "I told you they were in here!"

Emiko approached the policeman, whose knitted brow expressed skepticism because the garment seemed unusually small for a full-grown woman. "Those are mine," Emiko claimed, lying with a boldness that surprised everyone in the family, who all knew better.

"You wicked child!" Yua spat. "Those are not yours!"

Emiko held her hand out. "I came in here after my bath to see the garden before going to bed. I must have dropped my panties. May I have them, please?"

Bewildered, the military policeman handed the garment over before shining his flashlight out the window, where the strong breeze from an approaching storm flooded the room and masked the amorous aroma. Why would the girl leave a window open like that? "Let's check the garden," he said to his partner. "Someone in this house is a liar and I intend to find out who that is."

But the garden yielded no clues. When a thorough search of the house uncovered no additional evidence and no one in the family would speak, the police captain pointed at Yua. "Arrest that woman," he ordered.

"I've only done my duty!" she insisted. "Check the trapdoor in the pantry. They must have fled that way!"

Hiromi, bound by honor to his father, held his tongue and did not defend his wife. When she pleaded for affirmation, neither he nor Tadeo spoke in her defense. Cold silence testified to their disapproval.

The police captain, noting this, grunted. "Check the pantry for a trapdoor," he ordered. "If there's any exit there, follow it and report back to me."

But by the time the team found the entrance and searched the passage that led down to an open gate by the dock, Garrick had already rowed the old boat beyond visual range in the darkness. Brenna, sitting in the prow, calmed her racing heart with prayer as her weary husband worked the oars. She felt grateful for deliverance, knowing that she and Garrick had been betrayed, and yet saved, by the Nordan colonial family's duplicity.

A humid onshore breeze stirred waves that slapped against the rowboat's prow, a kind of punctuation to the steady, rhythmic squeak and swish of oars in the water. The muggy summer night quickly coaxed sweat from Garrick's flesh. Shirtless now, his strong body gleamed in the UV light as he alternately crouched forward, then leaned back, straining against the sea. The steady exhale whenever he pulled on the oars and pushed against the footplate, along with the flexing of powerful muscle in his upper back, arms and shoulders stirred sensual memories that ignited Brenna's desire.

Trembling, the Lithian woman looked away to regain control over her waxing libido. High above, storm clouds alternately veiled and then revealed the thin crescent of *The Handmaiden*, the smaller of Devera's two moons. With *Princessa* – the larger moon – still new, conditions favored Brenna's tetrachromatic vision. A few hundred yards away, she could see a long, low bluff that concealed the glow of Helsing, burning in the distance.

Nordan naval artillery had stopped before nightfall, but the evidence of its destructive power glowed in the night sky. A rare, anxiety-inspired inflection raised Brenna's voice as she spoke. "It doesn't look safe in Helsing right now."

Garrick paused to look down his right shoulder. Achingly tired and breathless, the brief rest wrought relief from endless exertion. Flexing his stiff hands, the soldier evaluated the burning city for several moments. "No," he agreed. "But the alternative is sneaking across the *Rio Attavela* into Kameron without papers."

Brenna thought about that prospect for only a moment before rejecting the idea. "I don't think that's wise. With the violence we've seen, I'll bet the Kamerese will lock down the border."

Nodding in affirmation of her wisdom, Garrick turned to face his bride. "They'll probably deploy troops to secure the south side of the riverbank," he added. "They'll take one look at me and shoot first."

"Then we'll have to go inland," Brenna replied.

Again, he agreed. "Maybe we can follow the river and find a remote spot to ford. As much as I don't like smuggling myself into a foreign country, I'd rather travel in Kameron than the coastal colony right now."

An idea dawned in Brenna's mind. "What if we let the current take us south, then row to shore on the other side of the river. That way, we can avoid attention at the border entirely."

Not knowing how fast the ocean current flowed, and not confident of their exact location, Garrick hedged. He felt so sore, the prospect of rowing for much longer discouraged his soul. "Let me think about it," he stated.

They drifted in silence for a few minutes, the boat's stern rising and falling in rhythm with the waves. While resting his weary arms and stretching his back, Brenna blinked away a tear. Her sadness, brought to the surface by evidence of fatigue in her husband's posture and body language, lay rooted in guilt for insisting they come to the music festival. While he'd brushed off her earlier admission of fault for this, Brenna understood the price he paid for tirelessly striving to keep them alive. He didn't complain, but that only made it worse for her.

The sounds of an approaching engine and a hull cutting through waves interrupted the woman's reverie. Unaccustomed to hearing that type of noise, and having little experience on the sea, a fearful quiver trembled through her shoulders. She glanced to the south with a gasp and warned, "There's a boat coming our way!"

While he could not see anything in the darkness, save for the orange glow of the burning city to the east, Garrick also heard the approaching noise. He set to the oars with renewed vigor, his youth and power focused on escape. But the engine sounds soon overwhelmed the melody of Brenna's lovely voice uttering desperate prayers.

Moments later, a speeding patrol boat flashed into his view. Evaluating its bearing, Garrick pulled hard on his right oar before resuming a frantic stroke with both arms in a desperate effort to avoid being hit and sunk by the bigger vessel.

Brenna screeched in terror as the patrol vessel sped by, its wake rocking the little rowboat hard, nearly spilling its passengers into the sea. Garrick, his heart beating fast and adrenaline overcoming fatigue, rowed furiously.

But the patrol ship slowed and made a wide turn. A very bright searchlight blinded Brenna as it passed over her eyes. Its operator swept the light back and locked its beam onto the dory. Letting go of the oars, Garrick held his hands aloft – feeling powerless and vulnerable.

An authoritative male voice, speaking curiously pronounced Kurian over a loudspeaker, ordered them to keep their hands up, remain still, and prepare for inspection. Shared fear rose between the young couple as the patrol craft turned, revealing a ramp on its stern.

Armed men, pointing their rifles menacingly, lined the aft deck. The eighty-foot vessel featured a 1.5 inch cannon, a pair of .75 caliber machine guns, a one inch rear deck turret and a pair of .50 caliber machine guns mounted in armored towers on the rear of its bulkhead. Resisting all that firepower would have been foolish, and with flight impossible, Garrick and Brenna complied.

A sailor tossed a line to the dory, which Brenna caught and hooked to the bow eye. An electric winch pulled the rowboat up the ramp. When the motor stopped, the lovers hopped out, leaving their *bug-out* bags behind. They climbed along a line of naval mines, realizing from the appearance of the vessel's crew that this was a Kamerese warship operating in Nordan waters . . . .

A sailor approached and searched Garrick for weapons before reluctantly moving to Brenna. Seeing that he didn't want to subject her to humiliation, Brenna raised her left hand to stop him. She bent slowly, lifted her skirt to reveal the concealed boot knife, then carefully removed it and handed the weapon to him, hilt first.

Nodding, the sailor thanked her in Kamerese and then stood aside as an officer approached. "What are you doing in the sea at this hour?" the officer asked in Kurian.

Garrick pointed at his chest. "Tamarian," he said. "I speak not," he continued in broken Kamerese, trying to explain that he couldn't respond in the local tongue.

"Do you understand me now?" the officer replied, switching into accented Tamarian with the ease of a multilingual child.

"Yes sir," Garrick said respectfully.

The officer raised his brow, noting a soldier's demeanor. His eyes moved and lingered on the man's companion, a little woman whose figure hung heavily on a slender, muscular frame. While windblown, he found her quite comely – save for a nasty scar marring the right side of her neck that told a sad tale of life-threatening violence. Her fearless glower and blue eyes that gleamed like cold fire were both belied by the body language of reticence.

When the officer turned his head for a better look at the injury, the young woman averted her gaze and turned away. Honoring her privacy, the officer addressed her companion. "Why are you two out at sea in the dark?"

"Sir," Garrick began. "We're trying to reach the Tamarian embassy in Helsing."

The officer narrowed his eyes in suspicion. "Don't lie to me, Mister Shirtless Tamarian who talks like a soldier out of uniform in the company of an itty-bitty Lithian girl with a wicked-sharp knife in her boot. I will ask you again, and I expect the truth. What were you doing at sea in the dark? Are you a spy? Are you smuggling?"

"No sir," Garrick stated, his fear of drowning displaced by a growing concern about being shot as a criminal. After introducing himself as a first lieutenant in the Tamarian Expeditionary Force, hoping the officer would view him as a friendly ally, he added, "We were on holiday at the Seashell Resort – north of Briminger – when it came under attack. We fled south, hoping to reach the embassy before the violence escalated, preventing us from entering the city."

"Then why are you in a boat in the dark?" the officer demanded for a third time, somewhat impatiently.

"We'd come upon a colonial fishing village just north of here when we heard sustained gunfire," Garrick responded, his lie so smooth it sounded like truth. "It sounded like a firefight and was getting closer, so we uh, *borrowed* the rowboat to avoid trouble."

While that story sounded plausible, the officer silently questioned the wisdom of vacationing at a resort in a volatile area like the Nordan Coastal Colony. "Show me your papers," he demanded.

"I'm afraid we left the Seashell Resort in a hurry," Garrick admitted, telling a partial truth with conviction equal to the earlier lie. "We have no identification in our possession. That's why we need to get to the embassy. They're expecting us."

Confident that the man's hillbilly accent was authentic, the officer turned to a subordinate. "Keep them under guard here," he ordered. "I'll get on the horn with Commander Saenz and see what he wants us to do."

One of the Kamerese sailors motioned for Garrick and Brenna to sit next to the bulkhead on the rear deck, close to the naval mines, one row of which were missing. His companion – who'd taken Brenna's knife – returned it wordlessly. These two men stood guard after the others departed to continue their duties.

Hope displaced fear in Garrick's heart. He took hold of Brenna's hand and pondered their situation as the patrol boat rolled in the waves. Gazing at the glow of Helsing in the distance, he spoke to his wife in Lithian, as quietly as the gusty wind and idling engines allowed. "We can't be in Kamerese waters," he told her.

Brenna nodded. Covering her right hand with her left while discreetly pointing at the missing mines she said, "Laying those in Nordan territory is an act of war."

"We don't actually know if that's their mission," Garrick replied, thinking the mines might be part of the boat's normal weapons compliment. However, Brenna's expressed concern sounded compelling, especially in light of the fact that Kamerese mercenaries had been involved in the bungled assassination attempt two nights earlier. "If it is, we need to get home in a hurry."

"Do you think they'll let us go?" she asked.

"If we'd been on the other side of the Attavela, they'd have reason to detain us. But Helsing is due east of our current location. This boat doesn't belong here, and everyone aboard knows it. If they take us back to base, they can't charge us with crossing a border illegally when we're in their custody."

Brenna thought about that for a moment. "If they *do* take us to Kameron, you could make a formal appeal to the embassy in the capital," she said. "That would be tough to explain without admitting that we'd been captured in Nordan territory."

Garrick shrugged, acknowledging the truth of her conclusion. "It would be our word against theirs. We can't prove where we are, but they know, and I'll bet that officer is wishing he'd rammed us right about now."

However accurate that statement may have been, Brenna felt dismayed by the suggestion. "You think they'll kill us?" she asked, wide-eyed and revealing amplified worry. "Would they shoot us, or force us back in the water and run us over?"

Squeezing Brenna's hand reassuringly, Garrick shook his head. "They're soldiers, not pirates, and they don't see us as a threat. They didn't search our boat, and that sailor returned your boot knife. I suspect they'll put us back in the sea tell us to be on our way."

While Garrick trusted the sailors' soldierly conduct, and the behavior of the men who kept them under guard affirmed his faith in their professionalism, after her experience with Kamerese rebels at *La Casa del Matados*, Brenna felt apprehensive. She kept her counsel to herself, leaning on her tired husband's shoulder and quietly praying for strength and safety. Moments later she felt his body relax as fatigue swept over his consciousness and he fell asleep, as she'd often seen him do between battles.

***

Artillery cracked in the distance, an ominous, familiar sound that slapped Garrick into alertness. Shouted commands in Kamerese stirred running feet into action. A geyser of seawater shot into the sky several yards to the north. A shock wave rippled through the waves. The bright lamps, which had bathed the loading ramp in white light, immediately switched off, and the powerful ethanol-fueled engines roared to life.

The patrol boat tore a curving path through the ocean as a flare arced overhead. Cannon fire screamed through the humid night. Racing on southeastern bearing, the Kamerese craft did not return fire, even after every sailor aboard manned their battle stations.

Several tense moments later, as the retreating vessel churned its way through the darkness, one of the sentries returned to the ramp. He pointed at the rowboat, urging the young couple to do his bidding in language that neither understood. He beckoned them into the boat as the patrol craft straightened into a dead run for Kameron.

Garrick and Brenna climbed into their borrowed boat. The sailor reversed the winch motor that held the dory in place and slowly unwound the wooden craft into the patrol vessel's turbulent wake, and then released the hook attached to the bow eye with an electric switch, abandoning the young couple to their fate in the waves.

Skidding hard over the top of the sea, the little rowboat bounced along the billows, rudderless and moving far faster than its Nordan builders ever intended. It had been constructed with care and designed for greater strength than was necessary for its intended use, which was why the dory survived the ordeal without breaking up. Brenna huddled with Garrick in the center of the craft as he clung to the gunwale with renewed strength.

Slamming into a wave that burst into a soaking spray over the bow, the rowboat's momentum slowed enough to nearly force Brenna and her weary lover over the stern. With the sea sloshing at her feet and gratitude for safety rising in her soul, Brenna used a small, onboard bucket to bail out the seawater before she paused to pray.

The rowboat settled into the swells, rising and falling with the rhythm of crests and troughs. Warm wind felt chilling on Garrick's wet flesh, yet he waited respectfully until Brenna finished her invocation before resetting the oars into their locks to resume rowing.

She noted his shivering with concern. Brenna unzipped her *bug-out* bag and removed a dry towel. Careful to avoid unbalancing the boat, she – with near mystical equilibrium – tiptoed toward him and carefully draped the towel over her husband's bare flesh, wiping away the sheen of moisture on his skin as another flare ascended into the windy heavens, revealing the ominous shadow of a Nordan warship.

They could both hear the sound of the big vessel slicing tirelessly through the sea a few hundred yards to the northwest. Its powerful searchlights swept over the surface, just missing the dory as it dipped into a trough between wave crests. Tension rose as Garrick labored at the oars, his heart racing at the prospect of being seen and blown out of the water.

Moments later, a loud explosion burst beneath waves at the bow of the Nordan ship, sending a column of spray higher than its superstructure. An alarm rang out as the frigate leaned away from the blast and turned, its emergency maneuver an effort to hurriedly change course.

"Mines," Garrick told Brenna. "That Kamerese patrol boat *was* laying mines . . . ."

But why?

Brenna watched the Nordan warship limp away, hoping in her innocent manner that no one had been injured in the blast. She whispered a prayer for the crew as the mechanical noise of the frigate gradually faded.

Watching her husband working the oars, Brenna tiptoed toward him again. "Why don't you let me row for a while," she suggested.

"I'm not complaining," he told her.

"I know," she replied with a sweetness in her tone that she reserved for him. "You've been doing this for hours. It's far past my turn."

Pausing to judge their position, Garrick could hear surf to the east. He'd not given her a turn at the oars because her vision under these conditions far surpassed his own, and he needed her to navigate, rather than row. Yet Brenna's fitness had been refined by years of intense physical training, and she was certainly no delicate feminine flower. Strong and well-defined muscle in her shoulders and upper back hinted at strength that belied her petite size. Further, Brenna's Lithian physiology endowed her with great stamina. Concerned about her in an unnecessarily protective manner, Garrick suggested, "Why don't we go ashore now and get some rest? We're far enough away from the village that we should be safe."

"Okay," she agreed. "But only if you'll let me row."

After gingerly switching places, Garrick rested his aching body and stared into the blackness, barely able to make out the white foam spreading on the shore. He hoped they wouldn't hit anything.

Brenna found working the oars awkward. Her legs weren't long enough to reach the footboard, forcing her to wedge her feet between the dory's tiller seat and the gunwale. With her legs spread like this, she had to work her thighs to keep her feet in place while pushing the oars back, and couldn't muster anywhere near the power of her husband's rowing stroke. However, she soon developed a rhythm that created slower, yet steady progress. With the tide coming in, the little boat gently rode the current toward shore.

Unable to see his own hand waving in front of his face, thanks to the heavy cloud cover obscuring *The Handmaiden* as she waxed in the night sky, Garrick suddenly felt his body pitching forward as the dory struck something heavy and unyielding. His momentum carried him into the sea, where he managed to gasp for breath before slamming into the cold water. Kicking hard for the surface with the confidence of an experienced swimmer, his right leg scraped against a steel invasion obstacle.

Brenna fell backward, landing in the rowboat's wet sump and smacking her head against its burden boards. The boat's momentum, amplified by the waves, dragged it along the obstacle's sharp edge, tearing a large gash in the dory's starboard side. Water poured in, drenching Brenna's face and threatening to drown her.

Reaching instinctively for something to grab so she could pull herself upright, Brenna felt frantic when her fingers could find no purchase. Bending her legs around the rowing thwart, the Lithian woman's core strength saved her life. Grunting upright in a singular, gracile motion, Brenna pulled herself above the surface as the dory settled beneath the water.

"Garrick!" she cried, gasping in panic and confusion. "Where are you?"

"I can't see a thing!" he shouted, turning toward the sound of her voice. "It's too dark. Are you okay?"

"Yes," she said in reply, grateful to hear the close proximity of his voice. While cloudy conditions dimmed the ambient UV light, his head and shoulders appeared above the waves nearby. "Are you hurt?"

"I'm fine," he told her.

"Can you come to me?"

"I can't see you!" he complained.

Brenna collected their floating *bug-out* bags, holding them in her left hand while pushing out of the dory with her feet. She uttered a brief prayer as her fingers touched the stricken rowboat and familiar power shuddered through her body. "Light!" she commanded.

And the submerged craft immediately began to glow. "I'm here," she announced.

***

Elvin Holmgren, waiting for the return of his younger companion, stared into the blackness, looking for Nordan Imperial Navy signals. He'd seen distant lights across the water, fire belching from a warship's gun, and not long later, a bright flash in the sea.

"I hope the lot of you drown!" he muttered.

He'd sent Ove, the preteen messenger boy, back to the militia command post to relay the news. While weary rebel Kurians rested after a hard day's labor digging trenches, preparing to defend their land against Imperial Marines they knew would be coming, Elvin believed his observations shouldn't wait until morning.

A militia commander, translating the whisperings of his trusted Kamerese advisor, claimed that the Nordans would need time to organize and send forces from their distant home islands. "This beach is the best location for an amphibious assault on Helsing," he told the militia members. "We either kill them in the sea, or freedom will die here on the sand."

Ominous words, but no one disputed Nordan military power. No one questioned their cruelty. No one dismissed their determination, either. The Nordans would come to take their colony back by force, and Kurian patriots had to stop them.

Ove returned, breathlessly reporting that he told the night watch what they'd seen. "They promised to pass the word along."

"So you didn't talk to the commander?"

The boy shook his head. "They told me he was sleeping. They weren't going to let me wake him up."

Elvin sighed. "I hope they don't regret that later."

Suddenly, something shiny caught Ove's eye. "What's that?" he asked, pointing into the sea.

When the old man turned, he saw light underwater near one of the defensive hedgehogs, along with at least two figures nearby. Was that an Imperial Navy demolitions team? "Send word down the line," Elvin warned. "The enemy is here."

***

Gunfire erupted on the beach. Bullet impacts peppered the water dangerously near the boat, and Brenna's impulse to flee left the light active on the dory when it would have been wiser to shut the magic down.

Knowing that she wasn't fast in the water, Garrick wrapped his right arm around his wife's slender waist and pulled her away from the stricken boat with a speed that belied his exhaustion. "Tell me where to go," he urged.

Brenna craned her neck to see over the wave tops, directing her husband to swim at an angle to the shore. Her skirt felt heavy and dragged in the water. His strong arm around her waist made breathing more difficult, while waves splashing over his right shoulder rolled across her face, leaving the hapless woman gasping for breath.

Pushing his strong body to the limits of exertion, Garrick held his bride close while using a recovery crawl stroke to swim away from danger. Moments after doubting that he could continue much longer, Garrick felt his waterlogged shoe reach the sand below. One stroke later he stood, pulling Brenna to her feet. Their pounding hearts beat in synchronous rhythm as the lovers held each other for a fleeting moment. Longing and relief aside, danger remained an ever-present companion as the gunfire died down.

"They'll search the beach," Garrick warned, taking his bag from her and slinging it over his shoulder. "We have to keep moving. We should stay at the tide's edge to cover our tracks until we find a safe place to head inland."

Brenna led the way, wearily sloshing through the gentle waves. As tired as she felt, the Lithian woman understood that her husband had to be feeling worse, since he'd done the bulk of the rowing after spending most of the previous evening pulling her through the sea. How long could he sustain this level of exertion before succumbing to physical exhaustion? Brenna kept her concern unspoken, expressing affection by squeezing Garrick's hand and whispering wide-eyed prayers of gratitude for his stamina, which blended into petitions for divine protection.

Onshore, she could see the glint of concertina wire, rows of angular, sharpened stakes and the slight discoloring of sand disturbed by hastily laid land mines. The waxing onshore wind and the sounds of surf slapping against wet sand masked the excited shouting of local men that rose as the gunfire died down.

Quickening her pace as flashlights activated and squads of men advanced into the sea behind them, Brenna led her husband northward. Nearly thirty minutes later, with the clingy, sandy fabric of her skirt chafing miserably against her thighs, the Lithian woman noted a series of small offshore islands ahead. Inland, the abrupt edge of the long bluff she'd seen earlier tumbled to the sea in a massive series of broken basalt boulders.

Brenna paused, watching and listening.

"What do you see?" Garrick asked.

"A place where we can find shelter for the night," she told him.

"I don't like being so close to a beach where angry Kurians are crawling around," he warned. "I'd prefer that we head further inland."

When she turned to him, her eyes gleamed in the darkness. Garrick remembered the first night he'd met her, and how he'd found the soft, blue glow disconcerting. Now, the sight wrought comfort, as he knew it meant she could see in what he considered complete darkness. "You need rest," she soothed in a gentle tone that conveyed her unspoken concern. "Let's find a place to sleep for a few hours. We can head inland at daybreak, when we both can see."

With fatigue and three consecutive nights of insufficient sleep weighing heavily on his eyelids, he wearily agreed. Curling up with her sounded better than a forced march, anyway. "Okay. Let's find a spot that can't be seen from the beach."

Once they'd climbed through the rocks above the beach, Brenna – having lost her towel in the accident – used Garrick's to dry her body before changing into clean clothes, willing water from her camisole, shaking out the sea salt, then wringing the moisture from her skirt.

After Garrick changed, he fumbled for his flashlight. With the beam on low, he led his wife on a hard climb up the bluff. Near its summit they found a sheltered spot beside a tiny waterfall where soft grasses had taken root. Moments later, Garrick fell into a soldier's sleep.

***

"What in the name of the Sea Devil are you doing?" Sergeant Blomquist demanded.

Old enough to be the non-com's father, Elvin spoke in a tone that sounded reproving, rather than respectful. "We saw light from the ghost boat. I'm sure an enemy commando team was clearing a path to the beach," Elvin explained. "I saw them in the water."

Appraising the ordinary little craft the men had dragged ashore, Blomquist shook his head. "Are you out of your mind? Have you been drinking?"

Elvin stood his ground. "The whole thing was lit up, plain as day," he testified. "Ask the lads. They saw it, too."

Affirming nods and grunts from the surrounding men confirmed Elvin's tale, but the sergeant remained skeptical. "There's neither magic nor threat here. This boat is older than you are. The Imperial Navy doesn't use hand-me-down dories in military operations. They'd have sent their people in on a power boat or a submarine."

"Then we'd have heard them coming," Elvin retorted. "They used this boat 'cause it's quiet."

"And yet, you claim that you could see it in the water, plain as day," the sergeant mocked. "Your enemy isn't stupid, but I'm not so sure about you!"

Holding his tongue, the old fisherman let the insult go. Maybe the sergeant didn't know as much as he led on. Elvin had seen some kind of ship with a good sized gun hit a mine offshore. A submarine would have to navigate through the same defenses to get in close, and it would have suffered a worse fate than the ship. He couldn't explain the glowing boat, but on closer inspection, the old fisherman saw Nordan features in the dory's construction. It had never been owned by a patriot.

"You've wasted time and ammunition," the sergeant complained. "Now, get back to your posts!"

As the men turned away Elvin noted a light-colored object floating in the shallows nearby. Curious, he waded in to pick up what turned out to be a towel. Near its bottom edge he found embroidery in the common, southern script that read, "Velez."

Where had he heard that name before?

***

Well after daylight began warming the rocks the next morning, a herring gull fluttered the grass. Hearing the sound of its wings, Brenna opened her eyes. "We're still alive," she told the bird in Lithian. "And I have no food to give you."

The bird squawked repeatedly in response.

Garrick stirred, then rested his head on Brenna's thigh and resumed his slumber. The interplay of light and shadow outlined his muscular shoulders, upper arms, neck and chest, reviving Brenna's desire. She longed to offer comfort, to arouse his ardor and feel his hands caressing her body, coaxing delight with fingertips, tongue and lips. She wanted to love him, and be loved by him, yet sensitive to his need for sleep and concerned that he'd collapse from exhaustion without time for recovery, she didn't have the heart to awaken him.

"Go away!" she ordered in a whisper.

Twisting its head to the side, the gull made eye contact with the Lithian woman before leaping into the air and flying off.

Making use of her time while Garrick slept, Brenna opened her heart in whispered prayers. She exposed the urges motivating her behavior – the never-expressed craving for applause she secretly struggled against; the pride of defeating lesser musicians in competition, and the pleasure she felt when others respected her skills. These self-centered impulses formed the foundation for a haunted mansion of rationalizations she'd constructed, motives that had closed her mind to Garrick's reasoning whenever they'd discussed attending the music festival.

She knew he'd forgiven her. He'd promised that he wasn't keeping score, and she believed him. Never once had he complained. Never once had he been short with her, despite exerting most of the physical effort expended in their flight from danger. Brenna felt grateful for his grace and blessed him in quiet intercession, thanking Allfather for the strength and stamina in her young lover's body. She expressed gratitude for his respect, his partnership, and his unwavering devotion.

Thinking of this made her realize that Garrick, though he professed no *belief*, had remained more true to his values than she could claim in recent weeks. His commitment to her success had proven faithful. She should never have questioned his motives, never harbored the wicked idea that getting out of their daily routine would ease his hypervigilance. In hindsight, his accurate evaluation of the threat environment, along with his foresight and planning, had helped save them.

Thus, Brenna arrived at a spiritual crossroads. Identifying the personal flaws that put them in danger led her to confess and repent of them. She vowed to love Garrick with less concern for herself, to honor his wisdom, experience and intelligence. He deserved as much.

Moving next to her family, Brenna blessed each one by name, starting with the youngest – her brother, Eren, who likely knew how to walk by now – then Camille, her teenaged, female sibling. As she prayed for her next-eldest sister, Cynthia, she heard Thea's voice in her head, as if the young woman been present and speaking to her. "Be wary of the one you remember."

What did that mean?

As her intercession proceeded, the long list of her loved ones slowly drew to an end. With her husband stirring, Brenna concluded her prayers and kissed him.

Hearing the boom of big guns offshore awakened the Tamarian soldier. While he loved the sensation of her lips on his, the need to flee compelled him to dress in haste.

Brenna pulled back, eyeing him with fervent longing as he pulled a shirt over his strong shoulders. Filled with frustration, she chided herself for bringing him here. They should have stayed home, where they could spend hours engaged in rapturous, undisturbed intimacy.

Distressed and distracted by the naval artillery, Garrick had already begun evaluating the threat. Resuming the shore bombardment suggested that Helsing remained a hot zone, with active engagements. Venturing into the city to look for the Tamarian embassy put them at significant risk, but they had little choice. Without documents, entering Kameron and booking a train passage to Marvic would be impossible.

"It's dangerous to head into the city, but we need to find a phone," he told Brenna as he rummaged through his *bug-out* bag for something to eat.

Dwindling food resources added urgency to their plight. A small caliber soldier's rifle made for a poor game harvesting firearm, and Brenna – a skilled hunter who could have provided for them – had lost her bow to the Nordans. They needed a way to legally and safely cross into Kameron before their supplies ran out. Given the exertion they'd already expended, going hungry would limit their progress and increase their vulnerability.

They ate a cold breakfast and filled their canteens in a shallow pool beneath the nearby waterfall. Garrick led his wife to the windswept summit of the bluff, where he could see broad fields leading from a low ridge extending southwest that concealed the mouth of the Attavela, to residential clusters fringing the outskirts of Helsing in the east. Over the ridge line to the south, linked by a massive bridge, lay Kameron, a country friendly to Tamarians. Studying the scene through his binoculars, Garrick determined that Nordan naval artillery was focused on targets near the northern edge of the city.

Offering Brenna the binoculars so she could comment on his thinking, Garrick pointed to the southern edge of town, where far fewer fires belched black smoke into the sky. "If we can find a working phone in that area," he explained, "I can call the embassy to arrange clearance for us to enter Kameron. At that point, we'll take a train to Desperado Falls, and then home."

"If we do that, we should stop in on Cassie and Jared," Brenna replied, the longing still welling in her eyes. Suppressing her yearning again, the Lithian woman looked away. "His family will be offended if they hear we came through without seeing them."

"In your current state?" he clarified, noting her arousal. "Shouldn't we get home as soon as we can?"

"They'll understand," she told him, handing back the binoculars. "One look at me and they'll know."

After saying this, Thea's warning message repeated in Brenna's mind. Following her husband eastward, Brenna silently wrestled with what the message meant.

***

The high ground overlooking the sea descended into forested land, where gnarled arbutus yielded to taller fir and cedar trees that offered relief from the Daystar's hot fury. While cooler air lingered beneath the tree canopy, as the couple trudged through ferns, hogweed and devil's club, humidity and exertion drew sweat from Garrick's flesh, staining the back of his now clingy shirt.

Their conversation thinned into quiet contemplation as the lovers hiked through dense undergrowth harboring spiny plants and swarms of biting insects. Garrick meditated on how to prove his citizenship to a border guard, yet he couldn't come up with plan likely to work. The language barrier complicated the task of explaining their situation to a soldier with an itchy trigger finger.

Not long later, they encountered a path. After pausing in silence to listen for movement, Garrick followed the trail to the southeast rather than tramping through the forest. Walking on a hard surface quickened their pace and provided relief from the unrelenting sting of flora and pestilent, buzzing, blood-sucking vermin.

The trail bent around a hill and intersected with a larger road. At that point, stone stairs led to a sanctum built among old trees, a place of significance to local colonists for reasons the travelers couldn't discern.

Its Nordan architecture evoked a similar harmony with the surrounding landscape and meticulous state of repair that Garrick had found striking in the village they'd visited the previous day. Yet the persistent squawking and squabbling of gulls at the summit warned of danger.

Concerned about ceding higher ground to bandits, Garrick readied and brought his rifle around before quietly ascending the stairs. As Brenna followed close behind, a familiar, charnel odor assaulted her senses, dragging unpleasant memories buried in her subconscious to the surface. In response, the Lithian woman nearly gagged.

Scavenging birds scattered noisily as Garrick paused before reaching the top of the stairs. Through the ensuing flurry of beating wings he pointed his rifle into a sickening scene of slaughter. Someone had brought nearly two dozen Nordan colonists, along with their children, to desecrate the shrine. They'd been stripped, bound and beaten to death in this sacred place of prayer. The bodies lay in contorted silence amidst dried puddles of their own blood. Swarming flies and evidence of avian feasting increased the indignity of the scene.

While Garrick did not ascribe to faith of any kind, he held his wife in high esteem and respected the belief system that gave meaning and power to her life. He'd attributed their miraculous deliverance at sea to natural factors – the uncommon, but not entirely unusual, respect for life among other intelligent creatures – yet he knew that Brenna *believed* Allfather had saved them. Viewing the world through a lens of faith, as she did, made witnessing this carnage in a holy place very disturbing.

The slaughter of these children reminded him of an incident during his last combat tour, when his platoon fell under an ambush by fighters hidden in a grove of trees. Vulnerable, exposed and losing men, Garrick ordered his mortar crew to fire white phosphorous at an enemy that he later learned consisted of young people and old men.

Waging war brought moral dilemmas like this into sharp focus. Basing his decision on tactical – rather than moral – considerations, he'd justified the deed as necessary to preserve lives in his platoon. He and his men shot and killed wounded children – badly burned by the chemical – as an act of mercy to stop their suffering.

Evaluating the brutal bludgeoning of unarmed, noncombatant colonists inspired tension between his professional soldiering ethic, which had eased his conscience concerning his own conduct, and the murderous scene which lay before him. Garrick held his breath, thinking about the kindness of the Nordan family who'd offered them food and shelter. What had these people done to deserve such terrible retribution?

Brenna retched, coughing and spitting as memories of her torment at *La Casa del Matados* inspired nausea. She felt Garrick's right hand caress her back as he handed her his canteen with the other. "I'm sorry," she squeaked, accepting the drink and swishing a gulp around her mouth before spitting it out. "I can't help it."

Feeling pity for her obvious discomfort, Garrick lifted his wife to her feet and pulled her close as fear and loathing trembled through her body. After kissing her forehead and confirming that she was okay, he quietly led her back to the path.

An hour later, passing through farmland and housing allotments that grew increasingly dense, the lovers found empty streets, boarded windows and eerie silence greeting them. Debris, the corpses of many colonial soldiers, and hastily erected defensive barriers testified to desperate fighting that had recently engulfed the area.

Power and phone lines lay on the pavement. Evidence of fire and vandalism multiplied as the lovers pressed deeper into the city. Garrick kept his left index finger parallel to his rifle's trigger guard. Progress slowed as he scanned roof lines, windows and alcoves for threats.

Brenna, with hunger rumbling in her belly and hypoglycemia shaking her limbs, held the handgun she'd taken from her *bug-out* bag. She carried a spare magazine for the weapon in her left hand, following her husband, listening and watching over her shoulder.

She paused as he stopped at a hoarding, where fresh notices had been posted. Photos of people – mostly Kurians, with a smattering of Nordan colonists – adorned the billboard. Several of these had been scratched out, including a face Garrick recognized from the shrine.

That didn't bode well.

Worse, in the upper right-hand corner, just beneath the overhang protecting the sign board from the weather, he noticed a poster with copies of the young lovers' passport photos. Garrick couldn't read the Kurian text, but their first and last names appeared in the common southern script near the bottom of the page.

"They're looking for us," Brenna concluded.

"That can't be good," Garrick added.

"Maybe we should move on," she suggested.

As he took down the notice and stuffed it into his pocket, she heard a mob of Kurians rounding a corner behind them and gently pushed him into action. Garrick led his wife behind the hoarding and crept to a nearby intersection without being noticed. Once the local boys turned a corner to the east, he began running northward.

While Brenna could easily outpace him on foot, she trusted his combat instincts and followed her man up a flight of stone stairs leading to an old section of the city. Here, narrow cobblestone streets wound through beautifully maintained insula buildings where shopkeepers had sold their wares for nearly three hundred years.

Scores of dead colonists – all of them men, lay slumped in doorways, or piled in frozen, contorted agony on the sidewalks. This fruit of rage, of imposed power over the helpless, had come quickly to Helsing. Coagulating blood suggested a recent time of death.

Knowing that they had to keep moving, Garrick shouldered into a shop, his rifle pointed and his finger on the trigger. Brenna waited at the entrance, scanning the street for threats until he emerged from the building. "No one's home," he told her, "and I can't find a phone."

Hiding her disappointment, Brenna followed him to another building, then a third, and then a fourth before a wonderful aroma led them to a bakery that happened to be open. As he charged through the front door, a balding, middle-aged man behind the counter raised his hands in protest and shouted something in Kurian that sounded vaguely like, "I'm a patriot!" to Garrick's ear.

Since Tamarian was not mutually intelligible, Garrick lowered his rifle and motioned with his hands, pantomiming the use of a telephone. The proprietor nodded, beckoning his guest to follow him around the counter. Jerking his head for Brenna to join him inside, the Tamarian soldier followed the portly man through an open doorway to the left.

The Kurian baker handed Garrick the receiver from a phone attached to a wall, wrongly expecting that he knew how to speak to the operator.

While Garrick struggled to communicate with the woman on the other end of the line, a tall blonde-haired lad – who might have been the baker's son – came downstairs. He stopped in his tracks, staring at Brenna with wide eyes and an open mouth. The young man said something that could have passed for an expletive in Tamarian, transfixed by the beauty of Brenna's body in motion as she put her gun away and approached.

Mildly annoyed by the young man's response – so oafish and yet typical – the Lithian woman rolled her eyes and stifled an acrid remark that he was unlikely to understand. Hungry and shaking, after retching her breakfast, she examined the pastries on display in a glass case, then pointed at a creamy *semla* and smiled sweetly.

The baker's assistant, flustered by her attention and eager to do something that might please her, blushed and stammered as he fumbled to reach her selection with a pair of tongs. Suppressing laughter, Brenna picked a coin from her magical *Auðr* and slid it across the counter. He nervously gave her the treat and, completely and shamelessly focused on her soft parts – as if he'd never seen the wiggle of a woman's bosom before – stammered Kurian gibberish as he clumsily dropped her change on the floor and bent to pick it up.

Brenna ignored him and devoured the delicious pastry with ravenous enthusiasm. When the baker's assistant reappeared, she pointed at another one.

Just as she bit into the second pastry, a group of laughing, insurgent fighters walked in. As the shock of seeing a dark-haired woman eating a sweet *semla* froze the men in place, she recognized the threat and acted swiftly. With the grace of a gymnast, Brenna abandoned the treat, hopped onto the counter – sliding her backside across its smooth surface – then dropped to the ground and raced toward her husband. Live fire traced her progress as small-caliber bullets punched ragged impacts through the bakery's back wall.

Garrick dropped the phone's earpiece and pushed the portly baker to safety. "Get down!" he ordered, raising his rifle and deftly flipping its safety off.

The baker's assistant screamed in terror.

With martial skill, Brenna tucked and rolled as three rounds from Garrick's gun slammed into an insurgent who'd scrambled over the counter. Confusion reigned and shouting erupted as Brenna burst through the back door with Garrick following a heartbeat later. He struggled to match her swift strides as the athletic woman raced around a corner, dashed up a steep street, and then turned again at an intersection.

"Wait!" he cried. "I can't keep up with you."

She paused with her back against a wall, her heart pounding. Brenna looked for an escape route in a section of town featuring multi-level plazas ringed by shops and derelict shrines dedicated to various deities in the Kurian pantheon. While Garrick caught his breath, she noted slain men – all Nordans – shot in the back of the head and laying in heaps around a central plaza. At its center, three Kurian collaborators swayed on a makeshift gallows.

Moments later, shouting voices arose behind them. A gunshot echoed through the narrow street, followed by the whistle of a bullet dangerously close to Garrick's head. Dropping behind a low wall that separated the plaza from a walkway, the panting Tamarian soldier brought his rifle around to honor the threat, while Brenna took cover and aimed her handgun. She prayed for deliverance, hoping they could escape without killing anyone else.

The angry insurgents stormed up a nearby street, determined to exact revenge. Their shouting rose over the pounding of booted feet on the cobblestones. A few guns rattled, wildly wasting ammunition that bounced across the plaza, spraying splintered stone fragments at tangents to their impacts. Against a Tamarian platoon, these men wouldn't stand a chance.

"We need to get out of here!" Brenna whispered in a worried voice. "There are too many of them."

"Let them get close," he advised quietly, just short of catching his breath. "They don't know where we are and I have an idea." Worried about a firefight in which he and his beloved were outgunned, Garrick reached into his *bug-out* bag for one of the grenades he'd taken from the beach. "When this thing goes off, we run!" he told her.

The men approached slowly and cautiously as they searched for their hidden quarry. As they came within range of his throw, Garrick pulled the pin and hurled the grenade over the wall. Wide-eyed and terrified, the rebels tried to flee before the grenade burst.

A bright flash, followed by a telltale hiss, released thick, choking smoke. This wasn't what Garrick had expected, but maybe that was better . . . .

As the Kurian rebels coughed and cursed, Garrick urged Brenna to flee. He arose with his rifle aimed, scurrying backwards in an orderly retreat until the enemies he'd just made recovered enough to fire their weapons, compelling him to run again.

***

Sergeant Tani Tsuneo, a longtime Imperial Army veteran, secured a street leading northeast from the plaza that the locals called *Helligdommen*. As part of an ambush, he sent sniper teams into the upper floors of two buildings that overlooked the plaza. Behind a sandbagged barricade on the street he'd set up a machine gun, with additional soldiers taking cover in alcoves to either side.

As his preparations neared completion, the sound of gunfire echoed between the buildings. Moments later he saw a dark-haired woman run across the intersection. At first, he thought she looked like a colonist, but as she paused, looking over her shoulder, Sergeant Tsuneo wrinkled his brow. Nordan women were typically more slender, and not as fit or shapely, as this one.

When he called out to her, the woman turned and made eye contact. She had strikingly beautiful blue eyes. Following her came a man who looked like a native. He pointed a rifle in the opposite direction of his flight, his posture and demeanor far too polished for a rebel. Noting that the woman had stopped, the man also paused, making eye contact with the Nordan non-com. He nodded and pointed to the west with his full hand – a signal common among military men.

But the Kurians had no army. Even the fanatical Old Guard were not real soldiers. Tsuneo remembered seeing a bulletin in the barracks describing two foreigners whom the Special Forces had been seeking. The Nordan sergeant, in a gesture of soldierly solidarity, jerked his head to the east, motioning for the foreign couple to flee. Yet as soon as they disappeared down a different street, Sergeant Tsuneo regretting letting them go. Why had he done that?

Trotting over to his radio operator, the sergeant ordered, "Get me the lieutenant."

Before he could carry out that command, an unruly group of insurgent fighters surged into the *Helligdommen*. Grenades and sniper fire pinned the rebels directly in front of the Nordan machine gunner's path, and the slaughter that followed lasted fewer than fifteen seconds.

***

Running beyond what felt like exhaustion, Garrick followed Brenna out of the city without further incident. Just as he thought his legs would betray his need to take another step, she stopped beneath a large tree at a burned-out farm. Brenna reached for him, holding his sweating body close until his racing heart finally slowed and he regained his breath. The aroma of her skin during *Y-Newen* quickened his already intense attraction to her. Receptivity shone in her eyes. One suggestive caress would trigger a response from her that he'd struggle to resist.

"Are you okay?" she asked, her concern evident in raised brows and a gentle, feminine tone.

Calmed by her demeanor and longing for the comfort she offered, Garrick stroked her hair before planting a kiss on her forehead – a fatherly gesture of affection among Lithians that she would not mistake for anything else. "I'll be better when we're safe, when we can be together without interruption."

Brenna – her flesh tingling as she struggled to sideline her craving – asked, "What about the embassy?"

"I couldn't reach them," he replied. "The operator didn't understand what I wanted, even though the word for Tamarian sounds similar in both languages."

Resting her head against his chest, Brenna tried to pray, but found herself distracted. She wanted him. While danger heightened her longing, he'd been right to kiss her forehead and she knew it. Nonetheless, frustration crept into her tone. "What should we do now?"

"Let's eat," he suggested. "We need time to think."

They'd only packed food for a few meals. In the interest of safety, Garrick didn't start a fire. Eating cold rations, while far less pleasant than hot food, renewed his strength and sated her hunger. Eating also provided a distraction that allowed Brenna to focus on gratitude for their deliverance. She prayed quietly between bites.

Unable to contact the Tamarian embassy in a city overrun with angry and ignorant insurgents, only three options remained for them. Garrick thought of heading northeast on foot, finding the main rail link with Marvic and following the tracks into Tamaria. However, the sheer distance involved in such an undertaking would require weeks of travel through hostile territory, and they didn't have provisions for such a journey.

Earlier, they'd discussed fording the Attavela somewhere upstream. While entering Kameron without identification would be risky, they had little choice. Garrick pulled the wanted poster out of his pocket. While their photostatic images looked remarkably sharp, he had no idea what the Kurian script said, and using it to prove their identities might bring more trouble. "Let's move on," he suggested, choosing the third option. "I'll try to talk our way across the bridge we saw from the bluff."

Brenna nodded wordlessly. The worry in Garrick's voice reflected declining confidence that they could make it out of the colony alive. After helping him clean their stopover spot in silence, Brenna took his hand in hers and held it to her heart – the sign of a sincere oath. "No matter what happens," she told him, "I choose you. I trust you. I love you now, and I will always love you. We're in this together, and if they don't let us over the border, Allfather with show us another way."

That endearing smile of his, an expression that had won and always warmed her heart, lingered on his lips as he bent down to kiss hers. "There's no one I'd rather be with than you," he whispered.

Young trees, thin and exceeding 40 feet in height after logging operations felled their ancestors decades earlier, grew along the southern edge of market garden farmland surrounding Helsing. Cedar stems stood in unnaturally straight rows more reminiscent of a planted field than a forest. While the shade promised relief from the relentless, humid heat, fear of the uncertain footing beneath its branches and the memory of irritating swarms of bloodthirsty bugs kept the lovers close to the road.

As they neared the bridge over the Attavela, clogged with refugees laden with their worldly possessions, Brenna heard the unmistakable sound of an engine approaching from behind them. A dust cloud rose in the wake of speeding wheels as a truck with a machine gun mounted on its rear deck raced forward.

Garrick led his wife into the trees on the western side of the road. Once they'd melded into the shadows, he readied his rifle. Armed Kurians dismounted after the vehicle came to a stop. Disorganized, brutal and hungry for violence, they swarmed through the crowd, separating men from their women and children with shouts and the threat of pointed rifles.

The Kamerese at the border stood by with their weapons drawn, but did nothing.

"We should get out of here," Garrick whispered. "I don't like the look of this."

Brenna had seen similar scenes before. Given that the slain Nordans in Helsing had all been male, she shuddered to imagine these defenseless men facing slaughter while sex trade slavery awaited the women and children. "Yes, let's go," she urged.

They fled westward, back toward the sea as the machine gun chattered behind them. Screams of horror and cries of pain faded as they picked their way between rows of cedar stems, moving as quickly as possible over the uneven ground. Struggling to keep up with his agile wife, Garrick pressed his aching body onward for what felt like a very long time as the planted forest abruptly gave way to much older, taller and thicker trees growing on a steep slope.

Brenna climbed tirelessly, her small body bounding uphill with enviable effortlessness. She stopped at a bluff overlooking the sea, waiting until Garrick reached her and regained his breath before she spoke. "I hear happy children down there," she told him in a hopeful tone. "You want to have a look?"

Garrick scanned the area with his binoculars and saw no threats. He found a well-worn path leading downhill and led his wife to the beach. The trail ended among large rocks that sheltered a private beach, where three children played in the water. Dark haired, except for the smallest – a girl whose long locks blended white and black – they were almond-eyed, with tapered ear tips. What were preteen Lithians doing here?

With a wave and a warm smile, Brenna called out in her native tongue and blessed them in the Name of Allfather. But rather than return the greeting, the children dashed to the tree line in a panic. Puzzled, Brenna looked at her husband in disbelief. "How rude!" she exclaimed.

"Maybe we should follow them," he advised.

But movement in 'the nearby trees whispered warning. A loud bang, followed by badly-aimed buckshot bouncing on the cliff nearby forced the lovers behind a rock. Garrick chambered a round, but didn't return fire.

Tense moments passed as Garrick slowly crawled closer to the cliff while his wife whispered prayers. As a slender, shirtless young Lithian man in filmy pants came out of the forest with a shotgun in hand, Garrick waited until the lad had moved away from shelter before standing in a firing posture and revealing his new position. "Put down your weapon!" he demanded in Lithian.

He knew this wasn't the right way to phrase the order, but in the heat of the moment, the cultural facility that Brenna naturally brought into Lithian conversation eluded him.

The young man didn't comply.

Brenna peeked over the rock. "You're in danger as long as you hold that gun!" she shouted. "If you put it down, we won't hurt you."

"You'd prevent me from protecting my siblings?" he replied, pointing the weapon at her. "You're trespassing on my family's land."

"Drop it now!" Garrick warned, his tone reflecting a dangerous, combat-trauma influence. But before Brenna had the chance to touch his shoulder and calm him, Garrick fired a three round warning burst that kicked up a spray of sand to the left of his target.

Terrified, having never faced an armed threat before, and distracted by a desire to not hurt the beautiful Lithian woman, the young man swung the gun around and pulled the trigger – his shot so ineffective that it missed even the nearby rocks. The lad dropped the weapon in terror and fled into the nearby trees. Garrick took aim and could have easily killed the boy, but Brenna pushed the rifle barrel down. "Please, Garrick!" she urged. "Think about what you're doing."

A different demeanor swept across the Tamarian soldier's face. He paused, exerting self-control as he slung the weapon over his shoulder and nodded. "You're right. But we have to follow him now."

***

In a clearing, less than 100 yards to the east and two dozen feet above the shoreline, stood a house built in the Nordan style. Its massive timbers and a tiled roof offered shelter for a wraparound porch that rose over a sturdy stone foundation. Huge, rusty chains hung from holes in its eaves, providing drainage.

A large vegetable garden occupied its south side. While the residence looked like it belonged to a wealthy colonial family, a tracking dish for hot water shone brilliantly in the daylight, while a vertical axis wind machine turned in a steady onshore breeze. Neither Garrick nor Brenna had seen any Nordan building with these features.

A muscular Lithian man with black hair carried a shotgun as he descended the porch stairs. Brenna dropped her bag as first her left hand, then her right, reached for her lips. "Oh, no!" she breathed.

A mutual expression of recognition morphed onto the man's face. "Well, well," he remarked, lowering the gun. "If it isn't lovely little Brenna Velez . . . ."

Garrick strode forward, hoping to rescue his wife from the obvious embarrassment she felt. He offered his hand in the universal gesture of peace and, speaking in Lithian, introduced himself.

"I am Belwyr," the man replied, squeezing Garrick's hand good and hard. "Why did you shoot at my boy?"

"I told him to put the gun down, but he didn't listen," Garrick replied confidently. "I fired in warning. It would have been just as easy to kill him."

Belwyr shook his head. "He tells me that he was only defending his brother and sisters."

"We're no threat," Garrick stated. "My wife greeted your children, they ran off, and then the lad with the gun showed up and shot at us without cause. Be grateful I didn't finish off the foolish boy on the spot. We're not here to cause trouble. We just need to get across the border."

Belwyr raised his brow while the corners of his lips turned down, his expression betraying disbelief that Garrick didn't quite understand. "Well, the crossing is about thirty minutes east of here . . . ."

"The bridge is closed," Garrick stated, lying with a completely straight face. "We just came from there."

With his gaze locked on Brenna, the Lithian man gestured for the young couple to enter. "Come in and refresh yourselves before you go," he offered. "Tell me your story. I'll have Eira brew us a fresh pot of tea."

Brenna, tight-lipped, picked up her bag, clung close to Garrick and said nothing. Her discomfort unnerved her husband, dangerously heightening his hypervigilance.

The children they'd seen earlier gazed from nearby windows as a slender woman whose long, black hair flowed over a lovely silk dress opened the front door. She introduced herself as Eira, and let her hands linger on Brenna's muscular arms as a sign of welcome and affirmation. The older woman, noting the obvious influence of *Y Newen*, scrunched her brow.

"You poor thing!" she said, her voice reflecting genuine pity. Knowing of Belwyr's historic interest in this strong and talented young woman, Eira lowered her voice. "No one in your condition should be running around like this. You need privacy. We have a room where you two can stay as long as you need."

Brenna felt nervous crossing the threshold. Belwyr's eyes followed her as the children – ranging in age from four to seventeen – lined up to greet their guests. His eyes admired her as they sat at the table for tea and lingered, even while Garrick relayed an abbreviated version of their tale. His eyes fixated on her as Eira led them upstairs, to a room in the attic with a patio view of the sea. Eira made their bed. Smiling at Brenna she told them, "Relax and make yourself at home. You're welcome here, and I'll see to it that your stay is pleasant and comfortable."

Garrick wondered why she would say such a thing. As the door closed, he caressed his wife and left a lingering kiss on her lips, stirring desire restrained by concern that he wouldn't want to love her after Belwyr's boorish reception. Garrick whispered in Tamarian to avoid eavesdropping ears. "You know this man. I can tell you two have history. What happened?"

Brenna shook her head, reluctant to tell the tale of a broken relationship between her and Belwyr until Garrick's persistence wore her down. She sat on the bed with a sad expression in her eyes and patted the spot next to her. "I met Belwyr at my last boys' choir concert, during that awkward age where *The Twins* were really growing. Before I put on my maiden clothes, my body became so distracting to the choirboys I had to resign as accompanist in favor of a younger pianist. It's a routine matter, but losing that position was hard on me.

"Belwyr came from a family in the southeast. We didn't know them, but his manners were good – at least in public. He came calling for me at home, but *Amair* said I was still too young for courting and sent him away.

"A few years later, I'd almost stopped competing at festivals altogether. Aside from *Umma* and my sister, not many Lithian women have a figure like mine. I felt the weight of leering eyes as men came to ogle *The Twins*, rather than appreciating my hard work and talent.

"Right about this time, Belwyr moved to Shirak with his uncle. He saw me at a concert, and because I was older by then, *Amair* permitted him to visit me. After a few months of acting like a perfect gentleman, he persuaded *Amair* to let me meet his uncle."

Brenna stood and walked to the sliding door. She crossed her arms as she continued. "He took me to an impressive and beautiful estate house overlooking the sea, just like this, a couple of miles outside the city. His uncle was wealthy, but had grown old, senile and quite deaf.

"I thought Belwyr really liked me," she continued, her voice quavering with emotion as she turned her head away, suppressing her physical response to the memory. "But after his uncle fell asleep, he attacked me like a predator. I begged him to stop, but he wouldn't. He pinned me to a sofa and tore at my clothes to get at *The Twins*. He held my arms in one hand and ripped the fabric of my favorite blouse until all the buttons fell on the floor.

"I fought back for all I was worth, but he was very strong and aggressive. He left bruises on my arms and scratches down my neck. I screamed, but no one heard me . . . ." Brenna's voice broke and her eyes dampened as she finally told him the tale.

Growing angry, Garrick arose, his hands flexing into fists. "I'll beat him to a bloody pulp if he lays a finger on you while we're here!"

"He won't," she asserted, calming him. Everyone can see that I'm receptive right now. He knows I'm yours. He knows you're mine. He had a chance to get what he wanted, but he was impatient and selfish. He didn't know I could will my camisole to harden like armor, and when I wouldn't let him fondle *The Twins*, or get his hands under my clothes, he started hitting me hard and pulling my hair, hoping I'd abandon my virtue. But I finally squirmed loose and pulled out my boot blade. He didn't think I knew how to use it, but I left my mark on his arm to prove than I can.

"After I'd cut him, he screamed at me. He called me a slut. He swore I was stupid for thinking anyone could love me. He said men would only want me for *The Twins*. His words broke my heart. I felt sick. I wanted to hurt him even more than I had, but my soul had been crushed and I'd been shamed. I took a bath in the sea to rid myself of his filth and ran home, crying the whole way."

Garrick stood, his sympathy mingling with indignation. "Only weak men disrespect women like that," he told her quietly. "I noticed how he stared at you. I thought his leering was ill-mannered, but his conduct is contemptible. I'm so sorry, Brenna. You deserve better."

"You *are* better," she said earnestly. "Allfather knew you'd love me. You're my gift. You're my blessing. All the men who came before you were more interested in *The Twins* than they were in the rest of me. Belwyr was the first to behave badly, but he wasn't the last."

Garrick swore, vowing in his heart to avenge Brenna's mistreatment. "I still want to hit him . . . . What did your father do when he found out?"

Brenna's expression morphed into a mischievous smile. "I'd never seen him so upset. *Amair* tolerated insults from lesser men, but he never shied away from defending my honor. He stormed over to that old man's house and warned him that if his nephew ever came near me again, he'd turn Belwyr into a eunuch."

Hearing this, and knowing Lord Velez, Garrick sputtered, "It's a good thing I earned his respect."

"*My* respect is what mattered," she replied, drawing near and laying her head on his shoulder. "You earned it. *Amair* told me I could tell love from lust by a man's self-control, and you were noble enough to keep your hands to yourself until I consented to your touch. What my *Amair* cared about most was whether or not I could trust you to honor my innocence when we were alone."

Garrick sighed, resting his cheek against her head, his fingers caressing her spine. "I was looking forward to a night of loving you, but after hearing this, I'm not so sure that's a good idea."

Determination filled her eyes as Brenna lifted her head. "There's no better revenge for me than loving *you* under his roof," she stated. "And I'll make sure I'm loud enough for him to hear. Eira saw his wandering eyes while you were talking, and she's no fool. He wanted us to leave, but she gave us a bed and told us we could stay here, knowing how I need you right now."

"So, you think we're safe?" he asked.

Brenna, remembering Thea's mystic warning replied, "We've crossed into his world. We have to be careful."

A massive thunderstorm advanced from the sea just after daybreak. Bright flashes of light awakened Brenna while her exhausted husband slept peacefully at her side. He did not stir when loud thunder crashed over the windblown water and rattled windows as the squall rolled inland. Hard rain hammered the roof while strong wind swept through the sighing conifers that bent and swayed in their yielding dance.

Unable to sleep, with a full bladder urging relief, Brenna wrestled into her camisole, willed it into place, and slipped into a skirt. She strapped her boot knife to her right calf, then tiptoed into the stairwell to find a bathroom. She could hear the happy noise of the youngest boy's banter with his older sister downstairs, while the aroma of spicy baked fish, along with the clinking of cutlery, suggested breakfast would soon be served.

Belwyr riveted his gaze the moment Brenna appeared on the stairwell and asked for the location of a toilet. Eira, wearing a thin robe, held her youngest daughter on her hip, smiled and pointed to the bathroom.

Terrified of insulting her host, Brenna prayed for wisdom as she relieved herself and washed her hands. Emerging into the hallway, the nervous woman glared at Belwyr, her cheeks hot with indignation, her heart pounding, and her eyes gleaming as the trauma of his attempted rape echoed in her body. "Your staring makes me uncomfortable," she announced, strongly implying he should stop without directly telling him what to do.

Struck by her daring, Belwyr looked away. "That was not my intention," he replied.

Brenna did not honor his remark with a reply. Her unspoken anger inspired the wide-eyed children to fall silent. Social tension thickened in the dining area.

"Will you join us for breakfast?" Eira asked in a maternally sweet tone. "We have plenty."

Lithians considered refusing an invitation rude, yet Brenna felt ill at ease in Belwyr's company and struggled to control the involuntary tremble in her fingers. Despite his apology, his thinly veiled contempt – worsened by his incessant leering – proved that Belwyr felt no remorse. Brenna could defend herself, but longed for her husband's presence to deter Belwyr's boorish behavior. Not wanting to offend her hostess, she offered a compromise.

"If you don't mind, I'll wait for Garrick," she stated. "He's very tired and still resting, but I'd be honored to pray with you and share a cup of tea."

"We don't pray," Ciaran, the eldest boy, remarked.

"Well, I do," Brenna responded, unwilling to let the teenaged boy's impudent statement stand. "Given our shared heritage, my faith should not offend you."

Eira glided to Brenna's side and touched her shoulder reassuringly. "Don't worry. You're safe here. If you want to pray, we'll respect you." She gestured to a chair, indicating where she wanted Brenna to sit.

Ciaran brought tea to the table, while his younger sister, Ilia, served the food, a convention followed by Lithian families who couldn't afford servants. Then Brenna bowed her head and blessed everyone present in the Name of Allfather, an act of grace she extended to the man who'd once mistreated her. Belwyr's expression reflected lingering discomfort after she'd finished.

"Why do you pray?" Ciaran asked. "Our people prayed for deliverance from the Azgar, but it didn't help."

The teenager's angry, accusing tone didn't scratch the armor of Brenna's faith. "If you ask a favor of me, am I obligated to comply?"

"It's not the same," Ciaran countered.

"That's true," she replied, calmly blowing breath over her tea to cool it down. "Allfather is sovereign. He's our Creator, and it's not our place to make demands. Insisting that God should serve us is the height of arrogance. So, if I'm not compelled to grant a request that you make of me, that very truth – to a much greater degree – also applies to Allfather."

"Then what's the point of praying if it doesn't do anything? You're just wasting your breath."

"You say this because you lack faith," Brenna responded. "The power in prayer is not in obliging God to honor my will, but in bending mine to his. The relationship is not about me getting what I want."

"Well, we don't need you to pray for us," Ciaran stated triumphantly. "We're doing fine on our own."

Brenna laid her right hand on her heart. "Blessing your family reflects a reality that lives in my soul. Why reject goodwill from a guest? What's the point of that?"

Eira raised her brow. This woman displayed wisdom and handled rude questions graciously. Belwyr had spoken badly of her, but like many assertions Eira had heard from him over the years, his testimony rang hollow. Despite his dishonesty, she loved him, always sought the best for him, and never took him to task in public.

Their private conversations, however, were a different matter. He would hear about this, for certain.

Understanding that his faith had long ago fallen away, Eira didn't want Belwyr to contend with Brenna in an area where the woman's passion and wit might make him look foolish in front of their children. "Tell us about your husband," she encouraged.

"What would you like to know?" Brenna asked.

"He's an officer in the Tamarian Expeditionary Army," Belwyr replied.

Surprised, Brenna turned, but didn't correct him. "How do you know about that?"

"The two of you are wanted for inciting terror," he replied. "I've seen posters with your picture on hoardings in town. That's why I wasn't surprised to see you."

Brenna looked away. "We've incited nothing."

Belwyr grunted. "So you say, but the authorities are offering a nice reward for your capture. Give me a good reason not to report you . . . ."

Stunned by that remark, Brenna's eyes burned with deep mistrust. "Are you blackmailing me?"

"Still holding a grudge?" he replied. "If I'd wanted to report you, I'd have phoned already and we'd have soldiers at the door. Instead, we welcomed you and endured the noise of your exuberant lovemaking for half the night."

"Then why make a threat?" she asked, defensively. "Eira invited us to stay. We're under your protection"

Belwyr shook his head. "I'm not threatening anyone. You baited me with your body. It was only natural for me to respond, but you attacked me with a knife. That's the truth, no matter what your *Amair* had to say about it."

Noting the anger lingering in Brenna's eyes, Eira held Belwyr's hand. "That was a long time ago," she said soothingly. "Let's wash away the bad blood, shall we?"

With his plans for vengeance in motion, Belwyr smiled at his guest. This time, his eyes lingered on the prominent scar that marred her neck. "I forgive you," he said, wondering where she'd sustained that injury.

The courage to reply in kind eluded Brenna. She couldn't let go of the visceral mistrust haunting her soul. Feeling self-conscious about her wound, she turned her head to make her neck less visible. "I'll pass that word on to my *Amair*," she replied.

***

Garrick awakened with a start, his dream of being pursued by hostile enemies ending abruptly as lighting brightened the room. A loud thunderclap followed, less than a heartbeat later. Brenna's place in the bed felt cold. With his back stiff and body aching, he sat upright and listened to orient himself to his surroundings.

He heard Brenna's melodic voice below, and sensing that she could use his support, he checked his rifle to make sure it was clean and ready, slipped into shorts and pulled a shirt over his head before trotting downstairs. A palpable tension around the breakfast table heightened his sense of danger, but Brenna appeared to be handling the threat well. "Are you okay?" he asked in Tamarian.

Knowing he'd need to relieve himself, she pointed in the direction of the bathroom. "We'll talk about this later. It's not safe here."

Ilia cleared dishes in silence. Her younger brother, Cedric, stared at Brenna with widened eyes until his little sister, Fiona, pulled him away to play in a large room at the end of the hall. When Garrick returned to the dining area, he noted relief in his wife's expression.

Ciaran served two dishes of eggs, spicy fish and vegetables, along with a small serving bowl of thickened cream to tone down the spice fire for Garrick. The young man loitered near Brenna, but possessing better manners than his father, didn't let his eyes linger for long.

"You can freshen our guests' room while they eat," Belwyr told him in a slightly conspiratorial tone.

The young man nodded, fetched a vial from the kitchen and a set of clean bedding before heading upstairs. Garrick, suspicious of Belwyr's intentions, noted the container and wondered about its intended use.

"So, what are your plans?" Belwyr asked.

"We thank you for your hospitality, but we need to be on our way," Garrick replied, stifling his distrust.

Eira hedged. "Your wife shouldn't be running around in a war zone in her condition," she counseled. "It's not wise. You need privacy and security."

"I'll be fine," Brenna countered gently. "I've dealt with this before."

"You'll attract unwanted attention from men," Eira warned. "Even our boys find you irresistible. If you stay here until your cycle is done, you'll be safe, with us."

"She's right," Belwyr stated. "If you leave our protection, you'll be in danger. You're in the wrong place at the wrong time. Who can you trust when the natives have a price on your head?"

Garrick stifled a rising indignation as Belwyr reviewed his claim concerning the bounty local officials had placed on them. "All we need to do is get across the river," Garrick replied. "Otherwise, we'll be okay."

Belwyr shrugged. "The river is in full flood and crossing is dangerous. With the bridge closed, you'll need help getting to the other side. You can take your chances, but I know people who can get you over there safely."

Suspicious of Belwyr's intentions, noting Eira's suppressed expression of displeasure, Garrick guarded his tone and concealed his emotion. "That's a generous offer, but we don't want to trouble you further."

The clever Tamarian possessed a soldier's reluctance to trust. While that attitude complicated Belwyr's plan, he could easily adapt. "There's a lot of pent-up anger toward foreigners in the colony," Belwyr explained. "For decades, the Nordans have stolen timber and mineral wealth. Their fishing boats are modern, equipped with sonar, and don't need to rely on the wind. They're harvesting so many fish there are very few left for local families. Hunger drives people to desperation, which is why you see burning piles of oil kelp and fighting in the streets."

Curious, Garrick asked, "How do you know all this? You're a foreigner, yourself."

"I manage the offshore fishery in this area for the colonial authorities," Belwyr admitted. "I calculate their quotas, but they have a growing population on their home islands and not enough land to feed them. They regularly exceed their catch limits, leaving little, if anything, for the native people. Doing this hasn't endeared the Nordans to the locals."

"That makes you a collaborator," Garrick stated. "We've seen what the locals do to people like you, and it isn't pretty."

"That won't happen," Belwyr claimed. "I've told the insurgent leaders why the fishery is in decline. I explained that harvesting oil kelp removes nursery habitat – which is why the young fish aren't surviving – and that over fishing is removing too many mature adults. The Nordans are destroying marine resources from both ends to feed their people and machines, but continually doing this will end badly for them. The resource is not infinite.

"Everything from their fishing boats to their navy runs on seaweed oil, and they don't give a damn that what they're doing hurts the Kurians. They take and never give back."

"None of that keeps the locals from coming after you," Garrick stated. "And you're in league with the Nordans, who won't take kindly to your duplicity."

"They have no idea what I'm doing, and they have no way of finding out." Then Belwyr added, "You're a military man. Think this through. The natives vastly outnumber the Colonial Garrison troops. They can handle the forces already deployed here. It's the Imperial Navy that they fear. They've told me so.

"Destroying the oil kelp trade creates fuel shortages that will limit what the Imperial Navy can do. The rebels have attacked transport barges and oil processing plants, which are essential in making fuel for the big ships, as raw kelp oil will gum the injection pumps of their engines unless it's transesterified first."

Garrick nodded, understanding the political and military implications, but not the process, as he'd had no education in that particular science. Belwyr's story explained the seaweed pyre he and Brenna had seen along the shore, and fit nicely into the larger, geopolitical picture. Stifling any expression, Garrick didn't respond.

Noting that the Tamarian soldier remained skeptical, Belwyr explained further. "The Kurians are justifiably angry. Nordan colonists take the best land and live here tax free, whereas natives pay heavy tribute. Restrictive laws that apply to local people don't apply to colonists. Military police and Colonial Army soldiers kill with impunity, arrest anyone who opposes them – including children – and then torture those people in their prisons.

"It's shocking the Kurians haven't tried to overthrow Nordan authority in the past. But now they feel like they have nothing to lose. They have weapons and training. Their population is fed up and their leaders are determined to push the Nordans into the sea."

"None of that makes you immune to their retribution," Garrick stated. "If you're so concerned about us, what makes you think they won't come after you? I look more like a native than you do."

"My face isn't on wanted posters," Belwyr argued. "If they'd intended to come after me, you'd have found my house empty, but they know I'm not part of the problem.

"Rest assured, the Nordans will come. They will use overwhelming force that the insurgents won't be able to resist without help from the Kamerese, who've been funneling Azgar weapons into the colony for months."

Hearing this, Brenna recalled the spent shells they'd found on the beach. However, the gun Garrick had taken from a dead insurgent wasn't an Azgar weapon. He said he'd seen that type of rifle while fighting the Tanarak on the Saradon last year. "What about the Vatherans?" she asked. "How are they involved in this?"

Belwyr couldn't have been surprised to hear her say this, but he feigned astonishment that she knew about Vatheran complicity. "The Vatherans cooperate with the Nordans because it suits them," he explained. "Transesterifying kelp oil requires methanol, which Vatheran gasifying plants produce from wood chips and electrolytic oxygen, using a catalyst. Bandits in the north steal Nordan lumber shipments and send the raw wood to Vathera in exchange for weapons. They're too far inland for the Colonial Garrison troops to intervene."

"If the Nordans need methanol to make their fuel oil, how do they get it?" Brenna asked.

"They buy from Kurian businesses in the north," Belwyr told her. "It's shipped down to the coast by rail."

"So, the Vatherans make money from gun sales and methanol," Garrick accurately concluded. "But why destroy the kelp oil, which you say will wreck their engines, when it would be easier to hit the tanker cars bringing the methanol down from Vathera?"

"Money is the root of international conflict," Belwyr said. "The people controlling the rail lines in the north are Kurian. The people controlling the oil kelp trade are Nordans. Who do you think the insurgents want to hurt?"

"Those distinctions tend to blur when the shooting starts," Garrick told him.

"Exactly," Belwyr concluded triumphantly. "And that's already happening. It's about to get much worse. If you're not careful, you lovebirds will get swept away in a very nasty conflict. That's why you need my help."

***

Ciaran felt his body automatically respond with arousal as he entered the guest room. His mother hadn't gone through *Y Newen* – the Lithian fertile period – since the year before they'd left Illithia, and so much time had passed since then, he'd forgotten that once familiar, sensuous and uniquely feminine aroma. Damp towels strewn on the bed exuded the strongest scent, though the bed sheets also carried that distinctive, seductive perfume. With pelting rain driving against the patio portal, he couldn't freshen the room's air without ruining the floor.

Llymah told him the Velez woman was a wealthy, lusty siren who strutted about, showing off her generous bosom to attract attention. That didn't seem right, given her conduct thus far. *Umma* had warned him that Brenna had no influence over her body shape, and that it had no bearing on her character. Further, their guest couldn't be in her current condition with the Tamarian man as her partner, and at the same time be as concupiscent as *Llymah* alleged. Lithian biology didn't work that way.

But the scar on *Llymah's* arm proved that what he'd said about the slutty Velez woman was true, didn't it? She wasn't shy about her sensuality, but that was true of all Lithians. Still, Ciaran wanted to please his father, and the Velez woman would pay for what she'd done to him.

Ciaran's role in punishing Brenna was both simple and elegant. Beneath the bed the young man found the Tamarian soldier's rifle. Quietly removing its magazine, he opened the kelp oil he'd brought up from the kitchen, held the weapon upside down and poured oil into its chamber, action and magazine. Wiping the rifle clean with one of the smelly towels their guests had used, he made sure no residual oil dripped from the weapon. Ciaran returned the rifle to where he'd found it and finished changing the bed. *Llymah* would be pleased at how easy that had been.

*****

Not long after Ciaran came downstairs with an armful of laundry, the clouds parted, the rain stopped and humid heat returned with a vengeance. Belwyr left to meet with his contacts and make his promised travel arrangements. He drove an old military truck through a muddy track in the woods, soon disappearing from view.

Brenna headed upstairs to pray, while Garrick lingered at the table with Eira, drinking tea. He'd briefly outlined his courtship, then turned the conversation on his hostess. "How did you meet your husband?" he asked.

"Oh, we're not married," she admitted. "That's why our children call him *Llymah*. My *Amair* managed the estate for Belwyr's uncle. I helped him with landscaping, and one thing led to another . . . ."

Thus, Garrick learned that *Llymah* referred to a man who'd sired children after taking his woman's virtue out of wedlock. This meant Eira was as biologically bound to Belwyr as Brenna was to him, but not spiritually affirmed.

Her smile, wistful and misty-eyed, brimmed with regret. She looked away, laughed nervously and then composed herself by sipping tea. "I had dreams as a maiden, but after meeting Belwyr – so handsome, so smart, so strong – nothing else mattered. I gave up everything to have him."

"What did your father have to say about that?" Garrick inquired, knowing that Lord Velez tolerated no inappropriate behavior toward his daughters.

"My *Amair* was . . . preoccupied," Eira admitted. "I gave myself to Belwyr of my own volition. I've made my choice. We have four children so far, and though I may never have another, he takes care of me."

Garrick's brow wrinkled. "Does he love you?"

"In his own way, I think he does," she replied. "Men are not always who they promote themselves to be."

Her tone suggested receptivity to an issue that had been bothering Garrick since they'd first arrived. "Your boys are curious, but they respect a woman's honor. Even the youngest one exhibits more self-control than Belwyr. Why do you tolerate him openly staring at my beloved?"

Eira tightened her lips and looked away again. A flash of personal pain washed over her face before she regained emotional control. "You should be alone with your wife right now. She is lovely, and Belwyr finds her impossible to resist."

Thinking carefully before responding, Garrick savored a sip of tea. "Brenna was a virtuous woman long before we first met," he said. "She reserved herself for me, even when mistreated. I expect Belwyr to honor your customs and keep his eyes fixed on you . . . ."

"Let's talk about something else," Eira stated abruptly, her tone sharper than Garrick had heard from her thus far. "Do you have any children?"

"Not yet," Garrick replied, shaking his head. "We have time, and I'm sure we will one day."

Realizing from his tone that she'd touched on a sensitive topic, and far more adept in the affective domain than he could claim, Eira used humor to diffuse tension. "Well, from what I heard last evening, I'd suggest it won't be long before you do." She smiled, knowingly, a little bit of envy creeping into her tone. "It sounds like you're very skilled at pleasing your woman. Brenna is blessed."

Garrick blushed. Lithians were remarkably candid about such things. "I have the honor of loving her," he stated. "And I am honored that she loves me."

Eira tapped her finger on the table. "Brenna prays over her meals while you wait for her to finish. She went upstairs for her morning devotion, while you stayed down here with me. Does it bother you that she's devout?"

"No," Garrick replied. "Having personal faith in the unseen isn't a problem. Insisting that I must think the same way is another matter, entirely. But Brenna isn't like that. She respects my point-of-view, which makes it easy for me to extend the same courtesy to her."

"You treat her with remarkable kindness," Eira said, a little bit wistfully. "Your high regard of her faith, the way you uplift her in your conduct and speech are all impressive. Your gentleness and tender regard for her is refreshing. I've never known a man to treat his woman this way – especially after he's wooed her into bed."

"Brenna deserves the best from me," Garrick told her. "She's a woman of sterling character, a woman of deep integrity who lives the faith she claims. There's power in her conviction. I don't have to believe any of it to see the impact that it has on her life.

"She always puts the welfare of others above her own, even at the risk of her life. I've watched her brave bullets and drag the broken bodies of men in my platoon to safety in the heat of combat. Her conduct consistently reflects the reality of her faith, of her trust. This is especially true in the way she treats me. Why wouldn't I honor her for that?"

Belwyr had described the Velez woman as petty and vain. He repeatedly claimed that Brenna thought only of herself, and because Eira had heard this so often, she struggled to relinquish her preconceptions. "That's high praise," the Lithian woman remarked. "Your wife is fortunate to have a partner who appreciates her."

Garrick finished his tea. "That works two ways," he explained. "Brenna inspires my confidence because she can trust me. I never have reason to question her loyalty, nor do I give her reason to question mine. She lifts me up when I can't stand on my own, and I'm blessed in the company of an intelligent, gifted and beautiful woman who's chosen to build a life with me."

Eira smiled, suppressing envy. "Then you deserve each other," she concluded.

***

Brenna called Garrick upstairs shortly thereafter. She pulled him into her yielding embrace and gripped his strong back with a feminine ferocity she reserved for moments of anguish, not sensuality. "We need to get out of here," she whispered urgently, in Tamarian.

Her reluctance to face conflict often resulted in an inclination to avoid confrontation, but this felt different. She seemed genuinely terrified.

Garrick reached for the door and shut it. "Let's talk about this," he suggested. "We need to be careful that what we do doesn't make matters worse by acting rashly."

"Belwyr's gone," she whispered in a desperate voice, clinging to Garrick while her eyes implored him to act. "We don't know what he's doing, and I don't trust him. If we slip away now, we'll be far away before he returns."

Hedging, considering the rain, Brenna's physical state, and his fatigue, Garrick replied carefully. "If Belwyr reports us to either the Nordans or the rebels, they can easily follow our prints in the mud. I'm sure you understand that no hunting hound will have any trouble tracking you right now."

Brenna couldn't admit that she'd come to this realization in the midst of her morning prayers. He wouldn't understand her trust in a spiritual connection that brought warning verses to mind when she faced danger like this. "You're dismissing my concerns!" she replied, anger rising in her voice. "For all we know, he might come back with a squad of armed men who'll shoot us on sight."

Setting aside his fatigue and choosing to trust his wife, Garrick kissed her. "Okay," he agreed. "Let's go."

***

From the bluff overlooking the northern edge of the cove, Special Forces Lieutenant Ohori Shoyo felt grateful that the rain had stopped. He longed to feel dry and warm in direct daylight, but suffered discomfort without complaint, unwilling to betray his team's position.

Through his binoculars he saw an armed man – tall, blonde-haired and fit – emerge from the upstairs patio door. He carried a Vatheran rifle in the manner of a soldier, and after checking the surroundings carefully, slung the weapon over this shoulder and lowered himself from the railing. He dropped to the ground behind the northern wall of the house.

Next, a small, dark-haired woman climbed over the balcony railing, dangling her legs into the man's open arms. He set her on the ground, and they rapidly melded into the edge of the forest surrounding the property, concealing themselves as they moved through the trees.

It had to be them. Lieutenant Shoyo looked over his shoulder at Warrant Officer Aki Yuichi, who operated the radio. "Report: *Tora* targets reacquired, moving south on foot. *Daburusupai* still absent."

Yuichi offered a short head bow before returning to the com tent to obey the order. On his way, he passed other members of *Ōkami Roku,* taking turns cleaning and drying out their weapons.

It wouldn't be long before they'd be fighting again.

***

Eira heard Belwyr's truck gearing down to navigate the last turn before stopping outside. Ten fully armed Kurian patriots and two hunters with dogs piled out of vehicle's covered bed. Eight men in pairs circled the house with weapons at the ready, while the other two stormed up the porch stairs and burst through the door.

"What's going on?" Eira cried in accented Kurian. "You can't come in here with your guns out like this. There are children in the house!"

The militia officer pulled out his sidearm and pointed it directly at her. "Quit your complaining, woman! Where are the foreigners?"

Eira lifted her chin, indicating upstairs as Belwyr entered. She glared at him angrily with her hands on her hips. "What have you done?" she demanded in Lithian.

"I'm collecting a bounty," he replied dismissively. "We need the money."

As the horror of his actions settled on her soul, Eira spoke the obvious transgression aloud. "Our guests were under our protection. You've betrayed them!"

"Shut up, woman! They're armed, dangerous and wanted. Slutty Brenna and her stupid soldier deserve what's coming to them. We don't shelter terrorists . . . ."

The men stomped back down the stairs and entered the kitchen. The officer threatened Eira with his gun a second time. "Where did they go?" he demanded.

"Put your weapon down!" Belwyr ordered.

Moving his arm leftward, the patriot spat, "Watch your mouth, Lithian scum. I have a good mind to waste you where you stand and let my men have their way with your woman, afterward."

Ciaran, who'd been in the back room when the Kurian fighters arrived, urged his siblings into the cellar for safety. With his heart pounding, he quietly closed the trap door over them and slid a rug over the opening to conceal it from the intruders. Then, he loaded and hid *Llymah's* shotgun in the back room before scurrying down the hall to save his mother from harm. "Wait, wait!" he cried. "The people you want were here this morning, I swear. If they're gone, I know how you can find them."

"Don't waste my time, boy!" the patriot warned.

"We have their laundry," Ciaran admitted. "Let your hounds smell their towels. They'll be easy to track, and they couldn't have gone far on foot."

Holstering his weapon, the insurgent fighter grunted in assent. "I didn't come here to play games, so you'd better be right, kid. Your life depends on it."

Ciaran, desperate to save his parents, nodded.

The patriot officer followed the young man to the laundry room, just off the kitchen. There, Ciaran produced one of the towels he'd taken from the upstairs bedroom. "Smell this," he suggested eagerly. "They didn't get much sleep last night, for sure!"

With his brow raised, the patriot fighter took a whiff of the towel and grunted. The attractive aroma aroused him, and if he could smell it, the hounds would have no trouble following the scent. He strode out of the house to speak with the hunters his team had brought along.

***

From the south-facing ridge separating the little cove from the Attavela's estuary, Garrick scanned the scene below with his binoculars. "Uh oh . . . ." he warned, watching as one of the local men offered a towel to the big, long-legged hounds bred to hunt bears. "They're using dogs on us."

"Let's go!" Brenna urged.

"I'll never outrun a hunting hound," Garrick stated. He limbered the rifle and chambered a round, finding the action a little stiff. "We have the high ground, and we're concealed. Let them come!"

"How many of them are there?" she asked.

"About ten," he replied.

"We're outnumbered and you want to fight?" she asked, incredulously. "This is the hill you want to die on?"

"We're not dying today," he promised. "They are. Make your shots count."

Below, the huge hounds oriented themselves and bolted for the bluff. The hunters, along with a Kurian fighter, followed behind. Garrick set up a crossfire by sending Brenna further to the east, where a large rock protected her from direct attack. He concealed himself in a spot with a good view of a clearing several yards below.

Given that the dogs gave the Kurians an advantage, Garrick needed to take them out first. As the creatures raced up the slope, he selected what he hoped was a fragmentation grenade from his *bug-out* bag. Calmly, the Tamarian solider waited for the right moment, pulled its pin, then tossed the handheld explosive just in front of the hounds, who instinctively approached it, sniffing. Their curiosity maximized the weapon's deadly effect.

***

Still awaiting orders, Lieutenant Shoyo heard a loud blast and saw smoke rising across the cove, followed by the pathetic whimpering of a wounded dog. The insurgents surrounding the house turned their weapons southward and began firing wildly into the trees, inadvertently killing one of their comrades.

Although he didn't have authorization, Shoyo seized the opportunity to act. He sent a four-man squad to the east while he led the rest of his team to the west, setting up a pincer movement and crossfire in the clearing that quickly felled four more of the insurgents, inciting panic among them. Terrified by the sudden appearance of a well-trained enemy, three of the rebels fled eastward, along the track that led from the cove to Helsing.

***

Startled by the gunfire, the patriot officer who'd threatened Eira retreated into the house, where he confronted Belwyr. "You lured us into a trap!" he snarled, drawing his sidearm for a third time. Before the Lithian biologist could respond, the officer shot him in the heart.

Eira screamed in terror. She died next.

Ciaran raced down the hall to the playroom before the officer could get a bead on him. The young man grabbed his father's shotgun, crouched in the corner, shouldered the weapon and prepared to fight. Believing the Kurians would kill him, the young man offered his life to protect his hidden siblings.

When the Kurian officer angrily kicked his way into the playroom, Ciaran blasted him in the chest with both barrels. The gunfire caught the attention of the lone surviving rebel fighter on the porch, who – after witnessing the Lithian lad kill his comrade – fired through the window and cut Ciaran down.

In the cellar, Ilia held her brother and sister in a tight embrace while the gunfight raged above. "Don't be afraid," she told them. "We're safe down here."

***

While the Nordan attack also surprised Garrick, he didn't panic. Steadying his rifle, the Tamarian soldier set his sights on the surviving dog, intending to put the poor creature out of its misery. However, his trigger felt sluggish and the weapon wouldn't fire.

Opening its chamber, he noted that the mechanism contained a sticky, gelatinous goo that smelled like the sea. Garrick swore, muttering murderous epithets under his breath. Brenna had been right about Belwyr's treachery. While Garrick recognized the wisdom of honoring her desperation to flee, his now useless weapon had to be thoroughly cleaned before it would work again.

A mercy gunshot ended the hunting dog's pathetic cries. Garrick heard the pair of older Kurian men arguing as they hid among the trees downslope. He recognized words that sounded like "trip wire" and "trap," along with epithets apparently directed at "patriots" being "dumb as rocks." Then men waited as a brief, but furious firefight around the homestead came to an abrupt end.

Garrick also heard Nordan voices below. He wanted to assess the threat they represented, but dared not move out of his concealed position as long as the Kurian hunters remained in the area. Controlling his fear response with deliberate breathing, the Tamarian soldier waited, listening, avoiding any motion that might draw attention to his presence while preparing for violent action.

Confident that Brenna would keep herself hidden, Garrick unsheathed the combat knife he'd taken from a dead rebel on the beach. If he had to dispatch the hunters, he'd need to do so without alerting the Nordans.

But that proved unnecessary. The hunters, rightly fearing for their lives, headed uphill to escape. Garrick watched them from the shadows as they labored to the summit with surprising stealth. Once confident that they'd not been followed, the hunters turned east and fled downhill, their rapid, noisy passage fading quickly.

Rising to full height and reaching for his binoculars, Garrick studied the scene around Belwyr's house. The Nordan Special Forces team moved the old truck to a position near the front door. Two men dragged Belwyr and Eira to the porch to photograph their bodies. After this, they loaded a radio into the truck, the team piled into the vehicle, and headed east along the track toward Helsing.

"Garrick?" Brenna called at length. "Are you okay?"

Startled, but relieved, he turned toward her. A sheen of sweat glistened on her face as she regained her breath. "Yes," he replied. "Did you follow them?"

Brenna nodded. "They went down to the river and headed east. I don't think we'll have to worry about them. What's with the Nordans? Where did they come from?"

As Garrick explained what he knew, they both turned at the heartbreaking sound of children crying. He felt his pulse quicken sympathetically. The center of Brenna's brow raised in concern. He collected his *bug-out* bag, as if preparing to leave, but Brenna – completely misinterpreting his intent – put her hands on his arms. "Maybe they're hurt!" she replied, worriedly.

Garrick shook his head as he handed the binoculars to his wife. "Have a look at the porch by the front door."

Brenna gasped as she recognized the horror of the scene. "Merciful God! Those poor kids!"

Thinking that perhaps they were the ones who should be merciful at the moment, Garrick replied, "They won't last long if we don't help them." He put the binoculars back in his bag, took Brenna by the hand and followed the trail downhill.

"You want to take them with us?" she asked.

Three distinct voices reflected the distress of newly orphaned children. "If we leave them behind they'll either starve, get shot, or wind up exploited," he explained. "Do you want that on your conscience?"

She wasn't surprised to hear him say this, as Garrick had always looked after his younger siblings. Yet somehow, his concern seemed oddly out of place in a war zone, where violence reigned and a man's compassion too often vanished like his shadow in the shelter of a cloud. While he'd never felt remorse after killing young Tanarak who'd attacked his platoon, Garrick's paternal instinct to protect Belwyr's children revealed core goodness of character that his wife had long admired.

While Brenna knew that they couldn't save every child from a cruel end, the irony of rescuing Belwyr's offspring pressed heavily on her soul. Yet the spiritual influence of living faith called her doubt and desire for retribution into account. Rescuing Belwyr's children complicated their escape and would dampen their marital conduct, but she believed it a necessary, moral choice.

Praying under her breath, Brenna let go of her resentment, of her desire, and the fear haunting her steps. *"Help us get home,"* she breathed. *"Help me set aside my anger, and have mercy on these motherless children."*

Garrick, speaking in Lithian, called Ciaran by name as he stepped onto the porch and through the front door. Ilia, her face twisted in severe grief and stained in tears, held her father's shotgun awkwardly as he approached. "It's okay," he said reassuringly. "We won't hurt you."

Cedric, the youngest boy, raced forward, threw his arms wide and leaped into Garrick's embrace. He sobbed in great shudders, completely incoherent and inconsolable.

Fiona, his little sister, climbed into Brenna's arms while Ilia put the gun down and buried her face in the Lithian woman's breast, weeping bitterly for a long time, her anguish dampening Brenna's blouse with many tears.

"Where's Ciaran, sweetie?" Brenna asked at length.

Sniffing and blubbering, Ilia pointed toward the play room. "They shot him in the back!" she cried.

A powerful, familiar sensation stirred in Brenna's spirit. "Let me see," she said. Lowering herself to one knee, Brenna set Fiona on her feet and walked down the hall with the sobbing four-year-old clinging to her skirt and Ilia holding her right hand.

Garrick, checking the stairs and outside windows for threats, followed close behind. He stepped into the play room and, noting broken glass on the floor, implored the barefooted children to stay away.

Brenna, eyes widened and heart racing, knelt at Ciaran's side. She touched his neck and felt a very weak pulse. "He's alive!" she announced. Turning to Garrick she added in an urgent voice, "I need the medical kit."

Fumbling through her *bug-out* bag, Garrick produced the first-aid box and handed it to his wife. She washed her hands and her boot knife with rubbing alcohol and paused to pray, *"Allfather, be glorified in me . . . ."*

Ilia held Cedric and Fiona close, watching carefully as Brenna began working on their brother. "Don't hurt him!" Ilia pleaded.

"It's okay," Garrick said reassuringly. "Gunshot wounds are nasty, but she's done this many times and you might not want to watch. Why don't you find clothes to wear and pack a light bag for each of you to carry?"

"Where are we going?" Cedric asked.

"Far away from these horrible people," Garrick replied, kneeling. "Don't be afraid. We'll protect you and care for you. Bring underwear, toothbrushes, and a towel."

Hearing this, and seeing Brenna with her knife in hand, terrified Ilia took her younger siblings into their rooms. The girl struggled to calm herself while packing.

When Garrick returned to his wife, he found her deeply engrossed in her work. "Three shots," she announced. "All through and through. It's a mess and he's weak. There's a lot of internal bleeding. I think at least one round hit a kidney."

"Can you save him?" Garrick asked.

Brenna shook her head. "Only Allfather can save," she replied. "I'll do what I can." Then she ordered the young Lithian to sleep, and he slumped into slumber.

For more than 40 minutes, Brenna desperately dragged Ciaran back from the brink. She cut him open, then found and restored every severed blood vessel. The boy's right kidney had been punctured, but after she stopped the bleeding there, she noticed that his stomach and small intestine had also been ravaged. Brenna used her singular bottle of sterile water to rinse away any acid.

Miraculously, the liver and spinal column showed no damage. As she worked backward – healing flesh with a touch – Brenna used tweezers to pick out small bits of window glass that had entered the wound. When she finished, no evidence of injury remained on Ciaran's body, but he looked very pale. *"Awaken!"* she ordered.

Slowly, his gaze met hers and his eyes widened. "Have you come to torment me?" he asked, weakly.

Brenna shook her head. "No. I'm here to save you."

Ciaran tried to swallow as raging thirst and a metallic taste lingered on his tongue. His body felt unnaturally warm in response to Brenna's touch. "It hurt like fury! I thought I was going to die."

"Not today," Brenna told him, gently wiping the blood from his lips with the young man's shirt. "Allfather is merciful and as long as you keep fighting, I *believe* you can pull through. Trust in Allfather and rest."

"Where is Ilia? Where's Cedric and Fiona?"

They're safe," Brenna assured. "You protected them, but I'm very sorry about your parents."

Guilt welled up in Ciaran's soul and a tear raced down the side of his cheek. "I betrayed you. *Llymah* wanted . . . I deserve to die . . . I'm so sorry . . . ."

"Shh," Brenna encouraged in a sweetly feminine way. "Save your strength. We have to get you to safety."

Ilia, trembling and weeping in the doorway with her brother and sister, moved aside as Garrick brought Ciaran a cup of water. "Who are you?" she cried, sniffing and crying while staring worriedly at the blood all over Brenna's hands, blouse and skirt. A mix of terror and wonder passed over the teenaged girl's face. "How did you bring my brother back from the dead?"

Cradling the young man's head, Brenna brought the glass to his lips and helped him slowly sip its contents. "I did no such thing," she stated quietly. "The power that restored your brother is not mine. It belongs to Allfather, who uses me to do his will."

"You're a witch!" Ilia accused. "*Llymah* was right!"

Brenna stood, spattered in gore and dripping blood from her elbows as she made her way to the bathroom. "You apportion Allfather's power to the agency of darkness," she replied. "Healing is not the enemy's work. You should know better than that."

***

While Brenna washed herself, Ilia supported Ciaran's slow climb upstairs. Garrick carried Belwyr and Eira to the bed he'd shared with Brenna the night before and laid them in a spooning embrace before covering them so the children could pay their last respects.

Brenna offered to pray. The children held hands at one side of the bed, with Cedric whimpering softly and Fiona crying loudly. Garrick listened to his wife skillfully employ her native language, soothing their sense of loss and pain with beautiful, hopeful and forgiving words toward a man who had caused her considerable pain. The mercy and grace that rolled off her tongue wrought hope in the heartbroken orphans solemnly clustered around their parents' deathbed.

When she'd finished, she asked each child to say a few words in honor of their parents, beginning with Fiona and moving up to Ciaran by age. As the eldest boy struggled to process the shock of losing his mother and father, as guilt for his role in betraying Brenna and taking away Garrick's ability to defend her devastated his self-esteem, Ciaran cried until his voice trailed off in raspy wailing that intensified the sorrow of his three siblings.

Every eye shed tears in solidarity. While she could have held onto her anger, relishing in the justice of her enemy's demise, absolution softened Brenna's heart.

Garrick, who knew childhood pain with the intimacy of long experience, quietly left the room during the prayers in order to compose himself. Brenna waited for a little while before she joined him on the stairs.

"Are you okay?" she asked.

"All of this hits a little close," he replied. "Your experience with that man creates complicated feelings about his family. That's not the children's fault, but our problems multiply the longer we stay in enemy territory."

Brenna nuzzled close, her hands caressing as she kissed his earlobe, gently pulling on it with her teeth, then teasing his neck with her lips. "What's your plan?"

Her touch felt electrifying and his heart pounded with longing, knowing that the emotional intensity of combat and of saving a life would heighten her responsiveness. Garrick brought his feelings under tight control. He naturally asserted leadership, sensing the need for decisive and wise action, and setting aside his marital interest to focus on escape.

"I can carry the little one on my back without slowing down too much," he said, turning face her. "The boy – Cedric – can probably manage a third of what we can do on our own, and Ilia should have no trouble keeping up with us. But Ciaran could barely make it up the stairs . . . ."

"Blood loss will do that," Brenna replied. "It will take a few days for him to regain strength."

Garrick shook his head. "We don't have that kind of time. As long as we stay here, we're sitting targets. All these bodies will begin to stink and attract scavengers. If we burn Belwyr and Eira in harmony with your customs, the flames and rising smoke will attract attention.

"Worse, the hunters may report what happened and lead rebel forces back here, looking for revenge. The Nordans themselves might pay us a visit. There's no way we can wait around for Ciaran to get better. We have to find a safe place to hunker down until he can travel."

"So we do the best we can," Brenna replied.

"We can use *Llymah's* research boat," Ilia said from the doorway. "It's strong enough for the sea."

Astonished, Garrick turned toward the girl. "Your father has had a boat this whole time?"

Ilia nodded. "He was a marine biologist. He used it to track the health of fish and oil kelp."

This statement revealed the full extent of Belwyr's treachery and desire to exact revenge on Brenna. She made eye contact with the teenaged girl, who backed away fearfully. "Can you give us a reason to trust you?" the Lithian woman asked.

Trembling, Ilia replied, " I think I'm the one who has to do the trusting. Your bad reputation and mystic power scare me. I worry you might hurt us, like you hurt *Llymah*, or sell us to the slave traders. But if we stay here, the rebels will come back and we will die. I don't like either option; but *Umma* trusted you, so I will too."

***

Garrick expected Belwyr's research boat to resemble a fishing vessel. Having little experience with seagoing craft, he felt disappointed when Ilia took him to a hidden shelter and showed him an inflatable boat with a wooden bottom. It only had seats for three adults and a driver, but once he'd removed all the equipment packed onboard, he felt that everyone and their bags could fit.

"Do you know how to drive this thing?" he asked.

"*Llymah* always let me drive it on the river, but not in the sea," she stated. "He said it was too dangerous."

Patting her on the shoulder, Garrick replied, "That's more experience than I have. Do you think you can to get us into Kameron?"

Ilia swallowed, afraid to disappoint the handsome soldier. No one had ever believed in her capabilities before and it felt a little scary. "I'll do my best," she promised.

Back at the house, Brenna packed dried fish, fresh fruit, bread and jam from the pantry into a cloth bag. Cedric took his father's shotgun and two boxes of ammunition. Brenna said it would be useful for hunting.

Garrick returned, pushing a wheelbarrow loaded with a heavy barrel of methanol that he'd taken from Belwyr's storage shed. "This will have to do."

Brenna frowned. "That stuff burns with a flame you can't see," she warned. "You'll need to be careful."

"I have an idea," he told her. Sensitive to the children's loss, he added, "But let's get the kids away from here. They shouldn't have to watch their house burn after what they've been through today. I don't want to amplify their trauma."

Ciaran sat in the wheelbarrow with the box of food as Garrick pushed him and their supplies to a small pier near the boathouse. Brenna wrinkled her brow when she first saw the craft that Ilia brought out of its sheltered mooring, but Cedric hopped in without concern.

"Stupid girl!" Ciaran complained. "You think you can pilot? We'll drown for certain!"

"Stop it!" Garrick spat in a commanding tone. "We need your help, not your commentary or complaints. Make yourself useful. Sit in the front and guide your sister."

Brenna held her tongue. This was not the way Lithian people spoke to one another, especially in light of the thin credibility her husband had with Ciaran, whose obvious resentment revealed significant mistrust.

Next, Garrick returned to the house, searching through the pockets and packs of the Kurians until he found a tactical terrain plat. Comparing it to his own map gave him an idea of fortified places they should avoid.

Afterward, he searched for a replacement rifle, checked it thoroughly and test fired the weapon. This rebel soldier also had a grenade launcher attachment with four warheads on his belt. He took them all.

Forcing his aching limbs to heft the methanol barrel upstairs, Garrick soaked the linen that covered Belwyr and Eira. He poured a trail of flammable liquid to the sliding door and set the barrel on the porch. When he came downstairs, Garrick opened every door and window to create a strong draft. Standing at a safe distance, he set up the grenade launcher and aimed carefully, firing the weapon at the methanol barrel. Its ensuing explosion created an inferno that quickly spread through the house.

Satisfied that Lithian cultural sensibilities had been met, Garrick trotted back to the dock. Lifting Fiona into Brenna's arms as smoke and flames from the burning house rose above the nearby trees, Garrick felt anxious to depart. "It's time to go," he told them.

Ilia, sniffling and repeatedly wiping her eyes dry, carefully navigated away from the pier and gently pushed the throttle down. The boat plodded through the cove's placid waters, but once she took them around the point, strong and swirling currents near the Attavela's delta drove the boat in circles, pushing it toward nearby rocks.

Ciaran snapped at her. "Stupid girl! We'll hit the rocks if you don't give it some power!"

Garrick's subsequent glower silenced him.

As Ilia gently added throttle, the boat's twin screws effortlessly drove the little vessel through the waves. Her boat handling skills proved more competent than her eldest brother had realized. Ilia cut across the currents in a curving S-turn that speedily brought them around the point and into a large side channel. With the vessel responding well to her input, Ilia's confidence blossomed.

The boat's twin outboard engines burned methanol with no smoke and far less noise than had the old Nordan skiff they'd taken en route to Chīsana Mura. This craft handled the braided streams that flowed through broad mud flats, scores of small, treed islands and gravel banks with ease. Gulls, herons, eagles and corvids took flight as the craft bounced over the turbulent waters.

Shortly after entering the main stream, Garrick noticed a Kamerese patrol boat on an intercept course. He handed his binoculars to Brenna. "We've got company," he warned. "And they're unhappy."

***

Alerted by rising smoke, the pilot of *Shīgōrudo* flew south to investigate. With the morning thunderstorms past and the Mageshima Garrison regaining control in Helsing, the airship's tasking broadened to identify and photograph insurgent positions to aid military planners.

Ensign Kenichi, dutifully working the optical sensors, had read a transcript of Lieutenant Shoyo's report and didn't expect to see anyone alive at the burning house of the Lithian traitor. Yet, movement caught his eye and he adjusted the lenses to get a better look.

"Lieutenant Ido!" he called. "I have visual contact with a man on the scene."

"Is he one of ours?" the officer asked.

"No, sir!" Kenichi replied. "I think it's the man *Tora* team had been watching."

"Are you sure?" Ido inquired. Various Intel resources had successfully tracked the foreigners all the way to Chīsana Mura, but only a single sighting in Helsing had confirmed their presence beyond there.

"I don't know for certain, sir. The round eyes all look the same to me. If I can find the woman, I will know for sure. She is . . . unmistakable."

Lieutenant Ido asked the pilot to circle over the scene. Dangerously close to Kameron, the crew had to ensure they didn't stray into hostile airspace. A well-placed rocket could easily bring the fragile airship down.

Ensign Kenichi used the optical scanner, following the foreign man down to a dock where he picked up a small child and handed her to a woman standing in a speed boat. He clicked the camera. "It's her," he announced. "The *Tora* targets are boarding a boat."

"Photograph its hull identification number," Ido ordered. "I'll see if we can get an asset on it."

***

Esteban Orozco had been touring defensive positions and reviewing battle plans with what passed for leadership among the incompetent Kurians. He felt frustrated by their ineptitude and cowardice, and had already grown weary of their commanders' excuses.

The garrison in Helsing should have been totally overwhelmed on the first day of battle, but the Nordans fought with legendary ferocity. Unable to wrest the radio tower, power plant and key infrastructure in the city from the tenacious colonizers, the Kurian rebels wanted to besiege the town and starve it out, rather than face the fanatical defenders in decisive battle. They didn't seem to understand that losses in war were inevitable.

Esteban believed that the longer the Nordans held out, the more likely they'd be reinforced and resupplied in sufficient quantity to drive the natives into the countryside. He'd heard rumors of food and ammunition falling from the sky by parachute. If the Nordans could do that with material, they could send men that way, too.

Now, observing a burning house and seeing the carnage of routed rebel troops below, he turned to the hunter who'd accompanied him. "You say the Tamarian man and his wife were here. Did you actually see them?"

The hunter shook his head. "They gave us this towel from their guest room," he said, producing the item from a backpack he carried. "They said the woman's in heat. Give it a whiff . . . ."

Skeptical and knowing nothing about Lithian biology, Esteban frowned as he took the towel from the hunter's hand. Startled as the sensual aroma from its fabric quickened his pulse, Esteban's eyes widened. "The family who lived here was Lithian," he stated, handing the towel back. "How do you know it wasn't the wife?"

"My hounds tracked the scent up that ridge," he replied, pointing. "I saw her scientist's wife in the house. The scent on this towel wasn't hers. Dogs don't lie."

Having heard the rest of the story, Esteban suspected that the Nordans may have captured or killed his prize. The latter outcome would work in his favor, but he needed proof of her demise. Turning toward his aide, Esteban ordered a sweep of both ridges overlooking the cove to search for her body. Once his men completed that futile task, he had them search the cove itself.

"Set your dog loose now," the Kamerese consultant demanded. "There are no more traps in the area."

Dutifully, the hound tracked the scent evidence straight to the dock and bayed mournfully.

***

"Cut your engine and prepare for inspection!" an authoritative voice called in Kurian over the loudspeaker.

Garrick, understanding the gist of the message, turned his attention to Ilia. "Stay as close to the colony shore as you can, and don't slow down!" he warned, shouting over the roar of the engines.

Ilia felt conflicted. She didn't like Garrick's tone and resented being told what to do, but the soldiers in the patrol craft were uttering threats and training their guns on the research boat. At length, they fired a warning burst across the bow with a .50 caliber machine gun. "What do I do?" she screamed.

"Just keep going!" Garrick ordered. "Let me deal with them. Did your father keep a camera onboard?"

Ciaran answered for his sister. "In the bin behind the driver's seat. But it's for taking pictures underwater. I don't think it works unless it's wet."

"They don't know that," Garrick replied, rummaging around until finding the camera. He made a scene of pretending to take photos of the patrol boat, their own heading, and their close proximity to the colonial shoreline. Knowing that the Kamerese had been mining Nordan waters, Garrick felt confident in his bluff.

It worked. Noting the camera from the bridge, an officer ordered his men to lift their guns. However, the patrol boat picked up speed, closing the gap until its course was nearly parallel to the one Ilia maintained.

"What do I do?" she asked, her voice betraying panic. "They want me to stop."

"They have no authority on the Nordan side of the river, and they won't want to provoke an incident," Garrick advised. "Stay your course. Can you go faster?"

The girl nodded. "I can, but it's scary. There's a lot of junk in the water, and the boat is fragile. I don't want to hit anything."

"I'll watch for you," Brenna stated. "I'll let you know if I see anything."

Given that Garrick had better visual acuity during the daylight, his wife beckoned him to the bow. Brenna caressed his back while speaking in Tamarian. "You're being rather assertive with the children," she warned. "These little ones are not your soldiers. They don't know you, and you have very little credibility to spend."

He felt she was being unreasonable, but knowing that he didn't like his authority questioned, he set aside his personal feelings and acquiesced to her wisdom. "Okay," he told her. "I'll be gentle."

Ilia pushed the throttles further and the little boat responded instantly, accelerating with impressive speed that left the Kamerese patrol craft behind. She shouted and raised her fist into the air as she passed under the high, rusting bridge linking Helsing to the Kamerese port of Luanca, on the south side of the Attavela's delta.

Ciaran held Fiona as their brother played with the underwater camera in the back seat. The young Lithian admired the way Brenna's breasts echoed the rhythm of the boat skipping over the waves. He remembered the negative comments *Llymah* had made about her, but now that he'd witnessed her conduct, none of those criticisms made sense. He saw kindness in her eyes. She handled his siblings gently, offering comfort and affection to children who were not her own. He heard respect and admiration in Garrick's voice when he addressed her.

Guilt rose in his soul again. *Llymah* had been wrong about Brenna, and Ciaran had been wrong to conspire in betraying her. He should have recognized that her sensuality, stirred by *Y Newen*, wasn't evidence that she'd ever been a loose woman.

Long ago, *Umma* had taught him how Lithian reproductive biology worked. Brenna's intense bond with the Tamarian soldier proved that she'd been a virgin on their wedding night. *Umma* had been right to trust the Velez woman. *Umma* had almost always been right . . . .

But now *Umma* was gone, and he'd never hear her wisdom or know her loving care again. *Llymah* was gone, and Ciaran would never benefit from his counsel and hard work again. The responsibility for looking after his younger siblings now belonged to him, and the burden felt heavy.

"You're crying," Fiona noted, wiping a tear from her brother's cheek. "Are you sad?"

Ciaran smiled. "I'm sad about *Llymah* and *Umma*," he told her. "But I'm glad you're here with me."

Fiona snuggled into his shoulder. "I'm sad too," she told him. "Let's cry together."

***

As the Daystar neared the horizon and the Great Eye rose in the east, the riverine landscape rose toward forested mountains. They'd passed villages, sawmills and canneries along the narrowing river when suddenly, the engines sputtered. Ilia realized she'd not checked the fuel level before departure, but sensitive about her brother's criticism, didn't want to admit it. "I'm losing power!"

"Try the reserve tank," Ciaran recommended.

Ilia turned a T-handle as the engines, starved for methanol, stalled. The boat lost momentum and gradually began drifting backward in the turgid, brown water.

Cedric awakened from a nap, his realization of danger creating distress that compounded his older sister's panic. Fiona complained that she had to pee. Ilia desperately cranked the engines until they roared to life.

Ciaran reached for Garrick's arm. "There's not a lot of fuel in reserve. We can't go much further."

With the Kamerese patrol boat still following at a distance and the river too wide to dash across, the only option that avoided arrest lay on the northern shore. Unable to speak much Kamerese, Garrick didn't think he could reason with sailors whose orders they'd defied.

Quickly consulting his map, the Tamarian soldier skillfully matched the land forms with an upcoming turn in the river and estimated their location. "There's a dock on the near side of that bend," he announced, pointing. "And it looks like there's a town not far inland. We can pick up more fuel in the morning."

Ilia anxiously drove the boat in harmony with Garrick's recommendation until Brenna, looking through the binoculars, noticed a large group of Nordan women and children sitting on the sand near the dock. Kurian men pointing guns stood around them. Chilled at the sight, Brenna gracefully stepped over Ciaran and spoke in Ilia's ear. "I don't think it's safe for us here. Let's find a beach further upstream."

Worriedly, Ilia sped past the scene. With Fiona insisting that she really had to pee, and the Kamerese patrol boat still stalking them, Ilia turned the speedy craft into a shallow back channel north of a narrow island after rounding the bend. She cut the engines and beached the boat on a sandy bank below a prominent rock formation.

Garrick surveyed the area, noting that an overhang in the cliff offered shelter, a commanding view, and could be defended. Still, with night creeping in from the west, danger felt close and he believed that only discretion, vigilance and prudence could keep them safe in this wild, isolated place.

The travelers hid the boat beneath a willow tree near the riverbank and unloaded on the shore. Ilia and Brenna covered its form with cut branches to conceal it from prying eyes while Garrick dug a toilet in the sand for Fiona, who really, really, *really* had to pee.

An eerie quiet, broken only by the gentle lapping of water on the shore settled around them. With no birdsong present, and no wind singing in the trees, the Tamarian soldier scanned for hidden danger in the foliage. He climbed the ridge with his rifle ready, taking time to scout an exit route to the north if a threat advanced from the river. Afterward, he felt satisfied they could rest here for the evening, but uncertain peril would haunt their steps until they crossed the river and left enemy territory.

Despite his rank and influence, Colonel Utemaro had been unable to find free assets that could track the *Tora* targets upriver. A long-planned civilian evacuation should have already taken place, but the logistical demands of such an operation had to wait behind tasks of an urgent military nature. No one had foreseen the scale and scope of the insurgency. No one anticipated the surprise it had achieved. Every military unit available had been devoted to saving the colony until a massive amphibious assault would forever end the Kurian folly.

But the Kamerese, and their Tamarian allies, had to be kept out of the fray. Kameron's huge, modern, and well-commanded land army represented a significant threat. And if Tamarian forces pushed into the northeastern valleys and cut off the rail links with Vathera, methanol supplies would abruptly stop. This would create disaster for the Imperial Navy.

Colonel Utemaro, a contemplative man, knew his nation's hold on the colony depended on handling the uprising without international interference. He'd planned the *Tora* operation to ensure that outcome, and it would be dishonorable to abandon such a noble endeavor.

To that end, the colonel had taken a trip by naval launch from the cruiser *Yakumo*, to Chīsana Mura, where Military Police had detained the colonists accused of offering aid to the enemy. While no evidence of the foreigners had been found, even after a thorough search of the village, neighbors confirmed that women from the family had been seen in the company of a young couple who fit the description of the *Tora* targets.

Tight security included a platoon of Royal Marines stationed along the walls and at the dock. Military Police, who stiffened as the colonel approached, stood around the perimeter. One of them bowed respectfully at Colonel Utemaro approached the front door.

"Sir! We have detained the family at your request. If you'll follow me . . . ."

The colonel entered the house without removing his boots, as the authority vested in his rank permitted trampling on this social convention. Compared to the humid heat outdoors, the generous shading and open windows of the home provided a much more pleasant place to conduct an interview. Colonel Utemaro sat in the honored seat of the tea room. Haruto, the patriarch of this family who looked no more than ten years older than the colonel, himself, stumbled in after being shoved through the portal.

"Honored sir!" the older man said, bowing low in a respectful greeting. "I welcome you to my humble home and offer my household to your service."

Colonel Utemaro gestured to the space on the other side of the serving table as one of the MP's brought in fresh tea. The two men exchanged pleasantries until the colonel brought up the foreign couple and asked to hear the story of the family's acquaintance. He listened politely as Haruto related the tale of the Sea Scorpion, the miraculous healing – which raised the colonel's skeptical brow – and the arrival of the military police.

"Why did you lie to them?" the colonel asked. "I have spared you interrogation, but you should have told the MP's what you've told me. Why did you not do so?"

"They would not listen," the old man replied. "I told the military police that we were sleeping. I asked them to return in the morning, but they rudely refused to comply. It was our intention to let the strangers rest for the evening and send them on their way.

"I'm sure you realize that were obligated by the kindness of these foreigners to extend hospitality. By her treachery against our guests, my daughter-in-law has angered our ancestors and brought shame to my family."

The colonel understood Haruto's sense of social obligation and didn't think it right to punish him for acting in harmony with his ethics. After hearing the truth, he sent the Military Police and Imperial Marines on their way, returned to the *Yakumo* within the hour and found an intelligence report awaiting his attention.

In it, he read that a veteran sergeant in Helsing saw a foreign woman in the company of an armed man fleeing from a rebel mob in the city. This report also contained the transcript of a radio message from *Ōkami Roku*. The last bit of evidence came from *Shīgōrudo*'s photographs, which proved that the foreign couple had taken a Nordan research boat upriver. The airship's commander showed initiative in following the vessel and photographing where it had stopped on the Attavela's north bank for the night.

The best opportunity to recover the targets now lay within the colonel's grasp. He just had to find an asset to retrieve them. Glancing at Liberty Call orders in his inbox, the colonel noted that *Ōkami Roku* was due for leave. Taking his pen out of its holder, Colonel Utemaro remanded that furlough, effective immediately.

***

Caring for children required more time and attention than Garrick and Brenna were accustomed to offering. The adjustment didn't start well. Getting the youngest ones to bathe in the shallow backwater, taking Ciaran to their campsite in the wheelbarrow, setting up sleeping quarters, digging toilet pits and finding clean water kept them busy.

Ilia prepared food in harmony with her habitual role in the family. By the time all these tasks had been completed, the Daystar had fallen to the horizon.

After Garrick entertained everyone with a funny story from his own childhood, he left the loaded shotgun in Ciaran's hands with instructions to defend the site from intruders and keep his younger siblings quiet and occupied. The young man grunted in grudging compliance.

"Will you be gone long?" Ilia asked.

"By nightfall I can't see anything," Garrick reminded her. "There's no point of patrolling in the darkness."

With that, the Tamarian soldier and his wife checked their own weapons before moving out to secure the perimeter in the twilight. While the need to ensure their safety superceded all other considerations, natural affection resumed between the lovers as soon as they were out of sight at the top of the rock formation. Here, a warm and lingering embrace affirmed their mutual commitment, edging dangerously close to passion. Garrick sighed, holding his woman close while listening to the silence of their surroundings. As the quiet persisted, the tension in his shoulders began to relax.

"Thank you for listening to me," Brenna whispered to her husband, running her hand up his back. "The young ones appreciate your gentler tone."

"It's hard to phrase commands without trampling on Lithian sensibilities," he said. "It's easier to give orders."

"You manage with me," she reminded him, gently.

Garrick smiled at her, reaching for his map and compass to shift focus away from his bride's sensuality. The ridge upon which they stood overlooked a narrow, valley to the north that had been gouged by a glacier in the distant past. Small dairy farms dotted the landscape. The tiny town of Trosa lay two miles west of their location.

The rebel map he'd taken showed a military hospital near the town where Garrick hoped to find methanol the next day. The hospital complicated matters. A dirt path from the dock – curiously labeled in Kamerese, *Camino del Contrabandista* – led to a road at the valley's edge. Garrick wondered what thing of value might be smuggled out of a place like this, but didn't give it much more thought.

To the east, old forest covered the long ridge that extended into three major mountain ranges, each progressively loftier. Tamaria lay on the far side of those perpetually snow-clad peaks, far too many miles away for walking. Showing the map to Brenna, Garrick concluded, "We can't hike that distance with small children in tow."

Brenna noted the proximity of additional mountains to the north, which blocked their path to the main rail line linking Tamaria with the coast. The Kurian town of Lyskevar stood near the headwaters of the Skellehaven River, where they'd first entered the Nordan Coastal Colony. That day already felt like long ago.

"Well, we can't keep traveling east," she stated, pointing at the map. "Even if we cross the river at night, there's nothing but forest and mountains in this part of Kameron. We need to head south, up the *Rio de Los Amantes*, to find civilization and catch a train."

Garrick understood her wisdom, but that tributary of the Attavela flowed through Kameron's populous northwestern province, creating an ideal invasion route. The Kamerese Inland Navy patrol boat they'd seen was one of many preventing the conflict across the river from spilling into their country. Pondering this dilemma, Garrick felt trapped. Fleeing a war zone like this sharpened his sense of distance from help and home.

"Maybe we should cross at night," he suggested.

Brenna shook her head, glancing at the moons. "*Princessa* is waxing and *The Handmaiden* is in first quarter," she observed. "By tomorrow evening, your eyes will be nearly as good as mine in the dark for two weeks.

"We also have to think about debris in the water during the freshet, especially in an inflatable boat. You can swim if we have an accident. I'd be okay as long as I'm holding on to you, but Ciaran is so weak he'll likely drown. Ilia might make it, but I don't think Cedric and Fiona will last long in the water. Can you carry them on your back and fight the current at the same time?"

That statement didn't require a response, as the truth she revealed in her question was self-evident. "What about the eclipse?" he asked her.

"That's three days from now," she replied. "It may be our best chance, but we'll be at the ragged edge of our food supplies, and these children are hungry."

"Then we'll have to hunt or fish," he told her.

Brenna left her concern unstated. Neither of them spoke the local language, and with their faces on wanted posters, recognition could prove fatal. Worry that painted her expression revealed underlying fear of being trapped, caught and captured, or killed.

Noting this, Garrick took her hand in his. "Let me think about it," he suggested. "We'll find a way."

The young couple carefully moved through dense ferns growing beneath an aspen and cedar canopy. They hiked along the ridge line to make sure no surprises lurked nearby before heading back to camp.

***

Concerned about the logistics of buying fuel and supplies in Trosa, Garrick discussed options with Brenna, Ciaran and Ilia. "We don't even know if we can find methanol in a town that small. The nearby military hospital concerns me, and I'm beginning to think we're better off to get back in the boat while it's dark and let the current take us downstream."

"What if the river pushes us out to sea?" Ciaran objected. "We need thrust to maneuver. Without the engines, we're taking a big risk."

"That's a good point," Garrick conceded, revealing how little he knew about power boats. "Then our biggest priority is getting more fuel."

"I'm sure a general store will have methanol," Ilia stated. "That's how we've always bought it."

"Let's hope so," Garrick replied. "But we have an additional problem. Neither of us can speak the local language, and our faces are on wanted posters."

"All of us know Kurian," Ciaran said. "Even Fiona could translate basic phrases for you."

"But you're too weak to walk all that way," Brenna interjected. "You need rest."

"I can go," Ilia volunteered. "It'll be okay. I even know the hand signs."

"Hand signs?" Garrick inquired.

Ilia crossed her fingers and tapped her chest twice. "Mist and Soil," she announced in Kurian.

Both Garrick and Brenna recognized the gesture from their encounter with the preteen Kurian boy during their escape from the Seashell Resort. "What does that mean?" Brenna asked.

"It's how people who call themselves patriots let others know they're in on the rebellion," Ilia told her.

Garrick shook his head. "I don't want to put you at risk. The people near your parents' house might know you're not Nordan, but you're slight of build and you have dark hair. It would be easy to mistake you for a colonist."

"I'll put my hair back," Ilia said. "They'll see my ears and know I'm not Nordan."

"Maybe," Garrick stated. "But it's risky. These people are trying to purge their land of anything foreign."

"That includes you," Ciaran countered. "Ilia knows the customs and language. You're better off taking her."

The teenaged girl made eye contact with Brenna for the first time since Ciaran's healing. When the Lithian woman nodded in affirmation, Garrick acquiesced.

Not knowing what the Kurian fighters in Smuggler's Cove would be doing, the closer they came to the camp site, the more vulnerable to discovery they'd become. The security issue nagged at Garrick's soul.

"We should get some rest," he suggested. "It'll be a long day, tomorrow."

***

Brenna struggled to fall asleep after her evening prayers. Lingering heat and high humidity left her skin feeling sweaty and sticky. She normally held Garrick's hand to her breast and fell asleep curled tightly in his embrace – a comforting posture for both of them – but his body felt like a furnace. Physical contact not only increased sweat and discomfort, in her current state it would likely lead to intimacy.

However, lovemaking, with the orphans sleeping nearby, would violate her culture's privacy values. Thus, hungry for Garrick's touch while honoring her upbringing, Brenna stewed in quiet frustration.

When she finally drifted into restless slumber, mind overflowed with memories of suffering, of being forced to watch rape and torture committed against other members of the Tamarian Expeditionary Force's medical staff haunted her dreams. Their shared experience as captives during the Kamerese civil war would soon extend to the Nordan colonists she'd seen on the shore. She knew the humiliating mistreatment awaiting those women as a firsthand witness to such inhumanity. Nightmares stalked her sleep until she awakened to calm her racing heart.

Sometime very late that night, Cedric awakened with a night terror. Garrick, quickly alert and behaving in a gently paternal manner that Brenna had never witnessed in him, took the boy in his arms and offered water to calm him. It worked. Brenna watched her husband hold the child until Cedric grew drowsy again.

Fiona wanted a reassuring cuddle until she fell asleep. Brenna listened as everyone drifted into slumber. She wept silently, again regretting she'd convinced Garrick that they should attend the ill-fated music festival.

Heartfelt prayers, whispered beneath a beautiful panorama of summer stars, bright planets, gas clouds and interstellar dust visible overhead, wrought just enough comfort for the grieving Lithian woman to finally fall asleep. Brenna curled up near Garrick, and though they didn't touch, she felt an ache in her heart and a longing in her flesh that only he could sate.

Hours later, Garrick awakened with purpose pulsing through his heart. With the Great Eye lingering in the west and the earliest light from the Daystar beginning to paint pink the distant mountain ridges, cool air from the sea belied the reality of another sweltering day ahead.

He gazed worriedly at his wife. She almost always arose for prayers before he awakened, but she looked so peaceful he thought it best to let her sleep. Quietly, Garrick pulled out a fresh change of clothes and crept away to empty his bladder and bathe in the cold river.

He returned carrying the speed boat's fuel tin. Ilia, had already awakened and was busily cooking a vegetable stir-fry over his gasifying stove. She smiled prettily.

Cedric poured hot water into ceramic cups for tea, wordlessly offering one to Garrick. Ciaran slumbered blissfully, while Brenna – whose beautiful eyes suffered from exhaustion and stress – held Fiona in a close embrace, gently rocking the child while softly singing an old hymn in Lithian.

"Are you okay?" Garrick asked.

She shook her head. "I didn't sleep well."

Garrick sat next to his bride, took her hand in his and kissed her. Despite her fatigue she looked lovely, and the aroma of her receptive skin intoxicated him. Brenna's rhythmic swaying, her soft voice and maternal demeanor led Garrick's imagination into a future fantasy where she might comfort their own daughter this way.

If only she could carry a child to term . . . .

"Maybe you should stay here and rest," he suggested. "I'll go with Ilia. It shouldn't take long."

His logic made sense and she certainly needed more sleep. Brenna pressed her shoulder into his and rested her head. "I'll pray for you," she promised.

After breakfast, Brenna encouraged Ilia to change into fresh clothes so she wouldn't look like she'd slept in them. Garrick braided the girl's hair to reveal her tapered ears, a skill he'd developed in the past when his sister, Kira, was young. He checked and loaded his rifle before putting Brenna's *Auðr* into his backpack. Handing Ilia the empty fuel tin, he held his wife in a tight embrace while their lips met and lingered. Her hands descended to his backside, while his traced a sensual path down her neck.

Ilia cleared her throat. "Do you two need to be alone for a while?" she asked.

Brenna relinquished her husband, who whispered endearing words into her ear before turning away. Her heart pounded for him. Her lower lip quivered and strong emotion threatened to spill from her eyes.

As they departed, Ilia said, "It's not good for you to leave her right now. She needs you."

"Let the adults worry about adult matters," he replied quietly. "Getting you to safety is our first priority."

With imploring eyes and a tone that testified to her sincerity Ilia added, "I'm just saying that you need to be alone with her. We all understand why."

He nodded, then set the wheelbarrow down, touched his finger to his lips to suggest she stop talking. "What do you hear?" he whispered.

"The dawn chorus, the wind, the river, and the sound of your breathing," she replied in a quieter voice.

"That's good. If the bird calls change to alarm up ahead, we'll know there's trouble. We need to listen . . . ."

She took the hint and fell silent, plodding carefully behind him as the handsome Tamarian wove the wheelbarrow through the trees, Ilia appreciated his faith in her and the way he kept her brother's endless criticism in check. He didn't act arrogantly, like the Nordan soldiers she'd seen. Garrick inspired her confidence as no other man had ever done for her.

Later, after he'd checked the path for threats and they'd descended to the road on the valley floor, she said, "I like the way you treat your wife. I hope I find someone like you one day."

Garrick smiled. "Be like her, and there's a good chance that will happen."

Ilia's tone hardened. "My *Llymah* talked about her all the time. He said she was the prettiest girl he'd ever met – talented and sexy, but treacherous. He showed us the scar on his arm and told us that she'd cut him, and then lied to her father as soon as she realized that he wanted her. *Llymah* said she couldn't be trusted, and warned me that I should never behave that way. We ran when you showed up because we'd seen your photos on the posters, and I was afraid she'd try to hurt him again."

"What he didn't tell you was that she was defending herself from his unbridled desire," Garrick replied. "You ought to know that she couldn't be in *Y Newen* with me if she'd not been a virgin when we married. You also know that forcing sex on a woman is wrong. Brenna's devout and sincere. There's no guile in her at all."

"Okay, you're right," Ilia conceded, still unsure that Brenna could be trusted. "Now that I've seen her in person, I understand why *Llymah* liked her so much. He always complained that *Umma* was too skinny, and I felt ashamed of the way he stared at Brenna's . . . ."

Ilia gestured to her flat chest with cupped hands, falling silent as her teeth pressed into her lower lip. She looked at Garrick for affirmation, then turned her head. "I didn't think Ciaran would live, and then suddenly, there wasn't a scratch on him. How does she do that?"

Garrick shook his head and shrugged. "She runs faster than I can, and recovers her breath in no time. She can see at night when everything looks dark to me. There's a lot she can do that I can't explain. None of that makes her spooky, just different."

"I see UV light, and I run fast, too," Ilia replied. "All Lithians can. But I can't heal wounds, and I've never heard of such a thing before. It's unnatural. I'm afraid to think of what she'd do with that power if she was angry."

"She's a warlord's daughter," Garrick explained. "Brenna learned how to fight with a bow and blade at a very young age. There's no question that she's deadly, but I tell you honestly that my wife is very reluctant to wield a weapon. She'd much rather heal than hurt anyone.

"Her conduct with you and your brothers should lay your fear to rest. She forgave your father without his contrition. From the moment Brenna heard your suffering, she opened her heart to care for you. I've experienced her honorable nature from day one, and I promise that she offers nothing but grace and love to you."

Ilia pondered this before responding. "The respect, kindness and affection between you two is unlike anything I've seen before. You're much nicer than *Llymah* ever was. He bossed my *Umma* around like she was stupid. I always felt sorry for her."

"That's unfortunate," Garrick replied. "The way a man talks about and treats his woman reveals a lot about his character. Your *Llymah's* attitude reflected his heart."

Casting her glance downward, Ilia muttered, "Well, he was wrong about a lot of things . . . ."

Knowing such disappointment from experience, Garrick cautioned, "That may be so, but your life is a gift through his union with your *Umma*. Think about what she admired in him, and remember the good he did for you and your family. Letting anger fester in your soul will make it much harder for you to find the love you desire."

"*Umma* didn't want to move to this rotten place," Ilia said, desperation rising in her voice. "Her family warned her to stay away from him. They didn't want us to leave, and we never heard from them after we came here. When the Azgar invaded, not one Lithian refugee migrated to the Nordan Colony with us. Not one!

"I left all my friends behind, and I'm always having to look after Cedric and Fiona. Ciaran hates it, too. Living here is lonely and boring for all of us.

"And worse, *Umma* felt trapped. She worried about our future and always felt sad, but *Llymah* didn't care. He had an important job. That's all that mattered to him.

"I miss my *Umma!*" she cried. Ilia began sobbing, and her voice rose in rage. "She'd still be with me if we hadn't been trapped in this horrible colony! It's all *Llymah*'s fault! I hate him! I hate him! I hate him!"

Garrick accepted the girl into his arms. "Hold on to your mother's memory," he soothed. "She will always live in your heart. Go ahead and cry. Let the pain go."

Ilia shuddered as anguish and regret trembled through her body. She wept, gripping Garrick's shoulders fiercely, muttering about her mother until the misery of her soul finally ebbed. At length, she let go and wiped her eyes. "I'm sorry," she sniffed. "I don't know what to do. What will happen to us? What's in store for our future?"

Witnessing her regain control, Garrick held his right hand over her heart, a gesture of a solemn oath among Lithians. "I will protect you, your brothers and your sister," he vowed, his gaze locked onto hers. "I will take care of you for as long as you need me. And I know that Brenna is equally committed."

Ilia smiled, her heart fluttering as she held his hand for a moment longer after he'd released it. As he picked up the wheelbarrow and resumed walking she asked, "What will you do with us when we get to Kameron?"

Garrick shrugged. "If we can find your *Umma's* family when we get there, maybe one of them can take you in. There's no guarantee that will happen, as records are scant and the Lithian people are scattered. Brenna's parents live in the northwestern corner of the country, and there may be someone in their social network who knows about your *Umma's* people, if they survived.

"It's also possible that someone may know your *Umma* in Hermosa, the area where Brenna's younger sister, Cassie, lives with her fiancé's family. I hear there's a large Lithian community up there.

"Having said that, I promise you that Brenna and I won't take any action without consulting with you and your siblings, first. As much as we'd like you to stay with us, we don't have room where we live, and getting you into Tamaria won't be easy."

Worried now, Ilia asked, "Why is that?"

"Because foreigners are unwelcome in my country," he replied. "I know it's ignorant and bigoted, but it's the way things are. Brenna deals with nonsense everywhere she goes, even though she's earned the highest honor my country bestows for courage in combat. If it's not her heritage, it's her appearance. That's just the way things are. We'd have to apply for permits, which isn't easy because we have no actual proof that you're orphans."

"Well . . . ." Ilia hedged, imagining the worst. "You won't just leave us, will you?"

"No," he said firmly. "We'll find a way, but I don't have energy to think about that right now. Let's get what we need, get out of here, and we'll worry about tomorrow when it happens. Okay?"

Ilia nodded, feeling uncertain as they passed fenced farms dotted with peacefully grazing cattle where the conflict seemed far away. Some time later, well after the Daystar had risen over the horizon, large tents appeared in a field outside the town. A red battle flag, featuring a double dragon and sword, fluttered in the breeze.

"That's the Old Order flag," Ilia announced, pointing.

Garrick, observing the camp's layout for a moment, gently brought her hand down. "It's a field hospital," he told her. "I saw it on a map I took from a rebel soldier. They've likely set it up here because we're out of artillery range. You'll only see suffering in those tents.

"If we stay focused and don't call attention to ourselves, anyone from that camp who sees us won't give us a second glance. Does that make sense?"

"Okay," Ilia replied, a nervous tremble creeping along the edges of her voice.

In the tense silence prevailing as they marched along, Ilia matched Garrick's soldierly pace without breathing hard or breaking into a sweat, just like Brenna. As they entered Trosa, he offered guidance on how to approach the transaction while they walked.

"I'd rather they didn't see my face, so I'll wait outside," he told her. "Get them to fill the fuel tin first, then worry about food."

"What about money?" she asked.

Garrick paused to remove Brenna's *Auðr* from his backpack. "How much will you need?"

Ilia shrugged. "How much do you have?"

"Don't worry about that," he told her. Garrick pulled out a coin. "What's this worth?" he asked.

"Not much," Ilia replied. "I'll probably need at least ten of those."

Garrick counted twelve coins into the girl's hand. "It's best if you avoid showing money until you've agreed on a price," he suggested, his Tamarian frugality on display. "If you need more, come and see me."

A cobblestone street featuring mature, broadleaf trees – offering shaded relief from the heat – curved through a picturesque cluster of cedar-clad, two storey salt box houses with slate roofs. Small storefronts graced some of these. A bakery, a bike repair shop, a seamstress, the local pub and a bookseller had their doors open.

Not a trace of Nordan architecture influenced any of these establishments. Garrick noted the Old Order flag in several windows before they arrived at a large, single story cedar building with a shaded porch. Household products, tools and barrels labeled in Kurian clustered around a well-worn bench near an open window.

"This is it," Ilia announced.

Feigning boredom, Garrick set his wheelbarrow against the hitching post and slumped on the bench. This gave him a good view of the empty street from both directions, and allowed him to eavesdrop on Ilia's conversation with the vendor, enough of which he could grasp to understand the gist of their discussion.

Glancing through the window, Garrick noted that Ilia combed the hair over her ear with her finger, a clever means of drawing the Kurian vendor's attention to her Lithian features. Her chatter quelled his suspicion, but because she was too young and childlike to sustain his interest, he quickly moved their banter to business.

Ilia gave the bearded blonde man the fuel tin. Garrick heard him question why a girl needed methanol, and how she – a mere child – intended to carry the load. She made an offhand gesture toward Garrick. "My friend has a wheelbarrow. He'll carry it for me."

The vendor turned his attention to the window, through which he could see Garrick's profile. "I've never seen that man around here," he said suspiciously.

"Oh, he's visiting us," Ilia replied.

"Really?" the vendor inquired. "From where?"

"He's from Tamaria," she said innocently, not realizing that she'd just betrayed him.

"Tamaria?" the man repeated, frowning. Then, turning toward a back room he called, "Solveig, take care of this customer. I have to make a phone call . . . ."

That was enough.

In one swift motion, Garrick arose and chambered a round in his rifle. He burst through the door with the barrel pointed at the vendor and his thin, blonde-haired wife. "Don't move!" he demanded.

Ilia, terrified, cowered to Garrick's left while the vendor and the frightened woman raised their hands. All of them felt intimidated by Garrick's soldierly demeanor.

"I need you to take off his belt and bind their hands, back-to-back," he told Ilia. "Make it tight!"

Shocked by the stridency of Garrick's tone, Ilia obeyed. Once she'd successfully tied the couple together, Garrick shut the door and pushed the hapless Kurians into the back room. He understood their whimpered pleas for mercy, but had no intention of hurting them.

Garrick found the telephone, motioned for the couple to sit, then turned to Ilia. "Can you call the Tamarian embassy in Helsing?" he asked in Lithian. "Once you've reached them, you can give the ear piece to me."

Nervously, Ilia complied. The frightened, bilingual child navigated the local telephone network with much greater success than Garrick had experienced in Helsing, and within a minute, she had the embassy on the line.

Once he'd identified himself, the embassy staff routed his call directly to the ambassador's desk. Relief rang through Elfriede Wagner's voice as she spoke. "Losing you and your wife would have sparked a major incident with the Nordans, who assured us of your safety here. Where are you now?"

"In a town called Trosa," he replied, briefly explaining his story.

Ambassador Wagner hedged, but only for a moment. "I know the bridge is closed, but you said something about a boat. Your best course of action is to cross the river and find your way to the Customs Agency in Luanca. Once you're out of the colony, we can arrange papers and transport home for you."

"That may be tough, ma'am. Kamerese patrol craft have already threatened us. Our boat has Nordan markings and tensions are high on the river."

"I understand, lieutenant. If the Kamerese take you captive, we'll work to secure your release. We have contacts in their military who will make sure you're treated well. Get to Luanca as quickly as you can. I'll arrange passage for you to Hermosa by train, where you and your wife can pick up new documents. From there, it's not far to Desperado Falls. That will be the fastest way to get you home.

"Know that your life remains under threat, lieutenant. The rebels and Nordans are looking for you, and the longer you stay in the colony, the more likely you are to be trapped."

***

As Brenna awakened from a nap, the absence of children's noise alerted her to danger. "Ciaran, where are your brother and sister?" she asked.

"They wanted to play in the water where you took them to bathe yesterday," he replied, weakly. "I figured you needed sleep . . . ."

She exhaled sharply, reaching for her boots. "And who's watching them there?"

"I'd have gone down if I could," he told her. "They'll be okay. The water's calm in the back channel and they both know how to swim."

Brenna pulled her sidearm out of her bag, loaded the weapon, made sure its safety was on, and then chambered a round. "I'll fetch them," she stated. "You'd do well to keep that shotgun handy."

As the Lithian woman descended to the beach, she prayed that she'd find the children playing safely. But Cedric raced up the trail, desperation in his expression and terror resonating in his voice. "A Kurian soldier heard us," the boy announced. "He hit me and took Fiona!"

"Oh God, no!" Brenna replied.

"Come and see!" Cedric urged.

She followed him to the shore, where booted footprints led westward, toward the dock where they'd seen Nordan women under guard the day before. "We were just playing the water," he admitted. "He came from over there. I tried to stop him, but he grabbed Fiona . . . ."

"I'll find her," Brenna said, reassuringly. "You'll be safe with your brother. He's waiting for you."

Brenna followed the boot prints around the ridge outcropping for a few hundred yards. With the ground rising sharply to her right, she ventured into the forest as the cove opened below her, scanning the prisoners until she noticed Fiona in the arms of a young woman and a group of girls who'd been separated from the older women. Counting fifteen armed men guarding the captives, Brenna slithered back to their camp.

"I need to find Garrick," she told Cedric and Ciaran. "While I'm gone, I'd be grateful if you'd pack everything up and be ready to leave."

"What about Fiona?" Cedric asked.

"We'll have to fight to get her back," Brenna replied. "But don't worry. Garrick knows all about fighting."

***

"Where's the methanol?" Garrick demanded.

Ilia translated, "It's in a shed behind the store."

Garrick took the vendor by the arm and urged him, along with his weepy wife – who repeatedly fretted that the Tamarian man would kill them both – out the back door. There, Garrick noticed a military truck similar to the one Belwyr had driven.

"Do you know how to operate that thing?" he asked.

Ilia nodded. "*Llymah* taught me."

"Well then," Garrick replied, tight-lipped. "We should be grateful. He may have just saved our lives."

He ordered the couple into the back seat. It couldn't have been comfortable for them, but it was necessary to keep them from running away. Garrick found a bit of rope and secured the man's neck to the front seat head rest. While he filled the fuel tin, Ilia retrieved the wheelbarrow.

After loading the truck, Garrick climbed into the front seat, holding the rope so that any significant movement choked the man. Ilia, who could barely see over the hood, pushed in the clutch and put the truck into gear. She backed into a water barrel she hadn't seen, grimaced, then nervously drove back along the valley floor.

At the trail, she paused to lock the hubs. Using low gear, she drove close to the summit before Garrick asked her to shut the truck off. Ilia activated the parking brake and left the truck in gear, just as she'd been taught.

"Good enough!" he announced.

Loosening the rope off the vendor, he asked, "How much do we owe for the methanol?"

The man, trembling in terror, told Ilia that he didn't want any money. He just wanted to be set free and begged Garrick not to rape his wife.

"I'm not a thief!" Garrick replied. "And I have no interest in your woman. How much for the methanol?"

He gave the man ten coins, set the couple free, returned the belt and truck's keys, and warned them not to retrieve their machine until the next day. Then, he ordered them to run off under threat of being shot.

They did so, with remarkable alacrity.

Ilia turned her head away and kept eyes averted. "You're scaring me," she said.

"No need to fear," Garrick replied. "I'm just responding to a change in the tactical situation. When you told that man I was Tamarian, he intended to report me. You're well aware that my face is on a patriot wanted poster. One phone call to the authorities, and we'd have an army chasing us down. We have to leave before those two get back and tell people with guns they've seen us."

Having witnessed Garrick's fearsome, soldierly aspect, apprehension tainted Ilia's perception. Her self-pitying concern about the demise of her mother faded as a deeper understanding of their plight – the reality that people wanted to kill her benefactors – dawned in her soul. She kept watch over the ridge as he unloaded the wheelbarrow and methanol, then followed behind while he struggled to keep his ungainly load from tipping over.

Brenna appeared on the trail, her light footfalls so quiet that neither Garrick nor Ilia had heard her approach. "We have a problem," she rasped.

Ilia felt her soul sink when she heard Brenna explain that Fiona had been taken. She blinked back tears as Garrick took a pair of binoculars out of his backpack, oriented himself to avoid a reflection from the lenses, and scanned the beach for what felt like a long time.

"I see her," he said. "And I have an idea . . . ."

Quick tactical thinking had served Garrick very well on the battlefield, and hearing his confidence brought hope to Brenna's heart. She'd long admired this trait of his. "What should we do?" she asked.

"I'll get the people with guns looking the other way as you sneak in and take the girl back," he replied. "I can cover you with the rifle, but we don't have much time. We'll be trapped here if we don't cross the river soon."

Together, they hurried back to their camp. Cedric had been busy, having already carried most of their things back down to the boat. Garrick took the heavy methanol tin to the shore, filled the fuel tank, then loaded the half-empty tin into the back of the boat.

"I'll need a signal that you're ready," he told Brenna. "Starting too soon will be as bad as starting too late.

"Take Ilia with you," she suggested. "She'll be able to see what you and the Kurians can't."

***

"Where are you?" Ensign Kenichi muttered to himself. "I saw you last night, and now you're gone." Could they have departed early in the morning? If so, with the Nordans aggressively patrolling the river, they could not have gone far.

"Do you have visual contact?" Lieutenant Ido asked.

"No sir. I do not," Kenichi replied. "But *Ōkami Roku* is approaching the target area."

"Keep looking," Ido ordered.

Scanning the scene again, Kenichi watched a group of armed rebels herding perhaps three dozen colony women toward a rickety dock. *What was this?*

After a closer look, Kenichi's heart skipped a beat. He checked again, just to be sure, before calling the lieutenant back over. "This child belonged to *Daburusupai.* I saw her in the company of the *Tora* targets, yesterday."

Ido set his face into the optic scanner. "Which one, and how can you be sure?"

"Look for the little girl with white and black hair," Kenichi responded. "She's unmistakably Lithian."

Lieutenant Ido raised his face, remembering the child from the photos Kenichi had taken the day before. "I'll contact the colonel," he said. "Keep looking!"

***

Garrick moved swiftly through the forest. He paused for only a moment to check that the path was clear before dashing across, seeking an optimal spot to survey the beach and dock from the crest of its slope. At less than 80 yards across, the entire cove lay within easy range. Better yet, the barren shore offered no cover.

Ilia watched him attach a device to the rifle and slide something that looked – at least to her eyes – like a ball of metal in the shape of a fruit to the end of it. His skill and speed at doing this testified to military training.

Next, he loaded a blank, raised an elevated sight at the rear of his weapon, then lowered the rifle, hoping it had been sighted properly. *But was Brenna in position?*

"Do you see the signal?" he asked, turning toward her, his attention quickening her beating heart.

"Yes," she replied. "There's a snag by the shore that's glowing like a star."

Garrick, seeing nothing out of the ordinary, shook his head in wonder. The advantage of surprise would create confusion. *Perfect.* "You'll want to cover your ears," he warned. "This will be really loud."

Aiming carefully, Garrick fired his first grenade into the sand on the western edge of the cove. The noise, smoke and geyser of sand – roughly 60 yards from his position – immediately drew everyone's attention. Gunfire erupted as the Kurian rebels fired blindly into the forest.

"Let's go! Let's go!" he urged. "Stay down and scoot!"

Ilia, her ears ringing despite having covered them, followed behind as Garrick moved east along the reverse slope of the ridge. He paused, loaded another blank and his second grenade. As four Kurians cautiously advanced toward the forest with their rifles ready for a fight, he aimed and fired his weapon directly at them.

Horror gripped Ilia's soul. Having never seen a body torn into hunks of smoking meat, she gasped and felt her stomach compress involuntarily. The outburst of violence she witnessed distressed her soul to the extent that the Lithian girl bent over and retched on the forest floor.

She felt Garrick's hand pull at hers. "Come on!" he urged. "We have to move!"

Gunfire peppered the sheltering trees. The voices of shouting men and screaming women overwhelmed the sighing wind, singing river and the bird chorus Ilia had heard at dawn. Chaos and terror wrenched the girl's heart until her lips quivered and a tear traced down her cheek.

Garrick, with his left shoulder aching from two grenade kicks, slapped a magazine into the gun before setting up in his third position. He selected burst mode, aimed and fired three rounds into a pair of Kurian rebels.

"How can you kill so coldly?" Ilia asked, her voice edged with bile and trembling fearfully.

"I'm a soldier," he replied in a matter-of-fact tone. "Killing is what I do."

That's when the distinctive sound of Brenna's handgun caught his ear.

***

She'd hidden in the trees near the water's edge for what felt like a long time. Tormented by bugs as she knelt in the shadows, Brenna had her handgun loaded and boot knife ready. She could hear Fiona crying as she watched the unfolding drama impatiently, waiting to take action.

A Kamerese boat named *La Bandida,* traveling against the current near the southern shore, made a rapid course change to dash across the Attavela. As it neared, the armed Kurians stirred, organizing their captives in preparation for departure. Fiona, sensing danger, began screaming in the arms of the young Nordan woman, who put a hand over the child's mouth to silence her cries.

"Come on, Garrick!" Brenna whispered.

The grenade explosion startled her. Many of the Kurian guards panicked as they sprayed the forested area to the west with indiscriminate gunfire. Brenna wanted to run out and snatch Fiona, but three armed men with dread fear etched into their expressions remained behind to guard their captives and prevent flight.

When the second grenade went off, the approaching boat turned into the current while its crew evaluated the situation. Four men uncovered its front deck gun, and panicky women began a stampede from the dock, looking for safety. In response, two of the armed men backed toward the forest and fired warning shots into the air before leveling their weapons at their captives. Amid all the noise and uncertainty, one guard stopped directly in front of Brenna. She could smell his sweat. With a single step backward, he stumbled into her crouching body.

Acting on combat skills that her great-aunt, *Malleah* Shevonne, taught her decades earlier, Brenna slammed the butt of her gun into the back of the rebel's head and jammed her hyper-sharp Lithian blade into his kidney, feeling gut-wrenching dismay at having to kill again.

His companion, noting his absence, called for him repeatedly. Hearing noise as Brenna discarded her victim's weapon, the nervous Kurian insurgent edged northward, near the place where the Lithian woman remained hidden.

She had to confront him. Brenna stepped out of the forest, and in the confusing moment created by her appearance, she shot his trigger hand rather than killing him. He dropped the weapon, clutched his wound and pleaded for mercy.

After tossing his rifle into the water, Brenna raced into the crowd with her handgun drawn, confronting a terrified Nordan woman who'd been trying to comfort the Lithian child. Fiona wriggled away, into Brenna's embrace.

***

Few of the Kurian rebels had used weapons prior to the insurgency, even for hunting, and it showed. Garrick, firing methodically, dropped them one by one, luring the survivors toward his position and away from his wife.

He saw Brenna's red shirt appear in his peripheral vision and trained his rifle to protect his beloved, bursting the brain of an insurgent who'd heard her gun fire and raised his weapon. Confused and frightened as the battle against an unseen enemy appeared to turn against them, the surviving rebels began racing for shelter in the forest.

With that unexpected outcome, Garrick scurried westward on the reverse slope of the ridge. He stopped to observe the chaos, then fired his rifle twice more.

Brenna and Fiona had vanished into the forest as *La Bandida* moved into the dredged cove. Someone on the front deck turned a heavy machine gun inland and began shooting into the trees.

"Go back to the camp!" Garrick told Ilia. "Find my wife and tell her to get everyone on the boat. This is getting ugly!"

Changing positions again, as .50 caliber bullets snapped through the surrounding foliage, Garrick loaded another blank and his third grenade.

***

What was this? An armed Kamerese boat in Nordan waters firing onshore? Ensign Kenichi immediately told Lieutenant Ido, who used the radio to hail the *Sumida*, an Imperial Navy patrol vessel assigned to transport *Ōkami Roku* to the area.

"Asset should be in visual range," Ido stated.

Kenichi could see the Nordan vessel's two-inch front guns train onto the Kamerese boat while awaiting permission to open fire.

However, something unseen exploded aboard the deck of the foreign craft and its machine gun fell silent. Men on the vessel began firing into the forest with rifles. People in the cove ran for cover as the airship banked hard to avoid flying into Kamerese territory.

During the turn, Kenichi caught a glimpse of a petite woman wearing a red blouse, running rapidly along the riverbank with a child on her hip. "Contact!" he announced. "I found the *Tora* woman!"

***

"Please, stop crying!" Brenna pleaded in Lithian as she dashed along the path leading to their camp. "You're safe with me. I won't let anyone hurt you. I promise!" Behind her, several Nordan women followed the sound of Fiona's voice. Brenna worried that armed rebels might be a short distance behind them, and that she'd have to kill again in order to escape. It all seemed out of control.

Ilia scurried down the trail. She made eye contact with her sister and opened her arms to take Fiona from Brenna. "Garrick says we have to go!" the girl stammered. "My brothers are behind me."

Fiona quieted in her sister's arms. Brenna pointed her weapon downhill. "We go together," she stated.

Ciaran, holding onto Cedric for balance, shuffled toward them as quickly as he could. "Cedric already cleared off and loaded the boat," he told Brenna. "We can leave any time."

Where was Garrick?

"Alright," Brenna stated. "Let's go."

She and Ilia scurried to the beach, where Brenna's handgun discouraged a cluster of Nordan women from approaching the hidden speed boat. Moments later, Ciaran arrived with his shotgun. He stood guard while Cedric and Ilia climbed into the vessel. The older girl expected the Lithian woman to board next.

But she didn't.

The Nordan women begged Ciaran to let them board, but he swore and pointed his weapon at them. As gunfire crescendoed in the west, they fled east, along the shore.

Brenna helped Ciaran into the bow. She could see *La Bandida* turning out of the cove. Once it got underway, they'd have little time to escape. Desperately, she scanned the surroundings for Garrick.

He wasn't there, and Brenna's heart pounded in desperation. What if he'd been hit? What if he was hurt? She couldn't rationalize leaving him behind as she pushed the boat from beneath the sheltering tree.

"Start the engines," she told Ilia. "If I'm not back in five minutes, or if there's any threat to you, take off without us. Go to Luanca and tell them your story."

"We need you!" Ilia lamented.

"Then pray for my safety," Brenna replied.

***

Sumida, an old Imperial Navy vessel, steamed upriver to intercept and impound the Kamerese slave ship. With its two-inch cannon trained on *La Bandida*, a warning to yield – uttered in accented Kurian – blared from its loudspeaker.

Ilia felt panic rising in her heart, watching helplessly as *La Bandida* turned into the shallow back channel where she waited. Someone on the deck shouted at her using language she didn't comprehend, but when he pointed his rifle, she understood the message.

Much to her siblings' dismay, Ilia turned the speed boat around and pushed the throttle down to avoid the impending threat. As bullet impacts splashed into the water, one struck the cowling of an engine and ricocheted, glancing off her cheek before it tumbled into the river.

While the injury didn't hurt, the sight of blood on her hand shocked Ilia into greater urgency. Turning left, then right, she presented a difficult target to hit, and the twin outboards quickly left the slave ship far behind.

Back on shore, Brenna paused on the trail to watch the speed boat vanish around the island. She felt trapped and alone. With a prayer on her lips she pressed onward until heated, Kurian-speaking voices gave her pause.

Moving into the trees, she advanced stealthily, quietly closing in on three Mist and Soil militia men armed with automatic weapons. The men stood around Garrick, arguing as he knelt on the ground with his hands held aloft. His shirt, bloodstained at its collar, drew her gaze to a gash on the right side of his neck.

When one of the men chambered a round and pointed the weapon at Garrick, her devotion to him compelled her to act. Outgunned, Brenna needed an advantage to tilt the odds in her favor. Discarding her bloodstained blouse, she quietly edged onto the trail with the gun behind her back, willing her Lithian camisole to loosen and become sheer enough to draw male attention.

"Hey boys! What are you doing?" she asked aloud, distracting the Kurian rebels, who'd been convinced that they'd cornered their quarry alone. Her lovely face, azure eyes and dark, fluttering hair shifted their focus entirely.

Stunned and gawking stupidly at her beautiful, feminine form – wrongly believing that the little woman did not represent a threat – the men lowered their weapons in near unison. Advantage gained, Brenna pulled her gun forward and coldly fired three lethal, close-range shots into the hearts of Garrick's would-be killers.

Momentarily stunned by the horror of her deceptive deed, Brenna locked her eyes on the fallen soldiers, the shock on their faces burning into her memory. Though her brutality shook the foundations of the Lithian woman's soul, she had no time for lamenting.

Garrick leaped to his feet, grateful that she'd saved him. "My brave, beautiful bride!" he whispered, reaching for her and planting a kiss on her lips. "Thank you!"

"You're hurt," she observed, wiping the blood away from his neck. "Let me help you."

"It's nothing," he claimed. "We need to go!"

Brenna stood on her toes. With a soft, lingering kiss, the gash from a broken branch marring Garrick's neck vanished. Warmth radiated from the place where her lips met his flesh, as it had the first time she'd kissed him.

Voices and pounding boots on the trail behind them compelled action. Garrick picked up a dead soldier's rifle while his wife willed opacity and full support from her camisole again. As Mist and Soil Militia members swarmed up the hill from the north, the shouted commands of their sergeants warned the lovers to flee. Brenna pulled her husband down the trail, her fleet and graceful steps crossing the beach near the placid, empty back channel.

"Where'd they go?" he asked, breathlessly.

"Ilia had to lose the slave ship," Brenna replied as guilt for killing threatened to spill from her eyes. "But she's terrified, and I'm sure she'll come back to get us."

And sure enough, the speed boat reappeared from the west, pausing near the spot where the Fiona and Cedric had been playing. Brenna splashed into the water. Seeing Ilia's injury, she climbed aboard and gave the frightened girl a healing kiss. Ilia flinched as Brenna's lips spread supernatural warmth into the maiden's cheek.

Four Nordan soldiers, advancing eastward from the cove, caught Brenna's attention. Feeling vulnerable in the fragile boat, Brenna gestured frantically for her husband to join them. She prayed for protection, understanding that Nordan soldiers were far more skilled with their guns than Kurian irregulars.

But members of the Mist and Soil Militia appeared at the top of the trail, their weapons targeting the Nordans, below. Garrick splashed through the shallows and threw himself aboard the boat as stray rounds peppered the stirring waters, dangerously near the inflatable craft. Raising his rifle, Garrick returned fire to force the Kurians down as the Nordans retreated toward cover. Doing this bought a few moments for their escape.

"Turn around!" Garrick urged Ilia. "Go! Go! Go!"

***

Wet and trembling, Brenna curled into Garrick's embrace at the back of the speed boat and briefly offered her lips to his. "Are you okay?" he asked.

Brenna shook her head, but didn't speak. The lovers snuggled together as she began to cry.

Seeing this, Ciaran called Fiona over. He cradled her against his shoulder and turned toward the bow. "Let's help Ilia look for things in the water," he encouraged.

Cedric, noting the lovers' behavior – mild as it was in the presence of the children – turned his head away, respecting their privacy without being asked to do so.

"I snuffed out four lives today," Brenna sniffed in Tamarian. "After I swore that I would never kill again, I failed, and failed, and failed, and failed . . . ."

Holding her close, Garrick let her express frustration without comment or judgment, knowing that her distress reflected the quality of her character. Arguing over the necessity of taking life would neither change her mind nor make her feel better.

Garrick, convinced that she'd acted with justifiable intent, had listened to his captors arguing about how best to collect the bounty on him. He also believed it was likely that Fiona would have been sold to some sick pedophile, had Brenna had not intervened. He soothed her pain with proximity, little kisses and gentle caressing as Ilia drove the speed boat around a forested island sheltering the back channel. While engine noise stifled Brenna's whispered, penitent prayers, the Lithian woman *believed* her cries were heard, even if she didn't utter them aloud.

Ilia turned into the Attavela's main current, where the Imperial Navy's river patrol craft loomed ahead. Its twin screws churned the muddy water into froth as the 160-foot vessel steamed in pursuit of *La Bandida*. Seeing the danger that *Sumida* presented, Ilia glanced over her shoulder and asked Garrick, "What do I do?"

Noting that the warship had a single machine gun mounted aft, and thinking the two-inch turret on its bow would be harder to use against a much more agile craft, Garrick advised, "Do what you can to stay in front of it."

But the *Sumida*, sustaining nearly 20 knots, closed the gap between the two vessels much faster than Ilia anticipated. The patrol craft turned to its starboard side, opening the angle between its heading and the speed boat. Without warning, its main gun thundered into action.

Wrenching the steering wheel to the left, Ilia jammed the throttles down. The engines responded with a burst of power that bounced the little vessel across the waves at the ragged edge of control, yet Ilia's quick reflexes and piloting experience overcame all danger as she trustingly followed Ciaran's pointing hand to avoid debris.

The round from *Sumida's* main gun arced overhead and splashed into the river more than a thousand yards distant. Garrick took out his binoculars and scanned the area upriver. The Nordans were targeting *La Bandida,* which had crossed most of the river and now lay well within Kamerese territory – an escalation that could lead to outright war between two very powerful nations.

Their next round struck the slave ship in the stern, penetrating below the waterline and into the engine room. Its explosion tore off the back end of the Kamerese vessel, flooding it with cold, murky water. *La Bandida* spun in the current, wallowing out of control as its fuel tanks erupted. Men leaped into the river just before the *Sumida* fired again, shattering and sinking the crippled craft.

Cedric – fascinated by the destruction – shouted excitedly as he witnessed the battle, while Fiona felt terrified by the roar from *Sumida's* gun. She screamed and cried. Ciaran soothed her as best he could, but as Ilia desperately weaved the research boat right and left, the exaggerated motion she created made him sick. Ciaran quickly put down his little sister, leaned over the side and retched violently.

Only the Nordans knew that *Shīgōrudo* remained overhead, vectoring Imperial Navy assets toward their targets. Also, the Special Forces commandoes they'd seen on the shore had a bigger, short-range speed boat of similar design to Belwyr's, which suddenly appeared to Ilia's starboard side. Unlike the research craft, this one had a mounted machine gun, which Sergeant Modo used to fire a burst well in front of the smaller vessel.

But Ilia proved to be quite clever. She slid her father's boat into a hard right turn that very nearly flipped it over. Despite a wobbly moment, the teenager regained control as her father's little craft raced behind the *Sumida*.

Sumida's passage soon revealed the targeted vessel again. Lieutenant Shoyo issued a warning over his boat's loudspeaker system. "You are ordered to stop by the authority of the Nordan Imperial Navy," he announced. "Refusal to comply will result your destruction."

"What do I do?" she asked in a panic. "They'll sink us if we don't stop!"

Garrick, who'd been scanning the surroundings through his binoculars, noted that the fireworks from *Sumida* had already attracted the attention of two Kamerese patrol ships steaming upstream roughly 500 and 800 yards to the west. "Go straight across the river," he told her. "Don't worry about the Nordans right now."

Brenna dried her eyes. "What are you thinking?"

Fumbling around in his *bug-out* bag, Garrick found an undershirt that needed washing. "We're trapped between an enemy and an ally," he told her, gripping the back of Ilia's seat as stood. Garrick held the shirt aloft and waved it vigorously. "Who's going to treat us better?"

Lieutenant Shoyo, observing this with incredulity, yelled at the boat's pilot. "Catch that boat and cut it off!"

As this collision of national wills played out on the broad waters of the Attavela, gunfire from the twin turreted *Fuerta Defensor* arced in front of the *Sumida*, forcing the vessel to rapidly change course. Her captain ordered her to flee for cover behind a large island near the river's northern shore.

Fuerta Defensor, one of a new class of littoral combat ships – larger and much faster than any river vessel deployed by the Imperial Nordan Navy – could nearly match the speed of Belwyr's research boat. Her modern armaments rivaled the power of oceangoing frigates and had been designed to counter Nordan naval threats along the Kamerese coast.

Her sister ship, the *Estrella del Norte*, held a bearing at the edge of the border, daring the Nordans to challenge her. She fired three rockets at *Shīgōrudo*, which exploded short of their target, but pushed the airship's flight path northward, over colonial territory.

With a closing speed approaching 40 knots, *Fuerta Defensor* passed in front of Belwyr's speed boat a little more than 20 seconds later. Her heavy machine guns targeted the Special Forces craft, whose pilot engaged in evasive maneuvers to save his vessel and crew.

Frustrated by his inability to successfully recover the targets, Lieutenant Shoyo ordered, "Abort!" In response, the boat's pilot set course for the *Sumida*.

Half a minute later, *Estrella del Norte* slowed as Ilia guided her father's speed boat alongside the larger vessel. Garrick secured a line tossed down by one of her crew. A few minutes later, an onboard crane lowered a rescue basket which could hold two adults. Garrick made a show of dumping their weapons, one at a time, into the water before climbing into the basket with Cedric and Ciaran, ensuring that no one on the Kamerese warship considered them a threat. His heart pounded fearfully, and his imagination raced to think of what to say as the crane lifted him and the orphaned boys up to the ship's deck.

Brenna, Ilia and Fiona took the next basket. When she arrived on deck, the Lithian woman wordlessly handed her boot knife to a Kamerese sailor, hilt first, then crossed her arms over her breasts and moved behind Garrick for protection against the leering she expected.

A slender, clean-shaven Chief Petty Officer named Diego Delgado approached Garrick with questions in Kurian. Annoyed that his captive kept referring to the skinny Lithian girl for translation, Delgado tried addressing Garrick in vulgate. Satisfied that the foreigner could understand and speak directly to him, Diego listened to the man's testimony with rising skepticism.

While Garrick's hayseed accent and soldierly demeanor underscored the truth of his identity, Delgado suspected the Tamarian wasn't revealing the full truth. "That's a wild story," the Kamerese officer stated. "If you'd really wanted to go to Customs, you'd have crossed the river near Luanca in your boat. Or, you could have walked over the bridge. If you'd done either of those things, we wouldn't be having this conversation."

"Your government closed the bridge," Garrick replied. "And I only received instructions from my embassy in Helsing by telephone this morning. You're speaking to an ally who fought for your country during the civil war. This conversation should be a lot more cordial than it is."

"Prove who you are and I'll believe you," Delgado retorted. "Until then, you're in no position to make demands on me, or my country."

Turning to his subordinates, Delgado spoke in Kamerese. "Take the captives to the brig. Let the woman stay with the young children. Keep the others separate."

Garrick objected, but Delgado ignored him and returned to the bridge. Forced to comply at gunpoint, the Tamarian soldier grudgingly descended a steep staircase and followed a narrow hall aft, through several bulkheads, until they arrived at the ship's brig.

The detail sailors treated Brenna with gentlemanly disinterest, presuming she didn't represent a threat. Locking his eyes on hers with a calm, strictly professional demeanor, one of the sailors placed Brenna, with Fiona and Cedric, in the first cell – a tiny enclosure with a steel lattice door that had a toilet, but no bed. The Lithian woman sat on the cold floor, processing sorrow as she cradled Fiona. Fearful Cedric, whose tendency to talk incessantly fell silent in the presence of the armed men, sat next to her, leaning his head on his rescuer's shoulder to seek her feminine comfort.

Ciaran and Ilia went into cells of their own. Garrick glared at his captors as they slammed the lattice door shut and walked away. He cursed, gripping the steel angrily, feeling betrayed, feeling trapped.

"I miss my *Umma*," Cedric complained. "I hate this place. I want to leave . . . ."

Sensitive to the boy's frustration, Brenna took his hand in hers. "Tell me about your mother," she recommended. "What was she like?"

His voice, edged with emotion, cracked hoarsely as he spoke. "She was always nice. She never had a mean thing to say about anyone. *Umma* took care of us, even when she felt sad."

"It sounds like she was a very good mother," Brenna stated. "I love my *Umma,* too."

Ignoring her, Cedric continued his complaining. "I wish we hadn't left Illithia. Everything was better there. We were happy. We shouldn't have moved to Kuriah!"

Brenna understood, but they were speaking in Lithian and cultural convention demanded that she not let that comment stand. "You and your family got away before the killing reached us in Shirak," she told him, remembering the terror of those days so vividly her hands began trembling. "The Azgar slaughtered everyone without mercy. It was the worst experience of my life."

"You were there?" Cedric asked, astonished.

Brenna nodded gravely. "You're lucky that your *Llymah* had the foresight to leave when he did. He spared you and your family a lot of sorrow."

"Why did you stay?"

"It took time to get people out," she explained. "My *Amair's* army stood with others to keep the Azgar at bay until our families could escape. I stayed behind to guard the portals, so enemy soldiers couldn't get through."

Cedric should have respected Brenna's condition and kept his hands to himself, but out of curiosity, he drew near and touched her neck with his finger. "Is that how you got the scar?"

Flinching, Brenna pulled away. "No," she explained, pushing the memory away to calm her racing heart. "That happened later . . . . Let's talk about happy things."

And for more than two hours, they exchanged pleasant stories. Their laughter ended abruptly as three armed sailors accompanied Chief Petty Officer Delgado into the brig. Intrigued by the aroma from Brenna's cell, he lingered there, staring longer than was polite – earning a hard glare from the Lithian woman – before moving over to where Garrick had been confined. "You have friends in high places, lieutenant," the Kamerese officer stated, motioning to have the prisoners released.

Diego glanced back as Brenna emerged from her cell with Fiona clinging to her skirt. The boy, also fearful of the stern-faced sailors, hid behind his eldest sibling. "We've moved your belongings to the upper foredeck, where all of you will be confined for now," Delgado told Garrick. "We also found a grenade and a combat knife in your belongings. You'll not be getting those back."

"What about my wife's boot knife?" Garrick asked. "It has sentimental value to her."

Wrongly confident that the little woman couldn't hurt anyone, Diego nodded. "I'll see that it's returned. We're keeping you under escort as long as you're aboard, as we can't have you and the children wandering around the ship while we're on alert. We've arranged for a launch to take you to Luanca when we reach the estuary."

Then, lowering his voice, Delgado added, "You're a soldier, so I'm sure you understand that we can't have unescorted females onboard – especially a woman in your wife's, uh . . . condition. We don't want any incidents."

"Then make sure nothing inappropriate happens," Garrick replied. He extended his left arm as Brenna slid into his embrace. Ilia moved to his side, seeking protecting from the implied hostility of the naval officer.

***

Shelling of coastal defenses had been going on without respite since shortly after daybreak. The necessity of moving beyond the range of Nordan naval artillery prompted Esteban Orozco and his retinue to visit the field hospital east of Trosa. There, he heard an intriguing report from the local Old Order commander, who recommended that Esteban interview the owners of Trosa's general store.

"They told me a wild story about a foreign soldier and a Lithian girl holding them at gunpoint," the commander said.

Esteban questioned the couple to confirm the tale. The part about a Tamarian seemed plausible, but their description of his companion couldn't be right. Brenna Velez was an adult woman, not a preteen girl. Also, Esteban knew that Lady Velez couldn't speak Kurian.

Confident that his elusive targets had to be nearby, Esteban intended to personally kill them, if necessary. He boarded a rickety, rattling truck up the road up to *Cala del Contrabandista*, where he learned that yet another disaster involving patriot forces had recently taken place.

In this incident, a group of local fighters had panicked and fled when attacked, scattering valuable slave captives whose sale would have financed more artillery and ammunition for the insurgency. By the time reinforcements arrived – in this case, Mist and Soil militia men from Trosa, alerted by the couple who ran the general store – the damage had already been done.

Worse, a witness confirmed that the Nordans shelled and sank *La Bandida*, a loss that complicated fund raising. Esteban's connection with the slave trade had been conditioned on discretion, which he'd now lost.

Heat, humidity and biting insects provided an appropriate backdrop of torment to Esteban's misery. He followed tracks left by the since recovered truck to a spot on the reverse slope of the ridge, then marched down to the beach with his men. Every slain Kurian rebel strewn along the shore, in the sand, and near the forest, had met his demise in a similar manner. With the exception of a group who'd blown apart by a grenade, every one of these men died in a single burst of well-aimed rifle fire.

What a waste!

Fernando, one of Esteban's men, called him over. "I found a survivor," he said.

A juniper thicket, bordered by wild grape and sword fern, grew in the shade of very old cottonwood trees, whose pale green leaves fluttered in a gusty breeze near the shore. Large red cedars, rising on the hill behind the cottonwoods, showed damage from .50 caliber gunfire. Here, Esteban met a trembling young patriot who'd wrapped his blooded hand with his shirt.

"What happened here?' Esteban asked.

"They were all over the place!" the young man said, frightened of retribution he felt certain would come. "They said this was easy duty, guarding a bunch of women. But they came for us with grenades and rifles. We fought back, we really did, but there were too many of them."

"What happened to your hand?" Esteban demanded.

"This lady came out of nowhere and shot me with a handgun," the terrified man replied. "About an hour earlier I'd heard kids playing and found a little girl over yonder. They told us that the young ones fetch a good price, so I brought her here. But I didn't know her mother would come after me like that."

"This girl was Nordan?"

The young man shook his head. "No. She had slanty eyes like they do, but pale skin, and naked as the day she was born. She had these pointy ears and two-toned hair. Can't say I've seen anything like that before."

"And what did the mother look like?"

"She was a little, dark-haired, blue-eyed thing with nice tits, and a nasty scar on her neck," the patriot said. "She killed Lukas with a blade in the back like an assassin, shot me in the hand before I could shoot at her, then went after her daughter and ran off. I tell you, that girl could move for being such a wee thing!

"Meanwhile, everyone else was trying to beat back the attack. The slave boat gave us covering fire, but it was too late by then. When the Nordans showed up, I hid."

"Did you see a blonde man with this woman, a husky foreign soldier with short cropped hair?"

The patriot shook his head. "Just her, and then the Nordans. They even brought a battleship. I didn't know a boat that big could come this far upstream."

His description fit the Velez woman, and the merchant's encounter with a Tamarian man meant that her husband had been here, too. They likely picked up the children from the Lithian traitor's house, which explained why a Kurian-speaking girl would be in Trosa. Little ones should slow them down, but damn the meddling Nordans for coming to their aid! And now, where had they gone?

"You need to get that injury treated," Esteban told the wounded soldier. Turning to Fernando, he ordered, "Get that hunter we had at the burnt house out here. See if his dog can pick up the woman's scent."

Then he sent the rest of his men on a search of the immediate surroundings, looking for clues of a Nordan unit operating in the area. What they actually found were four firing positions overlooking the beach, each littered with Azgar - stamped shell casings.

A few minutes later, the Kamerese mercenary discovered a grisly scene. Three Mist and Soil guards lay dead, from single shots, straight through the heart. The size of the bullet impacts suggested a handgun. Esteban shook his head. How had the Velez woman managed to get close enough to kill three armed men?

Javier, youngest of his Kamerese volunteers, found a jammed Vatheran rifle with a grenade launching attachment laying nearby – likely the source of the grenade attack and shell casings. Esteban concluded that the Tamarian soldier and his Lithian wife were entirely responsible for the incident.

If only the Kurian patriots could fight like that!

***

Colonel Utemaro meditated in his shipboard cabin to calm his frustration. The *Tora* targets eluded capture again, and he would likely face censure for his failure to successfully complete his mission. However, as his mind processed the reality, an idea of pure genius struck him.

He pulled down his writing table and composed a note to the acting Colonial Chief, requesting that he contact the Tamarian embassy in Helsing with the following message:

"Dear Madam Ambassador;

We are pleased to inform you that our forces have successfully escorted Tamarian national, Lieutenant Garrick Ravenwood and his wife, Brenna Velez, to safety aboard the Kamerese littoral warship, *Estrella del Norte*.

We thank you for notifying us of the peril they faced and assure you that we made every effort to ensure their safety during the insurrection."

He requested that the acting Chief sign the message and have it delivered to the Tamarian embassy. In doing this, he absolved the Nordan Coastal Colony Authority of any responsibility for the well-being of these pesky foreigners, now in Kamerese custody. It also insulated him from any political fallout, as his action protected the reputation of the Empire.

With that incident behind him, the colonel devoted his full attention to the planned amphibious assault and imminent recapture of the Coastal Colony.

***

"I'm not hungry," Ciaran said. "I'm not feeling well."

Brenna worried about the young man's welfare, encouraging him to eat so that his body could rebuild its strength. "It will take time for you to get back to normal," she told him. "Why don't you try a little fruit?"

Ilia – who'd developed an interest in hovering near Garrick – shared a sandwich with Fiona. As Brenna drifted to the railing, she felt her husband's strong hands slip over her arms and wistfully dreamed that they could leave all their troubles behind and share uninterrupted passion in peace.

"Are you feeling better?" he asked in Tamarian.

Brenna nodded. "I just need time to pray."

"Do you want me to leave you alone?"

She shook her head and pulled herself close. A subtle cedar scent lingered beneath Garrick's irresistibly masculine aroma. "I want you with me. I need you near."

Ilia, noting the lovers' behavior, took the hint and retreated – pulling Fiona along – without comment.

Feeling the tension in his wife's left shoulder, Garrick moved behind Brenna to massage away her stress. "You fret about killing because you have a good heart. I know you dream of peace. I admire that in you."

Brenna sighed, finally admitting a truth she'd kept hidden in her soul for a long time. "I wish there was a more noble purpose to our presence here than fulfilling my need to perform, to be seen and respected. I'd like to have done something more important than gratifying my desire to win another piano competition . . . ."

Garrick glanced at the orphans over his shoulder. "Belwyr's children were unlikely to survive on their own. Ciaran, in particular, would have died without your help. Isn't that more important to your sense of purpose than taking first place at a music festival?"

Brenna paused to think. "You've spoken truth," she quietly conceded at length. "My *Amair* says that good people serve as a check on evil, yet I can't honestly say that everything I do stems from pure and honorable motives. I know myself well. I have grave doubts."

"Ours is an imperfect world," he replied gently. "You ask a lot of yourself when you have little time for moral clarity. You expect to do right in the heat of every moment, where a quick reaction is the difference between life and death. But I understand your striving. Your turmoil reveals a nobility of character. I don't have the answers to any of this, but whatever you walk through – whether disappointment or triumph – I'll be at your side. My support for you is unqualified."

Feeling affirmed, Brenna pressed her body close, renewing courage from her husband's support and the strength of his embrace. She could always count on his steadfast advocacy.

Longing for seclusion, the amorous couple simmered in mutual desire as they lingered at the rail. Garrick trembled in expectation, anticipating Brenna's passion, her yearning for his intimate touch, the way her sensitive body responded to his lips and fingers. Warm wind, the roiling current, and the sound of froth churning at the ship's bow mingled with the sensuous aroma of her tanning skin, a hypnotic combination that belied the danger they faced.

Neither of them realized that one of the sailors leering at Brenna from the flying bridge belonged to *Los Patrones del Estado*, the shadowy organization that planned and carried out a terror bomb attack against the Tamarian palace gate several weeks earlier. While Brenna and Garrick had not been the target of that incident, they'd been present and narrowly escaped injury.

This clandestine consortium of wealthy landowners, bank executives, businessmen and intellectuals, desired an aggressive policy to contain foreign encroachment on Kameron's borders. Long aggrieved by the establishment of colonial holdings north of the Attavela, *Los Patrones del Estado* lavishly supported the Kurian insurgency in the hope of accessing regional resources and new markets after the overthrow of Nordan authority.

Without an armed force of their own, this society of Kamerese elites depended on mercenaries like Esteban Orozco and Able Seaman Santiago Méndez, who now craned for a better look down Brenna's camisole as the Lithian woman spoke to her husband, below. Santiago's father owned a large estate and two canneries whose profitability had declined because of Nordan overfishing.

Able Seaman Méndez recognized the lovers from a photo he'd seen while visiting home on a recent leave, and knew that these two were the targets of an operation to drag Tamaria into the upcoming war. Santiago had excused himself and dutifully sent a message to the *Patrones* commander – using the secure ship to shore transmitter – notifying him that the Tamarian soldier and his wife were aboard the *Estrella del Norte*. "Transfer to Luanca imminent," he'd written.

Too bad she would soon die. What a lovely woman!

As Brenna lost herself in whispered prayers, Garrick listened to the relentless, distant thunder of Nordan naval artillery. Instinctively aware of a fixed gaze behind him, the Tamarian soldier turned and looked up at the flying bridge. There he made lingering eye contact with a Kamerese sailor, who grinned wickedly.

***

"A message for you, sir," the Mist and Soil corporal said to Esteban. He did not salute, as the Kamerese advisors to the insurgency were technically not military.

Annoyed, Esteban snatched the envelope away. "You came all this way to give me a message I could have read when I returned to the inn?"

The corporal remained stoic and straight-faced. "They said it was urgent." He watched the Kamerese mercenary open the envelope and scan through the text. "I can drive you back right away," the Kurian soldier added. "They told me I should wait for you."

"No need for that," Orozco replied, folding the message into his pocket. Turning to Fernando he called off the search. "We're done here. Meet me back in Trosa after these dead are properly buried."

On the way back to Trosa, Esteban sketched a plan in his imagination. He had to make the killing look like it had been a Nordan operation, rather than a random crime. The outline he developed was more dangerous than the last, but wouldn't involve the cowardly Kurians . . . .

Esteban entered the local inn, where his wealthy benefactors had rented rooms for the combat advisory team. After reading through the ship-to-shore message with greater care, he secured the door and opened the safe, rummaging through it for passports and military ID he'd collected over the past few days.

"Lieutenant Sato," he mused, unable to read anything else, as only the man's name and rank had been printed in Kurian script. "This one will do."

Next, he wrote notes. A body and a uniform should be easy to obtain, now that people were actively killing one another. He knew of a derelict wharf where a boat might clandestinely deliver a body across the river, close to an inn affiliated with the slave trade. Finding a bomb required calling in favors – especially since he had little time to set up the kill – but that could be done.

For a fleeting moment he considered the children, who could not help being present during the operation, then pushed the moral problem out his mind. They'd represent collateral damage when they perished in the incident. That was too bad, but they were Lithian scum anyway, not the noble sons of Kameron, and terrible things happen in war . . . .

***

Careful to avoid revealing his suspicions of the ship's crew, Garrick questioned Chief Petty Officer Delgado in an offhanded manner. "Why don't you just let us take our own boat to Luanca at this point?"

If Delgado detected any guile in Garrick, he didn't reveal that conclusion in his facial expression or body language. "We have orders to sink any vessel with Nordan markings that enters our territory," he explained. "We want peace, but we're obligated to defend our border."

"I see," Garrick stated, musing that it should be a simple thing to make an exception for the short trip to shore. He suppressed a smirk, silently thinking that the act of mining Nordan waters didn't qualify as peaceful, either. The dishonesty didn't surprise him, but he said nothing about this to the officer, while Brenna – who remained focused on Fiona for the moment – missed the conversation altogether.

To his dismay, Garrick noted that the leering sailor from the flying bridge served on the launch crew that carried the refugees to shore. He concealed his concern fairly well, but Brenna noted his tension. She leaned her head against his shoulder and put her hand on his chest.

"What's wrong?" she asked, speaking in Tamarian.

"I'm not sure," he replied. "I've got a bad feeling about the man on the tiller. I don't like the way he stares at you."

Brenna glanced backward, noting that the Kamerese sailor in question unabashedly ogled her, making no more effort to avert his eyes than had been the case with Belwyr, who actually knew her. She didn't find the gawking unusual, but after their experience at the Seashell Resort, Brenna felt reluctant to dismiss her husband's instincts as paranoia. "What should we do?"

"Right now I don't know," he replied. "It may be nothing, but I'd feel better if we were armed."

The irony of his statement struck her, as she'd been the suspicious of the Kamerese since her captivity, while he considered them allies and felt more inclined to extend trust than had been the case with the Nordan colonists.

"Where are they taking us?" Cedric asked in Lithian.

Confident that none of the Kamerese understood the language, Garrick replied, "We'll find a place to stay in Luanca. I have to go to the Customs office and arrange new passports."

"What about us?" Ilia asked understandably concerned and apprehensive.

"Don't worry," Garrick assured her. "We'll take care of you."

While the girl's anxiety diminished with Garrick's declaration, Brenna worried about Ciaran, who looked pale and weak. For the duration of their boat ride to the shore, Brenna focused on his welfare in her prayers.

The unique combination of site and function created Luanca's gritty atmosphere, first manifest in the smell of fish and raw sewage wafting over the Attavela. Extensive dock facilities – including military moorage – lined the river's shore. Canneries, machine shops, oil processing facilities and various amusements – targeting the primarily male seafaring community – populated the strand.

Four armed men, all wearing uniforms, stood at the dock as the launch approached. Something about the way they handled their weapons didn't seem quite right. Brenna glanced at her husband, who nodded.

"What's this about?" Garrick asked aloud.

"It's your security detail," Santiago told him.

"Why do we need a security detail in an allied country?" Garrick pressed.

Santiago laughed. "Look around. Luanca's a rough town. We're just trying to keep you safe."

A service truck with an uncovered bed waited nearby. Once the launch tied up to the dock, the men formed a chain to load the refugees' meager belongings.

Santiago helped Fiona and Cedric into the truck bed. "We've arranged for a hotel," he explained.

"There's no need for that," Garrick stated. "Just take me to Customs. We can look after ourselves."

The Kamerese sailor shook his head. "Aside from that pathetic little knife in your woman's boot, you're unarmed. This is a tough place, she's lovely, and I've been ordered to keep you safe. You know about orders, right? It's not like I have a choice in the matter . . . ."

Garrick turned to his lover and spoke in Lithian. "Whose orders do you think he's following?"

"If we make a fuss, they might dispatch us on the spot," Brenna replied. "Those uniforms aren't right."

"I noticed," he told her. The piping and unit badges were not authentic, and the demeanor of these men, while strictly business, seemed mercenary. "Let's see this hotel of theirs . . . ."

Fiona wanted to know where they were going. Cedric, afraid of the grim faced men with guns, kept silent but stared with wide eyes. Ciaran seemed too distracted by weakness and unproductive nausea to care. He let Ilia fuss over him like their mother had once done. The girl trembled nervously as the armed men helped Ciaran into the truck bed, but she refused their assistance.

Garrick found this amusing, knowing that Brenna also hated being treated like an invalid. She bounded onto the deck with an effortlessness that reflected her athletic mother's leaping ability and huddled close to the children, willfully ignoring the men guarding her. Garrick climbed aboard, watching his surroundings closely as the silent, fuel cell-powered truck sped away from the dock.

While Luanca's smell improved further inland, its run-down business district featured many boarded shops where listless vagrants gathered. It did not look pretty near the river. Feral dogs, litter, liquor stores, strip clubs, dingy bars, pawn shops, graffiti and grimy workshops eventually gave way to a leafier neighborhood – initially with walled and gated compounds guarded by bored men wielding loaded carbines – where artisan papier-mâché studios displayed astonishingly realistic figurines and statues in their picture windows. Bead makers, hand weavers – who used very durable and watertight dune grass to create fine and beautiful basketry – formed a buffer between the grungy downtown and high-end, heavily forested properties stretching up the steep hills overlooking the Attavela. Many wealthy Kamerese managed their business empires from those heights.

Turning left, the road wound into a trendy business district featuring tea shops, banks, book stores, attorney offices and glass-fronted clothing stores offering the latest in pricey, Kamerese fashion trends. Patrons lingered on the patios of bustling cafes, sipping tea and enjoying local pastries. This area seemed too exclusive for the location of a Customs office.

The truck passed through this area and descended to the banks of *Rio de Los Amantes*, where a far lower scale district, dominated by aromatic, open air markets and street food vendors, lapped the water's edge. A gun shop and a general store stood nearby. Near the southern reaches of town, the truck stopped at an old inn called *La Posada del Descanso*. Its thick plaster walls represented a different approach to maintaining comfort in this climate than the airy, breezy, cedar buildings of the Nordan Coastal Colony.

Santiago urged the refugees to unload. "You can rest here for the night," he told them. "We'll take you to the Customs Office in the morning." He fawned over Brenna, offering to help her out of the truck. When she refused, Santiago positioned himself to peek down her camisole until stern-faced Garrick moved into his way.

While most men might steal a glance at a beautiful woman, Santiago made no effort to conceal his interest. He shrugged off Garrick's proximity, knowing the unarmed Tamarian soldier had no power to defend his wife. Very soon, this impotent visitor would die. Once that happened, Santiago planned to have his way with this beautiful, sexy little woman. He could hardly wait . . . .

"Everything's been arranged," he told her. "I'll come back for you in the morning." Then, holding Brenna by the shoulders, Santiago tried to kiss her cheeks in the manner of a Kamerese farewell.

She pushed him away firmly, resisting the urge to reach for her boot knife. "Don't touch me!" she insisted. "I'm a married woman, not your friend."

Santiago took that reprimand as if it had been undeserved, feigning hurt without objecting. Turning back to Garrick, he tipped his cap. "Tomorrow morning, then."

Ciaran, leaning against the inn's main desk, scowled. "He's got a lot of nerve!"

Brenna recalled that the young man's father had behaved far worse, but said nothing about the memory. "Let's hope we don't see him again," she replied.

Oddly, the staff expected their arrival. The clerk insisted they didn't have to pay for their rooms, either. Garrick, Brenna, and the orphans followed a porter beyond a locked door, down a dimly-lit hall that carried the musty scent of mold. Old, deeply-worn carpet and dusty wainscoting belied the fresh linens on the beds of two rooms at the hallway's end.

Recalling similar isolation at the Seashell Resort, Garrick felt uneasy. *What was going on here?*

While the inn had seen better days, the last two rooms – adjoined by a door that could be locked from both sides – featured a lovely view of the valley to the east. An iron-railed balcony overlooked grounds in desperate need of a decent gardener. Beyond its wall, the river's edge lay hidden beneath a canopy of tall trees.

After tipping the porter a full kroner – since Brenna's *Auðr* only carried the main currency of its current location – Garrick sent the children into the next room and with hands trembling in anticipation, shut the door to bask in Brenna's abundant passion . . . .

***

Not long after they children finished eating, they heard Brenna knocking on the shared door. Her dark, damp hair hung heavily on her shoulders and a lingering smile whispered of contentment. She gathered the orphans around, speaking quietly. "It's important that you listen carefully," she began. "We can't stay here. The men who brought us to this place are not real soldiers. They're standing at the exits to prevent our escape. Whatever they're planning can't be good. We have to leave."

Ilia's anxiety rose to the surface. "What? Why? You said you'd take care of us."

"Yes," Brenna replied, reaching for her hand and squeezing it reassuringly. "Don't be afraid. Don't worry. Garrick is brilliant at solving tactical problems."

"If these fake soldiers are guarding all the exits, how do we get out of here?" Ciaran asked.

"Leave that to Garrick," Brenna soothed, taking Fiona into her arms. "He's clever, creative and he's very good at outsmarting anyone who underestimates him. When he returns, we'll slip over the balcony and out the back. There's an old gate there, on a path that leads to the river. We won't need to be quick, but we'll have to be very quiet."

"What about Ciaran?" Ilia asked. "He's too weak to climb down on his own."

"Garrick will carry him if necessary," Brenna explained. "Wherever he leads, we follow. I trust him completely, and you should, too."

"Where's he now?" Ciaran asked.

A flash of worry crossed Brenna's beautiful face. "He's making arrangements for us," she replied cryptically. "I pray he'll be successful."

And while he'd held her as she prayed for him, Garrick didn't feel the need for her intercession. The idea that inspired her confidence developed in his mind well before she'd pressed her body tightly against his and whispered beautiful, supportive words to a deity he didn't believe existed. But he loved her enough to listen, interpreting her words as a gesture of support before relinquishing her strong, adoring grasp and leaving her with a loving, lingering kiss.

As he walked out of the lobby, one of the armed Kamerese stopped him. "Hey!" the mercenary shouted in vulgate. "Where do you think you're going?"

"Shopping," Garrick replied. "I have four hungry mouths to feed."

A guffaw and translation into Kamerese followed, the levity lessening suspicion. "What kind of man are you? Shopping is women's work."

"You're standing guard because Santiago said this is a rough town," Garrick stated, reminding them of their own lie in a manner that distracted suspicion from his personal prevarication. "I'd rather leave my woman behind a locked door, if it's all the same to you."

He continued on his way toward the open air market, ignoring the laughter directed at his back. For his plan to work, he needed a translator. Since young people were more likely to be bilingual, he approached three different men before finding an idle truck driver enjoying his dinner beneath a broadleaf maple.

"You want to earn some money?" he asked.

Lanky limbed, with blonde hair and pale green eyes, the young man stood. "I'm not on duty," he replied. Pointing a thumb over his shoulder, the youth added, "My truck is done for the day."

"I'm looking for a translator," Garrick stated, holding up a kroner. "I'll give you one of these every time we talk to someone who doesn't speak vulgate."

Motivated by the promise of easy money, the young man wolfed down his meal and afterward, offered his hand in the universal gesture of peace. "Mateo Meta, at your service," he said warmly.

Where had Garrick heard that last name before?

Their first stop was the general store. Here, Garrick picked up six envelopes, a pen and a train schedule. Next, they approached a middle-aged couple enjoying a local dessert specialty, who – after hearing Garrick's translated pitch and generous offer of money – agreed to help. He had them write their first names on an envelope, then gave each of them a kroner. He did this five more times.

Listening to Mateo talk about his family, Garrick recalled where he'd heard of the Meta surname. "Are you related to the mayor of Helena?" he asked.

"Yes!" the young man told him excitedly. "Alonso is an uncle on my father's side. I was born out there."

Garrick raised his brow at the coincidence. "I led the assault that liberated your hometown from Lord Navarro during the civil war," he explained, outlining the story of his first combat action as an officer, in which he'd been vastly outnumbered, yet prevailed because of courage and cunning. "My wife's family owns an estate near Helena."

"Lord and Lady Velez?" Mateo remembered, his eyes widened. "They're good people. My uncle brags that their land reform completely turned the region around."

"That's my wife's family," Garrick affirmed, proudly.

"What a small world!" Mateo exclaimed in genuine surprise. "I'd love to help. Is there anything more I can do for you?"

"That depends on how willing you are to face danger," Garrick stated. "It's a long story, but we need to find shelter that is both secure and discreet . . . ."

"My parents' villa is on a bluff overlooking the delta," Mateo told him. "They're away on business right now, so I'm looking after my *abuelita* until they return. The property is walled and has a guest house on the grounds. It'll be safe for you there."

"That's generous of you," Garrick stated. "We'd be grateful for the hospitality."

The two men arranged a time for Mateo to pick everyone up in his truck. "There's an old wharf at the river right behind the place where you're staying," Mateo explained. "Smugglers use it for the slave trade. I can pick up you and your people at the dock an hour after dark."

And thus, an important aspect of Garrick's plan found a willing partner – a stroke of good fortune. While Brenna wouldn't see it that way, Garrick didn't know how to explain the situation to her without starting a pointless argument, as he didn't like admitting that inexplicable things often happened when she prayed. Sometimes, he could imagine a rational explanation for events that she attributed to divine influence – as he'd done with the whale dragging them to shore. Sometimes, he could not.

He'd once watched in horror as an artillery burst knocked her to the pavement, only to witness the valiant woman scramble to her feet again without suffering a single singed hair. Situations like that defied logic, and he'd long ago given up trying to find rational explanations for every spooky coincidence common to his wife's experience. Garrick typically didn't comment on these strange occurrences. Brenna claimed a power that defied his understanding, and the Tamarian soldier didn't want to contend with her over its origins.

She'd draw her own conclusions, anyway.

At *La Posada del Descanso*, one of the soldiers approached to inspect his backpack. Garrick feigned offense. "You want to see the great deals I got?" he sneered. "Who's the woman now?"

After successfully passing the guards, Garrick stopped at the front desk, where he left six sealed envelopes in the care of the clerk. "These people will come tomorrow," he explained. "Please make sure that each one gets their package." He slid a kroner across the counter. "See to it there's no theft."

*****

Just before dark, a truck loaded with local police trundled along the road and stopped in front of the venerable inn. A score of well-armed officers deployed around the building with weapons drawn.

"Stand down!" the police sergeant shouted at the mercenaries. "You're under arrest for threatening conduct and disturbing the peace."

A tense and awkward confrontation followed. One of the outgunned mercenaries claimed that they'd been ordered to guard a group of refugees from Kuriah and fully intended to follow that order.

"Ordered by whom?" the sergeant demanded. "You want me to contact the garrison commander about this? Shall I get him on the phone?"

The mercenary remained stone-faced. "Messing with us is a really bad idea," he warned.

"Don't take me for a fool," the sergeant continued. "I don't know who you are, or what you're doing here, but only an idiot would mistake these uniforms for the real thing. I could entertain your little fantasy and make the call, but we both know I'd be wasting my time.

"I've had six complaints from decent citizens about you people playing soldier and waving weapons around. This is no place for war games. Tell your story to a judge in the morning. I have three times your firepower and reinforcements are but a radio call away. Now, stand down, surrender your weapons, and get in the truck!"

***

Santiago let his imagination wander. All evening long, he'd been dreaming about the Lithian woman. He imagined himself with her, possessing her, dominating her, fantasizing about how much she'd want him. He would make that happen, and if he did it all in front of the Tamarian soldier – forcing that arrogant prig to watch him enjoy the pleasure – the ensuing humiliation would bring satisfaction that few men ever experienced.

Confident that the presence of that lovely woman onboard *Estrella del Norte* indicated favor from his ancestors, Santiago praised them. He convinced himself that igniting her passions would represent another step on the path to greatness. He wanted her alive. Having such a beautiful woman at his side would elevate his social stature. The only thing standing in his way was a hick from the northern hills who'd never see his end coming.

The old wing of *La Posada del Descanso* had long served as the organizational center for slaves imported from the Nordan Colony. Runaways, criminals and girls snatched from the streets spent their first few days in Kameron there, recovering after being branded, and waiting for transport further inland. The inn's proximity to a wharf on the *Rio de Los Amantes* provided easy access for the slave ship, *La Bandida.*

While waiting for the hour to arrive, Santiago visited a downtown strip club, watching the women working there until the trap was set. He had more to drink than he'd planned, spent money on private dances, and with his judgment impacted by alcohol, lost track of time.

After wandering to the back of the inn near midnight, he looked for the gardener's ladder. It wasn't at the shed, where it belonged. Instead, he found it leaning against the balcony at the end of the building.

What was this? Were they stupid enough to think they could get away? Confident that the guards he'd posted ensured the amorous couple couldn't escape, Santiago ascended the ladder and quietly climbed over the iron rail. His heart pounded with anticipation. Sweat glistened on his flesh.

Moments later, he stood at the glass balcony door with his silenced sidearm in hand. Darkness enveloped the room, but the twin moons reflected enough light for him to notice that the bed appeared unoccupied. With his gun leading the way, the Kamerese sailor burst into a room that smelled like sex, and something *else* very erotic.

Where was she?

Santiago turned on the lights. The shower had been used. Wet towels littered the floor, but no toiletries lay on the counter. He tore open empty drawers and confronted a closet without clothes.

She wasn't here. She wasn't in the adjoining room, either. How had this happened? The lovers had been guarded by reliable troops, and they couldn't speak the language either. Where could they possibly have gone?

The perfect plan had been ruined!

Santiago tried to open the door and check other rooms across the hall, but the portal had been barred from outside. Angrily, he pounded on the door and cursed his bad luck.

Moments later, blinding light, a lethal concussion, and the impact of bursting steel fragments blew the door into ten thousand splinters, shredded Santiago's body, shattered glass and shook the building to its rafters. Intense heat ignited fire that spread across carpet, up the curtains and roared through massive, cedar timbers forming the roof trusses. The reserved wing of *La Posada del Descanso* glowed as ammonium nitrate burned like a furnace, pouring thick smoke into the night sky.

***

The sound of fire alarms drew Garrick and Brenna to the balcony. A panoramic view that stretched from the sea in the west, all the way to distant mountains in the east commanded the landscape in a strategic way to his eye, and an artistic one to hers.

"You were right about the bomb," she said quietly, watching flames and smoke rise in the east.

"I suspect we've become the targets of the same group who attacked the palace a few weeks ago," he told her somberly. "Bombing appears to be their specialty."

Brenna tightened her lips, grateful for their escape while the horror of being relentlessly pursued shuddered through her shoulders. "If so, they'll soon learn that we weren't there. Why are people so intent on killing us?"

"There must be an element to this we can't see," he replied. "We need to get home. We won't be safe until we're back in Tamaria."

"How do we know they won't look for us here?" she asked. "How many more incidents like this can we reasonably expect to survive?"

Stating this revealed uncharacteristic fear that belied Brenna's faith. Garrick squeezed her trembling fingers and spoke reassuringly to bolster her confidence. "Mateo says we'll be safe. There's a phone in the main house. We'll make some calls in the morning."

"You're sure he's telling the truth about his uncle?" she asked.

"I am," Garrick replied. "I didn't prompt him to start talking about his family. He seemed surprised and delighted to learn that you're a Velez, and refused to take money after I told him the story of liberating Helena."

"I don't trust the Kamerese," she murmured, turning away and crossing her arms. "There are too many factions in this country to know who's on what side."

While Brenna had a point, Ciaran desperately needed convalescence, Garrick's aching body demanded relief from constant exertion, and her *Y Newen* was nearing its height. Inside the walled compound they could rest, love each other without interruption, and carefully plan their escape. Caressing her hair and kissing her forehead, Garrick counseled patience.

"How do we travel without documents?" she asked at length, her worry persisting. "If you go to the Customs Office, our would-be killers will very likely be looking for you there. We have to avoid boats and trains, too."

"We'll call your sister," he soothed. Cassie Velez, engaged to a Lithian lawyer named Jared Hohner, lived at his parents' hacienda in Hermosa, a town not far from the Tamarian border. Jared maintained a friendship with the Kamerese sovereign, King Alejo, and for that reason, Garrick hoped that Jared's royal connections could ensure passage home without further incident.

Brenna stood on her toes to kiss her husband. Her eyes glowed softly in the darkness, imploring his affection as gentle wind brushed through her dark, silky hair. Moonlight spilled over her feminine form, painting her darkening skin in pale light and deep shadow. The lovely sight, the sensation of her soft flesh pressing against his, and the rousing aroma of *Y Newen* quickened Garrick's pulse. He caressed her heavy breast with his left hand while his right hand traced down her spine, coaxing a passionate response from her willing body.

"I want you," he whispered longingly.

"Then come and love me again," she encouraged.

***

Non-flammable plaster limited the fire damage to furnishings, carpet and charred rafters. Luanca's fire chief contacted the police by telephone, shortly after his crew quenched the flames.

"We have bodies," he announced. "The origin is clearly arson."

Later, as Oscar Ortega – Luanca's portly, balding and irritable Chief Investigator – arrived on the scene, he listened to the fire chief explain his findings. "What caused the blaze?" he asked.

The fire chief replied, "I'm sure it was a bomb. The front desk clerk told me there was a family staying down there, but we only found two victims."

That statement proved to be the first of many strange clues Captain Ortega discovered in his investigation. A door to the hallway that led to the scene had been blown open by the blast. Ortega noticed that the door locked from the outside, which seemed strange for an inn. Oddly, that detail was true of every door in the wing.

The foul odor of ammonium nitrate mingled with lingering smoke. At the end of the hall, fragments of steel casing and bits of wire testified to the fire's origin. A dead man lay on the floor nearby showed little impact from the blast. Damaged walls testified that the explosion occurred well above the floor level. This poor soul had to have been laying down when the bomb went off.

He'd also been shot, which meant he was likely dead beforehand. Now, why and how would that be?

Captain Ortega lifted the man's wallet and examined its contents, using his flashlight. *A Nordan officer? Why wasn't he in uniform?* Closer examination revealed that the face on the body didn't look like the one in the photo ID. The investigator scrunched his brow unhappily, as the evidence pointed to a hastily-arranged hit.

Water dripped from the ceiling in the room. Towels littered the floor and burned, disheveled sheets lay on the bed – the only clues that this room had been occupied.

The second body had been torn apart by blast and badly burned. Whoever he was, he'd been standing when the bomb went off. Nearby, Captain Ortega found a .35 caliber handgun with a silencer – an illegal modification in every Kamerese jurisdiction. Turning the body over, he checked its identification and raised his brow.

"Able Seaman Santiago Méndez," he mused. "What were you doing here, and why did you bring a weapon?"

***

At first glance, Rosalea Meta did not fit the diminutive term, *abuelita.* She stood taller than Garrick, had broad shoulders and a stout figure. High cheek bones, pale skin, green eyes whose beauty rivaled those of Brenna's youngest sister, Camille, in color and vibrancy, gave her an imposing appearance. All of Belwyr's children felt intimidated by the woman's stature, but she bent to her knees and spoke to Fiona in such a gentle, motherly tone, the child quickly let down her guard.

Rosalea knew no tongue other than Kamerese. However, the care she extended to her guests permeated her attitude, her tone and her actions. Affectionate touch, a smile that showed a thousand wisdom wrinkles, and a kindly demeanor reached into the refugees' hearts, soothing pain, loss and fear with unreserved generosity and abundant love.

She also knew how to cook. A bountiful breakfast featuring spicy *huevos rancheros*, cut fruit, fresh bread and dried fish, coaxed even Ciaran to eat a full serving. Rosalea beamed as Garrick expressed satisfaction with a thank-you in Kamerese – one of several phrases he'd learned during his deployment. Fiona, Cedric and Ilia each embraced the elderly woman after eating their fill.

"We appreciate your hospitality," Garrick told Mateo after the meal. "But we don't want to make extra work for your grandmother."

Mateo shrugged. "It gives her purpose. She loves taking care of people, especially children. Just let her do her thing, and she'll be happy."

The young Kamerese man rose to give his *abuelita* a kiss. "I'm off to work," he said.

"You come from a wealthy family and live in a really nice place," Ilia remarked. "Why do you need to work?"

"I don't," he replied. "My father started with one boat when he was young. Luanca had been a sleepy border town when he first came here, but now – thanks to him – it's the largest port north of Kameron City.

"He made that happen with hard work, partnerships with like-minded people, and a vision for opportunity. I'm going to do the same with transport trucks."

"Oh, I see," Ilia responded politely. "Good for you!"

Garrick inquired about using the phone. Mateo asked his grandmother to initiate the process of contacting the Hohner family and Kamerese Customs. Garrick also wanted to reach an exchange operator in Tamaria so that he could speak to his sister, Kira. Mateo offered the children the run of the grounds, giving Garrick and Brenna some much-needed time to themselves. "I'll see you all this evening," he said.

For Brenna, Rosalea reserved particular favor. She lavished the Lithian woman with attention. Once *abuelita* learned what treats Brenna liked to eat, she offered creamy, homemade pastries and sweet, milky tea that Brenna relished with gratitude. The Kamerese matron drew the lovers a hot, lavender-scented bath with soothing salts while she changed bedding and towels steeped in the tantalizing, erotic aroma of *Y Newen*. Rosalea set out fresh linens with a knowing smile and afterward, fussed over combing and braiding the younger woman's hair

The walled, forested grounds of the Meta estate offered Ilia, Cedric and Fiona opportunities for exploration and play that kept them occupied for hours. Ciaran, who felt better after eating a good meal, immersed himself in the library. Mateo's father had an excellent collection that included an entire section of titles in Lithian.

Brenna reached her sister at the Hohner hacienda and spent far longer on the phone with reticent Cassie than Garrick expected. When the women were done, Brenna handed the receiver to Garrick, who had an uncomfortable conversation with Cassie's fiancé, Jared.

"I'll do what I can," Jared promised at length.

But it didn't sound like much, and Garrick brimmed with resentment as Rosalea contacted an agent at Customs. When Garrick explained his need for replacement documents, the overworked officer – who understood little vulgate – rudely expressed exasperation. He didn't grasp what the Tamarian soldier needed and yelled abusively before slamming the phone down.

The misdeed pushed Garrick over the edge. All of the frustration he'd experienced since arriving at the Nordan Coastal Colony burst from his soul in pent-up fury. He swore loudly, threatening violence against the recalcitrant Customs Agent and uttering an expletive-laden lament about letting Brenna talk him into their ill-fated journey to the music festival before storming away.

She felt hurt, but didn't judge. Since he'd returned from his last deployment, volatile incidents like this had been gradually declining. Brenna soothed his anger with feminine grace, following her husband to the balcony where they'd lingered the night before. She quietly edged into his personal space, her proximity a calming comfort.

"I'm sorry about all of this," she said meekly.

Garrick tried to suppress his emotion, but it welled in his eyes and spilled down his cheeks. He sighed. "Please forgive me, Brenna. This is not your fault. I shouldn't take it out on you. That was wrong of me."

She acknowledged the truth of his statement with silence, pressing her forehead into his shoulder and nuzzling his arm as a gesture of forgiveness. Reaching for his face, she wiped away the tears lingering there and made longing eye contact that morphed into a soft sensuous kiss. "What did Jared say?" she asked, quietly.

Struggling to reassert control, Garrick caressed the back of her arms while taking in a deep breath. "He agrees that *Los Patrones del Estado* is after us. At my brother's wedding, he'd warned me to stay clear of them. Although he didn't say this directly, he's now insinuating that we're responsible for attracting their attention."

Brenna turned her head away, concern wrinkling her brow. An accusation like that would certainly stir Garrick's ire, especially because she knew it wasn't true. "That was an insensitive thing for him to say," she replied, worried that her husband's volatility would return, destroying all the mental health progress he'd made over the past few weeks. "He's usually more careful than that."

"I don't think he was being vindictive," Garrick told her, defending his soon-to-be brother-in-law in a manner that reflected respect. "He doesn't know what's going on."

While that was certainly true, Brenna felt miffed over the fact that Jared had spoken in a judgmental manner. "Exactly," she replied. "He's not here. He hasn't seen what we've seen. What does he know?"

Garrick bent to kiss her forehead. "It hurt to hear him talk that way, but I believe he's right. We can presume the Kamerese kill team at the Seashell Resort were mercenaries. That doesn't fit the pattern of a typical *Patrones* attack, but the blast outside the resort, and the bomb last night, certainly do."

If Brenna had not been in the throes of *Y Newen*, she'd have suggested getting a few pack mules, weapons, and heading east through the wilderness. With more than a month of summer remaining, children on mule back could easily travel 20 miles a day.

In her current condition, however, she was too easily tracked to seriously consider recommending that course of action. "Maybe we can book passage to Kameron City on one of the Meta family boats," she suggested. "From there we have a lot more options."

Garrick had never been that far south and worried that it would take them too long to get home, as he had to report to his commanding officer within a week. However, Brenna had a point. Their pursuers would be far less likely to imagine them fleeing that direction when they needed to head east. "I'll call my sister," he replied at length. "Maybe she can talk to someone at Fort Aeolus. If Algernon wasn't on his honeymoon, he could advocate for us in Kamerese."

"That's what Jared should be doing," Brenna stated, still annoyed at her sister's fiancé. "He should be helping, not blaming you for incidents beyond your control."

***

"So, the entire wing was empty, except for the last two rooms?" Captain Ortega clarified.

"That's correct," the manager replied nervously. "This old section is not up to current code, so we've locked it off until remodeling can be done."

Ortega scrunched his brow. *Did this man take him for a fool?* "Why were these last two rooms occupied, then? If the wing is not up to code, putting guests down there subjects the inn to a fine. Given that you had a fire in that area – with fatalities – I've a mind to have the city shut down your operation entirely."

"Captain, I'm cooperating fully," the manager stammered, clearing his throat. "I would appreciate some discretion from you. This is a delicate matter."

Ortega raised his brow. "Very well," he agreed. "Explain why you put guests in the back of that wing."

"We were full."

"Don't lie to me!" Ortega warned. Lack of sleep made him impatient, but not stupid. "I've seen your registry. Honesty is the sincerest form of cooperation. So why did you put guests – a family with children – back there?"

The manager's demeanor, his trembling hands, the sweat on his brow, the way he struggled to maintain eye contact, testified of a terror he did not want to articulate. "We have an arrangement," he explained in a low voice, glancing sideways. "We get a phone call. We make up the rooms and look the other way. We clean them when the guests leave. Money goes into the bank. That's all I know."

"Who calls you?" the detective demanded.

"I told you. I don't know. It's just a voice. They usually come through the back and I never see who's here. This time was different. They brought a man to the front desk – I heard he was Tamarian – a Lithian woman and four children. A sailor with armed men brought them here. He had them guard the exits and said he'd be back in the morning to take everyone away. That's all I know."

Ortega showed the military ID card of Able Seaman Méndez. "Is this the man?"

The manager nodded.

"Well that's odd, because he died here last night. There is no trace of a Tamarian man, a Lithian woman, or any children in your building. How can that be?"

"I don't know," the manager insisted.

At that moment, a middle aged couple arrived at the front desk. They conversed with the desk clerk, who slid an envelope across the counter. Captain Ortega had seen a similar exchange earlier in the morning and thought this looked suspiciously like a payoff.

After showing them his badge, the detective asked, "What's in the envelope?"

"It's a kroner," the gentleman told him, opening the envelope and presenting the coin.

"What's it for?" Ortega pressed.

"A foreign man offered us cash if we'd call the police and report men waving guns around the inn," he said. "We called the cops last night, and came here to collect."

The description of the man seemed consistent with one provided by the afternoon-shift desk clerk. "You say he was a foreigner. How do you know?"

"He didn't speak our language," the man insisted. "Mateo, the truck driver, had to translate for him. We don't know anything more."

***

Rosalea knitted in the parlor with rapture lifting her soul as she listened to Brenna play the family's grand piano. The Lithian woman poured such passion, such intensity into the keys, the elderly matron nearly wept. She'd heard many people play the instrument in her life, but had never known music to elevate her spirit like this. What a talent! What a delight!

Caught up in the emotion of the moment, she didn't hear Ilia enter. "Lady Brenna!" the dark haired girl called.

Brenna stopped her playing in alarm. "What's wrong?" she asked.

"We saw policemen at the gate, trying to get in."

"Where are Cedric and Fiona?"

"I told them to hide in the woods," Ilia stated.

The Lithian woman stood, placed her right hand on Ilia's cheek and kissed her forehead. "I would prefer that you stay with them," she encouraged. "I'll get Garrick. Don't worry. It'll be okay."

Rosalea, who understood none of this, arose with her heart beating fast. The girl's tone of voice, her anxious posture and Brenna's response gave the elderly woman an idea of a threat to their safety. She followed fleet-footed Brenna into the kitchen, where Garrick was on the phone with his sister, Kira.

"Sorry to interrupt," Brenna said quietly, her soft touch on Garrick's upper arm distracting him from his conversation. "Police are nosing around. Can you please deal with them?"

Rosalea watched the young couple's demeanor for signs of reconciliation. Had she not witnessed Garrick's angry outburst, she wouldn't have known a problem had arisen between them. He seemed delighted by Brenna's presence and paused to give his beloved a kiss.

Kira, hearing Brenna's voice, insisted on talking to her. Garrick handed the phone to his wife and beckoned Rosalea to follow him.

"What a relief!" Kira cried, her voice a rainstorm of emotion. "A story in the Capital Times this morning claims that you and my brother were killed in a bomb attack!"

How did that disinformation get all the way to Marvic so quickly? Brenna scrunched her brow as she explained their escape to her sister-in-law. "We're harder to kill than they think," she told Kira. "We're stuck right now, but Allfather will find a way to get us home."

Meanwhile, Garrick wordlessly escorted Rosalea to the gate. The men outside paused from their conversations as if caught in wrongdoing by a schoolmistress. One of them, a portly man wearing a suit that looked like it had fit a long time ago, waved in a friendly manner.

"What's going on, Captain?" Rosalea demanded. The matron could be very assertive. Her stature and her son's wealth and power in the community had a mildly intimidating impact on the police detective's entourage.

Captain Ortega, noting that the blonde man fit the description of the male guest at *La Posada del Descanso*, addressed the woman respectfully. "We believe your guests are under threat, *señora*," he began. "There are some very dangerous people who want to kill them."

"We have walls, a gate and dogs," Rosalea said, though the dogs were in their kennel. "Our guests are under our protection. They came here at night, and no one bore witness. As long as they're here, they're safe."

"*Señora* Meta, if I can find them, so can those who want them dead."

Rosalea put her hands on her hips. "Then what do you suggest?" she asked.

"I'd like to take them into protective custody," he told her, almost apologetically.

She shook her head. "You will do no such thing. They are my guests, under the protection of this household. There's no need for you to intervene."

"*Señora*, I understand your view, but the responsibility is immense. Perhaps it's wiser to leave the matter in my hands."

"Post guards outside the gate," she told him assertively. "Patrol the street if you like, but my guests are not leaving until they choose to go, and you are not bringing guns onto our property."

Witnessing her intransigence, Captain Ortega thought for a moment before offering a compromise. "Okay," he assented. "But at least let me post undercover officers around your house. This is for your safety, as much as it is theirs."

Rosalea considered the offer. She knew Captain Ortega, having watched him rise through the ranks since she'd first moved to Luanca. She respected his reputation for honesty, and had never heard so much as a whisper about corruption within Luanca's police department. "I believe in your integrity captain, but I can't let you bring armed men inside the gate. We have orphans present, and I don't want them further traumatized by men waving weapons around. You may post your police outside."

Ortega knew that the children's fate would be far worse if *Los Patrones del Estado* found them here. "*Señora*, our investigation suggests involvement with an unsavory group whom officials at the highest level would like to crush. Your whole household is under threat.

"This is a serious matter. A team of Royal Guards from Madera will arrive tomorrow and take over security. They would not be coming here unless the threat to your guests was significant. I will wait here for your grandson to return and explain the details to him."

Rosalea raised her brow. "He's coming home?"

"We've dispatched a squad car to find him," Captain Ortega told her. "I know it's inconvenient, but this is a national security issue, and we don't want any more violent incidents."

Darkness

The next morning Mateo sat with Garrick, Brenna, and Colonel Augusto Verano – the Regional Intelligence Chief for the Kamerese Royal Guard – in the family's formal living room."The Colonel is aware of your plight," Mateo explained. "He says the men arrested outside the inn, as well as one of the blast victims, are affiliated with a dangerous faction of powerful people agitating for our government, and yours – as our esteemed ally – to intervene in the uprising north of the river."

Colonel Verano, a tall, barrel-chested man with white hair and an impressive beard, made careful observations during the translation process, noting that the Tamarian lieutenant looked exhausted. Frequent yawning and blinking indicated a sleep deficit. Despite this, the soldier appraised his surroundings as if evaluating threats. Verano sensed an impatience lurking beneath his respectful demeanor, evidenced by tension visible in his shoulders, neck and jaw, suggesting that he wanted something done, and done quickly.

Lady Velez leaned on his left shoulder, her legs curled sideways on the couch while her husband's left arm held her in a protective embrace. The Lithian woman appeared small, fragile, and a bit sad. A lengthy scar on her neck testified to a haunting, terrifying past. Verano, who'd read her file, knew that a Kamerese rebel had been responsible for nearly killing her with a machete. That explained the suspicion in her tired eyes, and perhaps, had something to do with the soldier's vigilance.

Trust would be tough to establish with these two.

Both the Tamarian and his wife attracted affection from the orphaned children traveling in their company. The teenaged girl lingered in the soldier's proximity, infatuated in an innocent way that he tolerated graciously, but inspired the occasional sniff of impatience, eye rolling, and head shaking from his wife. The girl doted on the foreign man, racing to fetch tea and serving him Rosalea Meta's heated appetizers before offering anything to Lady Velez. Her focus on pleasing him resulted in her neglecting Colonel Verano entirely.

The bright-eyed youngest boy wanted to join the discussion. When he injected unimportant information into the conversation, a gently-worded remark from Lady Velez compelled him to play quietly with a toy truck at her husband's feet. His young sister sought comfort by sucking her thumb while laying her head on the Lithian woman's breast. This behavior suggested familiarity that stemmed from a trusting relationship. These children, even the eldest one – a slender lad who kept his nose in a book, only occasionally peering over it – had not been taken against their will, as the men arrested at *La Posada del Descanso* alleged.

Despite his obvious fatigue, the Tamarian soldier had been paying attention to Mateo's translation. "We've been dealing with this for days," he replied. "What happens between my government, the Kingdom of Kameron and the Nordan Colonial authority is not our concern right now. We've taken on responsibility for these children. We need to find their family, and we need to get home. Our only focus is on travel documents and safety."

Colonel Verano understood. "We've arranged an evacuation for you," he explained. "Our operatives believe the Nordans will soon launch an amphibious assault to re-take their colony. We have solid Intel that marine forces departed the Nord Islands weeks ago, and have now assembled offshore. We expect a lot of noise and fireworks north of the Attavela. While everyone is looking in that direction, we'll get you and the children out of here."

"How so?" Garrick asked. "If *Los Patrones* tracked us to Luanca, their agents may be watching the port, the roads and the train station, looking for us."

"We're using an airship," the colonel said.

Brenna, eyes widened, listened to the translation in rising terror. "Oh, no you're not!" she insisted. "I'm not riding in a floating bomb!"

"The lifting gas is hot air," Colonel Verano explained. "There is nothing about it that can explode. Once aloft, the airship is very quiet and will carry you to Madera, about 150 miles east of here. From there, we'll put you on a train for Valle Hermosa, where your brother-in-law lives, accompanied by a Royal Guard escort."

"This was his idea?" Garrick inquired.

Colonel Verano nodded. "*Señor* Hohner is a gentleman and friend of the court. King Alejo is personally interested in your safe return. We believe other *Los Patrones* agents are still operating in the area, and for that reason, it's best to conduct the evacuation in darkness."

***

Later, alone in their room, Garrick tried to soothe his wife's fear. "At least Jared advocated for us," he said.

Brenna conceded the point with a nod, but her lips remained downturned. When Garrick caressed her cheek she turned away. "That doesn't change anything," she countered. "Airships are dangerous and unpredictable. With our feet on the ground, we can rely on wit and experience. Once we're airborne, we're helpless."

If he'd suggested that she consider the rescue effort in faith that Allfather would protect them, he knew she'd argue against deliberately provoking divine intervention. "Presumption is self-centered and wrong," she'd once insisted. "Relationships don't work that way."

He didn't pursue that thought, uncomfortable discussing spiritual matters. Garrick couldn't deal with an accusation that he was trying to manipulate her, so he chose his words with care. "We face risk with every option," he stated, remaining safely within the realm of the rational. "Going by air eliminates a whole category of likely dangers. If we don't take the airship, we're stuck here.

"There are limits to hospitality, and the longer we stay, the greater the danger our presence creates for Mateo's family. That's the hard reality we face."

Shaking her head slowly, Brenna let out a shallow sigh. "I understand all of that," she stated. "I just don't like the idea of boarding a fragile craft that can get shot out of the sky, hit by lightning, torn apart by a storm, or driven into a mountainside by strong wind." She turned, put her hand against his chest, nuzzled his shoulder and tugged at the buttons of his pants. "I don't want to fall to my death. I'd rather raise a family with you."

Her sensual touch, the heat of her breath against his skin and the yielding of her breast rekindled the fire of his passion. "Then let's work on that."

Brenna let him lift her blouse overhead and willed her camisole to relax. He caressed her neck, shoulders and arms, steadily unlocking her sensuality. Garrick slid his hands down her waist, fervently kissing her lips while pushing her skirt to the floor. She deftly loosened shirt buttons as he reached beneath her camisole, gently caressing her soft breast with his left hand, starting at the side, working his way along the bottom, and ever so slowly to the front as her breath deepened and her right hand unfastened his pants. Their lips lingered for a long time while their hands heightened arousal in one another. He pulled her camisole over her head, then cradled and lowered her body until she rested on the bed sheets. Though sadness dampened her desire, Brenna pushed his head where she wanted his marital ministrations to continue, shut her eyes and whispered prayers of gratitude as she drifted into her lover's rapture.

***

"I saw the *Nagara* steaming up the river!" Cedric announced excitedly as the family sat for dinner. "And then I saw *Katori*. They're the newest near-shore ships in the Imperial Navy!"

"Nobody cares, Cedric!" Ciaran retorted, holding out his plate for a steamy serving of enchilada casserole and smiling at the spicy aroma of *abuelita's* main course.

"Well, he does," Brenna replied, not appreciating Ciaran's critical tongue, but wording her reprimand with a gentleness that Garrick believed the young man didn't deserve. She dipped her fork in the entree's sauce for a taste of its fire, letting the flavor linger on her tongue with closed eyes before turning her attention back to Cedric. "How do you know so much about Nordan warships?"

"I had a book," he replied. "Colonel Utemaro gave it to me the last time he came to visit us." The memory suddenly darkened Cedric's countenance as associated thoughts of his mother came to mind.

"The news keeps getting worse," Mateo stated. He watched Brenna bow her head and waited respectfully until she'd finished giving thanks before continuing. "Our ships are now on station to defend the border. I'd been hoping this ridiculous little rebellion would flame out in a day or two, and that cooler heads would prevail."

Garrick slathered his casserole in sour cream to cool its spicy heat. "From what we've seen, there's a lot of pent-up anger against the colonists. I suspect the Kurians will keep fighting, even if the Nordans invade to regain control of lost territory."

"The Nordans aren't monsters," Ciaran replied in between bites. "If the Kurians wanted to live peacefully, there wouldn't be any problems. They just need to do as they're told."

"Hmm," Garrick mused. "That's easy for an outsider to say. We've seen huge tracts of forest mowed down for timber. Freight trains full of extracted minerals are all destined for export.

"A colonial economy creates profit for the colonizers, while the resources that could pay for education and infrastructure fatten the accounts of foreigners. Even the farmland is under colonial control, and your father told us that the Nordans have been overfishing and stripping the seabed of oil kelp for decades. All of that fish and oil goes to feed the Nord Islanders and their machines. When hungry natives feel like they have nothing to lose and no future in the current status quo, they'll stop at nothing to get what they need."

"That may be true," Mateo added. "But the Nordans outclass the Kurians in every way. They're a clever and industrious people with a long history of success in combat. I hope they crush this insurgency quickly.

"The bridge has been closed for days. Commerce is dead. Now nobody can see Helsing's beautiful art and architecture. No one is going to the colony to eat its delicious food. Closing the border put a serious damper on my export business. I absolutely depend on trade."

"None of that is good, but don't underestimate human rage," Garrick warned. "Helsing has been shelled, shot, looted and burned. We stepped over the bodies of Nordan men who'd been slaughtered. We saw women and children rounded up for sale in the slave markets."

Brenna put her left hand on her husband's thigh as a reminder to constrain his emotions while she sampled the chickpea and green bean dish. While she found it creamy and tasty, Brenna listened helplessly as Mateo added fuel to the debate fire.

"All the more reason to end it decisively," he said.

Garrick rose to the challenge. "Violence has a corrupting influence. People who feel lonely and isolated gain friends and fellowship with others who take up arms. It fills a void in their souls. Regaining personal agency by killing and looting is addictive. Violence gives power to the powerless, control to those who've been controlled. Once that begins, ruthless and daring people who are skilled in delivering death will rise into leadership. They'll promote their success using brutality as a means to gain more power. They'll claim that the solution to their collective problems can be found in taking up arms against a common enemy, especially one they portray as inhuman.

"The Nordans look nothing like us. They speak and write in a language that's totally foreign. They're easy to identify, which makes them ideal targets for Kurian rage. What we've seen thus far will inspire retaliation by the Nordans and build a spiral staircase of escalating retribution. Destruction and death won't solve this conflict. Killing won't make it better. The only smart way to resolve the issue is to sit down in good faith and talk through the underlying problems before all of the colony's neighbors get dragged into the fight."

"You're a professional soldier. Why would you say this?" Mateo mused in astonishment. "It makes more sense to crush the rebellion with overwhelming force."

Garrick shook his head. "I'm speaking from personal experience. I come from a remote region and a dysfunctional family struggling with poverty and alcohol abuse. The army gave me a sense of belonging that I'd never known before. They trained me with a rifle until killing became a reflex response to every threat.

"I saw the same dynamic during the Kamerese rebellion, and witnessed its impact among the Tanarak on the Saradon Plateau. Belief in violence as an agent of change is like a religion. In the minds of the faithful, violence will cleanse all that is old, false and oppressive."

"That's not real faith," Brenna countered, putting her fork down. "That's a lie from a dark pit."

"I'm not claiming that it's anything like what you believe," Garrick replied. "But to those who think they have nothing to lose, violence has an irresistible appeal."

"There is always loss," Brenna added solemnly. "If not property, then life. My people endured unending conflict that touched me personally. I've lost loved ones in battle. The cruelty of loss impacts every family relationship. Untimely death creates a future haunted by regret and pain for those who survive. Glorifying violence is an ideology that denies life to anyone who opposes the powerful, proving its evil origin."

Garrick nodded. "That's why we stand against it."

Ilia scrunched her brow. "But if you're using violence to oppose violence, how is that any different?"

"That's a fair question," Garrick acknowledged. "Wealthy elites can distance themselves from the consequences of the hostility they fund by paying poor people to fight on their behalf. Usually, the powerful use war to make more money and expand personal control.

"My job is to make the cost higher than they're willing to pay. That's deterrence. It's why the Azgar gave up when they invaded Tamaria, and that's all the Kurians will try to do when the Nordans storm their beaches.

"This is not going to end well, nor will it end soon. The human capacity for bloodshed runs high among desperate people. It will bring ruin to everyone. Brenna's right. But unless the elites make meaningful concessions to those who've been trampled beneath their uncaring boots for decades – their demise will come. It's inevitable."

"You're depressing me," Mateo complained, pushing his plate away. "But if this pattern of retribution is true in your experience, how did the Tamarian Expeditionary Force prevail in Helena?"

"We weren't fighting to control oppressed people like the Nordans will be doing," Garrick replied. "We fought to liberate the locals and protect Tamarian interests, and we prevailed on the battlefield with better training, weapons, excellent logistics and determination."

"It's more than that," Brenna insisted. "My *Amair* didn't rely on force when he came to Kameron because he's not addicted to power. When we care for the powerless and oppressed, we act as people of the light, not the darkness."

***

The booming of naval artillery awakened Brenna very early the next morning. She gazed at the interplay of light and shadow on Garrick's muscular body while he slept, as muzzle flashes burst in the distance. Although she longed for him in that moment, she also knew he needed rest and quietly slipped out of bed.

Heat and humidity persisted through the night, but the ceramic floor tiles felt cool beneath her bare feet. Hoping to find some relief from the sultry ambiance of their room, Brenna opened the balcony doors and stepped out to pray.

Confident that she could not be seen up here, Brenna relished the ocean breeze brushing against her sweaty skin. She lifted her face to the starry heavens and breathed a whispered prayer in Lithian. *"I wish we'd never left home,"* she lamented. *"My pride is at fault. My need for affirmation baited a trap that I refused to see.*

"I put us at risk. I should have listened, but I didn't want to hear. Garrick's right to complain that I've put us in peril. I regret ignoring his counsel. I regret blundering into a situation where killing was the only way to save Fiona, the only way to save Garrick. I regret caving in to my darkness.

"Yet," she continued introspectively, *"your Spirit remains in me. You protect us from harm. You command the creatures of the sea and they obey. You brought me to the house of my enemy and crowned me with honor. You saved Belwyr's children through us and delivered us from the murderous schemes of evil men. You brought us to this house, and I believe you will lead us home.*

"Thank you for the Meta family, for Mateo and Rosalea. Thank you for Jared, who intervened on our behalf, appealed to the king, and arranged for safe transport. Thank you for Garrick, who has tirelessly labored to keep us safe. Thank you for his faithfulness, his skill and wisdom in battle. Thank you for the affection and respect of Belwyr's children. Remember their pain, and be their comfort in their hour of need.

"I am afraid to fly. Please give me courage.

"You are always with me. You are my hope, my strength, my future. You know the children of my womb before I conceive them. I pray blessings on them, the blessings of true faith, of health, strength, wisdom and happiness. I pray your love on them, my love on them, and Garrick's love on them for as long as they live, even before they first draw breath.

"May you bless this house and all who live in it. Prosper them for their kindness to us, for their protection and hospitality. Remember the Nordan family who sheltered us, the Kurian boy who let us go at the resort, the Nordan sergeant in Helsing who held his fire as we fled. Save them from the peril, the loss and the madness of mindless killing.

"Thank you for your unending patience with me, with my weak and wandering heart. Forgive me for acting in fear, for all the killing I've done, and for cherishing self-sufficiency over humility and faith."

Bright flashes, followed by the thunder of big guns and the fading roar of shrieking shells brought Brenna back into the moment. She shuddered, recalling the terrible pounding of Azgar artillery that shattered a frozen landscape, draining her courage and instilling terror.

Somewhere, on the far bank of the Attavela, the wrath of the Imperial Nordan Navy hammered men cowering beneath its fury. Somewhere, their helpless cries to mothers and wives rose pitifully in the din.

And somewhere in that dreadful darkness, the tears and weeping of those women would go unconsoled.

***

"I'm in the kitchen cooking!" Rosalea announced.

Mateo sat at the breakfast nook table. "It will be good when our guests leave," he told his grandmother. "You're working too hard."

With a pan of beans heating on the stove, Rosalea turned her attention to the eggs she'd set aside. "Taking care of people is not a burden," she replied. "I am not working too hard. The time will come for resting in the rocking chair. For now, I'm honored to serve."

She cracked the eggs and began mixing them in a bowl, adding a bit of cream and white cheese. Noting that her grandson had put on casual clothing she asked, "Are you not working today?"

Mateo shook his head. "There's no point. The army set up roadblocks in case the conflict spills over the border. I've packed my truck to evacuate us if necessary."

Rosalea shook her head as she used a whisk on the eggs, cream and cheese. "That's foolish talk," she replied. "The Nordans are only concerned with their colony."

"I'm not so sure," Mateo stated. "The soldier and his wife saw one of our ships laying mines in colonial waters. They also watched a Nordan ship sink a slave runner on our side of the river.

"Last night, a Nordan demolition team destroyed the bridge to Helsing. I just came from the lookout and noticed that the Nordan warships on station in the river have their guns pointed south. Our ships are lined up for battle as we speak. Under this much tension, something can break, and that would be bad news for everyone."

"Let's hope these actions only a precaution," Rosalea responded gravely. "Only fools want war."

"Colonel Verano believes *Los Patrones* sent a kill team after Lady Brenna at the Seashell Resort. If they'd succeeded, her death may have forced Tamaria into war against the Nordans."

Rosalea shook her head. "Who'd want to hurt that poor girl? She's sweet and kindly. She's young, pretty and in love. She comes from a noble and wise family. Why ruin what is good and beautiful in the world?"

Careful to avoid offending his grandmother, Mateo didn't comment on Brenna's beauty, her sensuality, or his envy of the Tamarian soldier. "It may not be right, but it's what they're facing. People know me, and people talk. As long as they're here, we're under threat, too."

"Don't worry, *mi'jito*," she soothed. "You were right to bring them home. If the king has sent Royal Guards to protect and rescue our guests, you know that these two are important to him. Our hospitality will look like loyalty to the king, and that's always good."

Just then, Brenna ran across the patio and pushed through the glass doors leading into the adjacent dining room. Sweat that glistened on her skin also soaked into the fabric of her workout clothes, creating a dark V shape down her breast. Observing this, Mateo concluded that she must have been running for a long time.

"I saw a company of soldiers deploying on the street, just outside your gate." she announced, panting to regain her breath. "I came here to warn you."

Rosalea urged the Lithian woman to sit, brought her a soft, clean cloth to wipe her face, as well as a glass of water. "Shall I make her the tea she likes?" the elderly woman asked her grandson.

After a brief translation, Mateo shook his head. "She thanks you, but says she needs to shower." He didn't add that he agreed, as her distracting, arousing aroma seemed more intense than he'd experienced before. Exertion and sweat amplified her appeal, which made it difficult for him to honor her dignity without deliberately looking away.

Brenna drank deeply and thanked Rosalea. "We'll be here for breakfast," she promised.

Mateo followed her outside, lingering on the flagstone patio a little longer than necessary to watch the Lithian woman bend to put on her shoes, then with mincing steps, descend the stone path to the guest house.

"What I wouldn't give to come home to a woman like her!" he mused quietly as she went inside. Turning away, he walked down the broad, curving driveway to the gate, where he caught the attention of a Royal Guard soldier.

"Please stay inside, sir," the man insisted.

"What's going on?" Mateo inquired, mildly surprised at how many Royal Guard troops occupied the street.

The soldier pulled his rifle around. He didn't point the weapon at Mateo, but the change in his posture and hardening demeanor indicated that he wanted to be obeyed, not questioned. "Don't worry, sir," the soldier said. "Everything's under control. Just stay inside, keep away from windows, avoid the entrance, and don't come out when it's dark."

***

Kurian rebels quickly discovered that the Nordans had no intention of cooperating with local defensive plans. Believing that it would take weeks for the colonizers to build force, they'd not known that their enemy's intelligence service had anticipated trouble. Someone in high authority ordered transport ships, laden with soldiers and supplies, out of home ports several days earlier.

Rather than storming the beaches west of Helsing, where insurgent commanders and their Kamerese advisors expected them to land – where the waters had been mined and barricades erected – the Imperial Second Marines landed an entire division north of the Seashell Resort without opposition. These men seized the highway, the rail lines, and cut off all access to Helsing from the north.

Colonial army units from northern coastal garrisons traveled south in long convoys, their columns stirring great clouds of dust. Their deployment, carefully timed to coincide with the invasion, bolstered the Marines and protected their exposed, northern flank.

Using four of their five airships, the Nordans dropped a battalion of Imperial Airborne troops to the east of Briminger. This force, tasked with disrupting resupply from the east, by attacking long-range artillery, and disabling communications, ran into heavy opposition.

Rear guard groups of Old Order, as well as Mist and Soil militias – men far more fanatical and utterly committed to killing Nordans than the irregular troops that made up the bulk of the rebel army – fought fiercely against their lightly-armed airborne adversaries. The Nordan counterattack stalled by midmorning.

Old Order forces held their ground at high cost for most of the day, but as Imperial Marines pushed down from the north, they found themselves outclassed, outgunned and in danger of being flanked. For this reason, the rebels performed a tactical retreat to reconsolidate their lines.

While this was happening, garrison units in Briminger broke out of their strongholds and pushed insurgents eastward in heavy fighting that made minimal progress until the threat of being cut off by the southward-pressing Marines forced the rebels to withdraw. All the while, a steady naval bombardment from the Attavela and larger ships at sea savaged the shoreline.

Poor communication – worsened by cut lines, Nordan control over radio stations and telephone exchanges – isolated rebel units all over the southern half of the colony, creating panic. This allowed garrison units in Helsing to regain dominance of the urban battlefield in the northern reaches of town.

This did not mean that the Kurian rebels faced defeat that day. Some of the insurgents fought the Nordans to a standstill in places already hotly contested, where they'd had time to build defenses in depth. East of Helsing, irregular militias backed by Mist and Soil troops prevented an encirclement maneuver, stopping the Imperial Marines cold – thanks to friendly artillery and the near-mystical zealotry of the Mist and Soil faction.

Two hours after lunch, a bell summoned Mateo to the gate. The Royal Guard soldier he'd spoken to earlier, awaited. "The pathfinders have arrived," he announced.

"Pathfinders?" Mateo asked. "What do you mean?"

A pair of tall Tamarian women whose uniforms featured Airborne shoulder patches stood to the side. Wisps of stray blonde hair peeked from beneath their caps, while pale eyes and lips drawn into tight lines portrayed a no-nonsense demeanor. One of them had a long, delicate neck and a penetrating stare, while the other carried a full-sized beacon over her broad shoulders. The woman's obvious strength had an intimidating impact.

The Royal Guard soldier gestured toward them. "They're the pathfinder crew for the attack airships that will take your guests away during the eclipse," he explained. "They need to brief everyone on procedures."

Mateo introduced himself to Technical Sergeant Annike Schaefer – the long-necked one – and Staff Sergeant Klara Becker, who carried the beacon like it weighed nothing. While Sergeant Schaefer ranked her colleague, she only nodded while extending her hand in the universal gesture of peace. Sergeant Becker, fluent in Kamerese, spoke on their behalf in a soprano voice that seemed almost comically feminine, given her height and bulk. Her hands felt solid. Her attitude exuded confidence.

The women followed Mateo to the main house, where Rosalea – noting fatigue in their faces and wrinkles that rumpled their uniforms – greeted them with kindness and offered the soldiers refreshment. "You've come a long way," she told them. "Why don't you rest awhile?"

Sergeant Becker accepted Rosalea's offer of tea with a caveat. "We don't have much time," she explained. Turning to Mateo, the sergeant asked, "Can you bring Lieutenant Ravenwood and Mrs. Velez here? We need to brief them on procedures."

Mateo hedged, knowing that the lovers had been locked in their quarters since lunch time. He didn't want to disturb them, thinking that a woman in Brenna's condition should limit her contact with the public. But he couldn't dissuade Sergeant Becker, and with the celestial junction nearing, acquiesced to her demand.

A few minutes later, looking a bit sheepish after interrupting the amorous couple, Mateo returned with Garrick. The Tamarian officer understood the necessity of a briefing, didn't complain, and entered the family room without extending his hand in a gesture of greeting. Mateo said, "Ladies, may I present First Lieutenant Ravenwood."

The women stood in deference to Garrick's rank, but because he was not in uniform, they did not salute. "A pleasure to meet you, sir," they each said in turn.

Now, since the language of conversation switched into Tamarian, Sergeant Schaefer took the lead. "We understand there's an observation tower overlooking a sports pitch at this location," she began. "We'll set up the beacon on the tower and mark the LZ beneath it.

"Due to the limited area for landing, an attack airship will come in to fly you to another location, where a longer-range Kamerese thermal airship is waiting. There is a gunner's seat and a storage area available on the attack airship. It may be a tight fit, but it's the only way for now. We'll follow you on the next flight."

Garrick shook his head. "That won't do. What about the children?"

The women glanced at one another, as if they should have known something, but didn't. "Sir? We understood that you and your wife are childless."

"They're not ours," Garrick replied. "But we're responsible for them and they'll be traveling with us."

"I'm afraid that's not possible, sir," Sergeant Schaefer replied. "There's only room for two passengers."

"So, you'll have to arrange for more than two trips," Garrick replied. "You'd better get on the horn with that, as we're not leaving them behind, and the eclipse is coming."

Sergeant Schaefer furrowed her brow. "Just how many children are we talking about, sir?" she asked.

"Four," Garrick replied. "Two of them are small enough to sit on an adult's lap."

"We can't accommodate children," Sergeant Becker stated. "The orders only specified you and your wife."

Garrick put his hands on his hips, displaying a sudden and serious change in demeanor. Mateo realized that the man was accustomed to being obeyed and didn't appreciate the push back. "Well then, sergeant, there's a phone in the hall. Make the adjustments now," Garrick warned. "We're not leaving without the little ones."

***

"Don't worry, ma'am," Sergeant Becker said, making very little effort to suppress the condescension in her voice. "The lift bladders on the attack ships are self-sealing. The undercarriage armor is a lightweight composite that'll stop a .30 caliber rifle round cold. If you want to shoot down one of these babies, you'll need a rocket-propelled grenade. But we'll climb out of range not long after we're airborne, and we're too fast for anything to catch us. You're safer in the air than on the ground."

"What about the wind?" Brenna inquired worriedly. Sensing a xenophobic taint in the sergeant's tone – a common Tamarian prejudice – the Lithian woman suppressed irritation and focused on her concerns. "I don't want to be dashed against a cliff."

Sergeant Becker, who presumed the lieutenant's rather young-looking, well-proportioned wife was entitled and not terribly bright, spoke to Brenna accordingly. The impatience in her attitude, informed by the limited time available to reassure the nervous woman that air travel was safe, might have been understandable had she not been so obviously bigoted.

"Its aerodynamic shape serves as a lifting body," Becker explained patronizingly, confident that the lieutenant's little foreign sex toy wouldn't understand. "It can't fly without upward or forward thrust. For that reason, the airship handles wind better than you imagine.

"And we don't have bad weather in the forecast this afternoon. It should be an uneventful trip out to Madera, where you'll catch a train bound for home."

Brenna, still envisioning a nightmare of fire and falling, frowned and looked away. "You say the Kamerese thermal airship uses no hydrogen. How does it fly?"

"Its air bags are heated by burners on the ground," the sergeant explained, somewhat disdainfully. "Hot air is less dense than ambient air. That what makes it float."

"So, it carries nothing flammable?" Brenna asked, concealing her irritation.

Becker shook her head. "No. Lift is controlled with ballonets, venting and ballast. They use fuel-cell powered electric motors for thrust, just like ours do."

Garrick, noting the anxiety in his wife's expression, rubbed her shoulder soothingly. "It'll be okay," he soothed in Lithian. "They have two airships coming. We'll split up the orphans and ride separately, so we can supervise the children. One of the airships will come back for Becker and Schaefer."

"What?" Brenna exclaimed. "You can't come with me? How am I going to handle going up there without you? It'll be fifteen minutes of absolute terror!"

"You're the bravest woman I know," he told her. "You'll face this like you've faced down deathwolves, the enemy in combat, the despair of being taken prisoner, and your worry about swimming in the sea."

"I can't run in the sky," she replied. "I can't fight, up there either, and you won't be with me. It's not like being in the water. How do you expect me to handle this?"

"In faith," he told her. With trust. That idea has sustained you for as long as you've drawn breath, and it will be your comfort in the clouds."

His words stopped her cold. She held her breath, then turned her head away. "Either you have greater faith than I thought, or you're beguiling me."

Garrick bent to kiss her, a lingering meeting of lips that raised eyebrows from the Tamarian women – who knew the couple were married, but disapproved of their public affection, in part because Brenna looked like a teenager in a full-grown woman's body, but mostly because neither approved of miscegenation. They exchanged a critical look while Schaefer shook her head.

"It's always been about trust," Garrick told his wife. "From the moment I first met you, until now."

Sergeant Becker frowned, thinking it rude that Garrick switched languages. His soothing tone annoyed her, too. Neither soldier knew that Brenna had earned the exalted title of Heroine of the Republic for valor in combat, presuming that Brenna was naturally timid. What was a handsome officer doing with a dainty foreigner who trembled at the idea of flying? They assumed that Brenna sustained his attention by virtue of her appearance, not her intelligence, sterling character and unending kindness.

"You have a problem, sergeants?" he asked.

Shocked by his attention and the sudden switch in language, the women stiffened in unison. "No sir."

"Good," he replied. "Let's get moving."

At the sports pitch, Cedric watched the shadow of the eclipse through a pinhole box projector he'd constructed. "It's happening!" he shouted.

Ciaran supervised, making sure his siblings didn't look directly at the Daystar while the celestial dance moved in slow motion in the western sky. *The Handmaiden* – the smaller of Devera's two moons – slid above the star's disk, while *Princessa* steadily edged across, blocking daylight.

"The first airship is coming!" Ilia announced.

Ciaran raised Garrick's binoculars for a closer look. The aircraft consisted of a tapered, cylindrical central fuselage flanked by a pair of gas bags, connected at the rear of the aircraft by a horizontal stabilizer and two vertical tails. Stubby, forward-canted wings, mounted amidships, contained powerful, gimbal-mounted lift fans. Forward thrust – necessary to keep the craft aloft – came from a rear-facing fan located aft of the fuselage.

Beneath the ship hung a .70 caliber rotary cannon on a ball swivel. This weapon was operated remotely by a rear-facing gunner sitting behind the pilot. It also had hard points on its wings for as many as eight rockets, but these had not been loaded for this mission.

Fully loaded, with its two-man crew, ammunition, ballast and aluminum spools for fuel, the airship could lift a far larger payload than could physically fit inside its skin. For that reason, weight balance did not enter into the decision about capacity. Passengers for this flight had to squeeze behind the pilot, one in the gunner's seat, and the other on the floor behind – in a storage space designed for gear, not people.

The airship flew in over the sea, descending rapidly. For a moment, Brenna felt sure that it would crash horribly into the ground, but its pilot flared the aircraft's nose and settled the 70 foot vessel onto the ground as gently as if laying an infant in its crib.

Brenna clung to Garrick, her heart pounding while Fiona held onto the Lithian woman's skirt. "I'll see you in 20 minutes," he told her. "You'll be fine."

"Ma'am," Sergeant Schaefer announced impatiently, "it's time."

Brenna nervously climbed into the rear-facing gunner's position, pushing a small backpack that contained essential belongings beneath the seat. She and Garrick had to leave their *bug-out* bags and most of their clothes at the Meta estate. Mateo promised to send their belongings to Marvic by train when the military / political situation became safe for him to do so.

Next came the flight helmet, which felt too big to be useful, and then the safety harness. Once Brenna had buckled in, Garrick handed Fiona to her. Ciaran squeezed into the limited cargo space at Brenna's feet. One kiss and whispered endearments later, the canopy came down.

The shadow of *Princessa* raced across the landscape, creating an eerie twilight that intensified far faster than any dusk Brenna ever remembered. The lift fans and main thrust pressed the Lithian woman simultaneously down, into her seat, and toward the back of airship. As her bosom compressed against the safety harness, Brenna held Fiona close and prayed. She felt heavy, then light, and then a little dizzy as the airship banked hard for the south, accelerating rapidly, as if fleeing from the darkness.

*****

With only six minutes remaining before daylight returned, the second attack airship landed on the Meta's sports field. Garrick held Cedric on his lap while Ilia curled into the cargo space.

Although he'd trained on and deployed from the massive hybrid transport airships operated by the Expeditionary Force, Garrick had never experienced such a fast, nearly vertical lift-off. He held his breath, knowing that his beloved would find the experience unsettling.

"Whoa!" Ilia exclaimed as the pressed-down feeling of leaving the ground rapidly changed to the odd sensation of near-weightlessness, accompanied by an exceedingly pleasant stirring in her loins.

Cedric wanted the pilot to do the maneuver again, but Garrick changed the subject by bringing up interesting facts about eclipses that he'd learned from his brother, Algernon. "The shadow of *Princessa* travels at nearly 4 000 miles per hour at this latitude," he explained. "There's a pattern to the timing and location of eclipses. Every 22 years, four months, a nearly identical event occurs because of precession."

"So, if I come back here 22 years and four months from now, I can see this again?" Cedric clarified.

Garrick shook his head with a smile, recalling Algernon's equal enthusiasm for celestial events. "A total of three cycles have to take place before an eclipse appears in the exact same place. That means you could come back here when you're older, but I'm unlikely to see another one like this in my lifetime, unless I'm traveling."

Thinking about the Tamarian soldier's demise made Cedric feel sad, as he continued struggling to process the sudden, shocking death of his parents. In his violent, tumultuous world, even Lithians – famous for their longevity – could be guaranteed a full life. "I'm sorry you won't see another eclipse," the boy said.

"Well, it's possible I'll see one," Garrick replied. "Seven eclipses occur in different places around the world every year. Sometimes it's *The Handmaiden*, sometimes *Princessa* – like today – and sometimes it's both moons.

"While I'll likely not live to see *Princessa's* shadow cover the Daystar in a total eclipse like this, maybe it'll be *The Handmaiden* next time."

"She's not big enough to cover the whole disk," Ilia stated. It wouldn't be as spectacular as this one."

"True," Garrick agreed, pleased that the girl showed interest in the natural world and had enough knowledge to understand its phenomena on some level. "But we're here right now, in the air, with a unique view that we may never experience again. We should savor the moment. In my case, this total eclipse is a once in a lifetime event."

***

The major actions intended to drag the Kingdom of Kameron into war had been carefully planned to create the appearance of Nordan aggression and maximize public anger. Esteban Orozco, confident that the Nordans were now fully engaged on the mainland, had quietly crossed the river during the night and – frustrated by the debacle at *La Posada del Descanso* – personally supervised the preparations for the operation's final stages.

He'd watched his men clandestinely plant explosive charges during the previous night in key locations – such as the radio station, the Customs House and the telephone exchange – to ensure maximum disruption. Agents in Luanca told him that the Tamarian lieutenant and his Lithian wife had taken refuge behind the high walls of the Meta estate, secured by a full company of Royal Guards. Contacts in the military reported that the Tamarian Expeditionary Force sent two attack airships to Madera by train – where they'd been quickly re-assembled for flight – to evacuate the targets from the Meta's walled villa in Luanca.

That was an outcome he couldn't have foreseen.

Esteban understood that the hybrid craft didn't have the range to reach this region from Tamaria – hence the need for rail transport – but not knowing about this shipment meant he'd not had time to arrange for sabotage. Adapting to the news, he equipped three of his volunteer squads with rocket propelled grenades to shoot the airships down. No one knew when the aircraft were due to arrive, but everyone involved had healthy respect for Tamarian firepower – having witnessed its devastating impact during the civil war – and approached their task with trepidation.

As planned, newspapers in Marvic, Tamaria's capital, had already reported that the couple perished in a tragic fire, but ensuring their demise would add to the outrage of Kameron's closest ally. *Los Patrones* concluded that cutting off the northern rail routes from Vathera was an essential step in crippling the Nordans, and only Tamaria was geographically situated to do this.

Many well-timed explosions erupted in the darkness during the eclipse, spreading fire and chaos throughout the port city. Bands of *Los Patrones* volunteers, wearing Nordan uniforms, attacked a bank, destroyed a water tower and clashed with Kamerese soldiers manning checkpoints, using ambush tactics that pinned the Kamerese troops in cross-fires as they fought back.

At the Meta estate, rather than fighting against regular army troops, the attackers faced Royal Guard soldiers who were better trained, better equipped, and fiercely loyal to the king. The battle against them went badly for the insurgents, who made no headway during more than six minutes of intense fighting.

But then the attackers experienced a momentary change in fortunes. As *Princessa* slid away from the Daystar and light returned to the landscape, an attack airship approached and landed behind the walls of the Meta estate.

A few minutes later, as the Tamarian aircraft lifted into the sky, the *Patrones* volunteers fired a hailstorm of rocket grenades that streaked from the ground like a swarm of angry hornets. One warhead struck the starboard wing, shattering its lift fan, scattering fragments of spinning blade through the gas bag and fuselage.

Sergeant Becker, crouched in the storage well, felt something smack her helmet hard. Sharp pain shot into her neck, right arm and thigh. She struggled to breathe amid the swirling chaos, cracked perspex and dizzying spin. Horrified, she saw arterial blood from her neck spray across the bulkhead.

Sergeant Schaefer, whose body had been shielded by armor and the gas bag bracing, activated the camera gunsight, turned the airship's underbelly cannon toward the threat, took aim, and pulled the trigger. The ship shuddered as .70 caliber rounds spat from its rotary barrel. Four insurgents fell as the battle took its final, fatal turn. Surviving attackers fled, firing rifles at the fleeing airship as they retreated.

With their rounds pinging off perspex, armor and metal bracing, Sergeant Schaefer reached to staunch Becker's bleeding in a desperate struggle against gravity and time. Distracted by the need to shoot back at the riflemen targeting the airship, she'd pulled a kerchief from her breast pocket and held it over Becker's wounded neck.

The pilot cut power to the wing thrusters, jammed the throttle down, and skillfully used rudder and elevators to adjust the ship's trim. With alarms blaring, he hit a button that flooded the stricken gas bag with flame retardant. The airship listed to starboard as hydrogen poured from holes in its rigid skin.

He could barely keep the airship aloft and believed it could not take another hit. With the aircraft racing southward as fast as the crippled ship could fly, the afflicted struggle of Sergeant Becker diminished. She turned pale and began feeling cold.

"Stay with me!" Sergeant Schaefer pleaded. "Don't let the darkness win!"

***

Something had gone wrong. Stirring crews at the rendezvous point – a hastily created airfield located on a high, grassy, windswept bluff overlooking the ocean – serious chatter among the Royal Guards and the readying of fire and medical crews testified to a reality that had inspired Brenna's fear.

No one approached Garrick to explain the disaster. The lovers and their orphaned companions were left to draw their own conclusions in worried silence.

Hot air filled a large thermal airship that remained tethered to the ground some distance to the east. Like its Tamarian counterparts, the craft could not fly without forward momentum. Yet with gusty wind buffeting its huge surface area, the great ship swayed in rhythm with the flowing air, tugging at its grounding anchors.

What should have been a fifteen minute flight bled into twenty. Neither Garrick nor Brenna could respond to Cedric's questions and Ilia's anxiety. They all stood, gazing northward, waiting, until Garrick saw the afflicted airship. "Uh oh . . . That doesn't look good," he said.

Brenna held her breath watching the broken aircraft land, worried that it might crumple into wreckage and burst into flames. Yet the stricken machine hit the ground and skidded to a curving stop without further incident.

As the fire and medical teams raced forward, Sergeant Schaefer and the pilot climbed out of the open canopy. Tense moments filled with animated banter ensued as the medical staff went into the cockpit. A few minutes later, they removed Sergeant Becker's body from the cargo compartment.

Garrick watched the surviving Tamarian soldier approach. "Permission to speak freely, sir," she requested.

"Permission denied," Garrick stated flatly.

Anger rose in the sergeant's face. She turned away from Garrick and vented at Brenna, instead. "This is your fault!" she spat. "Becker's dead because you're a timid little coward. You might be a minx between the sheets, but that's all you're good for. We should have left your *sicklian* spawn behind. The world be better getting rid of worthless scum like you!"

"Sergeant, you're out of line!" Garrick warned, moving between the angry woman and his wife. "If you want to lay blame for a combat loss you'll do it to me, and you'll do it after you've cooled your hot head. The call to run three trips instead of two was mine, not hers.

"Save your diatribe for the After Action Report. I'll deal with you when you're rational. Now, get out of my face or you'll be dealing with a lot more than your personal grief."

Seething and red-faced, her fists clenched and jaw held tight, Sergeant Schaefer backed down. She stormed off toward the airship muttering muted curses as the crew prepared Sergeant Becker's body for transport.

Brenna's lips quivered. Feeling responsible for her role in the their recent struggle, staggering under the spiritual trauma of taking life after vowing to never do so again, she struggled to suppress hurt feelings. A singular tear raced down her cheek as Garrick embraced her.

"I'm sorry about that," he soothed. "You don't deserve her poison."

Brenna shook her head. "I feel awful about the sergeant. She'd be alive if it weren't for us."

Garrick stroked her silky hair with his left hand. "Everyone who wears a uniform puts their life on the line for others. Becker knew that. She volunteered for the mission, and as tragic as her death may be, risk is part of the job. Schaefer's vitriol is a product of personal darkness. It has nothing to do with you."

His words and the strength of his embrace encouraged her. Brenna shut her eyes and whispered a brief prayer of forgiveness – which she didn't feel like uttering, but knew was the right thing to do – and for the softening of her attitude toward the Tamarian sergeant, before slipping out of Garrick's grasp and turning away. She whispered a prayer for atonement from all the death resulting from her decision to compete at the festival.

Since none of the Kamerese crew spoke Tamarian, Garrick had to find someone fluent in the Azgar Vulgate who could translate the boarding procedures. One of the crewmen, an older non-com officer whose tanned face had been wrinkled by long exposure to daylight, admired Brenna and the orphans in a friendly, fatherly way.

"This is a commercial transport craft," he explained. "The procedure for boarding passengers involves walking on the scale, then sitting where the steward says. The weather is fair and the wind is from the sea. It should be a boring flight to Madera."

Brenna certainly hoped so, but the boarding didn't fill her with confidence. The ship, though tethered, swayed and bounced in the gusty wind. Each of the orphans went to the scale separately – with Ilia insisting that standing on the metal plate was a game, so that Fiona would do it without being held.

But the little one cried for Brenna and screamed when the crew tried to take her away. After much animated conversation, the steward gestured for Brenna to step on the scale and hold Fiona. Then, he led her down the narrow aisle of the passenger compartment and seated the Lithian woman – with Fiona in her lap – right behind Sergeant Schaefer, who remained angry and whispered vile epithets over her shoulder.

Behind Garrick, Ilia shared her spot with Cedric, while Ciaran had a seat to himself across the aisle, directly aft of Brenna. The cabin door clanged shut as other crew took their places elsewhere, in areas not visible to the passengers.

After waiting what felt like a long time, the ground crew finally released the airship's tethering lines. With its thrust fans blasting, the great craft lumbered into the wind, gradually picking up speed until its wheels left the ground and the sound of their friction faded into memory. Unlike the precise, gravity-amplifying maneuvers of the Tamarian attack craft, the smooth, gentle roll and pitch characteristic of the thermal airship felt a lot like standing on a luxury liner sailing through calm water.

Once aloft, the great ship turned eastward and climbed to its cruising altitude of 1 500 feet. The steward allowed everyone to release their safety buckles and wander about the passenger cabin. The aft gondola section featured a rounded couch set beneath three large windows, which offered a panoramic view of the landscape. The children persuaded Brenna to join them there, where the calm sense of controlled flight settled her nerves enough to enjoy a beautiful landscape below.

Garrick took the opportunity to confront the sergeant. He ordered her to stand, stepped into her personal space, and vented just enough anger in his tone to terrify the non-com. "I have additional details you might want to include in your After Action Report," he told her.

Dread of facing consequences for wrongdoing arose in Sergeant Schaefer's mind. She found the handsome lieutenant's demeanor intimidating, knowing that his rank gave him power she could not contend against. "And what would those be?" she asked, trembling in anticipation for the dressing-down she expected to receive.

The officer did not raise his voice. His grey eyes locked onto hers and did not move away as he spoke.

"I'd like you to include that you've insulted the courage of a woman who's earned a Medal of Valor. I'd like you to mention that you've disparaged the heritage of a Heroine of the Republic, who led a combat mission to rescue Tamarian hostages during the Kamerese Civil War. In that mission she faced modern weapons, yet dispatched 19 rebels using only a recurve bow and a longsword.

"That woman, whom you so casually dismissed, earned the respect and admiration of every man under my command. They called her *Little Sister*. I've seen her crawl forward – under heavy fire – to save the lives of wounded men with whom I've had the honor to serve. They stand when the woman whom you so arrogantly disrespect enters a room. I hope – for your sake – that they never read or hear about what you've said to her. If they do, you can expect the kind of treatment from them that good soldiers reserve for traitors and deserters.

"Include in your report that you referred to orphaned children as *spawn*, implying that she and her people are vermin. Yet I'll tell you something important, sergeant. My wife comes from an honorable family whose ethics and concern for others far outshines any integrity that I've seen or heard out of you since we met."

Sergeant Schaefer struggled with shame. "You're right, sir," she admitted. "My conduct was inappropriate."

"Then henceforth, you'd better think twice about the sentiments that so easily roll off your tongue," Garrick replied, unrelenting in pressing his point home. "I get that you want to honor Sergeant Becker, but her memory isn't served by the torrent of foul bigotry I've heard from you."

"I'm sorry, sir.

"I'll accept that," Garrick stated. "But you have some relational fence-mending to do with my wife."

The tall sergeant nodded. "Yes sir. Right away, sir."

But as she approached the aft lounge, Ciaran and Ilia stood in her way. "Don't worry, Lady Brenna," Ilia said in Lithian. "We'll protect you from that mean woman!"

"It's okay," Brenna told them. "Let her talk."

Sergeant Schaefer couldn't sustain eye contact. She let her gaze fall to Brenna's breast, which made the reticent Lithian woman feel uneasy. Brenna crossed her arms over her bosom as the sergeant stammered about behaving badly and speaking words she claimed to regret.

The Lithian woman nodded. "I forgive you, sergeant," she said, quietly and sincerely. "Go in peace."

***

Madera, a small city located nearly 150 miles from the sea, thrived because of its proximity to a vast forest. Unlike the logging operations in the Nordan Coastal Colony, all harvesting in this region followed strict conservation guidelines. This, coupled with regular clearing of underbrush and debris, maximized yields and minimized damage from tree-cutting and wildfire.

Local timber grew lofty and straight, thanks to long summer days and abundant rainfall, creating demand for regional lumber and chemical products derived from waste wood and sawdust. Initially, the town had been located at the terminus of a rail line linking the region to Kameron City in the south. In later years, the Kamerese government extended that track all the way to Luanca.

Completing the rail network, the main east-west connection ran to the Tamarian town of Desperado Falls. This also made Madera an important regional transportation hub, which diversified its economy and brought investments in construction, more than doubled the number of high-tech chemical plants, ore processing facilities, hotels and tourist ventures, as well as many businesses that served the needs of local people.

The Royal Guards selected for escort duty – all of them women, as Garrick had told Jared over the phone that Brenna was in *Y Newen* – arrived earlier by secure train at a location south of town. Their commander believed that *Los Patrones* operatives would be unlikely to look this far afield in search of their targets. The thermal airship made its uneventful approach early, thanks to a strong tailwind.

Two armored locomotives waited on the siding. One would ensure no surprises awaited on the line ahead while maintaining contact through a radio link with the second engine, following about a mile behind. This locomotive pulled four lavishly-equipped armored passenger cars that featured sleeping berths, as well as a dining car, a lounge, and an observation car with an overhead dome.

Sergeant Schaefer offered a terse farewell with the Tamarian pilots. All three soldiers stayed behind to prepare the surviving attack ship for transport on a regular train, bound for Desperado Falls the following day.

Ciaran, who now felt stronger and much more like himself, followed his siblings onto a passenger car. A porter led him and Cedric to a comfortable berth of their own, mistakenly thinking that their sisters needed privacy.

Grateful for the additional room, and knowing that Cedric would spend most of his time in the observation car, Ciaran plopped into the lower bunk and gazed out the window while the train began its eastward trek. As he processed the events leading to this train journey, the young man focused his ruminations on Brenna.

Aside from his own mother, Ciaran hadn't spent much time in the company of adult Lithian women. While his memories of Illithia had faded, they remained clear enough to conclude that he'd never encountered a woman like Brenna before. He had scattered recollections of maidens in translucent gowns, yet most of his memories featured awkward interactions he wished he could forget.

Brenna – despite being visually spectacular and optimally alluring in the midst of *Y Newen* – had favorably impressed the young man with selfless conduct and intelligence. The stories that *Llymah* related had initially led Ciaran to draw conclusions about the woman that faded in the bright light of her actual behavior. Now, her beauty didn't matter. His experience of her healing touch and gentle manner, contrasting with the ferocity of her effort to find and rescue Fiona, crafted a new, more nuanced and far more moderate, perspective toward her.

For this reason, Ciaran hadn't been surprised to hear the Lithian woman forgive the angry Tamarian soldier for her rude behavior, as Brenna never once said anything negative about *Llymah,* despite the ugly history she shared with him. While he never asked her to explain the story from her perspective, Ciaran concluded that *Llymah* had not been truthful, a troubling reality he hated to admit.

And Garrick, whose skill with a rifle could easily have ended the teenaged boy's life on the beach, ranked as the most competent man Ciaran had ever met. Every plan, every action and every result worked exactly as Garrick had intended. The man's wisdom and uncanny ability to solve tactical problems could not be questioned.

Moreover, the soldier never felt threatened by his wife's many talents. He listened to her, honored her and defended her from any threat. His conduct reflected deep respect, an appreciation of her character – as manifest in his tone, demeanor, and the very gentle affection he offered to her – consistently demonstrating a partnership that transcended physical attraction. He adored her as a complete woman, a trait that Ciaran admired, wishing his parents had been as mutually supportive.

He'd also observed that where Brenna felt shy, Garrick's charisma sheltered her in its shadow. Where she felt uncertain, her husband naturally reinforced her confidence with decisiveness. Where she was kindly and soft-hearted, he was disciplined and resolved. And, judging from the light laughter frequently wafting from the adjacent berth, they shared humor and playful conduct that Ciaran had never heard from his own parents. Belwyr and Eira argued incessantly, and had essentially lived separate lives under the same roof.

As the train sped eastward, crossing over low ridges crowned in forest, snaking along broad river valleys dotted by farms, ranches and picturesque towns with broad squares and tall buildings, Ciaran dreamed of loving a girl like Brenna. He imagined a partnership with someone beautiful, smart and kindly . . . .

For Ilia, who wistfully remembered her homeland and had long resented having to leave it, the eastward journey filled her young heart with a magical sense of returning to somewhere she belonged. Yet even as the distant mountains called to her spirit, Ilia begrudged the Tamarian soldiers for mistreating Lady Brenna. Her brow furrowed at the thought of living among such people.

What was this mystical attraction she felt? Enchanted by the rising landscape, Ilia let her imagination drift. How would it feel to love a handsome, strong, confident, and a little dangerous – yet inspirational – man like Garrick? At the end of this journey, could she find someone who'd treat her with the same consideration that the handsome Tamarian soldier offered his wife?

Cedric recited 1 703 facts he'd learned about the forest from reading books, but Ilia had fallen into a pleasant reverie and wasn't listening. Fiona raced from side to side in the dome car, as if taking in every possible angle of the landscape. She was tired and a little grumpy, but too excited to sleep.

While Ilia fantasized in the dome car and Ciaran dreamed in the berth next door, exhaustion battled against Garrick's passion. His desire sated for the moment, the soldier held his lover's soft body close and savored her profoundly comforting, womanly form as she rested in close proximity.

"What are we going to do with the orphans?" she asked at length, tracing her finger through his chest hair. "As much as I'd love to have them stay with us, we don't have room for that many children."

Struggling to stay alert, he caressed the back of Brenna's right arm. Despite her fitness and muscularity, his wife's skin felt soft to his touch. "Jared told me that Valle Hermosa has a thriving Lithian community, with hundreds of families living in the area. They have enough young people for schools and a lacrosse league. He made it sound like it would be best for them to stay there."

Brenna's lips morphed into a little frown and her brow wrinkled. "I'm not sure how I feel about that," she admitted. "I've grown quite fond of Fiona. It'll be hard for me to leave her behind."

Garrick nodded wearily. "I'd love to have a daughter or two. The older one will take your family name, and the younger one will take mine," he replied.

"Oh, I think Ilia would prefer to have your name," Brenna teased, gently poking his areola with her fingertip "She likes you!"

His body stirred at her sensual touch, despite his fatigue. "I'm not suggesting we adopt the orphans," he said deliberately, rolling onto his elbow and locking his gaze onto hers. "Ilia may like me, but she's not ours. She's not like you. I want nothing more than for you to carry, nurture and help me raise children of our own. You're going to make a marvelous mother, and I want to leave a family legacy that's better than the dysfunctional one I inherited from my parents.

"I want my daughters to carry my name, and sons to know with confidence that they're loved. And I want children who will love, honor and take care of you long after I'm gone."

While she felt a little sad to hear him say this, as a soldier's wife, Brenna secretly faced the terror of living as a lonely widow. He might meet his end in combat before their mutual dream of raising a family came to fruition, a possibility made more vivid by the sudden, shocking death of Sergeant Becker. "We don't know the end of our story," she stated. "I trust that Allfather does, and _believe_ he'll grant our desire in time."

Garrick leaned forward to kiss her. "We only have this moment," he replied. "Nothing beyond what we have, here and now, is guaranteed. We hold the past in our memory and the future in our dreams. Right here, right now, this is all I really know: I love you, and I trust that you love me."

She turned over as he snuggled close. Moments later, she felt his hand relax on her breast as the gentle, side-to-side sway of the tireless train speeding into deepening darkness lulled her handsome lover to sleep.

Two long days confined between their berths, the dining car, and the observation lounge escalated small conflicts between the orphans into major squabbles. Ciaran became impatient with his younger siblings, while Ilia – weary of having no time to herself – bickered at her older brother for not looking after the younger ones. "You only care about yourself!" she complained.

Some of this resentment, along with unspoken desire, eroded respect for Brenna. While the girl never overtly vented her frustration, the way she avoided conversation at mealtime, averted her eyes and addressed the older woman curtly testified to unspoken irritation.

In an effort to restore relations, Brenna initiated conversation up in the observation car. "How have I offended you?" she inquired.

Ilia shook her head. "It's nothing," she claimed.

"That's not true," Brenna replied calmly. "You're acting like you're upset. We understand that it's hard to lose people you love. It's hard to leave your home behind. It's hard when you have to grow up fast because of circumstances beyond your control. But I want to make sure I'm not making matters worse for you."

Unwilling to reveal complicated feelings for Garrick that blended innocent admiration with a longing she neither understood nor accepted as noble, Ilia avoided admitting her envy of Brenna's marital conduct. "I'm just tired of being cooped up," she claimed. "I need to get out, breathe fresh air and stretch my legs."

"Do you need us to mind Cedric and Fiona for awhile?" Brenna asked. "Would that help you?"

Ilia nodded, though she doubted it would. "I need some personal space," she said.

Brenna patted her on the knee and wordlessly withdrew. Stepping into the lounge car, she accepted Fiona into her weary arms and sat next to Garrick as Cedric repeatedly ran the length of the lounge car. "That didn't go very well," she announced in Tamarian.

"The girl's probably depressed," he replied. "We've all experienced the emotional let-down that comes from feeling safe again, and she's had a lot of time to think for the last day or so. Given that she's naturally prone to anxiety, I suspect her brooding is making matters worse."

Fiona, watching her brother run, wiggled out of Brenna's lap to join him in a rather loud game of tag that rattled everyone else's nerves. A stern warning from Garrick temporarily quieted the mayhem, but not for long.

"Cassie told me the Hohners have horses," Brenna said. "It'll be therapeutic for Ilia to do some riding."

Observing the high-energy play of the two youngest orphans, Garrick slowly shook his head. "By the time we get to Valle Hermosa, we're all going to need therapy."

***

By mid-morning the train turned away from the *Río Vieja Bruja* and raced across a broad grassland with far greater speed than had been safe in the mountainous terrain to the west. Vast herds of ungulates grazing beneath snow-clad ridges to the north stirred unpleasant memories of Garrick's last deployment on the Saradon Plateau. He held Brenna a little closer, but said nothing.

She noted the tension in his body and recognized the sad expression on his face as indicators of renewed combat trauma. While she longed to soothe away his pain, the obligation they felt to supervise the youngest orphans demanded attention. Brenna could hear her husband exert self-control as Cedric insisted that they play a game of word scramble.

Despite the vocabulary limitations common to adult learners of non-native languages, Garrick's proficiency with Lithian delighted the young boy. Yet Brenna could tell that her husband's heart wasn't in the game and sensed his relief when the grassland climbed into a steep, dry valley ringed with high foothills. Oak forests covered the lowlands, leaving the arid hilltops uncovered – an ideal place to build Lithian light forges. Here, the train slowed to enter the station at Hermosa, and their Royal Guard escorts secured the platform before saying goodbye.

Acacia Velez, whom everyone called Cassie, waited on the empty platform. The prettiest and most delicate of the Velez sisters, she wore a thin, pale-colored Kamerese dress that fluttered in the warm breeze. Although she'd seen her sister at Algernon's wedding only weeks earlier, the maiden embraced Brenna tightly and held her for a long time. The sisters kissed before Cassie relinquished her grip and stood on her toes to greet Garrick.

According to custom, he kissed her cheek and expected her to back away. But Cassie put her arms around his neck and gave her brother-in-law an embrace that spoke of deep concern and relief far louder than any words she might have said.

"Where's Jared?" Garrick asked.

"He's working on a case and couldn't come," Cassie replied. "I'd have brought the car, but there's not enough room for everyone. We'll have to walk. Is that okay?"

"You're driving now?" Brenna asked, surprised, yet thinking that after being confined on the train for so long, the walk would do everyone some good.

Cassie smiled sweetly and nodded. She thanked the Royal Guards in Kamerese, which also surprised Brenna, as Cassie seldom spoke to strangers, and hadn't learned Kamerese until she'd moved here. A lot had changed in the young woman's life since they'd last had spoken privately, and Brenna sensed her sister needed to talk.

Ciaran, eyes widened and mouth agape, stammered a greeting. He'd thought Brenna was beautiful, but Acacia shone like a bright star – even when standing next to her lovely eldest sister. Cassie – amused by his response, but suppressing laughter – allowed him to flounder. "I'm honored to meet you," he managed to say while staring at her dark, waist-length hair. Despite the fact that she was not wearing a maiden gown, he struggled to exert control.

The young woman shook her head wordlessly before turning her attention to Ilia, Cedric and Fiona. She beckoned her retinue to follow, not speaking again for the twenty-minute walk. She led them along a cobblestone road shaded in oak trees that wound through a prospering town. They passed tidy, brightly-painted buildings with boutique store fronts, and a picturesque stone plaza that hosted farmers' markets. A fountain simmered in the late afternoon heat. Its flowing waters called to Cedric and Fiona, encouraging a pause to allow the little ones a few, joyous minutes of splashing around.

The Hohner estate featured an extensive flower garden with shady pergolas, trimmed shrubbery and original statuary cast in bronze or carved in marble. The two-story manor house featured copper shades sheltering large windows. Three tracking dishes provided heat for the villa, its greenhouse, a spa and an outdoor pool.

Cassie stopped before they passed beneath the 12-foot arch leading to the front door. "As you know, Jared's *Amair* is very conservative," she reminded Garrick quietly. "He'll take one look at my sister and lock both of you in an apartment until it's time to go. Just a warning . . . ."

While Garrick appreciated the patriarch's respect for marital privacy and longed to spend undisturbed time with Brenna, they needed to work on securing documents and finding a family for the orphans. The latter, in particular, required research and exploring social connections that would be impossible in isolation. Garrick also felt uneasy, worried that with war brewing on the border, he would soon find himself deployed to the colony, leading his platoon in combat. As much as soldiering gave him purpose, he dreaded the prospect of leaving Brenna a widow without children for the rest of her long life.

Moments later, Caoimhin – Jared's *Amair* – set down his pruning shears and approached with both hands extended. "Welcome!" he proclaimed, his eyes moving from Garrick – whose ethnicity he disdained – to Brenna and lingering there as he evaluated her physical condition. "It's good to see you again, my dear! How is my favorite pianist? Did you win the competition? We hear you had quite an adventure. I'm delighted that Allfather spared your life in that godforsaken colony!"

And he continued this nearly seamless monologue until Brenna introduced the orphans. Caoimhin, the father of eighteen children, presented himself in a paternal manner that established his interest and trustworthiness.

"You sir, look like a fine young man," he said to Ciaran. "We have good schools, a thriving temple, and many maidens for you to meet." The patriarch put his hands on Ciaran's shoulders, smiled and winked. "I'm sure you can find a place for yourself here in Hermosa."

Ciaran, blushing, accepted the counsel graciously and felt relieved when the elderly gentleman's attention shifted focus to his sister.

"Oh, my beautiful young lady!" the old man exclaimed as he focused on Ilia. "We have horses that are excited to meet you!"

Cassie rolled her eyes and discreetly made a shoveling motion to her sister. Brenna sputtered with immediate understanding.

"And you, my handsome boy!" the old man continued, addressing Cedric. "I hear you're interested in science. My grandson, Rowan, is in charge of the whole town's infrastructure. He's got a tour of the light forges set up just for you. And later, you can also see our state-of-the-art water recycling systems, our technology museum, the Institute of Advanced Learning and . . . ."

That's when Áine, Jared's mother, came out of the house. "Oh, look at you!" she exclaimed, wiping her hands on her apron. "Aren't you adorable!" She scooped Fiona into her arms with maternal confidence so powerful, the little girl basked in the woman's affection as if Áine had been her own grandmother.

Then, turning her attention to Brenna, she smiled. "I'm so glad you've come, my dear." Then after glancing down Brenna's body, she lowered her voice. "I see that you're ready to start on a family of your own. Don't you worry! We have a wing set up for you that has everything you need. Cassie, be a dear and show these young lovebirds the way . . . ."

While she didn't ignore Garrick, having expressed disapproval of his marriage to Brenna before their wedding, the matron did not speak to him, either. Áine acknowledged his presence with a nod and a little frown.

Acacia, whose personal will melted against her duty to comply, offered her hand to Brenna and led her elder sibling beneath a long pergola graced with ripening table grapes. The path beneath led to a door on the north side of the house, facing hilly pasture. Cool air flooded down from the upper floor, where a suite with a private balcony overlooked high foothills and lofty, snow-clad mountains rising like a forbidding wall in the distance.

"Can I talk to you?" Cassie asked. "It's important."

The two young women left Garrick to refresh himself in the washroom, and retreated to the balcony. Ignoring the padded outdoor seats and a recliner, Cassie leaned against the balcony rail and collected her thoughts before speaking.

"What's on your mind?" Brenna asked.

"It's hard to say this without sounding like I'm some horrible, spoiled and ungrateful brat," the young woman began. "The Hohners are saintly people, they mean well and I love them, but they're rigid with their expectations and nearly impossible to please.

"Áine wants me in maiden clothes, even though no one else in Kameron wears them. She says it's disgraceful that I'm covered up like this because the neighbors might think that I'm having sex with Jared before we're married. She expects us to be totally chaste, and worries that any sign of affection between us will be misinterpreted."

Brenna's tone hardened. "Your private conduct with Jared is not her concern. You've courted for a long time, and it's not her business to judge you!"

Anger rose in Cassie's expression, a rare emotion, given her naturally gentle disposition. "I'm the good girl in our family. I'm the dainty, dutiful virgin who always does what's right. You and Thea get away with doing whatever you want, but I'm always waiting for my time to come."

"Thea?" Brenna inquired. "Has she given herself to Caerwyn already?"

Cassie shrugged. "I don't think so, but he's all over her, and I mean all over . . . ." She placed both hands on her little bosom for emphasis. "She's refused an escort. They disappear for hours on end and come back looking rumpled. She likes how he makes her feel, wants to please him, and can't resist her desire much longer."

"This doesn't sound like envy," Brenna remarked. "It's more like you're torn between doing what people expect of you, and where your heart is calling."

"Yes," the younger woman rasped. "The Hohners have no servants. They're getting too old for hard work, so I'm doing dishes, scrubbing floors, washing laundry, cleaning bathrooms, barns and working on the grounds. They're rich. They can afford hired help, but as long as I'm here, I'm unpaid labor. They say it's for my own good."

Brenna disagreed. "That's not fair, Cassie. They shouldn't be treating you like this. Have you spoken to them about hiring someone to take on the cleaning?"

"How can I?" Cassie complained. "Jared picked me over you because I'm demure and dainty. He doesn't like all your muscle and says your breasts are too big, but he once told me that he'd have overlooked that if you hadn't been so fierce and headstrong. He's too gentle for someone like you. He dreams about a docile and submissive maiden, and would have been crushed by your independence. Well, I'm the quiet, submissive girl in our family. He chose me because I'm the woman he wants.

"I love Jared's parents. They're devout people, but you'd never tolerate what I've had to do around here since I moved in. You're the fighter in our family, not me."

Pulling her sister into an embrace, Brenna felt the younger woman shudder and sob until Cassie pulled away. "Sorry for crying. Everyone can see you're in *Y Newen*. You need Garrick, and I'm wasting your time."

Brenna held onto Cassie's hand. "Before you go, please think carefully about what I have to say. If Jared's parents are like this now, nothing is going to change after you marry. They'll still expect dutiful behavior, but at that point, you'll have no way out. If you're going to leave, you have to do it now. If you need a place to stay, you can come home with us."

"That's thoughtful and sweet," Cassie replied. "But you don't need a weepy sister hanging around. Your body is ready and receptive. Your aroma is so compelling, Garrick must be mad with desire. I don't know how Belwyr's boys can be anywhere near you right now . . . ."

"They're not like their father," Brenna told her. "But hear me out. Algernon and Bronwyn are away on their honeymoon. Garrick's little sister has a place in town where she's staying. That means the house on Superstition Mesa is empty right now. If you need somewhere to go, I'm sure Kira would open her home to you until I'm out of my cycle."

Cassie sucked on her lower lip and shook her head. "I love you for caring about me and having my back. But I don't want to leave," she said. "I love Jared and I want him more than anything. He's a decent man who honors and adores me. He makes me feel like I'm the center of his world, and we're going to build a future together."

Brenna's expression took on a warrior's mien. "Then why doesn't he advocate for you? Why is he permitting his mother and father to treat you like a slave?"

Her word-order choice sounded strange to Cassie's ear. Brenna had lived in Tamaria for so long, she instinctively spoke of Jared's mother first, as if she were head of the household. Cassie, struggling to put feelings into words, found herself stammering, gesturing with her hands in a futile effort to explain her feelings.

Brenna put her hand on Cassie's arm. "Honoring Jared's parents isn't about suppressing your own will, quashing your gifts, your talents and sidelining your future. They should support you, not control your life.

"This is totally backwards. You're not a servant girl. Áine and Caoimhin have no right to exploit you. It's neither fair, nor healthy. The longer you stay here, the more resentful of their control you'll become. How does this nurture your relationship with them?"

"If we got married, we could leave," Cassie blurted out. "Jared's legal firm is doing well. His contacts with the Royal Court give people confidence when they need help. We can afford our own house and I could start up my graphic design business again. Some of my clients from Shirak have settled in the area, and I'm a better artist now than I was back then.

"But everyone expects me to live here at least four more years before Caoimhin will grant me the right to marry his son. Jared lived with us for that long. It's our custom, and it's only fair.

"Now that Thea's finally given up on Algernon, her passion with Caerwyn is growing. The longer they're together, the worse it is. She's pressuring *Amair* to let her get married, as he consented with you and Garrick. While everyone understood that we had to wait for you to marry first, it'll be humiliating if Thea marries before I do."

"So *Amair* and *Umma* know what's going on with Thea and Caerwyn?"

Cassie nodded. "Yes. He makes Thea feel pretty, not like an awkward, top-heavy maiden no one wants. I thought we could talk about this while in Marvic, but you were distracted by all the drama in Bronwyn's family.

"*Amair's* refused permission thus far. Thea says she's trying to hold back, but she's been lonely a long time and you know how hard it's been for her to attract the right kind of attention. Caerwyn is a good man and would probably wait, but if she gives in to her desire, *Amair* will have to assent to their union in order to protect Thea's honor and the reputation of her children. That's what everyone said about you behind your back . . . ."

Brenna wanted to feel angry at Thea for essentially blackmailing their father like this, but Brenna hadn't gone through the extended, traditional Lithian courtship period with Garrick either, and a sacred force moving in her heart reminded the young woman that she'd have gladly given herself to him long before they married, had he not consistently halted progress in their private conduct. She could hardly blame her sister for feeling the same way.

"So, your heart is being pulled in different directions," Brenna concluded. "You love Jared, he's good to you, yet his parents compel your servitude, rather than encouraging you to pursue your gifts and talents."

Cassie nodded.

"You're respecting our traditions by living here for the proscribed courtship period, while our hot-blooded sister pushes the boundaries of accepted conduct. But unlike you, she's struggling to control her sexual desire."

This time, Cassie shook her head. "I'm no example. I want Jared as badly as you wanted Garrick," she admitted. "I remember you telling me how you felt. I want to please my beloved like Thea's pleasing Caerwyn. It's a burning coal in my heart. *Umma* says I'll have plenty of time for that after we marry, but I'm tired of being the good girl – especially when I know what Thea's doing."

"How does Jared feel about all this?" Brenna asked.

"When it comes to the way he behaves when we're alone, I suspect he's equally conflicted," Cassie told her. "We haven't talked about this, but I know he wants me. There's an urgency to his response when we're alone." Her dark eyes raised to meet Brenna's, then her gaze darted away. "You know what I mean . . . ."

Brenna nodded. "I do. I know it's tough to wait. That's why you're not supposed to be alone with him."

Letting an impatient sigh, Cassie shrugged and rolled her eyes. "The Hohners won't let me have a servant, so I had to leave Sioned behind. She'd be a big help, but I'm here by myself. What am I supposed to do? Every option I consider is constrained by duty, yet if I do what is right – what is expected – I face years of aching knees and worn knuckles, frustration that we can't act on our passion, and the prospect that Thea will act on hers long before I do. For all I know, the two of you will be raising families while I'm still waiting for my wedding."

Brenna tensed as her sister unwittingly hit a sore spot. "The best outcome would involve releasing you from the traditional courtship period so you can marry, ending your servitude, and getting your own place with Jared before Thea gives her virtue to Caerwyn."

Cassie turned her head away. "That would be nice, but if I compel them by having sex with Jared before we marry, his parents will disown us. It'll ruin our reputation in this community and make matters worse."

"Let me have a word with Garrick," Brenna suggested. "He understands duty and he's clever when it comes to solving problems."

***

Just before dinner, Garrick poured tea for his wife on the same balcony where she'd earlier conversed with her sister. Although Brenna liked her tea with cream, Garrick preferred it straight out of the pot.

"I don't get why Jared can't advocate for Cassie," he said. "They've been together for 12 years. At this point in their relationship, he should be the one defending her, not us. It's baffling, unless he approves of what his parents are doing. And if that's the case, she should leave him."

Brenna took a sip of tea before responding. "If it were that simple, she would have. But she loves him, and family ties make it very hard to broach the subject with such conservative people. Jared's also the youngest of their children, which limits his credibility with them."

Garrick put his cup down and leaned back in his chair. "You were already an adult when his mother approached your father about courtship. At that point, you were a celebrity in piano circles and everyone knew you were no pushover. If his mother figured you'd be a good match, she ought not object to Cassie sticking up for herself. You'd have never tolerated nonsense like this."

"Yes, but Cassie isn't me," she countered. "In a confrontation, she gets flustered and will stammer and wave her arms around. When she's frustrated – like she is right now – that makes everything worse. Cassie feels duty-bound to not complain, so it's possible that Jared doesn't even know how miserable she is."

"What kind of a relationship is that?" Garrick exclaimed. "She can't express herself to her fiancé, and he's too afraid of mommy and daddy to stick up for her?"

"It's not fair to compare them to us," Brenna stated. "My sister has always been quiet. I think she said more to me in one talk than she has in years. She won't debate. We can't change her."

Garrick sighed. "How are his parents going to react when you offer to pay for their cooking and cleaning?"

"I don't know," Brenna responded. "But Áine was also a concert pianist. I occupy a place of honor in her heart, said she was disappointed that Jared preferred Cassie over me. She's resented that for years, so she projects contempt on you, like she did at our wedding."

He remembered, and nodded in response.

"It would have been a bright star in her crown for Jared to court me because she and I share a passion for the piano. I'm sure the only reason she hasn't asked me to play for her is that I'm in *Y Newen*, and she thinks we should be having sex every waking moment."

Garrick rolled his eyes. "Alright, if they agree to you paying for a cleaning crew, that should be enough," he stated. "We have no business meddling in their affairs."

Brenna shook her head. "Servitude isn't Cassie's only issue," she reminded him. "Cynthia and Caerwyn are complicating everything right now."

Holding his ground, Garrick said, "I don't see this issue as our problem. I get that Caerwyn is terrified of losing Thea, but if he's stirring her libido – knowing that once they have sex, she'll be bound to him – he's a selfish man who isn't worthy of her. Where's his self-control?"

"Have you listened to Algernon?" Brenna asked. "He described my sister's libido in more explicit terms than I cared to hear. She's lonely, she's bustier than I am, and you know that most Lithian men prefer slender partners. They may lust after *The Twins*, but they don't want the rest of the girl who grew them.

"Caerwyn is gentle with Thea. He might be consenting to passionate conduct because he's afraid he'll lose her. But she's been worried that she'll grow old wearing maiden clothes since she first put them on.

"Algernon lusted after my sister, but she told me that he never laid a finger on her while they were alone. If Caerwyn did that, she'd throw herself at him more desperately than she did with your brother. Unlike Algernon, Caerwyn has no other courting option. He likes curvy women, and Thea has plenty of what he wants."

Scowling, Garrick tightened his lips. During the wedding ceremonies with Brenna, he hadn't appreciated what he considered Algernon's inappropriate conduct toward Brenna's *not-so-little* sister. "Why won't your parents sit down with the two of them and lay down clear expectations for their behavior as a couple? That's what needs to happen here."

Impatiently, Brenna returned her cup to the serving tray, stood up and stormed into the bedroom. "You should know better than to talk like that!" she exclaimed. "Thea's 20 years old. Our people don't treat adults that way!"

Garrick wasn't about to relent. "Well then why do Jared's parents treat Cassie like they do? This hiding behind tradition is stifling effective communication and breaking down trust. No one in this household can say what they're really thinking because they're duty-bound by a rigid set of customs that won't allow people to be who they are. This is ridiculous! We're arguing over something that isn't our problem . . . ."

Sorrow flashed over Brenna's face as she lowered her voice. "It's my problem because I love Cassie. I love Thea. And because you love me, it's your problem too!"

Caught in a revealing truth, Garrick sat on the bed. After a moment of introspection, he spoke in a calm, controlled voice. "I'm sorry," he told her. "I'm not listening as I should, and you don't deserve my anger."

She moved to his side, laying her head against his shoulder. "And I shouldn't be trying to force my will on you, either. Please forgive me, Garrick."

He kissed her lips and took hold of her arms. With trust re-established he whispered, "Okay. I have an idea."

***

After dinner, Garrick persuaded Jared to help him clean dishes. As men brought all the plates and serving bowls to the sink, Brenna herded everyone else into the parlor to hear her play an impromptu recital on Áine's long-neglected grand piano.

Steeling himself to broach the delicate topic of Brenna's sister, Garrick decided a forthright approach was best. "Doesn't it bother you that Cassie's unhappy?" he asked, calmly enough to avoid offending his host. "She feels like she's being exploited like a slave around here, and you don't appear interested in alleviating her misery."

Jared paused. "Is that what she actually told Brenna?" he asked in a biting tone. "Or is that a conclusion you two have drawn on your own? In either case, you're totally misunderstanding the social dynamic.

"When I brought Cassie home after your wedding, the contrast between my *Umma's* mental state when I left five years earlier, and when I returned, upset me. I couldn't believe how she'd declined.

"*Umma* would forget she was cooking and leave a pot on the stove until all the liquid had boiled off. Once, she burned herself on a red-hot pan. She's left cleaning rags too close to the heating element. We've had two or three fires in the kitchen since we returned. One was so bad it could have engulfed the whole house had I not been here.

"The place was a mess. My parents were very neat and clean people in their day, but now *Umma* can't see when there's dirt on the floor. The furniture is covered in spills left behind from being sloppy with tea and wine, and worse, my parents were sleeping in bedding that hadn't been washed in months. Laundry hadn't been done for weeks. It stank in here. They smelled bad, too . . . .

"No one ever compelled Cassie to cook and clean. She took on those responsibilities without anyone making demands on her. My beloved is a thoughtful and kindly woman who lives her faith through acts of service."

"So, you're okay that she's unhappy?"

Jared shook his head. "Of course not! She's mentioned getting people in to care for my mother, but she'd never told me she was feeling miserable. Until Brenna brought it up at the dinner table, I didn't know the extent of the problem. I suspected she was a little sad, but when I talked to her about it, she explained it's her duty to be a good daughter-in-law. Cassie is never as forthright with me as she was with Brenna this afternoon."

Garrick handed Jared clean plates at a far more rapid pace than the Lithian lawyer could dry them. The soldier knew a thing or two about washing dishes. "You were pretty quick at shooting down the idea that we pay for a kitchen and cleaning crew," Garrick stated.

"While I appreciate your willingness to help, it's my responsibility to look after my parents, not yours," Jared replied. "There's no reason why I can't bring people in to look after them. Now that the issue is out in the open, I'll deal with it."

Scowling, Garrick paused from his task. "You honestly didn't know that Cassie felt so displeased?"

"I didn't," he asserted earnestly. "In all the time I've known Cassie, I've only heard her complain twice. Once was in Shirak, when the Azgar blocked supply routes into the city and we ran low on food. It got so bad we were eating once every other day. The second was while we were in Kameron City during the riots. She felt terrified by the violence and hated it there. Aside from those two incidents, she's never whimpered about a thing."

"Well, she certainly doesn't talk very much," Garrick stated, now realizing the role Cassie had played in her own hardship. "That complicates matters for you."

"It's never been a problem in the past," Jared stated, a little defensively. "Maybe she was afraid to tell me, worried that I'd think she was being selfish. Maybe she thought it wasn't right to speak up, or that I wouldn't support her. I don't know. I can't read her mind. She's terribly shy, and won't advocate for herself with anyone other than Brenna, who's always fought on her behalf.

"But when it comes to recognizing pain in others, she takes action right away. Whenever she sees that something needs to be done, she's on it. Cassie is the most selfless person I've ever met. I can't believe how fortunate I am that she loves me."

"Okay, you're right," Garrick conceded. "We've misunderstood the social dynamic at play with household service, but she's also concerned about her sister, Thea."

Jared blew a hard breath between his teeth, slowly moving his head back and forth. "Yes, our passionate sister Cynthia complicates everything."

"I'm less interested in talking about her than I am in urging you to reconsider your plans with Cassie," Garrick stated.

"What concern about my future is your business to discuss?" Jared countered. "Tread carefully, brother."

"It's not my intention to offend," Garrick replied gently. "There's a long form poem in your holy books about Brídin and Osgar, two young people desperately in love during a time of crisis."

"What of it?" Jared inquired, noting that Garrick consistently mentioned female names first. "I don't see how the story applies to my situation."

"It does," Garrick affirmed. "Cassie and you have behaved in harmony with your traditions, but like Brídin and Osgar, you find yourselves in a situation where sustaining traditional expectations is unreasonable, due to external circumstances."

Jared grew a little impatient. "My mother's mental decline is no reason . . . ."

"That's not what I'm talking about," Garrick interrupted, his assertive tone silencing Jared's premature defense. "War is coming. I'm not talking about a minor skirmish that'll be over in a month, or the ritual conflicts of Kamerese insurrection that flare up now and then.

"This one will be huge and unpredictable. We've already seen blood on the warpath – a lot of it. Combat is underway among the Nordans and their colony as we speak, and Kameron is already involved. We know that a Royal Navy attack boat was laying mines in Nordan waters. We've seen evidence that Kamerese mercenaries are advising the Kurian rebels and funneling weapons to the Old Order, and the Mist and Soil Militia."

Furrowing his brow in thought, Jared said, "King Alejo would never support this. There must be some factional, back-channel nonsense going on."

"It's only a matter of time before it spirals out of control," Garrick continued. "The Nordans have already sunk a Kamerese slave runner in the Attavela, and the bomb attack against us in Luanca involved at least one Royal Navy sailor. As we left, someone shot at and nearly downed one of the attack airships sent to rescue us.

"This conflict also involves the Vatherans, and if Kameron formally engages, you can bet Tamaria won't be far behind. It won't be long until every nation on the west coast – and their allies, like the Heran Islanders – will be dragged into conflict."

"What does this have to do with us?" Jared asked. "I'm no soldier. I know nothing about fighting, and my people are refugees here."

"It means the young men from this community will be drafted into the king's service. They may not know anything about combat either, but the army will train them, just as it did with me, and will also do with you.

"Kameron has to defend its territory in the south and the east from the Azgar. The garrison troops preventing another outbreak of the civil war have to stay in place to deter southern warlords from re-arming. If this conflict gets as big as I'm certain it will, conscription is right around the corner."

"I'm a lawyer, not a soldier," Jared countered. "I'm 18 years older than you are, and I wear glasses because I can't see without them. No one's going to draft me."

"You don't know how modern armies work," Garrick warned. "The Judge Advocate General will snap you up faster than you can blink. They'll need men like you who know the law, and while you may never see combat – and I sincerely hope you don't – war has a way of claiming victims who aren't directly involved in the fighting.

"You're fit, and you look no older than I do. The army doesn't care that you're hitting 40, as long as you're able to serve, and Lithian longevity will work against you. A big war means a long war, and modern weapons make for heavy casualties. They'll be drawing men from isolated towns like this one, and the expectations for immigrants to do their duty in service of the crown will be impossible to resist."

Jared felt his heart pounding. He'd never considered being involved in the military. "What does this have to do with the story of Osgar and Brídin?" he asked.

Garrick pulled the plug out of the sink, allowing the soapy water to drain. "The star-crossed lovers in your ancient poem married before he went to war, defending his clan. I recall that Osgar received a priestly dispensation to marry Brídin and stay with her until she conceived."

Eyes widened, Jared nearly dropped the plate he was drying. "You think we need to bump up the date for our wedding?"

"Yes. It's your duty to do so," Garrick replied.

***

Cassie had been right about Caoimhin. He'd had Ilia cleaning out the family stable, and an hour before breakfast the next day, Brenna and Garrick had watched her emerge from the paddock, her bare feet, calves and thighs smeared in horse muck as she carried her neatly folded clothes to avoid getting them dirty.

"A little work never hurt anyone," Garrick stated, respecting Ilia's privacy by turning his back. Lithians found this rude, but it harmonized with Tamarian values. "If it gets her mind off her misery, there's no harm done."

Brenna didn't respond, but her sister's lament spoke with greater conviction, and her loyalty to Cassie ensured that any criticism of Jared's parents found fertile ground in Brenna's mind. Additionally, the mild disdain the Hohners reserved for Garrick seemed every bit as bigoted as the contempt she routinely experienced in Tamaria. The longer she and Garrick stayed as guests, the more obvious their disapproval of her marriage to him became.

A knock on the door brought Brenna out of her reverie. She pulled a robe over her shoulders as shirtless Garrick arose to answer the door.

Cassie and Jared stood beyond the threshold, looking rather uncomfortable. Lithians typically honored the privacy of married couples in their fertile season, so this interruption carried an unspoken urgency. When Garrick invited them in, the Lithian maiden immediately opened the double doors to freshen the air in the room.

Jared handed Garrick a newspaper. "You were right," he said, pointing at the headline while reaching for Cassie to avoid looking at Brenna. "Kameron's Ministry of Defense announced a general mobilization this morning. They're moving four divisions to the northern border."

Garrick shook his head. "So, it looks like *Los Patrones* will get their way after all. You told me King Alejo was opposed to this. What happened?"

"I don't know, but I suspect that pressure to address the Nordan Colony's conflict had been building in the House of Lords. Knowing about the *Patrones* plot, the king resisted the hawkish clamor from parliament. But new powers in the constitution give the legislature the right to mobilize the army in response to perceived threats against the Kamerese people. King Alejo doesn't have veto power in a situation like this."

Brenna shook her head in irritation. "And so young men will die to assuage the egos of old men. Again, the poor will pay the price for the ambitions of the rich!" She stood and stormed out to the porch, muttering under her breath, strong emotion rising in her eyes.

"We live in a fallen world," Jared continued, as Cassie rose to comfort her sister. "I spoke to my parents about moving our wedding date. When *Amair* saw the headline, he agreed."

"Well, that part is good news," Garrick replied.

"Yes," Jared agreed. "But now there's something else. After hearing about the war declaration, my parents told me they want to adopt the orphans."

Hearing this, Brenna turned around. "Bad idea!" she snapped. "With all respect due to your parents, they can't even look after themselves anymore. I know your mother loves little ones, but these children come from a very dysfunctional family, and they don't know how to love.

"How are they going to deal with Ciaran, who has a snarky attitude, adamantly denies faith, and pushes every responsibility for the little ones onto Ilia's shoulders? The girl needs friendship among other young women. How is she going to develop those ties when she's busy parenting her siblings and mucking out the horse barn?"

"I'm not suggesting their idea is an ideal solution," Jared replied. "But we've only found a handful of people who might be related to Eira. Belwyr has no living relatives, other than the orphans, themselves. Let's think of my parents as a back-up plan."

"If that's what you're thinking, they'd be better off moving in with my family," Brenna countered.

"They have their hands full with Thea right now, and Eren is at the age where little boys get into all manner of mischief," Cassie added meekly. "I don't think sending the orphans home is wise."

She had a point, which Brenna conceded with eye contact and a nod. "Ciaran and Ilia need to adopt a social community of their own, where they can learn from others and grow out of the negative, selfish dynamic we've witnessed between them," she explained.

"It would be best for all of Eira and Belwyr's children to stay in Hermosa, where they can integrate back into our society, where Cedric and Fiona can attend classes taught in our language."

"They could do that staying here," Garrick replied.

Brenna glared at him, remembering how badly Jared's mother behaved at their wedding. The elderly woman had already lost her social filter and uttered many gaffes that had neither been solicited, nor welcomed. Áine had been very critical of Garrick. *How could she offer a woman's wisdom when she couldn't guard her tongue, or even properly care for herself and her household?*

"I need your support," she said in a nettled tone.

"Okay," he affirmed. "Let's hope that at least one family Jared found will be willing to take them in. If that doesn't work, we'll have to send them to your parents and hope for the best. Like you, I'd rather see them settled here. I think this will be a good place for them."

***

Rising heat motivated Brenna to skip her morning run and wear a spaghetti-strapped top and a skirt that hung higher on her strong legs than was her custom after getting married. Garrick wore shorts and a muscle shirt, which exposed a lot of skin to burning UV light.

The town of Hermosa had two distinct neighborhoods, separated by a dry runoff channel that emptied into an ephemeral lake further south. Precipitation pushing up against high mountains near the Tamarian border drained mostly through an east-west valley network linking the northernmost regions of Western Kameron with the massive and turgid Angry Bear River. Rainfall in this region occurred mostly during the summer, as moist air from the sea rose on its eastward journey, dropping its gift in hard, heavy showers.

A rolling parkland, dotted by wealthy ranches and high-tech light forges on the hilltops, supported a growing and vibrant town whose residents had swollen with Lithian refugees. Its remote location and lack of river access had traditionally kept its population small. But a rail link with Tamaria meant that when the Lithians arrived – bringing business networks, wealth, technology and practical know-how with them – access to markets located east and the south created the obvious prosperity that Garrick and Brenna witnessed in this beautiful place.

Mutually annoyed after Caoimhin scolded Brenna about leaving the cozy apartment while she was still in *Y Newen,* the lovers labored up a steep, tree-lined street to a branch office of the Tamarian embassy – a facility built to handle refugee claims for Lithians fleeing the Azgar invasion. With little immigration interest among the people here, this office mostly handled business permits – usually import / export certificates – and opened only a few days per month. The staff traveled here from the Tamarian entry port of Desperado Falls, roughly an hour to the east by rail, and returned home at the end of the workday.

The moment the young couple walked into the embassy office, the lead guard called attention and everyone stood to their feet. While this gesture of respect always embarrassed Brenna – who didn't feel that she deserved the honor – its familiarity soothed edgy feelings over Caoimhin's relentless criticism. Garrick appreciated the positive reception, given the fact that Sergeants Schaefer and Becker had both been far less cordial. A young man brought tea, with cream for Brenna and plain for Garrick. Someone had done their homework . . . .

As it had always been among Tamarians, Brenna's appearance inspired gawking and staring. Yet now, the combination of her face, her form, and the chemistry of her aroma made matters worse. The men working at the embassy extension knew she was a Heroine of the Republic, but didn't know her personally and could not appraise her appearance through the moderating lens of her good character. Brenna felt awkward interacting with the staff who greeted them and lingered to ask questions.

Noting this, the embassy's chief officer – an older blonde woman wearing a pair of earrings whose gemstones matched the color of her bright eyes – came to the Lithian woman's rescue. She pulled Brenna out of the line, uttering a mild warning that everyone should get back to work. "These two are not here to tell stories," she said.

Gesturing toward her desk in a polite manner, the woman continued. "We're expecting you, and we're glad you made it out safely. The Capital News published your photos, along with a boilerplate article claiming you'd both been killed. It's good to meet you and confirm that wasn't true. That's some nasty business going on at the coast."

Nodding, Garrick replied in the weary tone of disbelief and despair. "Yes, ma'am. Let's hope we don't get dragged into it."

With introductions out of the way, the young couple proceeded to a desk where the chief officer processed their declaration forms. "After we take your photos, we'll prepare a temporary entrance permit you can use to get home. I'm afraid you'll have to re-apply for passports and provide the necessary documents to get it done."

Despite her professional manner, she seemed genuinely apologetic about the inconvenience. "When can we pick up the permits?" Garrick asked.

"We'll have them ready this afternoon, sir," she replied, standing and extending her hand in the universal gesture of peace.

"Very well," Garrick replied. "We appreciate the work you're doing on our behalf."

The woman smiled. "It's my duty, sir."

***

So many refugees from Shirak had settled here, Brenna could not walk around, visit a shop or admire something in a store window without someone recognizing her, seeking an autograph, or excitedly presuming she'd come to play a surprise concert. Garrick had never realized the breadth of her popularity as a pianist, and despite her obvious condition, local residents lingered to chat and ask for her autograph.

"You're famous," he remarked.

In a hidden corner of her heart, the affirmation and respect Brenna received from people who acknowledged her hard work and talent touched a craving for approval that she only revealed in prayer. It felt selfish and wrong.

Thus, Brenna carefully suppressed the desire she experienced for applause, believing it revealed a defect in her character. While she trusted Garrick and honored his integrity, the Lithian woman only hinted at her personal flaws – even with him. Instead, Brenna hid behind her reticence, feigning that she preferred anonymity.

And Garrick, oblivious to the truth, awkwardly ran social interference on her behalf. As they walked through rising heat to Jared's office in the town center, he told people that his wife had an urgent appointment and couldn't honor their desire to chat. Garrick made no favorable impressions doing this, yet Brenna found his desire to protect her so endearing, she didn't stop him.

Jared had saved for well over a decade to start his own law firm. His renovated building included an architect's office, an accountancy enterprise, the local lacrosse league headquarters, a high-tech tailor – with light-powered machinery that bonded fabric into custom shapes without any seams – along with a cheese and wine vendor. Judging from the small space his offices occupied on the top floor, Garrick mused that Jared probably made more money as a landlord than as a lawyer.

Since Brenna had missed her morning run, she and Garrick took stairs to the eighth floor. Passive ventilation kept the stairwell cool enough to permit climbing in comfort, and they arrived at their destination free of additional sweat.

Brenna had to wait for Garrick to recover his breath, using the time to flirt with and tease her husband. She wiggled her hips, raised the hem of her tank top to a daring height, kissed him with rising fervor and encouraged his eager hands to wander.

Hearing feminine laughter and a male voice in the stairwell, a hefty Kamerese woman wearing large, round glasses opened the door. She was dressed in a silky, floral-patterned dress and carried a fan in her left hand, which she fluttered once she realized that she'd interrupted a private moment.

"Heavens, you!" she said in deeply accented Lithian, turning away as Brenna pulled her tank top down and slid from her husband's grasp.

Embarrassed, the Lithian woman wanted to melt into the floor . . . .

Garrick extended his hand in the universal gesture of peace and introduced himself, while red-faced Brenna hid behind his broad back. "We're here to see Jared."

The woman shook her head, keeping her gaze averted and holding the door open while muttering disapprovingly in Kamerese. "I think you come about children," she said at length.

"Yes," Garrick replied, adeptly handling the Kamerese legal clerk with far greater ease than he'd experienced among the Lithians.

"My name Martina," the woman stated, leading them into her office. She was friendly, but her poorly articulated Lithian pronunciation made her difficult to understand. "I looking for you for children. If you please . . . sit."

She clearly had the same issue with commands in her second language that Garrick struggled to overcome. Brenna unconsciously moved a chair for her husband that enabled him to keep an eye on the exit, then wordlessly sat to his right.

"You are sister of Miss Acacia?" Martina asked.

Brenna nodded.

Martina smiled in genuine admiration. "You beautiful both." Then turning to handsome Garrick, whose sculpted shoulders and broad chest attracted her attention, she continued, "But they talk little. I don't know how you . . . understand . . . ?

"Okay, I find eight relatives . . . maybe. Names and homes here," she said, offering a list of address. "You go and speak."

Garrick reached for the paper and offered it to Brenna. "Do you know any of them?"

Brenna read through the list and shook her head. "These are Eira's family. They came from the east. It's a rural area where farming and fishing were more important than industry. I'd only been through a few times on tour."

Hearing the Lithian woman speak, Martina looked up. "So, you talk!" she exclaimed. "You need taxi? I call."

"No, that's okay," Brenna insisted. "We need to speak to the children, first. They may know some of this family, and we want to respect their preferences."

Martina raised her brow. "Then we finish." She stood, her duty accomplished, and offered her hand. The Kamerese woman watched playful sensuality resume as the lovers returned to the stairwell. She shook her head.

***

"You said you were going to take care of us!" Ilia spat in an accusing voice. "Now you're dumping us off with some shirt tail relatives who we don't even know!"

Cassie watched Garrick's demeanor closely. She could tell he'd thought this through, as he wasn't fazed by Ilia's attitude and remained calm, despite the girl's fury.

"We're doing what we said we'd do," he replied. "We're looking after your interests, as we have from the moment we knew what happened to your parents. Nothing has changed since you've been in our care.

"Now, I've already told you that I'm likely to deploy soon after we return home. Our place is too small for so many people, and we're unlikely to get clearance for you to live behind the palace wall."

Ilia began to sob. "Just take me, then. You can leave the rest of them . . . ."

Ciaran swore at her. "You'd dump all the responsibility for looking after Cedric and Fiona on me? Thanks a lot, little sister!"

"It's not like you lift a finger to help!" Ilia screeched. "It wouldn't hurt you. It's always me that gets stuck with the babysitting, while you go off and do your own thing!"

"Both of you need to stop this right now!" Garrick said in a commanding voice. He turned to Ciaran as silence prevailed. "Your sister has a point. She takes the brunt of child care. You're shirking *your* duty to your siblings, and that needs to change, starting right now. It's time to grow up and be responsible, to be a man. It's time to leave your boyhood behind."

Ciaran trembled indignantly. He wanted to respond, but lacked the courage to challenge the Tamarian soldier. He should have accepted the rebuke gracefully, but the young man brimmed with old resentments and couldn't bring himself to acknowledge the obvious truth of the older man's counsel. Intimidated by Garrick's anger and the raw truth of his testimony, Ciaran crossed his arms and fell into sullen silence, glaring at his sister.

Turning to Ilia, Garrick warned, "Don't ever turn your back on your family. There will come a day when they're all you have, and for you, that day is coming sooner, rather than later."

Lithians did not speak to each other this way. Cassie held her breath, exchanging a glance with Áine, who seemed visibly distressed by the social acrimony. With Brenna outside minding the little ones, Cassie felt the disapproval of her future mother-in-law and wished she had her older sister's support. While everything Garrick said was true, his manner wasn't helping.

"So, instead of grousing about your situation, the two of you should be setting an example for Cedric and Fiona," Garrick continued. He picked up the paper he'd received from Martina. "Let's go through this list of your mother's people and see if you recognize their names. We're including you in this process, not dumping you off without a proper transition. Now, the two of you can be a part of this, or I'll do it on your behalf. What will it be?"

Ilia sniffed. Her lip trembled and she began to cry. "I'm sorry," she sobbed. "I don't mean to be selfish!"

That sounded like her mother, Garrick thought. When the girl wrapped her arms around him, Garrick patted her back but did not encourage further contact.

Ciaran glowered, snatching the paper away and studying the names Martina had written while his sister wept on Garrick's shoulder. "Some of these people were not in *Umma's* family," he said at length. "If they're related, it's distant."

Reading further he raised his brow and added, "This woman might be *Malleah* Ceridwyn. If so, she's our mother's sister. I've only met her a couple of times, but I'd know her if I saw her again."

Brenna had a widowed aunt with the same name.

"Then, we'll start with her," Garrick said.

***

Contact began with a telephone call. Garrick spoke to a man named Owain, who was Ceridwyn's husband. Leery of the story Garrick told, Owain agreed to meet him and Brenna at a tea house not far from Jared's office. "If possible, I'd like to see a scan of these children you say belong to my sister-in-law," the man suggested. "I'll take it to my wife and discuss it with her."

While he sounded excessively suspicious, Garrick didn't find Owain's request unreasonable. Cassie retrieved the family's scanner and took several still images and an action sequence of the orphans with sound, which she subsequently recorded on a crystal disc small enough to fit into the pommel of Brenna's boot knife.

Cassie drove her sister and brother-in-law to the tea shop in the tiny, four-seat auto carriage that belonged to Jared's father. She'd been right when she'd told them the vehicle didn't have room for everyone. Garrick had to bend himself awkwardly to get into the back seat. While he didn't object to being crammed into a small space with Brenna, the late afternoon heat reduced the delight of proximity to his beloved, creating a sweaty ordeal instead.

Near the tea shop, Cassie parked in a back alley and went to see Jared. Garrick took Brenna by the hand, leading her into a quaint little tea house on a street corner. Inside, cool air caressed their sweating skin, and the aroma of fresh tea, accompanied by recorded piano music, welcomed the young couple. They sat near a window, ordered tea, and waited for Owain to arrive.

"You think he'll show?" Garrick asked.

"I'm more concerned that I know him," Brenna stated. "One of my biggest competitors at festivals in the south was an older boy with that name. It might be him."

No sooner had she uttered the statement, than Owain came into the tea house. Wide-eyed, Brenna set her teacup down and instinctively pulled her hair around to cover the prominent scar on her neck. Garrick turned to see a slender man dressed in field workers' garb lock his gaze on Brenna and shake his head.

"It's really you," the Lithian man said, smiling broadly. He would have embraced Brenna – a greeting ordinarily permitted by Lithian custom between people who'd not seen one another in a long time – but he could see and smell that she that was in _Y Newen_ and politely kissed her hand, instead. "I'm delighted to see you again."

Garrick stood to greet him. Owain had good manners, but expressed only passing interest. The man reminisced with Brenna for more than an hour.

"I remember your bare feet struggling to reach the pedals," he said wistfully. "You were astonishing, even as a little girl. And later, I traveled to Shirak and saw you at one of the boys' choir concerts. You were blossoming into womanhood. The boys couldn't keep their eyes off you."

"She still has that problem," quipped Garrick, drawing a chuckle from the other man. "But we really need to talk about the orphans."

Accepting the change in topic, Owain turned his full attention to Garrick. "We haven't seen Eira in years," he admitted. "We'd heard what Belwyr did to Brenna, and after we learned that Eira gave herself to him, the shame my in-laws experienced led them to break off contact.

"Now, you tell me that my sister-in-law and her godless lover left four children behind. We are not people of means. Why not just care for them, yourself?"

Brenna's heart pounded. How could he talk about his wife's family like that? She knew he could be conceited, yet he'd accepted defeat graciously every time the two pianists met in a competition.

But she didn't need to contend with her rival. Garrick took the lead. "I understand your people have a tradition," he began. "When Lachlan met his demise in battle and Tanwen perished from a wasting disease in her despair, his brother took in eight or ten of their orphans and raised them as his own. I believe that story sets a precedent for your duty as their uncle, does it not?"

Surprised to hear a foreigner speak so confidently about an obscure story from a rather arcane, spiritual book, Owain raised his brow. "How do you know of this? Are you a convert?" he asked.

"No," Garrick stated, shaking his head. "But I love a woman who *believes*. I'm familiar with Lithian lore because it's important to understand her culture."

Owain nodded. "Very well. If you have the disc, I'll take it to Ceridwyn and we'll contact you in the morning."

***

The meeting with Ceridwyn went well. She looked a lot like her sister, and demonstrated the same degree of kindness they'd seen in Eira. Ceridwyn felt excited about meeting Brenna – expressing admiration of her skill as a pianist – but knowing what Belwyr had done, expressed surprise to learn that Brenna had taken on responsibility for looking after his orphans.

Kindly Ceridwyn embraced her sister's children warmly, assuring them that they would be welcomed and cared for in her home. She and Owain had seven young ones of their own, ensuring that Cedric and Fiona would have cousins with whom they could play.

This lifted the childcare burden from Ilia and also let Ciaran off the hook for shouldering his own responsibility. He felt quite smug about his unexpected fortune and didn't hide his delight well. But when the moment arrived to say farewell to Brenna, the young man broke down and wept on her shoulder.

"Thank you for everything!" he told her, releasing pent-up guilt and shuddering with deep emotion as he spoke. Unable to think of anything further to say, Ciaran offered his hand to Garrick in the universal gesture of peace, and wordlessly turned away.

Ilia acted strangely, as if unconcerned about her future and the imminent departure of her benefactors. "I'm fine," she said in a matter-of-fact one. She didn't say want to say goodbye, suppressing her emotions and laughing in an odd way that Brenna suspected had more to do with coping than processing her feelings.

Cedric and Fiona latched onto their rescuers one last time before Ceridwyn beckoned them to go with her. The transition into their new family went seamlessly for the youngest orphans, yet this arrangement didn't end the lovers' duty to Belwyr's children. Their obligation of care would endure for more than a decade.

Jared, who drew up the adoption papers, explained that Owain and Ceridwyn could not afford to take the orphans in without help. "They'll need subsidies," he explained. "I've set up a trust through a local bank that has ties to credit unions in Tamaria. An orphan's charity here in Hermosa has agreed to a sponsorship, but the family will still need your help, as the charity's assistance won't be enough to support four more hungry children."

And thus, Brenna became duty-bound to support the offspring of a man who'd assaulted her when she was a maiden.

***

Feeling anxious to return home, Garrick arose just after Brenna finished her prayers early the next morning. He stripped the bed, washed the tea service, showered, and then called his little sister, Kira, while his wife went for her daily run.

"It's getting tense around here," Kira told him. "I read about Kameron. Everyone thinks war is inevitable."

"Let's hope cooler heads prevail in the Senate," he replied. "We have no business meddling in this matter, and if we deploy, the Vatherans may mobilize against us."

"Bron and Algernon went up there for their honeymoon," Kira reminded him, fearing that she might lose her twin brother. "There's no way to warn them."

Hearing this, Garrick felt sick. "Bronwyn can understand and read the language," he replied at length. "Hopefully, she'll pick up on the idea that something's amiss and they should return home right away."

"Can you ask Brenna to pray for them?" Kira encouraged. "I'm really worried!"

"Of course," he responded. "We'll see you soon!"

Garrick relayed the grave message to Brenna when she returned. She'd been happy about going home and bought flowers as a thank-you gift for the Hohners' hospitality, but when she heard what Kira had told him, a sad expression formed on her lovely face. "Algernon was clever enough to survive the war in Kameron," she said. "I will pray that he and Bronwyn survive this one, too."

Brenna spent a long time in the shower, inspiring Garrick's unspoken impatience. When she realized he didn't appreciate the delay, she packed hurriedly.

The Hohners offered a rather tepid farewell, their displeasure of Garrick seeping through body language and facial expressions in a way that telegraphed unrepentant disapproval. Brenna felt hurt by their behavior.

Oblivious to this, Coaimhin promised to spare no expense in hosting Jared and Cassie's wedding in a few weeks. "We're having the invitations printed up today," he announced, speaking to Brenna directly. "We'll be sure to send yours along as soon as it's ready."

Garrick thanked the Hohners graciously, suspecting that professional responsibilities would prevent him from attending. He quietly said so to Jared before they departed, then mused to himself that it was probably for the best. Áine and Caoimhin were not likely to complain if he was unable to attend their son's wedding.

Cassie drove the lovers to the train station and wordlessly bid her farewell with teary eyes and lingering embraces. She stayed on the platform, waving as the locomotive slowly pulled away to the east.

After what seemed like a very short ride, the train pulled into the station at Desperado Falls, where Garrick and Brenna presented their new documents at Customs. Entering Tamaria proved an effortless and welcoming process, as the agents had been told to expect them.

From there, they waited on the siding for over an hour to catch a northbound train, a rail journey that passed familiar sights, heightening Garrick's anticipation. The Angry Bear Gorge, with its frothy waters tumbling restlessly to the sea, and the volcanic triplet of snow-clad peaks called the Three Orphan Sisters served as beacons for the homeward journey.

Garrick recalled, during the climb through the famous spiral tunnels, that this was where Brenna had finally agreed to marry him, two years earlier. He felt grateful for her faithful and formidable partnership, especially in a crisis. Her unwavering trust in his leadership, her willingness to share her life and her intimate gifts with him, inspired personal confidence.

As the train turned for its final approach into Marvic, Tamaria's fortress capital, Brenna – who missed the affection and attention that Belwyr's children had offered to her – gazed at the ripening grain fields fringing Superstition Mesa, land that faithfully yielded its increase year after year. The farmers could not compel their crops to grow, yet trusted in a miraculous process that sustained them. Brenna shut her eyes and breathed a prayer, trusting that Allfather heard her longing, would honor her faith, and make her womb fertile.

Beautiful and charismatic Kira, Garrick's younger sister, met them at the train station with a shriek of joy, strong embracing and grateful tears for their safety. Noting the daylight burns on her brother's flesh and the obvious impact of *Y Newen* pushing through her sister-in-law's blouse, she wondered aloud when they'd found any time to spend outdoors and nodded, knowingly.

When her brother laughed off the ribbing, a wistful smile appeared and lingered on Kira's beautiful face. "It's been a long time since I've seen you happy," she told him. "I know you weren't excited about leaving, and I'm sorry about the trouble on your journey, but I think that going on this little holiday was good for the two of you."

Brenna, her eyes brimming with regret, left that comment unanswered. She gazed at the familiar surroundings with a hint of resignation reflected on her face. While she endured undeserved scorn among many who lived here, the scent of cool, pine-scented air and thunderclouds piling high against the mountains to the north wrought a sense of safety that she hadn't felt since the night of the kill team attack. Despite the city's thin air, its all-too-short summers and cold, snowy winters, Marvic – Tamaria's capital – felt like home.

Yet for Garrick, reading billboards on hoardings that clamored for retribution against a nation whose people most Tamarians had never met, and overhearing conversations on the streetcar, or at nearby tables in Kira's favorite restaurant, revealed an ugly public mood. Ill-informed opinions and outright bravado – all fueled by effective political propaganda – felt sinister.

How did groups like *Los Patrones* reach so deeply and effectively into Tamarian society? It seemed obvious that very powerful people wanted war and were successfully manipulating public opinion. Thinking about the horrors of combat, Garrick felt distracted during dinner. Kira chatted incessantly, as if making up for lost time during their absence. She had obviously missed the company of her brothers, Brenna, and Bronwyn.

Garrick interrupted her near the end of the meal. "When do Bronwyn and Algernon come back?"

"Next week, if they can make it," she told him.

Unable to sustain eye contact, Garrick looked away. "I hope I'm still here for that," he said quietly.

Ever the keen observer and aware of Brenna's condition, Kira noted longing between the lovers, and understood that they needed time alone. Kira smiled at Brenna and went home after they'd finished eating. She didn't tell them the bad news about Bronwyn's brother, thinking they had enough to worry about at the moment.

Walking slowly through the lingering twilight, Garrick and Brenna crossed Equality Park to the palace gate. Here, they checked in with the Defenders for the first time since leaving for the coast.

"What happened to your sidearm, sir?" Sergeant Siefert, who knew the couple very well, asked.

"That's a long story, sergeant. It's in the hands of a Nordan Lieutenant now. I'll need to get a new one."

In the mail Garrick found a warning order and a summons from Dr. Bauer, the regimental psychologist, urging an immediate appointment. As he and Brenna both knew the reason for these messages, not a word broke the moody silence that thickened between them as they strolled through the lofty redwood grove toward home.

Later that evening, in the privacy of the idyllic music manse where they lived, Brenna cut her husband's hair. She carved a dragon pattern into the short stubble on his head – a reminder that she loved him fiercely.

Alone in familiar and comfortable surroundings, with no threats or responsibilities impeding their conduct, the lovers finally expressed the full, uninhibited extent of their shared passion. Hours later Garrick finally fell asleep, holding Brenna's breast with his right hand. She curled into his embrace, wishing that they'd never left home, clutching him close all night long.

In the morning after breakfast, she pressed her body into his, doing everything she could to delay his departure. "I wish you didn't have to leave," she muttered, a pleading tone reflecting turmoil also manifest in the strength of her arms, imploring fingers, and her reluctance to release him.

"We've not deploying yet," he replied, meeting her lips with his. "We don't know when that will happen. Let's enjoy whatever time we have left. Please don't be sad."

But she couldn't suppress a string of strong, complex feelings arising from her soul. As Brenna watched him from their front door, a tear raced down her cheek.

Wearing his uniform again, Garrick checked out of the palace gate and caught a streetcar from the Victory Street Exchange up to Fort Aeolus. His first stop was at Dr. Bauer's office, where, as expected, he went through a brief evaluation that cleared his return to his unit.

Not long later, when summoned to meet Captain Richter, his new commanding officer, Garrick stood at attention with his eyes riveted on the paneled back wall. He saluted stiffly. "First Lieutenant Ravenwood, reporting for duty, sir!"

8 November 2020

08:38

Thank you for reading **Blood on the Warpath.** Please take a moment to offer an honest review in an e-mail. This doesn't have to be lengthy – a sentence or two is plenty:

robert@newadventure.ca

Reviews are very important to independent authors. Thank you for taking the time to do this.

Other titles in the Deveran Conflict Series include:

The Edge of Justice

The Long Journey

Crisis

Ceremonies and Celebrations

Dreams and Missions

The Inquest

Secrets and Whispers

Learn more about the World of Devera at

www.newadventure.ca